Echoes of Stone and Fire

Hannah's Heirloom ~ Book Two

Rosie Chapel

First printing 2016
ISBN 978-0-9945053-3-0

Ulfire Pty. Ltd.
P.O. Box 1481
South Perth
WA 6951
Australia

www.rosiechapel.com

Cover artwork by E.H Rodgers

For my parents,
with all my love.

For my three beautiful sisters,
always in my heart.

Acknowledgements

Heartfelt thanks to Helen for all your hard work on the covers and
your tireless efforts in promoting my books.
I am endlessly amazed by your vision.

Grateful thanks to Janet, Moira and Jane.
Your help during the editing process was invaluable,
your patience and support is much appreciated.

Echoes of Stone and Fire

Hannah's Heirloom ~ Book Two

Chapter One

Spring AD78

The great ship was anchored off Ostia, a port city in the Tyrrhenian Sea on the west coast of Roman Italy. We had been travelling for a long time and I was looking forward, very much, to standing on ground that didn't move underneath me. It was mid morning and the sea was beautiful today, quite calm and the most incredible blue. The sun sparkled on the water, which was so clear that you could see right through the shoals of colourful fish all the way to the bottom.

This made a change from the squally weather we had suffered for most of our sea journey. The ship had been tossed relentlessly, something I had found exhilarating; much to the amusement of Maxentius and Marcus who had been sure I would be terribly seasick. I had spent hours at the prow of the boat, watching the waves crash along the sides of the vessel and often right over the rails.

We were far removed from Masada, Herod's great citadel on the edge of the Judaean desert, which had been our home for the past eleven years. The place where I had met, healed, fallen in love with and, against all the odds, married my Maxentius, Garrison Commander and one of three Romans wounded in the Zealot ambush of AD66 and then made captive; the place where I had given birth to Claudia, our only child; and the place where we had survived a siege, a massacre and the storming of the fortress by the Roman army.

After they had breached the defences, the Romans set about rebuilding Masada where they could. Some areas were too badly damaged and simply abandoned, but much was salvageable, to the joy of the Roman engineers who took great pride in their efforts to restore the fortress. Maxentius had been asked to remain as commander of the new garrison now assigned there, which suited us. I had no desire to leave, for despite the horrors that we had endured, it was still our home.

My name is Hannah, I am a Hebrew woman and a physician and my life was turned upside down by a secret only my husband knows.

Once the dust settled and before we could resume our normal lives, there was the not inconsequential matter of the bodies scattered across the plateau. The large number meant that it would have been an impossible task to bury them all and we could not just leave them to be pecked at by carrion birds. In the end it was decided that we would cremate them, which we did in as dignified a way as possible.

It was very hard for those of us who had lived there for so long. I had known many of them all my life, treated most of them at one time or another and two of them were members of my family. While not necessarily friends, my two Romans had enjoyed, eventually, a cordial relationship with their erstwhile enemy. Surprisingly, the Roman soldiers were compassionate to my anguish and did what they could to help me deal with the remains in a considerate manner.

Liora and Efraim, my brother Aharon's children, understandably were very upset when we told them of the death of their parents. Unable to leave their destiny to an avenging Roman army, Aharon and Raizel, his wife, had taken their own lives, but I had persuaded them to let me have their children. Despite Liora and Efraim's distress, their own innate ability to cope with shock more easily than adults, as is often the way with children, came to the fore and they got over their loss far more quickly than I did.

Of all of us, it was Aliza who struggled to come to terms with their deaths, for Raizel was her daughter and she had known Aharon most of his life. Thankfully the presence of her grandchildren helped her through the darker days and, though it took many moons, she did begin to smile again.

The other two little girls, Gavriella and Sarah, whom I had found by complete chance all alone on the night of the massacre, had found a home. When news of the fall of Masada reached Jerusalem, their mother's brother had risked the journey across the desert to see whether any members of his family had survived. Although devastated by the loss of his sister and her husband, he was very thankful that I had saved the girls. He told me that he and his wife had been unable to have children and that the two girls would now have a home with them.

He was a gentle and kind man and it seemed there was quite a large extended family, so I hoped those sweet children wrapped in the warmth of such caring kin would soon forget the trauma that they had experienced. I was happy for them and, although would have made them part of our home, was secretly relieved that I wasn't putting Maxentius in the awkward position of being responsible for two more children.

During the transition period, while the fortress was being rebuilt, there was much for me to do. The soldiers were always injuring themselves on one thing or other — fallen masonry, burnt wood, flying debris — and I was constantly required to bind wounds, dress lacerations or remove splinters. These men of war seemed to respect me, not just as the wife of their commanding officer, but also as a healer in my own right, treating me with deference and over time, becoming quite affable.

As when I had first met Maxentius and Marcus, I realised that these soldiers were just men, doing a job that they had either chosen to do or been, for want of a better word, encouraged into. Their basic requirements were the same as every other — food, warmth, shelter and safety. It was just sad that they had been part of a conquering force that had devastated my land. However, I was nothing if not a realist. I was safe, happy; I had a place to live and was with my Maxentius. That would do me very well thank you.

Claudia was our joy and she grew quickly. A cheerful and healthy child who, once she was walking confidently, I rarely saw during the day. Her cousins, Aliza, Marcus or one or two of the soldiers who had taken on the role of guardians, were always looking after her. As far as she was concerned, they were all her willing slaves and she had them wrapped round her little fingers. This meant that I was free to look after anyone who needed me, either due to injury or sickness without worrying that she would come into contact with infection. It also allowed Maxentius and me to steal the odd private moment together knowing she was well cared for.

Marcus, the second of the three soldiers whose injuries I had treated and who had remained captive along with Maxentius, never changed. He was unfailingly positive and happy with his lot and had become very important to me not only as a trusted friend, but also as he had taken the place of my brother whom I had lost in the massacre. When he wasn't helping with the building projects, Marcus worked his beloved garden beds, persuading a large number of the auxiliaries to help him and his crops flourished. We had many more mouths to feed now, but, thankfully, most preferred to eat and sleep in the camps below.

It is testament to the efficiency of the Roman army that within a few weeks of its arrival, those areas, which were not too badly damaged, had been made eminently habitable. The ash, soot and grime were removed and, where possible, furniture restored. The upper tier of the Northern Palace and the administration building where my clinic had been were the first to be deemed ready, followed by the Western Palace and one or two of the smaller buildings. The armoury was, of course, restocked, but guarded round the clock. There was no way the Romans were going to be caught on the hop twice.

To our reckoning, it was over four years after the fall of Masada when Maxentius was recalled to Rome. His orders were to take charge of a small force of soldiers posted to the port city of Pompeii in the Bay of Naples following some severe unrest. It was a huge wrench leaving this place, but Maxentius was excited about seeing his homeland again, especially as his family lived near Pompeii.

Marcus would be coming with us, as would quite a large number of the legionaries who had been living here since the Romans retook the fortress. They would make up the majority of the peacekeeping force under Maxentius' command. At thirty and eight years, Maxentius was quite the veteran having seen much action and I think he was hoping that it would not be too arduous a task to preserve the stability of a small city.

It took a little while to pack our belongings, but we didn't have much, mainly clothes. I had toiled long and hard to restock my medicines, oils and balms and, although I left a plentiful supply for whoever would be dispensing treatment, the rest I was determined to bring with us. You never know when such things might be needed.

Eventually, there was nothing left but to say goodbye. I hoped some day we would return, but in my heart I knew it was unlikely. Life was about to change in ways none of us expected.

Our journey had taken several weeks; months even, since leaving Masada, travelling by land and sea. I did miss our home, but was looking forward to discovering the country of my husband, although the thought of meeting his family was somewhat nerve-wracking. I was a Hebrew woman, not the highborn Roman lady his mother would have likely preferred. Although, since he was not supposed to be married anyway, maybe they wouldn't be too upset with him. I could only hope.

From Ostia we would travel up the River Tiber to Rome and, after a short stint there, when Maxentius would have interviews with his superiors, we would go on to Pompeii. The main body of the garrison that Maxentius would command was housed outside the city's boundary, but its headquarters were within the walls. We, along with a small number of soldiers, would have accommodation above and alongside the offices, allowing for an immediate response if necessary.

As I stood on the deck, leaning over the rail, gazing out towards the harbour, Maxentius came to join me, smiling at my expression of wonder.

"It is something to behold isn't it? A great port city. Although, this is nothing compared with Rome." He leaned down and kissed my nose, pulling me close to him. I nestled in the crook of his arm, feeling my heart flip-flop in my chest, as it always did when he was near me. I looked up at his ruggedly handsome face.

"They will go well do you think, your meetings? Is this formality normal when a general returns to Rome?"

"It is a requirement to present a report to your superiors, they need to understand the nature of the place you have come from, whether there are ongoing threats, whether it is peaceful, all manner of things. So yes, my Hannah, this is quite normal."

Unaware of army protocol, I had been worried about this summons to Rome. Did it have anything to do with Flavius Silva granting us citizenship and approving our marriage? I was concerned that these things would be undone and Claudia and I would end up as slaves or worse. I voiced my fears as we admired the view.

"There is nothing to fear my love, Silva was empowered to grant you those honours and our marriage is ratified. The meetings are simply procedure." I sighed with relief, although I would probably not be completely certain everything was approved until we were safely in Pompeii.

I could see the new harbour, which had been built, so Maxentius told me during the reign of the Emperor Claudius. Constructed not only to service the needs of a Rome that was rapidly expanding, but also to protect ships from both the treacherous current at the mouth of the Tiber and the destructive storms, which often lashed the bay. We had to transfer to a smaller vessel to travel up to Rome, as our large troop carrier could not navigate up the winding river and its size meant it was unable to dock. Our transport was expected imminently and, with Roman precision, we noticed a boat approaching.

Aliza and Marcus came over with the three children and, gathering our few belongings together we were ready to be helped into the craft with little delay. The children thought this smaller boat was great fun, although I was moved to comment that if they didn't sit down and behave, they would end up swimming all the way to Rome. This settled them somewhat but didn't do much to douse their enthusiasm. The sights and sounds fascinated them, so much colour and movement and noise, very different from our quiet life on Masada.

The journey up the River Tiber was uneventful, if rather long and it was dusk by the time we reached the wharf where our boat docked. Three sleepy children needed to be coaxed up the gangway and the soldiers who had accompanied us carried our things, which would be delivered to our accommodation at some point. We were escorted to a spacious house somewhere in the city — Maxentius called it a domus — and it appeared to be well set up with everything we might need, including an incredible amount of food.

Being very tired, however, we saved our explorations until the morning. I managed to get the three children to settle in one of the bedrooms and then we four adults enjoyed a goblet of wine in the quiet of the evening. We chatted for a little while, but exhaustion was clear on all our faces, so we finished our drinks and took ourselves off for a relatively early night.

I stood with Maxentius in the cool of our room, looking out of the window. The sky seemed to have fewer stars, although my husband indicated that this was due to all the light thrown up from the town around us. I felt myself sway, partly from tiredness and partly from being so long at sea. Maxentius pulled me to him and kissed me gently. I leaned against his chest, fumbling absently with his clothes. Suddenly I needed him and, attuned to my every emotion, he responded, his hands roving over my body, lifting my tunic and shift over my head. Naked, we fell onto the beautifully comfortable bed, letting our fingers work their magic, the restless heat of passion ignited.

I was endlessly amazed that the desire we had known when we first fell in love had never burnt out. We had known each other for over eleven years, had been married for eight of them and although our love had deepened, the passion was still there. I missed him when he wasn't close and my heart never failed to beat faster the minute I caught sight of him. It was as though we were two halves of a whole, one unable to exist without the other.

That's not to say we always agreed with each other. I am not your typical meek and biddable wife. As I had told my brother years ago, I am impulsive, feisty and headstrong, but I would never turn away anyone who was hurt or in distress and I would do anything to keep my family safe. Despite all these things, or maybe because of them, Maxentius loved me and I would give my life for him.

Our lovemaking was unhurried but intense, after which we fell asleep wrapped in each other's arms, as we did every night. Sometimes I feared that if he let me go, I would disappear — after all, it has happened before.

Chapter Two

Unaware of what was unfolding almost two thousand years away, Max and I were discovering the fascination of Rome, revelling in the ancient city. We had come for a holiday and, surprisingly, given my love of anything connected with Ancient Rome and Max's love of its archaeology, neither of us had been here before. For long enough, its name had been enough to stir my imagination, conjuring up a world of gladiators, chariot races, vast amphitheatres, soaring monuments, political intrigue, huge armies, great battles, victorious generals and its notorious rulers, all culminating in one of the greatest Empires the world has ever known.

On arriving, I was enchanted that the heritage of Rome is not set apart, tidily sectioned off away from the main city; rather it simply exists everywhere. You never know what you will come across; one moment you are walking down a busy shopping street, the next you are in front of Trajan's column. While heading to the Piazza Navona to enjoy a coffee or check out the markets, you realise you are passing by the Pantheon. Rome and its history envelop you, becoming as much a part of you as breathing.

My name is Hannah Wilson and a little over a year ago I accompanied my best friend Max Vallier to Masada, in an attempt to trace the origins of a ruby clasp, a gift I had received from my long-dead grandmother. While helping with the archaeological excavations, I began to experience strange dreams relating to the storming of the fortress by the Jewish Zealots in AD66. Initially putting them down to my vivid imagination, eventually I discerned that I was actually experiencing the events as they unfolded, but through the eyes of my ancestor. As I was trying to deal with all of this, I realised I was falling for Max who, it seemed, had been in love with me for quite some time and was just waiting for me to catch up.

Unable to stop what was happening to me, my two worlds melded. In the ancient world I was suddenly caring for three Roman soldiers who had survived the attack but were now captive, while back in the modern world I was finding artefacts that tied me to my ancient counterpart. Following an accident, which knocked me unconscious, some part of me slipped into the world of ancient Masada. With no real recollection of my ancestor's life before this, I had to rely on instinct and the knowledge of what would happen to the citadel, to save those I loved without changing history.

To complicate matters, my ancestor, also called Hannah, fell in love with one of the Roman soldiers, Maxentius, which could have had deadly consequences. Thankfully, I — or she and I — were able to overcome many obstacles and the last connection I had with her was as she fell asleep, safe in Maxentius' arms after the Roman army had retaken the fortress. Even though long weeks had passed in this world, equating to six years in the ancient one, my Max had waited for me. His love had been strong enough to bring me home.

The clasp — the clasp is gorgeous, a deep red stone nestled in an intricate setting of burnished metal. I had received it twice, once from Maxentius, who gifted the clasp to me — okay, well not really me, the other Hannah — on the birth of their daughter, which is how, nearly two thousand years later, it came back into my possession, the gift from my grandmother. I believe it has magical powers, don't ask me to prove it, I can't, it's just a feeling.

Over a year after those events, it was late October and we needed this break. We had both been very busy and, had not seen as much of each other as we would have liked. I had hoped that on our return from Masada we would be living together, sharing our lives in much the same way as we had begun to do during that fateful holiday. It hadn't quite turned out that way. Max had been seconded to an engineering project in America and I had ended up travelling between several museums to promote upcoming exhibitions. Despite the fact that we had talked almost every day, it wasn't the same as being together.

When I'd worked it out, I realised that we had probably seen each other only half a dozen times over the last eighteen months and I was finding the separation a little too much to cope with. After my experiences on Masada, I felt adrift when Max wasn't close by to ground me. My head was full of memories that I couldn't share with anyone but him and I still struggled to deal with the loss of what seemed to be six years of my life. Even though I knew it wasn't my life and that I hadn't actually been there, the voices from my past were never far from my consciousness.

We had eventually told our parents that we had become more than just friends, simply because it was obvious that something had changed between us. We hadn't gone any further ahead with finding a house though, or even one of us moving into the other's flat. I worried that we would drift apart, that too many things kept getting in the way. I missed the cocoon we had at Masada, the deliciousness of only us knowing, the newness of it all, secret smiles, stolen kisses and passionate lovemaking. A month of being in a coma aside, it was the best time of my life. I wanted to recapture those moments before we let life intervene and lost it all. We had both waited too long.

This holiday had been a spur of the moment opportunity. One of Max's friends, Edward, with whom he had been on previous archaeological digs, had an apartment in Rome and was looking for someone in England, where he would be attending a course, who would be willing to do a house swap. It was too good to turn down; Max jumped at the chance and offered Edward his flat, which happened to be reasonably close to where the course was being held and as a further inducement his car.

Edward had duly arrived in England three days previously, had handed over the keys to his home along with all the details about how to find it, best places to eat and so on. After a night in London, we had landed just over twenty-four hours later and the minute we had stepped out of the apartment, I was enthralled. I have never particularly liked big cities, I find them overwhelming, but Rome was like nowhere I'd been before. It has a magic about it that ensnares the senses, interweaving the past and the present, bewitching the visitor with its history. Giotto di Bondone, an Italian painter of the Early Renaissance, described Rome as '...the city of echoes, the city of illusions and the city of yearning.' His sentiments mirrored mine perfectly.

I wanted to see everything; the ruins, the basilicas, the museums, everything. Suddenly I was like a child at Christmas;

I felt my tensions draining away, everything I love about Ancient Roman history was right here. We had spent the last two days just walking around, getting our bearings, enjoying being able to have a coffee near the Trevi Fountain or a glass of wine in the Piazza Barberini, without worrying about having to be anywhere at a given time.

Today we had found our way to the top of the steps by the statue of Marcus Aurelius, in the Piazza del Campidoglio and Max had stopped to take photos of the Theatre of Marcellus from this great vantage point. While he was clicking away, I followed my nose and went out through the gap between the buildings at the rear of the square. Laid out in front of me was the Forum Romanum in all its glory.

I could not get my head around it, it was just there, right in front of me and its magnificence took my breath away. I was riveted to the spot, you could have probably left me there all day and it still wouldn't have been enough. My mind started to imagine it, as it would have looked in antiquity, from its humble beginnings as a meeting place, to the awe inspiring judicial and administrative centre of the Roman Empire.

During the Late Republic, the population of Rome grew rapidly due, in no small part, to the arrival of people from new provinces along with an influx of army veterans as well as landowners who had lost everything in the civil wars — all seeking new lives in the city. The existing centre for administration, the Forum, proved inadequate for the inundation of people, so Julius Caesar had proposed a radical expansion. This had the dual effect of allowing administration to be handled more efficiently while impressing the citizens of Rome with his munificence.

Other Emperors also saw fit to add to the complex, each trying to better or at least equal his predecessor. Today, their ruins lie nestled between the Palatine and the Capitoline Hills, hinting at the remarkable ingenuity of the Roman architects and builders and the Emperors' whose power created it.

Dragging my mind back to the twenty first century, I heard Max come up behind me.

"Look at this." I said spreading my hands out. "Just look at it, it is absolutely astonishing. I cannot get my head around the fact that I've just walked through a gap in the buildings and this is here. There should be trumpet voluntaries or banners, or something, heralding the utter awesomeness that is the Forum." Max laughed at my enthusiasm.

"It's certainly incredible! Shall we start looking round now, or wait 'til tomorrow?" Glancing at my watch I noticed that it was nearly three o'clock.

"Tomorrow." I decided. "Then we can spend the day without rushing at it."

"That's what I'd hoped you'd say. I can feel a gelato, or a beer, or both calling my name, 'specially if either can be enjoyed on a very comfy chair." Smiling, he took my hand and pulled me close, kissing me gently. I felt my heart quicken, as I kissed him back. We stood a little longer, his arm around me, my head on his shoulder, looking out over the ruins. Then, reluctantly in my case, turned to head back towards our flat.

On the way we spotted a street bar and ducked in for a beer. It was endlessly fascinating watching the world go by in Rome. The crazy motorcyclists, the tourists exclaiming at the sights, the locals immune to the beauty all around them - well maybe not immune, but so accustomed to it that they no longer noticed. I loved it, full of colour and life and sound, its vibrancy contagious. The beer ran into dinner with wine, it was so relaxing and I think part of me was holding off the moment when we would return to the flat. I was nervous, but for why I couldn't tell you.

The bar was quite close to where we were staying and in a lovely part of the city, so it was still quite early when we arrived home - well our home for the next three weeks anyway. Situated near the Spanish Steps and on the fourth floor, it was a large, airy apartment and from the main room, we had a stunning view over the roofs of the city. I love roofs and the colours of the ones outside our window were glorious. Soft yellows and reds, browns and creams, in the dying light of the day their shades were muted, but no less beautiful and, in the distance I could make out the dome of St Peter's Basilica, I was entranced.

I knew I was playing for time, I was afraid that the moment wouldn't come. Then Max came over to stand behind me and, lifting my hair kissed the back of my neck. Frissons of delight began their dance up and down my spine and my breathing quickened. I didn't move, letting him weave his spell, he turned me to face him and murmuring my name, continued kissing me. His hand curved round the back of my neck, tilting my head up; I loved it when he did this, it was so intimate and he held me so gently, as though afraid I might shatter.

Max drew me close, our bodies fitting together, curve for curve and I could feel the flame scorching along my veins, but it wasn't enough. I needed to feel all of him and in tune with each other we somehow ended up in the bedroom. I hesitated for just a moment, he smiled that slow toe-curling smile and my heart thumped against my ribs.

I leaned into him and let my hands find their way up his shirt, slowly undoing the buttons, letting my fingers glide across his skin. It had been so long since I felt connected to him that I did not want this to be a frenzied rush. His shirt undone, I kissed his chest and the hollows at the base of his neck, loving the shudder that rippled through him as I did. Removing my top, he ran his hands back through my hair to cup my face, reclaiming my mouth with his lips.

His kiss was harder now, more intense, his fingers ran up my back, stroking me, he slipped the strap of my bra down, sliding his fingers between the silky material and my breast, teasing across the sensitive skin. I gasped, needing more. Somehow, our fingers fumbling, we removed the rest of our clothes, hands teasing across warm flesh as the fabric fell away, material floating to the floor. I let my hand slide over his thighs caressing him, his need for me was obvious and it still amazed me that I had the power to make him desire me.

"Please Max, we've waited long enough." My voice was barely a whisper, but he heard, he always heard. He kissed me again, hot and fierce, his tongue searching, his hands roving, somehow we were on the bed, my body arching into his, desperate for him to take me, but he held back. His hands wandered down my body, his fingers working their magic and taking me to new heights of ecstasy.

I ran my hands down his back and along his waist, making him groan as I brought them back up over his stomach, my legs hooking over his, holding him to me. Just when I thought I could not take any more, he moved me under him and entered me. The fire that had been flaming through me became a conflagration and I needed to consume him, this man whom I loved more than life itself. He took me higher and higher and I never wanted to come back down. Finally, after what seemed like forever, our breathing eased, our hearts slowed and we came back to earth.

"Hannah, oh my darling girl I have missed you." He sighed against my hair. Looking at him, I noticed how dark his eyes were and unbidden a memory popped into my head, 'They were like pools of night, so dark I might drown in them.' No, not now, not here, this is my time.

"I've missed you too. I love you Max, more than I can ever tell you. Please let's not have another year like this last one. I've been so afraid that you were growing away from me, that your work would be the thing that finished us. We had barely begun our lives together and you were gone..."

Max put his finger on my lips, following it with a kiss and then said —

"I cannot imagine my life without you in it, you are the reason I get up everyday and the only person I want to see when I come home at night. I have hated being away so much this year, every time I had to say goodbye, I saw beyond your smile, the smile you hoped would fool me and I knew how it hurt your heart that I was going away again. Even when we're apart and I know you're not with me, I feel you beside me. I counted the hours every day while I was in the States 'til I could call you at some kind of reasonable time."

I murmured against his lips —

"I wouldn't have cared if it was unreasonable." He started kissing me again, softly and tenderly, running his hands through my hair with one hand and pressing me to him with the other. The spark re-ignited and flared, our kiss deepened, growing more intense. The slow burn became a firestorm, desire rocked through me and I gave myself over to the exquisite torture Max was inflicting with his fingers and his lips. A lifetime later, when we had both got our breath back we lay wrapped together, my head resting in the crook of Max's neck, his cheek laying against my hair. Tired now, we talked for a few minutes and just as I fell asleep I heard him whisper —

"I love you, Sunshine."

I smiled.

Chapter Three

My hand was resting on the wall of a large structure, I couldn't work out where I was, I must have taken a wrong turn. It was very cold and seemed to be late afternoon; the daylight was fading and the air misty. Keeping my hand on the cool stone to make sure I didn't step too far away from the one solid thing near me, I looked around. The building I was touching was curved and very high and, opposite me, about twenty feet away there was another structure. This one was square and from it I could hear voices and the clash of what sounded like weapons, muted by the fog.

Light glowed from the centre, which looked huge. As I walked towards it, a group of young men came out of a doorway, talking and laughing, their warm breath creating little white clouds in the chill air. They didn't notice me and I waited until they had disappeared before I ventured closer. The door was standing open; there was a short corridor, opening onto what, at first glance, appeared to be an enormous peristyle courtyard, which I followed round. In the centre was a swimming pool and, at either side, large open squares surrounded by trees, where men were practising all kinds of sports. Huge torches were scattered around, lighting the grounds most satisfactorily.

In my hand was a cloth bag. Glancing into it I could see rolls of material, balms and salves. Was I coming here to treat someone? Was someone injured? I couldn't tell. Surely I should know? I carried on walking around looking for someone who could tell me why I was here. Then a voice called me over.

"Are you the medica? I nodded. "Over here please." I followed the voice and came to a halt by a group of young men surrounding another who was unconscious on the floor, bleeding quite heavily from a cut to his leg.

Memories kicked in and I realised what was happening, but was still unsure whether I was dreaming this. Half of my mind was confused. This wasn't Masada, where was I? Pushing the thought to the back of my head, I asked —

"How did this happen?"

"He was training with the javelin and somehow it flipped, cutting his leg."

"Please move back a little, I need space to work. When did it happen, how long ago?"

"Not long, less than a quarter of one hour, you arrived more quickly than we expected."

"I do not live far from here." Then, turning to the task at hand, I asked. "Please will someone get me a bowl and a pitcher of clean water?" One of the youngsters ran off, returning quickly with what I needed. Using it first to wash my hands, I refilled the bowl, added salt and, soaking one of the cloths in it, began to clean the wound. It wasn't too deep but it was long and the mud from the point on the javelin had lodged itself nicely inside the cut.

The poor boy had come around as soon as I had started to work on his injury. He was pale and shaking and I tried to be gentle. After several minutes I had cleaned away all the dirt and could examine the wound properly. I looked at the young man.

"What is your name, Sir?"

"Appius Horatius." Shakily.

"Well, Appius Horatius, I think we can save your leg, but this might sting a bit." I winked at him and he smiled, just a little. Pulling out a jar of salve, I got a large dollop on my finger and pushed it deep into the wound, making sure any excess coated the sides. Then unrolling two of the bandages I found in my bag, I folded one to cover the cut and used the other to bandage it securely.

As I finished, the pain obviously became too much and to my patient's total embarrassment he was very sick. Squeezing his shoulder, I offered him a drink of water and asked whether now that I had finished, the pain was lessening. He nodded weakly and his friends gathered round to carry him into the changing rooms. I glanced at his trainer who was waiting nearby.

"I will return in the morning, that wound will need re-dressing. Make sure he stays warm, it is cold this evening."

"Thank you, we are indebted to you for coming so quickly."

"It was nothing, how often do these men injure themselves?" I asked, interested.

"Not often, they can be clumsy and awkward when they start training and small injuries are common. This is the worst one we've had in quite a while."

While he was talking, a thought struck me and I asked whether they had a regular physician.

"No, we just find the closest one."

"How did you know I practised medicine?"

"One of the youngsters saw you the other day helping an old man who had fallen injuring his arm and thought you lived quite close by. He said he would try you first."

"Well I am pleased to help and I was just thinking that maybe we could be of service to each other. Rather than search the town for a healer who is free, maybe I could be the one you call first. I am only a few streets away and can be here quickly. I could also visit regularly, so even small concerns could be dealt with straight away and, if you paid me a small amount for each treatment, I could put it towards medicines, bandages and so on, which would be used only on your students."

He ruminated on this for a few minutes then said —

"It sounds feasible, I will ponder your suggestion tonight and you will have my answer when you come to check young Horatius."

"Thank you, I appreciate your consideration. I hope the rest of your session is uneventful and I will see you in the morning. Oh..." as I was turning, "...is there a better way out? I am not quite familiar with the layout of the Palaestra and in the gloom missed the main entrance. I came through what looked like the students' door." He pointed to the opening opposite where I had come in.

Thanking him, I nodded and took my leave. This was much quicker and I made may way back along the misty path to our home in half the time, where I hoped Maxentius, having finished his day, would be waiting for me. The breeze was picking up. I could hear it rustling through the pines and hopefully it would disperse this dank fog.

The house was warm and welcoming, a fire burnt merrily and several oil lamps had been lit. Maxentius was sitting in a chair with Claudia on his knee telling her a story that was making her chortle with laughter. Liora and Efraim were sitting at a table playing some kind of game and Aliza was cooking dinner. They looked up as I came in and Maxentius came over to take my cloak.

"You are wet through, my love, where have you been?"

"I was called to the Palaestra, one of the boys had gashed his leg on a javelin. Honestly, how he did it I have no idea." Smiling up at my husband, I raised myself on tiptoe to kiss him, he held me close retuning the kiss with interest.

"You should change, your tunic is damp too and you do not want to get sick." Knowing he was right but enjoying the moment, I reluctantly relinquished my hold and went to our bedroom to find dry clothes. Claudia bounced in after me telling me about the story and what they'd been doing while I'd been out. Apparently Aliza had let them help prepare dinner so who knew what that would taste like!

Once changed, I sat on the bed and she crawled onto my knee. I loved these moments, just her and me; they were so precious as she getting too big to want cuddles from her mother. I hugged her to me, resting my chin on her curly hair as I told her about the misty weather and the boy I had just treated. Sensing movement, I glanced up to see Maxentius leaning on the doorpost, he smiled across the room and my heart flipped.

He came and sat next to us on the bed, drawing us into his chest and I could feel his heart beating steady and strong against my back. We remained like that for several minutes, listening to Claudia's chatter, until Aliza called us for dinner and the moment was broken — so few of them now. Maxentius spent long hours with the peacekeeping unit and Claudia was usually in bed by the time he got home. Still, at least we were all together.

A knock at the back door heralded Marcus who joined us most evenings for a meal. He lived next door, in rooms over the headquarters, which was in reality a conveniently situated house, requisitioned for the purpose, as the main barracks were outside the city walls. He came in with treats for the children, who swarmed all over him in glee. He still reminded me of the Pied Piper. Everywhere he went he was a magnet for small fry and always had time for them, he never ceased to amaze me. I generally found other people's children annoying or spoilt and, if they didn't behave respectfully or appropriately, I tended to avoid them, but Marcus took it all in his stride.

As either Aliza or I were home much of the day, we had not taken any slaves as servants. I found it difficult to accept that we were entitled to them and it did not sit well with me, especially as many were from conquered countries, one of them being my own. Slaves had been part of the set-up when we'd been in Rome, but I was never comfortable with it. In fact I had found Rome wholly uncomfortable in every aspect, being huge and full of people. I spent more time worrying that I would lose the children than anything else. Thankfully, our sojourn there had been brief and I had not been sad to leave it behind, finding Pompeii much easier to navigate. There were far fewer people to start with and many had fled after the devastating earthquake about sixteen years earlier, yet to return. Those remaining, whom we had met, seemed friendly enough.

There were too few of us to require servants anyway, we had been living in Pompeii for over six months and so far Aliza and I had managed all the domestic chores between us, making it hard to justify having extra help. Aliza did most of the cooking, as I was hopeless, but I did the cleaning and washing, so it worked well. It also meant that at meal times, it was just us, we didn't have anyone else in our home and we could talk without fear of anyone overhearing. This was something we appreciated, especially as often our discussions involved political or civil unrest and trust was hard earned here.

After dinner, I got the children ready for bed, sitting with them for a little while. The three of them shared a room, our home wasn't small, but Claudia preferred the company of her cousins to a room on her own. I'm sure they got up to mischief when we closed the door, but as long as they were quiet, I wasn't overly worried about it. The rest of us enjoyed another goblet of wine and chatted until it was quite late. I told them about my conversation with the trainer and they thought it was a good idea, suggesting that I also ask at the gladiators' barracks, as they were always injuring themselves. I didn't want to step on the toes of other physicians, but it was worth a visit, if either Maxentius or Marcus would come with me. It probably wasn't somewhere a woman should be without an escort.

Our chatter moved to less mundane matters, mainly the unrest that continued to brew in the city. It seemed to be simmering under the surface and was hard to trace the source. The latest theory was that it was linked to those who had sided against Vespasian during the civil war nearly a decade earlier and, according to my two Romans, Pompeii was quite the melting pot for the resentful and disillusioned.

"You need to take care when you are in the city, Hannah. These riots can blow out of nothing and I do not want you to get caught up in one."

"I will, but I am not going to let the possibility of a riot stop me from going about my daily life. If they make us fear stepping outside of our homes, they will have won. Also, I am not a soldier, I am just a woman. What threat am I? I cannot imagine I will have any problems." Words that would come back to haunt me soon enough. We talked for a little longer, then Marcus left for his own apartment and we tidied up and went to bed.

Maxentius mentioned his concerns again as we lay together under the bed covers.

"I meant it Hannah, please be careful and take note of anything which seems odd or unusual. These people do not care who they hurt when they are part of a mob and if the children are with you..." I put my fingers to his lips and told him that I would never deliberately place them in danger and I would do as he asked, as long as he did the same.

"For you are more at risk than I, it will be the soldiers they want to fight, you are the Emperor's representatives."

"Fair point and I am always vigilant, my love." He blew out the oil lamp and as the darkness enfolded us, we slept.

Chapter Four

I couldn't wake up, the bed was so comfortable and warm and I felt as though I hadn't had enough sleep. Someone was shaking my shoulders and telling me it was time to get up. Ignoring them I tried to snuggle back down, but suddenly the covers disappeared and the cold air did what nothing else could.

"Nooooo...not fair...I need more sleep." Grumpily, I opened my eyes, straight into a pair of dark green ones glimmering with amusement. My jaw dropped and the amusement changed to concern.

"Hey, Sunshine, what's wrong?" Fighting back sleep, I sat up and stared around me — modern apartment, clean minimal lines, picture window, what *was* wrong? Max was looking at me in puzzlement. "Come on, Han, give." I gazed back at him, trying to pin down my thoughts. Then, hesitantly, unsure of their reception...

"...I had a dream..." the words hung there, innocent enough, but loaded with meaning.

"A dream? Do you mean a regular dream or one of your dreams?" knowing the answer before he even asked. Why else would I have been so shocked when I looked into his eyes? Even though they were the same as Maxentius', I could still tell one from the other, it was something indefinable, except to me.

"I'm sorry," I whispered, reaching for his hand, "I didn't ask for this." He had hoped that when we left Masada, this was all finished with, but I hadn't been so sure. It hadn't felt like the end, more like just the beginning, but I hadn't had any 'events' in the last year and had started to think maybe I was wrong. "I don't know why, I don't even know where they are. It isn't Masada, but it's Roman..." and aiming for levity, "...just make sure there are no stairs for me to tumble down." He grinned and leaned across to kiss me, quick and hard.

"I know you didn't ask for it, Sunshine and, I'll watch out for low-flying steps." He kissed me again and suddenly the cold air wasn't a problem any more.

After a leisurely breakfast, during which Max quizzed me about my dream, trying to work out what it meant and failing

— it would keep — we set off for the Forum. The walk to it from our apartment was lovely, only about twenty minutes, down the Via Conditori, onto the Via del Corso, around the Piazza Venezia and along the Via dei Fori Imperiali. I loved rolling the names of the streets around my tongue, they sounded so seductive and laden with promise. We strolled, hand in hand and as we passed the Capitoline Museum, the ruins of the Forum came into view through the tall umbrella pines.

The scene from above had been incredible enough, but to be down at eye level was nothing short of astonishing. I was spellbound. For a student of classical antiquity, whose passion is all things Roman, this is the Holy Grail. I began to hurry, not wanting to waste another moment outside of this complex. Max laughed at my enthusiasm, but I could tell he was just as captivated and his love of archaeology would now be fighting with his desire to understand the ancient engineering.

Paying for our ticket, we walked down the long entry pathway, coming onto the Via Sacra, next to the Temple of Antoninus and Faustina. For several minutes we just soaked it all in, the immense Domus Tiberiana rising up majestically behind the House of the Vestals, the remaining columns of the Temple of Saturn soaring over the Arch of Septimius Severus and everything in between. It was so awe-inspiring that I wanted to cry; I did not have enough adjectives in my vocabulary to describe the emotions that flooded through me. Where did we even start? Looking at the map we had been given with our ticket, we decided to start under the Temple of Saturn and work our way towards the Palatine.

One or two sections were closed for either for conservation or protection and a few areas where archaeologists were working were also off-limits, but most of the complex was accessible. My camera barely stopped, it was a good job I had brought an extra battery. Max was as bad — there was just so much to see. We almost forgot to stop for lunch but, thankfully, just outside the entrance there was a street vendor who sold sandwiches, so we could eat and run.

Back into the Forum, we made our way up to the Palatine Hill, making sure we stopped to view the vast Basilica di Massenzio and the Arch of Titus on the way. I hesitated at this last monument, for the depiction of the Sack of Jerusalem struck a chord and I studied it for a long time. Dredging through my memory I recalled that this arch was the first unreserved demonstration of Roman impressionism and an innovation of the Flavian age — the reign of Vespasian and his two sons — mid to late first century AD. On either side of the passageway the intricate friezes depict two successive moments of a triumphal procession. One panel portrays Titus on a chariot preceded by a crowd of lictors, or magisterial attendants; the opposite shows the spoils of war from the sack of the Temple of Jerusalem.

The illusion of light and depth had been achieved by deep drilling, creating dark shadow and high relief. A slight curve in the background of both panels gives the impression that the procession comes towards the onlooker. The slightly bent knees of the figures carrying the spoils of war are also leaning forward, implying weight and progress as they move towards the distant arch. It was incredibly beautiful, but it hurt my heart. I, through the eyes of my ancestor, had witnessed the aftermath of this destruction: refugees stumbling into an isolated fortress, followed eventually by an avenging Roman army.

Despite the warmth of the autumn sun, I shivered and Max came to stand beside me gazing up at the reliefs.

"You okay, Sunshine?" I nodded, but he wasn't convinced, putting his arm round my shoulder and hugging me close. "Come on, let's keep going, this can't be doing you any good." I hugged him back, relieved that he understood. Walking up the gentle slope to the top of the Palatine Hill, we meandered through the Casa di Livia and the Casa di Augusto — queuing to admire the remarkable frescos — then back around to the Domus Augustana and Domus Flavia including the immense Stadium of Domitian; this last considered more likely to have served as a private sports ground and garden than a public stadium. Even today in their ruined state, the scale of these structures is extraordinary; they must have been magnificent when first built. By now we had been in the complex all day. It was late afternoon and as the Forum closes at five, we knew we had to leave but it was hard to drag ourselves away.

"We can always come again," said Max. "We've got three weeks."

"I know, but I don't want to leave, it's so evocative. You can almost see the people who lived here walking through these buildings, I never expected to feel like this."

"I'd be more surprised if you didn't, given your love for Ancient Rome and your connection to it." I looked at him enquiringly, he didn't usually talk about the 'other me,' but he didn't elaborate and I was loath to spoil the moment. Grinning, he squeezed my hand and pulled me up off the bench we'd been relaxing on.

"Ooof, my feet are starting to throb," I moaned, "I can't walk far."

"We've got to get home somehow and I'm not sure I can give you a piggyback all the way up those steps." Laughing at my pained face. "Come on, we'll stop for a drink on the way, that'll help."

We meandered back down the hill, stopping to watch some of the archaeologists at work. I knew Max was itching to join them, but was managing to restrain himself. Just as we were about to set off again, we heard a familiar voice hailing us. Astonished, we turned round to see Geoff and Nate walking towards us, big smiles plastered all over their faces. We hadn't seen them since they left Masada and although we had been in sporadic touch through emails, neither of us had a clue that they were in Rome.

"What are you guys doing here?" asked Geoff as they reached us, shaking hands with Max and kissing me.

"On holiday mate. You?"

"We're helping on this plot, then next week we're off to Pompeii, how about joining us?"

"I'm not sure..." I started to say, as Max said —

"Really, do you think it'd be possible?" I looked at the three of them excited about the prospect of working together again and smiled, a little wistfully. There goes our holiday, I thought; now it'll be all archaeology. Max turned and caught my expression before I managed to hide it.

"Oh honey, I'm sorry, that was thoughtless. We don't have to go, but imagine the chance to see the parts of Pompeii that tourists can't get into, such an opportunity." I gazed into his eyes, how could I say no, it wouldn't be fair and at least I might get to help. It was just that as Pompeii had been mentioned, I suddenly had the strangest feeling about it, not foreboding as such, more a sense of unease, although I couldn't put my finger on the reason.

Pushing it aside, I beamed at him, infusing enthusiasm into my voice.

"Why not, it'd be fun, as long as I can help." The other three grinned back and we agreed to meet later for dinner to thrash out the details.

"Just don't go falling down stairs again, Hannah, its bad for your head." Geoff chuckled at his wit and the two of them waved as they made their way across the dig site. As we turned to leave, I felt cold and, it wasn't anything to do with the afternoon breeze. What had I let myself in for?

In the couple of hours we had before we needed to go out again, I managed to fill in my journal, yes the same one I had with me at Masada, those pages now tucked away safely in the side pocket. I had taken care to jot down where we'd been, but needed to be more detailed. I had also brought my clasp with me, unwilling to leave it in my flat. In fact it had become my habit to take it everywhere, a bit like putting on a watch, or picking up your phone. Don't ask me why, I can't explain, but it's like my shield. My grandmother called it a talisman, I feel the same and that I'm vulnerable without it. Sorry, didn't mean to get distracted there...once I'd committed as much as I could remember to paper, I had a quick shower, feeling much more refreshed, although I have to admit that my feet were still sore.

Thankfully, we didn't have to walk far as we met that evening at a café near the bottom of the Spanish Steps. It was one that had been recommended and turned out to be a great choice. The food was fantastic, the wine cheap, but excellent and the service superb. We discovered that both Nate and Geoff could speak Italian, which delighted our waiter who could not do enough for us. By the time we were enjoying our post dinner Limóncello, we had sorted out the trip to Pompeii.

We would go by train, since neither of us wanted to drive and Geoff had invited us to stay at his place; seems he had a holiday home in the modern town. I felt a little uncomfortable at the thought of sharing his home, thereby losing some of our freedom, but he finished up by saying that Nate had offered his spare room, leaving us the run of the villa. Bless them, I think they knew I was struggling a bit with the suddenness of it all and had tried to make the move to Pompeii as attractive as possible.

"Are you sure? I asked gently. "That is so generous, but it's your home, we could stay in a hotel. It's not really fair for you to leave your house, just for us."

"It's my pleasure, Hannah. Seriously, we've already decided so there's to be no argument. We asked you to join us, we can't expect you to pay for a hotel as well." Nate has a huge place and he rattles around in it, the pair of us will be fine there." Nate was nodding, agreeing with his friend.

"Well, if you're certain," I was still hesitant and Nate put his hand on my arm.

"Take the offer, Hannah, we wouldn't have made it if we didn't mean it."

Capitulating, I grinned at the two of them who looked like they'd just scored the winning goal in a footy match.

"You two are incorrigible, thank you so much." Max was laughing at me and I punched his arm. "Okay, you win — this time." The rest of the evening was spent discussing the site itself. There were several areas they would be working on and I let their words wash over me, I would help wherever they wanted me to. However, the more they talked, the more uneasy I felt, I just wished I knew why.

I was quiet on our way back to the apartment, Max talked about the following week and I let his soothing voice calm my disquiet. Halfway there he stopped talking and stood still and, in a world of my own, I carried on for several steps before I realised he wasn't next to me any more. Hadn't we been holding hands? I looked down and then back, he was waiting, half in shadow, watching.

"Max?" He came slowly towards me.

"I wondered whether you'd notice if I wasn't here."

"What do you mean?" Bewildered.

"You're in another world Hannah, I've been talking away for the last ten minutes and you haven't said a word."

"I was enjoying listening to you, I love hearing your voice and I didn't realise you wanted me to reply." Puzzled, I tried to fathom his expression, but couldn't in the darkness. "I'm sorry, what have I done?"

"Tell me what's going on in your head. Ever since we met Nate and Geoff you've been sort of disconnected, does it have anything to do with that dream you were telling me about this morning?"

Sighing I shook my head.

"I don't know, the mention of Pompeii this afternoon made me feel quite strange. I can't explain why, because I know I want to see it, but something's niggling at me. I realise that you don't like talking about what happened to me, but you're the only one who knows and I think this is part of it, or the next bit of it, or something. You waited for me, was that all for nothing? Oh...never mind..." my voice trailed away and frustrated that I couldn't seem to find the words that would help him understand, I turned away, not wanting him to see my face. Annoyed with myself as useless tears began welling up, tears I didn't want him to see. He was the one I thought I could rely on, the one person who said he believed me and now I wasn't so sure. The time we had spent apart had changed us and I feared we would never recover what we had found at Masada.

Max wasn't going to let me off that easily however and spun me back to face him, lifting my chin so he could look at me properly.

"Why do you think I dislike talking about it?"

"You always change the subject and I know it bothered you, when I told you about my, well the other Hannah's, life. That there was a man whom she loved as much as I love you, I was part of that and it can't be easy for you. You have to know it wasn't 'this me' who fell in love, but it worries me that you can't get past it, that this will break us and I'm so afraid I'm losing you. Even this holiday, I thought it was going to be the chance for the two of us to reconnect and then suddenly its all archaeology and digs and other people..." deep breath, "... oh, I know that's selfish, but it's how I feel. I can't help it, I've missed you so much." Then, like a dam breaking, it all came tumbling out; there on a quiet back street in the middle of the most magical city I had ever seen.

Everything that had built up over the last year while he'd been away. Things I hadn't wanted to bother him with on the few occasions he'd been home, because we had so little time together and I didn't want to spoil it. Then, sighing I said quietly, "If anything, my love for you is deeper than it was last year, it fills my life. I know you said last night that you feel the same, but we have been apart for so long, I'm afraid that what you feel is the memory of what we had, not what we have now."

My voice was hoarse with unshed tears and I was trembling with the force of my emotions, but I held his gaze, watching his eyes, those eyes that reflected his soul. Then he spoke, his voice enveloping me like a warm blanket.

"Oh Hannah, when will you learn, I'm never letting you go, I have waited too long to hold you, to kiss you, to love you. Yes, we've been apart, but that only made me more certain that we were meant to be together. You are my other half. Do you think for one moment that if I no longer cared that we would be together on this holiday, or that I would have made love to you last night? What kind of man do you take me for? I would never string someone along."

He paused for a moment.

"I change the subject because I worry about you, about how it affects *you*, not me. I am more than happy to nut it out if you need to, but you get so upset when you talk about it. I think you've decided in your muddle-headed way that I can't handle what you went through and, if this unease is anything to go by, may be about to go through again. You're pushing me away, so that if I do give up on you, you can't be hurt." I looked at him, was he right? Was I pushing him away? Confused, I mulled over that thought, maybe he was right. Why on earth would I do that?

"Why would I do that to you?" I whispered, one solitary tear finally escaping my eye. "I have no desire to live without you, why would I push you away?"

"Because you are terrified that you might slip back in time and never be able to find your way home and if you push me away, you will save me from the heartache of losing you."

"Really, do you think I'm that clever?" Trying to smile

"I don't think you even know you're doing it, Hannah, it's just your way of trying to protect me, but I don't need it, I'm a big boy and I want to do the protecting, you just need to let me."

Tears were falling freely now, just falling, and I gazed at my love hoping I hadn't ruined everything.

"Oh God, Max, I didn't...surely I wouldn't... please forgive me..." It was barely a breath, then, "...protect me, please protect me." I reached blindly for him, stumbling a little, but he was there, he was always there, he caught me to him, holding me close, murmuring my name over and over.

"I'm here, Sunshine, I'm here."

Chapter Five

He held me close for a long time, then we walked the last few minutes back to the apartment, my head was aching a little, but I felt better. Once inside and curled up with a glass of wine, we carried on talking. It was as if we had broken through an invisible barrier, one we'd unknowingly erected, preventing us from sharing small anxieties, allowing uncertainty to fester.

Our weekends together had been so rare, that neither wanted to bother the other, even things that were seemingly inconsequential and easily dealt with, hadn't been addressed. It was very cathartic, like a weight rolling off my shoulders and I felt lighter and happier than I had in months. A bottle of wine and copious cups of tea helped and somewhere around dawn we fell asleep on the sofa, curled up together, finally on the same page.

Several hours later, I woke up to find Max, resting on his elbow watching me, he smiled his slow smile and my heart thudded in response.

"Morning, Sunshine, sleep well?"

"Better than I have in months." I smiled back, lifting my head to kiss him. "How long have you been watching me? Sorry if I snored."

"No snoring, although you do make delightful snuffly noises when you're about to wake up." I blew a raspberry at him.

"Do we have to go out?" I asked hopefully. "I'm quite comfortable here."

"Really, on this couch? I'm fine with that, but if we're staying here, we'd be way more comfortable in bed." Inviting.

"Sounds blissful. I know we should go out and discover more of Rome, but I really don't want to today. Today I want it to be just us, here, away from the world."

"We're on holiday, Hannah, we can do anything we want."

"This is what I want." I said showing him — so much for the bed.

A most delectable while later, we made breakfast — well, to be fair, it was more like brunch — and then sat with a second cup of very delicious coffee. Say one thing for Edward, he had an amazing coffee machine. I stretched out on the sofa twirling my feet absently, pondering the trip to Pompeii; it still bothered me, but somehow, after last night, less so. Maybe it was my own fear that had blown it out of proportion, whatever it was, I was happy to let it lie for the next few days.

Max came and sat at the end of the couch and lifted my feet onto his knees, he hadn't done that since...

"Do you remember the last time you did this?" I smiled lazily. Max looked at me questioningly. "The last time you lifted my legs onto your knees." I watched as he thought about it, his expression told me he'd worked it out.

"Why yes, I do remember, that was the night we..."

"The night we...wanna try for a rerun?" I winked lasciviously and pouted, Max smothered a laugh, tickling my feet. "No, it wasn't the night you tickled me, oh," trying to extricate myself, giggling, "ok, yes actually it was. Oh well, if that's all you remember, I might as well go and get dressed."

Moving my feet and starting to get up, I was prevented by Max who had other ideas. Pulling me towards him along the sofa, he carried on tickling me mercilessly until I had no strength to fight him off. Hiccupping with laughter I was helpless, when he suddenly changed tack and gently kissed me. It was like the touch of butterfly wings, yet instantly the heat surged through me and, unable to stop myself, I moaned.

"Max..." my voice dying off as he turned me to him, running his fingers through my hair and scattering kisses all over my face ... and we had our re-run.

The day passed in much the same way, we talked, we laughed and we made love. I'm pretty sure that at some point we had food, but for the life of me I can't recall what we ate. Our rediscovery of each other was all I remember. We did spend a little time rehashing my dream and what it might mean. I still couldn't work out where the other Hannah was, except that it was definitely not Masada and nowhere I was familiar with.

I contemplated, briefly, whether any record had survived relating to the army career of Maxentius, even a short inscription might help. I knew that we had detailed histories of many Roman generals because they had also been in public office, could he have been one of them? There was also the slim chance that Maxentius' diplomata, or discharge certificate had survived, assuming he lived long enough to reach retirement. Usually carved into a bronze tablet, fragments of over a thousand had been found. Although mostly from the Roman frontier provinces, I knew one had been discovered in Pompeii — Pompeii again — I tried to ignore the unease that word evoked! I would have to do a proper Internet search and in my heart of hearts I knew I was clutching at straws, but it was worth a try. Then we stored it away, to be dealt with if necessary, but no more today, today was about the present.

By the evening, we were ready to face the world again and ventured out for dinner. We had been warned that it was costly to dine out near the apartment, being so close to the Spanish Steps, but we had not found this to be the case. We returned to the place where we had eaten the night before and it was just as good. We both had pasta and shared a carafe of red wine, finishing up with a Limóncello. It was so relaxing, not having to worry about getting up for work the next day, or being home by a particular time, although, if the light in Max's eyes was anything to go by, we wouldn't be lingering very long.

We had an early night, the next day we were planning to visit the Colosseum and wanted to be there early to avoid the crowds. Warmed by the wine and tired from our...errr...activities of the day, I fell asleep almost as soon as my head touched the pillow.

It was a beautiful morning; the sky was bright blue and the air, crisp and cool, so much nicer than the heat of summer. Winter was nearly upon us, yet the trees refused to accept the change of season, continuing to provide a blaze of colour, their bright autumnal shades like jewels in the morning sunlight. I walked along the path towards the Gladiators' School. Maxentius was unable to come, but had asked one of his officers to accompany me, as he was concerned about me being there on my own. The soldier, whose name was Gaius Petronius Faustus, had become my regular escort and a very friendly young man. He had only been in the army for about five years and had already seen conflict in Judaea, although he hadn't been at Masada.

We chatted as we walked and while I understood that this might be seen as inappropriate, it didn't worry me. My status in this world was unusual, my husband was an army general and, even though many soldiers married, technically it wasn't allowed and their wives remained unrecognised. I was a Hebrew physician a rare job for a woman and, even though I had been granted citizenship and our marriage had been approved, we didn't really fit into a class, something I was very happy about.

This morning's visit was to find out whether they would consider allowing me to be part of their medical team. I had done my research and knew that they used medici, or physicians, who checked the gladiators for any medical problems and treated them if they were injured. These combatants, were an expensive commodity to be treated with care and although I realised that they probably already had a regular team of physicians, it was worth taking the time to let them know of my skills.

I was a little nervous; I had never been anywhere like this and I struggled to understand the attraction of the gladiatorial games. Despite the glory and popularity that many of these gladiators achieved, fights to the death between humans, or between humans and animals were abhorrent to me. Even more so, when it was used as a way to execute prisoners. I'd seen enough of it in real life; I certainly didn't need to have it as entertainment. There had been several games since we'd arrived in Pompeii, but I had not attended any and they were no more scheduled until the spring. Seemingly during the height of summer and the depth of winter there was a brief hiatus, as the extreme temperatures had proved unbearable for audience and participant alike.

Arriving at the main entrance to the school, we entered and found ourselves in a cool atrium, which opened onto large colonnaded courtyard, not dissimilar to the Palaestra I had visited several days ago. We waited and after a few moments a tall man with grizzled features came across to meet us. He had the bearing of a soldier and I discovered later that retired soldiers often became gladiators and if they managed to survive, their trainers. I let Petronius tell our host why I was there, explaining that I was a highly trained physician, who had treated Roman soldiers at Masada and was now one of the regular medici at the Palaestra.

"The men who live and fight here are not like those who play at sports. My gladiators are hardened warriors, prisoners, slaves, the condemned and the disreputable. It is no place for a woman." His response was less than encouraging.

"Sir, I have lived among those who were prepared to take on the whole of the Roman army and then when they realised their intent was futile, killed themselves. I have treated many men, both soldier and rebel for wounds that even your gladiators may never have inflicted upon them. I grew up in a city where civil unrest was normal and during my training saw what damage men can do to each other. I understand that this place is not somewhere that most women should see, but I am not most women. If you would but give me a chance, I will prove to you that I am more than capable of treating any wounds and should a fighter be too gravely injured, I can help to make their passing as painless as possible."

It was a long speech and I was not sure whether my words were making any difference. The man just looked at me, impassively, so taking a deep breath, I tried my trump card. "My husband is Lucius Maxentius Valerius, the commander of the garrison here in Pompeii, he would vouch for my skills. I saved his life." On hearing Maxentius' name the soldier's expression changed.

"Maxentius Valerius is here? Since when? I must see him, he may not remember me, but we fought together in Parthia. Then he was dispatched to Masada and I, having reached retirement, was recalled to Rome." His countenance took on different aspect as he was talking and realising that this could be my way in, invited him to dine with us that evening, thereby giving the two men a chance to reacquaint themselves. He was happy to accept and after telling him where we lived, we took our leave. Better to let him think about what I had asked and then maybe talk it over with Maxentius tonight, rather than try to force his hand.

Petronius and I walked slowly back to the headquarters. On the way, we were confronted by a group of rough looking men, who did not care that I was a woman and Petronius a soldier, crowding us off the pavement. Their belligerence was unusual, I had not encountered anything as violent as this since our arrival, not even in Rome where there were far more people. This must be what Maxentius had warned me about. Petronius made sure I was safe and we hurried home, but it was something I did not forget quickly.

That evening our guest, whose name was Secundus Tullius Rufinus, arrived promptly and with a flagon of quite excellent wine, which we had with our meal. I had given the children their dinner earlier, so we adults could talk without interruption. As usual Marcus joined us, but Aliza chose to eat with the children and then retired to her rooms for the evening, for she was not very comfortable with my plans. Maxentius did remember Tullius and they regaled us with tales of battles for most of the evening, some of which, I'm sure were exaggerated.

Later, after much food and several goblets of wine, their talk turned to local matters and Tullius revisited the question I had asked him that morning.

"I am loathe to allow your wife to spend time in the gladiators' quarters, Maxentius Valerius. While some of the men are free born or soldiers who have chosen this life, there are also prisoners and slaves. They spend their days training and you know that their fights are often to the death. This can lead to unrest within the school and brawls are not uncommon. I would be concerned that your wife might get badly hurt." Maxentius pondered this and then said.

"You may have discerned that Hannah is not your typical Roman wife, however she does not place herself in harm's way deliberately..." looking across at me with an amused smile on his face, "...I presume her services will only be required if a gladiator was injured in the arena, or after any brawl has been subdued?" Tullius nodded. "Then I cannot imagine her being at risk. Further I would ensure that she was always accompanied by one of my men. The danger to her would be minimal; she is probably more likely to be crushed underfoot by a street gang than hurt by one of your gladiators. If she were to treat a sick man, I would imagine that he'd be isolated from the others to prevent the spread of disease, again reducing any risk to her person. However, I do not expect you to accept her help just because we fought together on the battlefield." He paused for a moment and then continued.

"Both Marcus and I were badly wounded at Masada when the rebels overran the fortress and our comrade Sergius grievously so. Even knowing we were an enemy of her people, she did what she could to save us all, preventing the rebels from simply finishing us off and risking her own life to do so. She fought for many days to save Sergius, refusing to give up hope, but in the end his injuries were too severe. Even after his death, she showed courage and respect by asking for and receiving permission to perform funeral rites on this man, a Roman and a captive. She continued to provide the utmost care for Marcus and me, along with many of the rebels who had attacked us, until we were healed. My wife will go to great lengths to make sure anyone who requires it receives the best treatment. She was trained by a first class physician in Jerusalem and the Jews are renowned for their surgical skills."

Maxentius' knowledge of what I did and how the sick or injured should be cared for, not only surprised Tullius, but me also. I knew he respected my work, but that he remembered everything astounded me. I smiled across the room at him, my heart in my eyes and he winked back at me. Marcus put his opinion in too and by the end of the evening Tullius was persuaded. He did point out that it would have to be approved by the other doctors, but as he was the lanista, or overall manager, he didn't think there would be a problem.

He said he would send confirmation of my appointment in due course. I thanked him, told him not to be a stranger and without thinking gave him a quick hug, forgetting that here this type of behaviour was unseemly. I would never learn! Thankfully he took it in good part, thanked us for an interesting evening and departed for his quarters.

We three turned back into the house and finished our evening off with a goblet of calda, a warm drink made up of water, wine and spices, very welcome on these cold nights. Marcus left soon after and Maxentius and I went to bed. We lay talking quietly for a little while. I was still very impressed with what he said to Tullius and told him so.

"I am proud of what you do, my Hannah, why should I pretend otherwise? I will never forget what you did for us at

Masada; it took great courage to stand against your brother and the other elders. Please take care though; there is a savagery to these gladiators. Even though they may befriend each other, ultimately their job is to kill. It is difficult to retain any humanity in such circumstances."

"Trust me, my love, I will be very careful. I just want to help." Lifting my face for his kiss, I pulled him close, soothing his concerns, the best way I knew how.

At some point during that night, there was an ominous rumble, like the roll of thunder but a long way off. I woke up to feel the earth trembling and knew it to be an earthquake, I had experienced mild ones back in Judaea. Maxentius slept on, but I wanted to check the children. Tiptoeing into their room, I watched them for a moment, they were undisturbed, their little faces flushed with sleep. I lifted the window covering a little to let some fresh air through, for the room felt stuffy.

Everything seemed calm again, but as I gazed across at the dark mountain, I had a sense of disquiet, a subtle shift in my awareness. Padding quietly back to bed, I slipped beneath the covers. Still deep in slumber, Maxentius rolled over and caught me to him; I snuggled in trying to calm my unease, eventually falling asleep.

"NO!" I bolted awake, nearly falling out of bed in my haste. It was still dark and the clock said 4.30am. The clock? Confused I looked around me, realising I was in Edward's apartment. What had woken me? My head felt fuzzy, but I recalled something about an earthquake. Had we had an earthquake? No, we couldn't have done, there was no sound, or movement, or panic, no sirens, all was peaceful. As my heartbeat settled, I remembered — it wasn't me it had happened to. Had it been a dream, or was I 'visiting' again?

"You okay, Hannah?" I had woken Max.

"Sorry hon, it was a dream, I didn't mean to wake you, go back to sleep." Sleepily, he pulled me to him, wrapping his arms around me, fitting me to his body.

"Was it one of those dreams?" Drowsily.

"I think so, but we can talk about it tomorrow, go back to sleep." I patted his leg and settled against him. He tightened his hold, kissing the back of my neck and nuzzling my hair, I felt my heartbeat quicken — I'd just got it to settle down. How could he do this to me when he was virtually asleep?

"Max..." I whispered, "...are you asleep?" No answer, well dammit all, that's not fair. I started to roll over, I couldn't lie that close to him, my body was responding to his touch. There'd be no getting back to sleep if I didn't move.

"Where do you think you're going?" He murmured, his hand running along my thigh.

"You were asleep...uhhhh..." as his hand reached my waist, "...make your mind up."

"I was, but now I'm thinking awake could be more fun." He turned me to face him and kissed me for a long time, gently and tenderly. His hands began their dance over my skin and I moved against him, trying to get closer. I ran my fingers down his back, curving round his thighs, then bringing them back up to trail along his chest. He trembled, his body pulsing to my touch, his kiss deepening, while his fingers fluttered over my stomach causing delicious shivers to race along my body. I succumbed to the ecstasy of his touch and simply floated away.

Chapter Six

We did, eventually, get back to sleep and woke again when it was full daylight. We lay together for a little while, just enjoying the comfort of being in each other's arms. However sightseeing called and quickly, we showered and dressed, deciding to treat ourselves to breakfast out. We had been in Rome a week and were heading off to Pompeii the next day. I couldn't believe what we had managed to fit in, the Colosseum, the Vatican Museum, the Baths of Caracalla, numerous churches including San Clemente with its stunning Mithraeum, not to mention several museums and art galleries.

However, despite all these remarkable sights, it was the Pantheon that captivated me. It had been my favourite building since I'd studied ancient Roman art and architecture at university and, seeing it in the flesh, so to speak, merely added to my fascination. So yes — you've guessed it — now you get to read about it.

The current Pantheon is thought to be the third incarnation of Marcus Agrippa's original wooden temple built in 27BC to commemorate Octavian's (the soon to be Emperor Augustus) victory at the Battle of Actium. This temple and its successor were destroyed by fire in AD80 and AD110 respectively, eventually being rebuilt in stone during Hadrian's rule, somewhere around AD120-5. Hadrian retained the original inscription, possibly as a mark of respect for the victory at Actium, or more likely as a symbolic gesture linking him to the Imperial Augustan line. Built on what was, in antiquity, the Campus Martius, the Pantheon would have towered over its surroundings, a highly visible landmark. Today it nestles in a dip, the modern city slightly higher — an indication of the changing ground level since ancient times.

Approaching from the back I was unprepared for the impact of this astonishing building, even though I knew what it would look like, for it seems rather nondescript — a curved brick structure adorned with the odd piece of decorative marble. On reaching the front, however, the sheer size of the building is breathtaking. Sixteen soaring granite Corinthian columns support a rectangular portico, which bears the famous dedication with the immense dome rising behind the triangular pediment. Despite re-appropriation, long ago, of all the exterior bronze, marble and gold, the Pantheon is still stunning.

Under the portico, the great bronze doors open into a circular interior, which is a marvel of engineering. A cylinder, topped with a hemisphere, the height from the floor to the tip of the dome exactly matching its diameter. Clever use of niches between the supporting wall buttresses, along with the coffers in the ceiling, belies the weight of the structure, giving the impression that the dome simply floats, effortlessly, above your head. The massive proportions making the visitor feel quite inconsequential.

In the centre of the dome, the oculus draws the eye and, other than the door, is the only source of natural light. Open to the elements, the floor beneath gently slopes away allowing drainage after the rain. The interior marble is largely original, sourced from across the ancient Roman world at no small cost, creating an illusion of luxury. Despite this, today an elegant simplicity is retained, allowing the building itself to impress, rather than its decoration.

Although originally dedicated to 'all gods,' the Pantheon was reconsecrated in the seventh century into a Christian building, honouring one god and has remained so. An active church and subsequently the burial place for several famous Italians including Raphael, Vittorio Emmanuel II and Umberto I, which probably explains why the Pantheon is the best preserved of all ancient Roman buildings.

For me, with my passion for anything connected to Ancient Rome, seeing a building such as the Pantheon, in its original position, more or less intact and being able to walk the same floor on which Emperors trod millennia ago, makes the past seem more tangible. Not that I particularly needed that, given what happened last year, but whimsically, I imagined that echoes of antiquity still whispered within the walls. The architecture of this incredible monument confirming the innovation of the Romans, seamlessly united with an interior modified to include Christian heritage, is for me the essence of history.

Max was just as impressed, the elegant engineering of the building kept him engrossed for hours, which was a good job since I spent just as long walking round it, or sitting in front of it drinking coffee. Plus, every time we walked anywhere near I had to detour past, just so I could see it again. I know — I was obsessed. On this, our last day for now, we revisited some of our favourite haunts, starting at the Trevi Fountain, then detouring passed the Column of Marcus Aurelius, making our way through the back streets to the Piazza Navona where we had lunch, stopping here and there to check out the souvenir shops.

On through the Jewish Ghetto to the Theatre of Marcellus, coming back round to the Largo di Torre Argentina and its cat sanctuary. By sheer coincidence — yeah right! — we ended up at the back of the Pantheon and as we were setting off for Pompeii the next morning, I persuaded Max to have one last — for this week anyway — walk past 'my' building.

In the square and the little streets running off it, there were several lovely restaurants, so we decided to have our meal in one of them, giving us the chance to see the Pantheon floodlit — I know, back to the obsession. I chose a pasta dish and Max opted for a pizza. Although the evenings were cooler now, we decided to sit outside and watch the world go by and since the café had a portable heater, we didn't get chilled.

Seeing the Pantheon at night is just as magical as it is during the day, especially as most of the cafés and shops are open into the evenings, their lights reflecting across the huge structure. The fountain standing in the middle of the Piazza della Rotonda in front of the Pantheon is also floodlit, the whole area full of life and movement. I found it hard to drag myself away.

"C'mon Hannah, we'll be back in a week, you can do this all over again." Max pulled my hand. "We've still got to pack and we need to be up quite early, so we really should go." Smiling at him, I nodded and with one last glance, left my ancient leviathan to the night.

On our way back to the apartment, Max asked about my dream. I'd almost forgotten about it until then, we'd had such a busy day. I told him everything, especially that it seemed as though they were in Pompeii and that this was maybe why I felt so uneasy.

"I can't think what could be happening that is making my mind connect, what could be so important, that I'm having dreams again?" Just as the words left my mouth, I realised precisely what was so important, as did Max for we spoke together —

"Vesuvius."

"Oh, no, this is awful! What if they're there when it erupts? I have to warn them! Good grief do you hear me? How am I going to do that? So far its just dreams, I'm not really involved, not like I was on Masada."

"Maybe this is just the start? You dreamt about what was happening on Masada before you were there so to speak. Maybe this is just like a warning that things are about to change" Listening to Max, I marvelled at our conversation. We were talking about the impossible as if it was an everyday occurrence.

"I guess I'll have to let it unfold, like I did before. I would need to know what year it is and how long they have, maybe they're only visiting, although it seemed as though Maxentius was commanding the garrison there. Oh dammit! When we left Masada I felt that it might not be over, but since nothing has really happened lately, I rather hoped it was." I knew I was speaking too quickly, my words a stream of consciousness rather than anything coherent. Thankfully Max is used to it and let me vent, just putting his arm round my shoulders drawing me close.

"We'll be okay Han, try not to worry, just tell me if the dreams get more ...well...real." We talked it over a little longer, but as neither of us really knew where it was leading, we just stored it away for future discussions. Maybe that was all I would see, maybe it was already over, not that I believed that for a second, but it was easier for my head to handle it that way.

By the time we'd decided what to take with us, we found we only required one suitcase and a couple of backpacks. Since we were coming back to this apartment, we could leave anything we didn't need and meant we could travel light. Setting our luggage aside for the morning, we had one last glass of wine and then went to bed. Max fell asleep almost instantly, but I lay awake for a while mulling over the dream and our conversation. What was it that I needed to know, was it the eruption, something else entirely, or both? Didn't matter how long I rolled it around my head, I was none the wiser, I would just have to follow my own advice and let it play out. Eventually, after tossing and turning for well over two hours, I finally fell asleep.

The room was cold and dim and smelt of sweat and dirt. There were two men in it, one was sitting in a chair that looked like it was woven from thin strips of wood and the other was lying on a bed. The room itself wasn't small and the furniture was not crowded in, but there was not much light. Two beds, two chairs, a cupboard for storage on top of which rested a large bowl for washing and an oil lamp. There was a sort of bucket made of rope and sealed with pitch, standing on the floor near the doorway, which may or may not have been for their overnight toilet. I decided not to look closely.

The man on the bed was pale and clammy; apparently he had sustained a nasty gash to his side while training. Tullius had sent for me because this man was a prisoner and, as such, expendable. I think, in reality, he was testing me. I had brought my bag of remedies and had even thought to pre-mix some of my salve before I left home, just in case.

Petronius had accompanied me and I was glad of his presence, even though there were two guards stationed outside, for although the atmosphere in the room was not quite hostile, neither man was particularly welcoming. For a start, I was 'just a woman,' what could I possibly know about healing? Smiling hesitantly at my patient, I told him with both words and actions, in case he did not understand me, that I would need to examine his injury, but that I would be careful not to hurt him. He nodded sullenly and turned his head, ignoring me completely.

Sighing, I knelt down next to the bed and lifted his tunic, using the thin sheet on the bed to cover him from the hips down. The wound was deep and jagged, I don't know what kind of weapon had caused it, but it required more than just a quick clean and a bandage. I would need to remove the ragged skin from the edges of the wound and pack it open allowing it to heal from inside out.

I asked the man his name, it was easier than calling him 'you' all the time.

"Darius." He replied in flat tones. I explained and demonstrated to him what I would have to do and asked whether he understood. He looked at me impassively and merely nodded again. I asked Petronius to make sure that Darius really knew what I meant and he confirmed that he did.

Shrugging, I also asked whether he would like a sip of my poppy draft to help with the pain, but Darius shook his head. They were hard these men, but this would be agonising. Rooting through my bag I found my knife and placed it on a piece of clean cloth, asking Petronius to get me a pitcher of clean water and a bowl. I shifted my position, allowing the light from the doorway to filter into the room and lifted the oil lamp off the shelf, placing it on the chair next to the bed. It still wasn't very bright, but it was better than no light at all.

Petronius came back quite quickly, by which time I had laid out my jars of ointments and salves. After washing my hands, I refilled the bowl with water, adding some salt and a few drops of vinegar, having discovered that this mix was better than just salt. Soaking a piece of sea sponge — much more absorbent than cloth — with the liquid, I squeezed it into the wound. Darius grunted in pain and clenched his teeth.

"I'm sorry," I said to him, "but this is not the worst part, are you sure you would not like a little of the poppy juice?" He still shook his head. "Well you are a stubborn one." I smiled. "Let me know if you change your mind." I carried on washing out the wound until I was sure it was clean right to the centre, then dabbed the edges with a mixture of oil and mandragora, in the hopes that it might dull his pain just a touch. I asked Petronius if he would hold Darius still, as I didn't want him to jerk when I removed the damaged skin.

Petronius held the prisoner's shoulders while I gave him a twist of cloth to bite down on and then I began to slice away the ruined flesh. I felt Darius tense as the knife entered the skin and he was unable to prevent a groan. I worked as quickly as I could trying to spare him as much agony as possible, but it was a delicate task and I didn't want to rush it. The room was silent;

the two guards and the other prisoner watched, in what appeared to be, horrid fascination. Finally I was satisfied that I done everything I could to neaten the edges of the wound. Darius was sweating now and his heart rate was sky high.

I removed the twist from his mouth and patted him on the arm, smiling encouragingly.

"That's the worst over. Now I just need to pack and bandage it." He just looked at me, unable to speak. With infinite care, I pushed salve into the wound and covered it with a piece of cloth soaked in the same mixture. Then I bandaged it firmly in place. It would need stitching eventually, but not until the wound had begun to heal from the centre. Once finished, I found a goblet on the cupboard and poured a small amount of the poppy draft into it, mixing it with some wine.

"Drink this, it will help you rest." Acquiescing, finally, he nodded and I held his head while he swallowed it all and then helped him to lie back on his bed.

Going to the door, I motioned to one of the men standing guard in the corridor.

"Please could you bring me two clean sheets?" I asked. "This man's bed is covered in dirt and blood, he cannot sleep on it with such a wound." Although seemingly astonished that I would ask them to do my bidding, one of them went to find the sheets, coming back within a few minutes, holding what could barely be described as clean bedding, but at least it wasn't covered in blood.

I would need to talk to Tullius, for if these gladiators were as valuable an asset as he claimed, they needed better domestic care. I had no doubt that they received decent food — these men were well fed — but the room was dirty and their bedding looked like it had never been washed. An unclean living environment can cause horrible infections and was so easy to prevent.

Petronius helped me change the bedding and I told the guards that I would take the dirty linen, wash it myself and bring it back the next day when I came to check on Darius. The floor of the room was filthy, so I dispatched the other guard to get me a broom and some more water. On his return, I swept the room as thoroughly as possible, then using a pile of old cloths I had with me for washing wounds, washed the floor, adding vinegar to the bowl of water. Four of the men — the two gladiators and the two guards — were amazed, while Petronius, familiar with my behaviour, was unfazed and helped me by lifting furniture and refilling the bowl when necessary.

Eventually I was satisfied with my efforts and went to wash my hands. Rolling the dirty sheets into a ball, I stuffed them into a second pouch, replacing all my equipment and bottles into my bag. I was tired now, it had been hard work, but I thought I had done enough to save this prisoner. He was nodding off; the draft was working its magic. I asked the guards if they could take me to the lanista.

They escorted us back through the maze of passageways to a small office at the front of the accommodation. Tullius was sitting behind a desk, working. He looked up at our entrance and dismissed the two guards.

"So, Hannah, wife of Maxentius, how is my gladiator?"

"I think he will live, although I will need to check on him over the next few days." He bowed in acknowledgement. "However, there is something we need to discuss. The rooms where these men sleep, are they all like the one I have just been in?"

"I would imagine so, why?"

"They are unclean, the floors are dirty and will become a breeding ground for disease. They should be swept daily and washed at least once a week. These men are training in dusty conditions and then dragging it all back to their sleeping quarters. Also, their sheets are grimy and in desperate need of a wash. Even those of your men who are physically fit could get very sick if you do not do something. Fresh air should be allowed to circulate through all the rooms and they need to learn to wash themselves, especially their hands, frequently."

I drew a deep breath.

"I know this might prove difficult to start with, but if you persuade the men to clean their own quarters, they will get used to it, it will take only a few moments and they will be much better for it. You told me that these gladiators are like prized possessions, please do not waste them."

I stopped, unsure whether I had overstepped the mark, as I am wont to do. I knew that in my earnestness to make this man understand what I was proposing, I probably sounded overzealous and I did not want him to feel as though I was forcing his hand. Tullius rested his elbows on the desk, steepling his fingers and studied me for a long moment.

"I will think on your suggestion, Hannah Valerius and maybe we will be able to discuss it in more detail when you come back to check on the Dacian. I can show you through this complex and you may be able to offer other ideas that may benefit my school." I was astonished; had I made progress? I beamed at him and dropped a brief curtsey.

"Thank you, Tullius Rufinus, I appreciate your time and consideration. I will see you tomorrow."

Waving his hand he dismissed us and we walked out, along the corridor adjacent to the training square and out onto the main street. Once there I let out a huge breath.

"Oh my goodness, I cannot believe he listened. I hope he lets me help."

"You are either very brave or quite insane." Petronius replied. "I cannot believe you dared say that to him, he is an important man here in Pompeii, you took a risk."

"I will not let his men fall victim to disease if I can help it, Gaius Petronius. These gladiators cost a lot of money to feed and clothe and train. There is no point spending so much on these details, to ignore basic domestic cleanliness, it would be completely illogical. One always complements the other." I sighed. "Well, we shall see what happens tomorrow."

We walked the rest of the way in companionable silence, the day was very cold, it had snowed overnight and its whiteness crunched under our footsteps. Petronius said he would meet me the next morning at the fourth hour. Before I went inside, I decided to go round to the Palaestra, which was only minutes from our home, to check on Appius Horatius. His wound had healed up nicely and I was glad to see that his injury had in no way hampered his activities.

His trainer, Aulus Ennius Balbinus, who had accepted my proposal to act as regular medica, was there and we chatted for a few moments about how his charges were doing. Despite the onset of cold weather, they were all fit and healthy and there would be no more games now until the spring, hopefully reducing the risk of any of them suffering a serious injury. I confirmed that I would check them at regular intervals, but otherwise would await his summons.

Finally I returned home, my house was quiet, no one else was there, a rare luxury. I poured myself a goblet of water and sat with my feet up on the long seat, letting my thoughts run free. Unbidden, I remembered the woman in the white room. For a long time I hadn't felt her, but recently I had become aware of her presence. She must be well, despite appearing to be deeply unconscious when I last dreamed about her. I ruminated over why she felt near to me now, especially after what I had divined the last time she was part of my thoughts. Strangely enough, I missed her.

Chapter Seven

We woke to the alarm the next morning, my dreams had been confused and I felt rather wrung out, as though I had barely slept. Hopefully I could snooze during the train journey. We had a quick breakfast, tidied up, then left making sure we had locked everything securely. For ease and convenience, we took a taxi to the station, arriving with about half an hour to spare. Max texted Nate to let him know we were on our way and what time we were due to arrive in Naples; then we grabbed a coffee and waited on the platform. The train, which was very fine, arrived promptly and once clear of the city sped through the countryside. The rocking movement was soporific and I was soon fast asleep again.

The dream I had been having returned. I could see Hannah sitting in an airy room, curled up on what looked like a sofa, quite alone. After a while the door opened and three children accompanied by an older woman walked in. The children hurled themselves on Hannah, all talking at once and I realised that it was Claudia, Liora and Efraim, which meant the older woman was probably Aliza. With a jolt, I worked out that Claudia looked to be around six or seven years old now. That must mean over four years had passed since I last connected with this woman who was part of me. It was strange seeing them again and I wondered where Maxentius was.

My dreams were not dreams then — more a perception of her life. Hannah was treating gladiators at the school and the young sportsmen at the Palaestra; that hadn't been my imagination. What about Vesuvius? If it was over four years since the massacre at Masada, the mountain would erupt in less than two, maybe sooner. How could I warn her? As I was chewing on this problem, the door opened again and both Maxentius and Marcus walked in. I think my breathing must have stopped, Maxentius hadn't changed. He didn't look any older and still had that charisma that I — well the other me — had fallen in love with so long ago. I'd forgotten how tall he was, how his dark hair fell in an unruly mop, despite being tied back with a piece of leather, how his deep green eyes twinkled when he looked at her...me. He was utterly mesmerising and I could see by Hannah's response to his entrance, that her love hadn't dimmed one iota.

Feeling like a voyeur, I tried to wake myself up, but couldn't seem to manage it. I wasn't there, I was watching this from a distance, the edges of the scene were hazy and I needed to wake up. Panicking a little I shook my head trying to dissolve the picture and suddenly I was awake. Max was shaking my shoulder, talking to me, asking what was wrong. I waited until things came back into focus, before I spoke.

"It was another dream, this one started last night and carried on when I dropped off."

"Tell me." I did so, explaining the dream of the night before and how it had concluded just now. The previous dreams hadn't seemed so close, more like a distant memory, clouded by time. Although I knew who was in them, they were shrouded, misty figures, enough to make me aware, but not enough to feel that our lives were entwined again. This was different, this felt like the dreams I had had at Masada. Something was stirring, but what?

We continued to talk about it for the rest of the journey, which wasn't very long at all. We were on a high-speed train and it swallowed up the miles. Arriving at Naples, we collected our suitcase and went onto the main concourse. It was bedlam; there were people everywhere and we knew there was a local train that went out to Pompeii, but had no idea which platform it departed from. As we were gazing at the notice boards, trying to work it out, we heard a shout. Geoff was walking towards us. Oh the relief!

"Come on guys, I've got the car parked out here in the drop-off zone...better than trying to work out the trains." We hurried out of the station into the sunshine. It was a beautiful day, especially for that time of year. We had been very lucky with the weather so far, not a single day of rain and the forecast was for it to continue. We piled into Geoff's car, which he had managed to park right at the entrance. The drive was uneventful, if you can ever call being on Italian roads 'uneventful,' by which I mean that we arrived at Geoff's home in one piece.

He had a lovely villa, three bedrooms, two bathrooms and an open-plan kitchen/living area. The garden was quite a surprise. Colourful bougainvillea, protected by the high walls to which they clung, contrasted beautifully with the dark green box hedge delineating gravel pathways and borders. A pergola at the far end, harbouring a wrought-iron outdoor setting, was covered in wisteria and, although at the end of its flowering, was still quite beautiful. Within the little bordered squares, lavender and rosemary sprouted. It was a welcoming and relaxing space; I could imagine us sitting under the canopy of wisteria drinking wine and watching the moonrise.

"Did you do all this, Geoff?" I asked, waving my hand at the garden.

"I did actually, it's turned out alright don't you think?" With this massive understatement and without waiting for my reply, he turned to take us through the rest of the villa.

"It's glorious. I'm just amazed that you found the time, what with lecturing and archaeological digs, it must have taken you ages."

"It is a work in progress," he agreed. "I've had this place for about eight years, some of the plants were already in, the bougainvillea and such, but I marked out all the beds and planted the borders and trained the wisteria. I find it very relaxing after a busy semester. No one knows me here, I'm just Geoff and it gives me a sense of purpose, to come down during my breaks and see how the garden is doing."

He smiled quite shyly. Despite his bluff exterior, Geoff was essentially quite a private person; it always amazed me that, on top of being a well-regarded archaeologist, he was a very busy lecturer. Having to deal with all those students and other scholarly necessities, although an expected part of academia, was in my eyes an evil that must be borne to allow him to pursue his first love.

He showed us into the second of the three bedrooms at the back of the villa. It was a light and sunny room in shades of lemon with French doors opening onto the garden. The bathroom, decorated in soft blues and cream, with brass fixtures, was next door. His own bedroom could be found at the other end of the long corridor running through the centre of the villa, off which all the rooms opened.

The whole place reminded me of an early summer's afternoon, the soft palate of colours throughout the villa creating a delightful space. Explaining the oven and microwave and telling us there was a bottle of wine in the fridge, he said he would let us get settled and then he and Nate would come over later to take us out for dinner. I hugged him before he left, thanking him for his generosity. He grinned and patting me on the arm, took his leave.

Max and I stood there for long moments, in the middle of the living room, taking it all in, what a lovely place to spend a week. Eventually, we went along to the bedroom and unpacked the suitcase, making sure everything was tidied away, before going out into the garden and down to the pergola. I could hear the soft humming of bees as they filled their little pouches with nectar from the flowers. The breeze wafted through the trees cooling the air and the scent from the lavender was sublime.

"This is just gorgeous, Max, do you know how far we are from the ruins?"

"Not sure, can't be that far though, I don't think anywhere in Pompeii is too far from the ruins. No doubt we'll find out tomorrow." He draped his arm over my shoulder, pulling me close and I rested my head in the crook of his neck. I could have stayed like that for hours just sitting, then realised that we could. We had nothing to do, nowhere we needed to go and having taken such an early train, we had most of the afternoon to ourselves.

"Is there anything we have to do, like go and buy food, or drinks, or anything?" I murmured, hoping the answer was in the negative.

"Probably not, we'd have to check the fridge, but knowing Geoff, he's probably set us up for a couple of days 'til we work out where the closest shops are. I reckon we should eat out most nights and I know you can buy food inside the site — there's a café — I spotted it on the map we were looking at yesterday."

"Good one, so we only really need breakfast stuff then and maybe a few nibbles just in case." I love snacks, and always have a supply in the house; you never know when the urge might take you. Max grinned down at me, knowing my penchant for crisps and peanuts.

"Come on then, let's see what we do have and what we might need. Grab yourself a pen and we'll make a list."

Much later, having discovered that a bottle of chilled white wine complemented a lazy afternoon in the garden very nicely thank you, Nate and Geoff called around to take us out for dinner. We could walk there and on the way they showed us the local shops, bars and restaurants. It was an interesting town, I expected it to be far more commercialised, since it surrounded such an incredible archaeological and UNESCO listed site, but it wasn't. In fact, if it wasn't for the ruins, you would barely even notice it — just a small, quiet Italian town nestling under the still forbidding Mount Vesuvius.

We had a lovely meal in a quaint restaurant, where our two hosts were obviously regulars. The owner brought us extra dishes, that we 'just had to try' and persuaded us into a luscious dessert, a vanilla pannacotta, drizzled with a mixed berry coulis followed by a glass of Limóncello. I was so full by the time we left, that I wasn't sure I'd be able to walk home. We had spent most of the meal talking about the dig that we would join tomorrow. Geoff was in charge, which I found comforting; at least I knew him and how he liked to work. There were a couple of buildings where they wanted Max to assist, one of which was situated next to a fullonica, or laundry and apparently had some incredible mosaics. I would be helping with recording in some of the houses that had recently been declared safe for access.

There was a huge concern that the weather, time, tourists and mishandled early excavations were causing the site to decay; so much of the work was now restricted to conservation and preservation rather than actually digging stuff up. This meant that the investigations were on a much smaller scale and our group was only fifteen people, including Max and me. There was also great excitement because in some areas, using modern technology, archaeologists were able to get below the AD79 layer, allowing them to begin tracing the long history of Pompeii and its development as a Roman city. I was hoping that I would get the chance to assist in one of those areas, even if it was just logging their progress.

Nate and Geoff saw us safely back to the villa, worried that we might take a wrong turn in the dark and, refusing our offer of a hot drink, carried on to Nate's house. The air was still mild and filled with the heady scent of jasmine. We let ourselves in and decided to sit on the patio with a cup of tea before heading off to bed. The sounds of the night here were quite different from those of Rome, much quieter, although we never quite seemed to escape the distant sound of sirens. Eventually, the soft air, full stomachs and weariness from a long day were too hard to fight and sleep called, so after washing our cups and locking up, we called it a night.

My dreams drew me back to my other world. I could see her going about her daily routine, playing with the children or walking through the markets; searching for new herbs and oils, or wrapping bandages into neat rolls. It was all so familiar, yet Pompeii was a world away from Masada. Would I be able to help?

Chapter Eight

Vaguely aware that I was reconnecting with my other self, I had been enjoying a very pleasant and, unexpected, sleep in when suddenly I was awoken by the clattering of feet along the hallway and before I could move to stop it, three not so small children landed on the bed. Aliza came bustling in after them, apologising for their lack of manners. They had just had breakfast and wanted to see me before they went off to the market.

Smiling, I told Aliza not to worry and that they could stay with me while she got herself ready. The children were chattering about where they were going what they might treat themselves to with the coin Maxentius had given them. He was a pushover with these three, him and Marcus both; it was a good job Aliza and I were not quite such easy marks, or they'd be spoilt rotten.

Soon they were gone and the house was quiet. I got up, washed and dressed. I had to go back to the Gladiators' School this morning to check on my patient and wanted to get my things ready before Petronius arrived. It was unusual for our home to be so silent, like yesterday afternoon, when I had arrived back before anyone else. The quiet reminded me of the woman again, she had been in my dreams last night, but I didn't know whether that was because she had been on my mind, or there was another, less comfortable, reason. Pushing it aside, I continued to prepare for the day, slipping into a fresh shift of pale green and a tunic in a darker shade, hoping that the deeper colour would hide anything questionable that I might come into contact with.

I smiled to myself as my choice of tunic suddenly reminded me of how clothing had become a whole other level of complication since we arrived in Roman Italy. On Masada, the isolation inevitably restricted our options and we were used to simple, yet well worn outfits, so while we were in Rome, we had decided to replenish our wardrobes. I was astounded and totally bewildered at the range of attire that was available. Cloaks, dresses, jewellery, along with all manner of accessories could be purchased, or made to order. I had tried to conform to the current fashion, but found the style worn by married women uncomfortable. I bought a few to comply with what I'd be expected to wear if we ever mixed in exalted circles. For everyday attire, however, I had asked the tailor to copy the clothing I had brought from Judaea, in a way that wouldn't look too out of place in Roman society.

The choice of materials was considerable, but I eventually managed to pick several I hoped were appropriate. Then I was expected to choose accessories. For someone who had never owned a piece of jewellery in her life, oh except for my cloak clasp that Maxentius had given to me, it was all a bit overwhelming and I ended up with very few pieces. Cloaks, something we hadn't needed often on Masada, would be essential here during the colder months and Maxentius had persuaded me to purchase four. Two heavy winter ones as well as two in a lighter material, all fashioned in a way that gave me a hood.

As if this wasn't enough, there were the hairstyles, which I found far too elaborate so, once again, eschewing this current trend, I simply plaited it, before twisting it up onto my head. As we didn't have any servants, I had no-one to style it for me anyway. Also, due to my work, I didn't need my hair to be floating around my head in ringlets and curls. It would annoy me or worse, get covered in blood and dirt and, I'm sure no one would take me seriously as a physician if I swanned in looking like I was modelling the latest fashions. All this had made deciding what to wear and how to wear it, somewhat befuddling which amused Maxentius no end.

It wasn't quite so cold this morning, so I chose one of my lighter cloaks, knowing that the walk would warm me. Petronius arrived promptly at the fourth hour and we talked quietly as we made our way back to the Gladiators' School. Tullius was waiting for us and said we would take a tour of the barracks before I went to treat the Dacian. I smiled and nodded, quite excited about getting to see round this rabbit warren of a place. Petronius followed at a distance, close enough for my protection, but not so close that he would hear our conversation and I appreciated his discretion.

The two story high building, which surrounded the large training area, was enormous. There were over sixty rooms where the gladiators slept. Kitchens, laundries and what was possibly a clinic or medical room were housed at the back on the ground floor. There were rooms for weapons and rooms where the special clothing worn in the arena was stored. When they were not in the arena, the men wore simple woollen tunics.

The complex was very well set up and I was astonished at the efficient layout, commenting on it to Tullius. He seemed pleased with my praise. Then we began a systematic tour of the sleeping quarters. As I had suspected, this was an area in need of a thorough overhaul, but I would need to put forward my recommendations with tact — not my best characteristic.

The rooms were all quite spacious and would have been airy if the windows had been larger. I understood however, that they were probably this size to prevent anyone from escaping through them. The doors were thick wood, with vertical bars on the outside. Each room was exactly like the one I had been in yesterday, two beds, two chairs, a storage area with a jug and bowl on top and the rope and pitch bucket by the door.

Several rooms on the upper floor were larger and the furnishings were of a slightly better quality. These, I learned were for the best gladiators or the primus palus. These men had survived many fights and had earned considerable status within the hierarchy of the school. Also the building had sustained some damage during the last big earthquake and these upper level rooms were newly repaired, giving them a brighter, fresher look.

On the lower floor, while some rooms were similar to those on the upper level, there were many that were obviously for prisoners of war, or criminals. The squalor was atrocious and I was surprised any of them lived long enough to get to fight, although that may have been the point. Nevertheless, I was not prepared to let Tullius get away with such treatment; it was inhumane and could besmirch the reputation of the school.

I studied each room carefully, mentally noting the good and the bad in each one, feeling like I needed to put a positive spin on things where possible. As we walked passed those holding the prisoners of war and criminals, they looked up, eyes dulled in defeat, their ankles shackled, knowing that they had been reprieved only to die as entertainment. Regardless of their status, my heart ached for them.

Reaching the penultimate doorway for this section, I peered in, trying to assess the state of the room, when my eyes locked with those of the man sitting on the bed nearest the opening. I heard a hiss as he glared at me with an implacable hatred. The world began to spin, images flooded my mind and I had to put my hand on the wall to steady myself. It couldn't be? It couldn't possibly be?

I felt nausea rising and motioned to Tullius that I needed fresh air. Petronius was immediately at my side, helping me into the daylight. The training ground was just to our left and we were out into the open very quickly. I leaned against the wall, taking deep breaths, trying to stop the sickness, while Tullius asked one of the guards to get me some water.

"I am so sorry," I said, trembling from the shock, "I humbly beg your pardon for such a display of weakness."

Tullius looked any me in consternation. Yesterday I had calmly sliced the broken skin off one of his gladiators without turning a hair and today merely the sight of a prisoner made me sick.

"It is nothing, I know you are not weak, what was it that made you feel so unwell?"

"The man in that room, the one on the bed close to the door...do you know his name?" Avoiding his question.

"He was brought in with a group of Jewish prisoners from Jerusalem. He has been here for two years. He is not a bad fighter, but he is a very angry man. His name is Tobias."

"Oh by all the gods, why?" If anything I had gone whiter. Petronius wanted to call for a litter to take me home, but I waved his concerns aside, I would feel better in a moment or two. I just needed to get my head round what I had seen.

"You look as though you have seen a ghost, Gaius Petronius is right, you should go home."

"No, I must check on Darius, his wound will need cleaning and redressing. I cannot leave without doing that. Please, this will pass, I just need a few moments." Without thought of whether or not it was appropriate, I slumped to the ground, leaning my back against the wall and trying to steady my breathing.

64

It was passed the sixth hour now, we had been busy in the school and the sun was high, but the day was not too warm. I watched the pines swaying gently, their needles whispering in the breeze; it was a soothing sound. I felt my heart rate slow down and my body stopped trembling. Tullius had brought some water, which I gulped down and a small platter of food — bread, olive oil and dried fruit — which I nibbled at, still seated on the ground.

Eventually I felt able to stand and Petronius helped me up. I dusted down my clothing and asked if there was somewhere I could wash my hands. Taking care to avoid Tobias' cell, Tullius escorted me to the Dacian's room, then left me in the care of Petronius and the two guards, saying he would be in his office when I had finished.

Darius seemed much the same, although I thought that his features looked less pinched. He acknowledged my presence with a grunt and I told him I needed to check his wound. Opening my bag, I pulled out everything I would need and, after washing my hands again, undid the bandages. Removing the swatch of linen soaked in salve, I gently wiped away what remained in the wound. Then filling a bowl with water, salt and vinegar repeated my process of the day before. Carefully, I washed the wound out trying not to hurt the man, but it was deep and required a bit of digging about before I was sure it was clean, there was no sign of infection and I heaved a sigh of relief.

The edges of the injury where I had removed the skin were starting to scab over and, knowing this would itch, rubbed them with a thick dollop of honey to try to soften the raw flesh. Then I pushed fresh salve into the gash, covered it with a new piece of material also soaked in the same mixture and re-bandaged him. He was gritting his teeth and when I offered him some of the poppy juice, he drank it without hesitation. At least this way his rest would be undisturbed, reducing risk of further damage. His bedding was not unclean, so I thought it would not do any harm to leave it another day. The man had had enough and he needed to sleep.

"I'll be back tomorrow," I said quietly. He turned his head to look at me properly and said something in a low voice. I had to bend close to hear him, but I didn't understand the words.

"He says 'thank you'," said Petronius, I glanced up at him astonished and smiled.

"Really?" Petronius nodded. "How do you know that?"

"I was in Dacia for a time, I know a little of their language." I was ridiculously pleased and without thinking, patted Darius on the arm.

"My pleasure," I said. Petronius translated for me and Darius nodded. Maybe I was making progress; maybe he was beginning to trust me. It was a start.

Tidying my things up and checking the room one last time, I said goodbye and our two sentinels walked us back to Tullius' office. Before they left, one of them muttered something to their manager, who looked troubled.

"My guard tells me you chat with the prisoner and think nothing of touching his arm, is this true?"

"I told him I'd be back tomorrow and apparently he thanked me, to which I replied that it was my pleasure. I patted his arm without thinking, it was just a gesture," I replied holding his gaze, daring him to tell me off.

"You must have care Hannah Valerius. These men are prisoners, they have no scruples. The Dacian would not think twice if he thought you could be used as a way of escape."

"I understand, Tullius Rufinus, but my job is to heal these men, nothing else. If someone thanks me, it is polite to respond in kind. He may be a prisoner, but he is still a human." Tullius grunted.

"That is not always the case, some of these men have committed acts that calls their humanity into question, why else are they in my school?" I conceded his point, but commented that I had to look beyond the person; otherwise I would not be able to do my job properly. He nodded, not so much in agreement as in understanding. The tension lightened and we were able to move past it and talk about what I had seen on my tour that morning.

For the most part, the accommodation was well set up, the rooms large enough, especially the new ones and not too stuffy. It was mainly just the floors and bedding. In an effort to seem less judgemental, I told him how impressed I was, before offering suggestions about how to keep a clean house.

"These men need to be in peak condition to fight, therefore every care must be taken to ensure they cannot be brought down by sickness. Change their bedding once a week, get the sheets washed properly, send them out to a laundry if you have to, or employ someone who knows how to do it. Get the men to sweep and wash their floors once a week. Offer them an incentive, extra rations, or extra wine, even extra coin. For I know they are allowed to keep rewards when they win a fight. It does not require a big change and things will be much better." I watched Tullius while I spoke, trying to determine what he thought of my ideas, but his face was expressionless.

I waited and after a few moments he replied —

"I think your proposals have merit, easy to implement and will not change the arduous schedule of training they must continue with. I will begin tomorrow and we will see how it goes. Thank you Hannah, it has been good to discuss this with you."

"Thank you for listening, I will be back sometime tomorrow to check on the Dacian, I assume owing to his injuries he will not be on the practice field?"

"Not yet, but he cannot lie abed for long."

"Wounds as bad as this one take time to heal, please do not try to rush it, or he will get worse." Then I remembered Darius was a prisoner, they probably didn't care whether he keeled over in practise, one less mouth to feed. Sighing with the futility of it all, I smiled and nodded to Tullius, who stood while I left the room.

"Are you sure you will be able to walk home, Hannah? I can call for a litter." Petronius was still looking worried, but I assured him I felt better.

"The fresh air will do me good and it isn't far. It is a lovely afternoon and I do not feel comfortable in those litters, I always think they will drop me." I grinned at him and he smiled back, probably thinking I was a nut case.

"That man..." tentatively, "...do you know him?"

"Yes, I'm afraid I do. I may be able to tell you how soon, but I must tell Maxentius first. He needs to know before anyone else, it is his right and he also knew him." I changed the subject and the rest of the walk was uneventful.

Petronius said goodbye at my door and agreed to escort me again the next day.

"Thank you Petronius, you are most kind to help me this way."

"I am glad to help. You remind me of my sister and I would not let her walk into a place like that alone." He blushed and left quickly. I smiled after him and went inside. It was quiet again, I was getting lucky with this, but today I did not want to be on my own; I needed Maxentius and debated as to whether I dare interrupt his day. Deciding that I dared, I went out through the back door, along a passageway and in through another door, which connected our home with the headquarters of the garrison. I found my way to Maxentius' office, but he wasn't there, neither was Marcus. Dammit!

Returning home, I sat for a long time on a bench in the garden, unable to focus on my other tasks. I knew I should probably check on the boys in the Palaestra, but I was reluctant to leave the safety of my house. That anger, that hatred, it was a tangible force and I felt as though it had followed me. Memories of that afternoon haunted me occasionally, but now they flooded back with a vengeance. I could smell him; I could feel the cold blade of the knife that he had used to hack at my hair and remembered his determination to break me.

I had been sure he was dead, nobody ever told me what had happened, just that he would never bother me again. I should have checked and then this might not have been such a shock. I did not intend to let him stop me treating the gladiators, but what if he were injured or sick, would I be able to care for him? Would it be acceptable to defer to one of the other medici? I would only need to treat him, if he was hurt on the days I was scheduled to be on call. I just had to hope that never happened.

Chapter Nine

I had no idea how long I was there, but suddenly I became aware of noise and movement in the house and knew I needed to pull myself together. Getting up, I realised I was cold and the sun was going down; I had been sitting for quite a while. Going back in, I noticed my three children and Aliza busily doing something in the kitchen. Claudia saw me and came running over for her kiss, followed by Liora and Efraim. I hugged them all and asked whether they'd found anything nice at the market. Efraim had seen a chicken that he wanted to bring home as a pet and it had taken Aliza all her powers of persuasion to get him to leave it there. The two girls thought he was crazy; who wants a smelly chicken in the house?

I had to agree with them, although maybe we could have a few in the garden, especially if they were egg-layers. I mentioned this to Efraim who thought it was a marvellous idea.

"We need to think about it properly though, we can't let them wander all over the garden, they will scratch up the plants, then Uncle Marcus will be angry and you don't want that do you?" The three of them looked horrified. Uncle Marcus angry! I don't think they'd ever witnessed such a thing. It had the desired effect and they stopped talking about it for a little while.

My two Romans came home late that evening, the children were already in bed and Aliza had retired to her rooms, but I had waited up. I needed to talk to them and even though I would have preferred to tell Maxentius when we were on our own, I didn't think my news should wait. I gave them their meal and poured them a goblet of wine each, then sat watching them.

Their day had been busy, several gangs had been having running fights in the streets and the garrison had been stretched trying to suppress them. I asked them whether they considered this to be the whole point, to see whether the garrison had enough soldiers to quell this kind of action. It might have been a trial run for something much bigger. They had also thought of this and Maxentius had sent a message to Rome asking whether they could assign him some more men.

"How was your day, my Hannah?" Maxentius asked, while demolishing his meal.

"Some good, some not so good. I enjoyed being shown through the Gladiators' School and I checked on the Dacian prisoner whom I treated yesterday. Before I got to him, however, something quite unsettling happened." Something in my voice caught their attention and they both stopped eating to look at me.

"What happened, Hannah?"

"I was checking the rooms where the prisoners of war and the criminals are sequestered; they are quite filthy and really need to be sorted out. Anyway, as we were nearing the end of their row of rooms, I glanced into one and there was a man sitting on his bed watching what we were doing. Without intending to, for they do not need to be gawped at, I looked at him full in the face…" I could feel the nausea rising again and had to stop speaking. Taking a deep breath I continued, "…it was Tobias."

My words fell into the silence. I almost expected them to echo. Neither man moved nor spoke. I was trembling again.

"His anger and hatred Maxentius, it was like a living thing. I have never felt so afraid in my life. It was worse than waiting for you lot to breach the walls at Masada and far more terrifying than when he tried to...to..." I couldn't finish my sentence, the sickness threatening to overwhelm me. The two men looked at me, trying to process what I'd told them; they didn't want to believe it either.

"I thought Aharon said he would never bother you again?" Maxentius said.

"He did say that and I thought he meant that Tobias was dead, but I never asked, I never checked, I didn't want to know and now he's here." I shot into the kitchen where I found a large bowl and was very violently sick. When it was over, I took the bowl outside and cleaned it, then washed my face and rinsed my mouth out with water, to which I'd added a drop of mentha. It did the trick and gave me a few moments to gain control. Coming back to the main room, I saw that both men looked worried.

Maxentius came over and held me close, then pulled me over to his favourite chair, sat down and lifted me onto his knee — it's a good job Marcus is used to us.

"What do we do?" Marcus asked

"I don't think there's anything we can do. He is under lock and key at the Gladiators' School. I have to hope that if he falls sick or is injured, it's not on any of the days I may be called upon to treat him. I'm not sure my ability to set aside what people do or who they are extends to him. I just wanted you to know. After I saw him today I became rather unwell and, Petronius wanted to call for a litter to bring me home, so either he or Tullius may tell you. I wanted to get in first."

I relaxed into the warmth of Maxentius' body, his arms were around me and I felt safe again. The two of them talked for a while longer, then Marcus took his leave. I was nodding off; by this time it was very late. Maxentius carried me through to our bedroom, then went back to secure the house. By the time he got into bed I was virtually asleep. He kissed me gently and folded me into his embrace. The last thing I heard was his whisper —

"I'm here, my Hannah. I will always protect you."

I was trying to run from the horror that was chasing me down and, panic-stricken, I realised I was coming to a dead end. There was no way out, he would find me here, he would find me, then he would finish what he had started and no one knew I was here. Frantically looking around for some way of escape, I wondered whether I could get over the wall. It wasn't very high and the stone looked as though I might be able to get some grip. I began to climb, but he caught me, dragging me by the arm and, as he spun me around I saw his face, so full of hatred. I struggled trying to fight him off, hoping I could dodge passed him and get out of the alleyway, but he was too strong. I began screaming and yelling for anyone, anyone at all to rescue me.

"Hannah, Hannah, come on, you need to wake up. Hannah!" Still in the throes of terror, I tried to push away, my hands flailing, they were caught and held — this was it.

"Hannah, Hannah!" The voice was strong and calm, it didn't sound like it belonged to someone with murderous intent. "Come on, Sunshine." 'Sunshine,' that was familiar, surely a bogeyman wouldn't call me Sunshine? Forcing my eyes open, I gazed up at two deep green eyes in a very handsome face. "Hey baby. Finally! That was some dream. You've about destroyed the bedding with all that thrashing, not to say how bruised my legs are going to be." I stared at him, waiting for the terror to subside.

"You know who I am, right?" Half jokingly, he waited for me to speak, but I couldn't make my mouth say the words he wanted to hear. "Hannah?" Smile fading, he leant back, letting me sit up. I didn't recognise the room, where was I? Shaking my head trying to clear it, I blinked and looked again, waiting for something familiar to catch my eye. Nothing. "Hannah, we're in Geoff's house in Pompeii, remember?" I looked at him for a few more moments, then suddenly it all flooded back; I knew where I was and who he was.

"Max? What happened?" My voice trembled.

"I have no clue, sweetheart, you started yelling and screaming and fighting me. I couldn't wake you. I don't like that feeling, I know what it means."

"I was being chased, I couldn't get away, he wanted to kill me — well not me, her. Max, it was Tobias."

"What? Isn't he the one who...?" Unwilling to finish the sentence, he went on, "I thought you thought he was dead."

"I did, I assumed that was what Aharon meant when he said he'd been taken care of, but I — she — never asked for any more details, it was too painful."

Max lay next to me on the bed, wrapping me in his arms and asking me to tell him everything I could recall. It took a while, it seemed as though I had been seeing what the other Hannah did for a day or so. The images or dreams were getting clearer, closer. I was aware that when this had happened last time, I had slipped through time and was rather unnerved by the possibility of a repeat performance.

"Maybe it'll just happen in dreams. Last time I was unconscious, can't see that happening again, there's no Naomi here after my blood."

"We'll just have to take care, so no climbing up onto dodgy looking ruins." Max winked at me to lighten the tension, I started to relax and the dream began to fade.

After a few more minutes, we got up, it was only around six o'clock, but apparently the archaeologists started early and we didn't want to be late on the first morning. After enjoying a leisurely breakfast and noting what we'd need to pick up from the shop on the way home, we collected our backpacks, shoving in cameras, hats and, finally, waterproofs. Despite the dry forecast, the weather had a tendency to be unpredictable at this time of year.

We were at the entrance to the ruins by eight; Nate met us there and took us along to meet the others. They seemed like a nice crowd and, to my delight, included Sebastian, who had been with us at Masada. After shaking hands with Max, he gave me a hug, asking how I was and checking the back of my head for lumps.

"Cheeky bugger." I grinned. "Be nice...or I'll make you do your own recording." He grinned back and we moved off towards the areas we would be working in. Max would be helping with the mosaics somewhere over by the Forum and I would be with Nate and Sebastian in some of the insulae off the Via dell'Abbondanza. Agreeing to meet up for lunch at the café, we went our separate ways. The three of us were lucky, as the houses we'd be concentrating on were quite close to the gate we had come in through; some of the others had quite a walk.

The aim of this dig was to record which houses had been in the process of renovation at the time of the eruption in AD79 and whether we were able to gather any information about the earlier history of the town. Once we had recorded what was visible, we would be looking for what was invisible, using ground-penetrating radar (or GPR), resistivity and magnetometry. I had absolutely no clue how to use any of these, or even, except for GPR, what they meant, so I would be simply photographing and recording anything they asked me to. Still it was quite exciting to have access to areas that were not open to the public at the time.

The insulae that we were investigating had already had significant work done. It was what was underneath that was important, but we needed to measure that against the state of the buildings as they stood now, as some had deteriorated over the past several years and also whether they had been undergoing any repair work at the time Vesuvius blew its stack. So our task was threefold and it was fascinating. We didn't stop until lunchtime and, even then, we took only half an hour — barely enough time to walk to the café and buy something, never mind sit and eat it. Max, along with the two he was working with, met us there and, as I had found on Masada, everyone was very enthusiastic about what they were doing.

We worked late into the afternoon and by the time Max and Geoff walked down to meet us it was well after four. Reluctantly and as the light was starting to fade, we packed up, but had achieved a huge amount. We were recording everything in the three stages, saving all the remote sensing until last and then we'd do all the houses in one go, negating the need to lug in heavy equipment every day. We walked out of the site chatting about what we'd done and as we passed a very inviting looking bar on our way along the street, decided we needed a drink before dinner.

Over a cool beer, we talked about the site. There was much to do and, hopefully, the efforts going into conservation would save it from the ravages of time. It had survived so long hidden from the world, well protected under layers of volcanic debris and would be a travesty to lose it because of damage inflicted by the elements. Claims of administrative mismanagement with funding, several building collapses owing to the water seepage and lack of routine maintenance had caused grave fears for the future of this site.

However, there was still hope, especially now the plight of Pompeii had come to worldwide attention. We would just do as much as we could in the time allowed; every little helped. I also hoped to be able to spend at least one day actually touring Pompeii. It was a long way to come to spend all the time working and miss out on its wonders. Maybe we could fit in Herculaneum and Oplontis too.

Since we were comfortable and the bar served food, beer led to dinner, after which we said our goodnights and went our separate ways. We stopped at the shop to pick up some supplies and then wound our way through the back streets, home. It was a lovely evening, quite chilly, but the sky was clear and full of stars. Reaching the villa, we went in and unpacked all the food, including enough crisps to feed a small army. Max made a hot drink and, having turned out all the lights save one dim lamp, we curled up together on the sofa, looking out across the garden. Tired after such a long day, we were in bed quite early and sleep claimed me as soon as the light went out.

The dreams came again. She was closer now and I knew it wouldn't take much for me to slip back to her.

Chapter Ten

It was several days after my encounter with Tobias before I had the chance to return to the Gladiators' School. I had been busy with other matters, not least of which were three children who had fallen victim to some kind of stomach upset. I was pretty sure they had eaten something they shouldn't have and deserved what they got, but they were very sorry for themselves. I also needed to be sure it wasn't something contagious, for I could not risk carrying sickness into any of the places I visited to treat the injured or otherwise unwell. I had sent word to Tullius who had one of the other medici keep an eye on Darius.

The morning was dull and grey, it had been drizzling with rain since the day before and I pulled up the hood of my cloak, in an attempt to keep my hair dry. The ever-faithful Petronius accompanied me and we chatted about what he had been doing since we last met. The protests had gained momentum and the garrison had been kept very busy trying to make sure what started out relatively peacefully did not turn into a full-blown riot.

The soldiers were simply rounding up the agitators and placing them in a kind of holding cell until they calmed down, before removing them from the city. Occasionally, if damage had been done to property, some were brought before the magistrate and usually fined. So far there hadn't been any reason for harsher punishment.

We arrived at the school, to be met by one of the guards, who told me that Tullius would like to see me before I left. Nodding, we followed him along to the Dacian's room. I heard the sound of men practising in the large yard and hoped my skills would not be needed there today. Darius was sitting up and looking much better. His skin was not as pale, the clamminess had gone and, surprisingly, he acknowledged my presence.

The wound was healing well and I would need to stitch it soon; pulling the sides together would give a much less delicate scar. I showed Darius the needle, demonstrating what I had to do, explaining that I would probably do it in two days' time. He nodded.

"It will hurt," I said, "but it is the best way for a fighter like you, it will make the skin stronger."

"I agree to this," the Dacian replied, stumbling a little over the words. I smiled at him thinking that he didn't really have any choice, but happy that he understood.

After cleaning and re-bandaging the injury, I checked the room. The floor was not quite spotless but had been swept and washed. The sheets were clean enough; I would make sure they were changed after I had stitched the wound anyway. It seemed as though Tullius had kept his promise. I sighed with relief; this was one not-so-small battle won. Telling Darius I would see him again in two days and not to practise yet, we left the room.

On our way back to Tullius' office we passed a gateway into the yard where training was in progress. I stopped to take a quick look. There were several wooden poles against which the men were practising sword techniques — thrusting, cutting, jabbing and slicing. Petronius told me that they used wooden swords, which were often heavier than the real weapons, to build their strength. They seemed very agile and adept, despite the rain-soaked ground, which had turned the yard into a muddy puddle.

As we watched, I became aware that one of the men was looking in our direction, ignoring the guard who was telling him to get on with his training. I realised the man was Tobias and my heart sank; this could not end well. I pulled at Petronius indicating that we should go when I heard a voice shout my name. It was in Hebrew. It could only be Tobias. I turned back to face him.

"Why are you here, whore? Is it not enough that you get me beaten nearly to death and then banished? You then have to turn up here. Did you wish to play some more?" His tone was arrogant and full of malice. The rest of the men stopped what they were doing and fell silent, watching. The guards started to close ranks in case this got out of hand and, Petronius tried to make me leave the yard. I just stared, debating with myself whether or not to respond.

"Oh come, Hannah..." taunting now and spreading his arms out as if including the other men, "...tell my esteemed colleagues here what you did, that you allowed a Roman prisoner to take you but refused me, a man of your own race. You let that scum touch you, yet you screamed when I tried to do the same. I can see your hair has grown back, it is a shame I cannot repeat my actions, a scalping would be well deserved." A gasp went up from some of the men, who I assumed were also Jews and therefore understood his words. This insolence would likely earn Tobias a dust-up with the guards, but I was strangely unmoved. The nausea I had felt when I first saw him did not return and although I wanted to punch his lights out, I refused to be drawn.

I held my ground and his gaze, my face expressionless. He snarled, angry that I had not buckled under his words; presumably expecting me to faint, or weep, or have a fit of the vapours and he lurched towards me. He was shackled, making his movements clumsy, but he was determined and had there been no guards, could have reached me relatively easily. I did not move, other than to straighten my shoulders and raise my chin. Petronius was desperately trying to get me to leave, but I shook my head.

The guards were on Tobias before he had taken five strides, gripping his arms and preventing him from coming any closer. Without thinking, I walked out into the square, stopping less than a foot away from my tormentor. Heaping as much contempt into my voice as I could muster, I said —

"I hope you can learn how to die with honour, Tobias, son of Reuven, for you have not lived with it." Turning on my heel, I walked out of the training ground, head held high, back ramrod straight. Tobias spat at my retreating figure before being hauled away by the guards.

Petronius was looking at me in shock, his mouth opening and closing like a stranded fish. I winked at him as I passed by, sailing on into Tullius' office. One of the guards was already there, explaining what had just happened. I waited until he had left, before sitting opposite Tullius in one of the chairs near the large wooden desk.

The elderly man looked at me appraisingly. I knew my colour was high; it is not very nice being called a whore in front of a large gathering of people, even though most of them were prisoners. I also knew it unlikely that Tobias' insults would remain within the confines of these walls. A confrontation like that would be juicy gossip, especially once they knew the identity of my husband. I did not want to let him down, but I was not going to cower behind him either.

"So, Hannah, wife of Maxentius, what was all that about? Do you feel able to tell me now?"

"I suppose I have no choice. Tobias has forced my hand," I sighed. "It is not a pleasant story." Petronius made as if to leave and I put my hand on his arm, halting his steps. "You should hear this, Petronius, at least that way it is not second-hand news, exaggerated out of all proportion to please the scandalmongers." He sat in the chair next to me, as for only the third time in this life I told what had happened that afternoon, so many years ago in a quiet room of an isolated fortress in the middle of the Judaean desert.

I showed them the scar on my neck, which was still visible and pointed out that we had assumed Tobias to be dead.

"This explains your reaction the other day when you saw him." Tullius stated. I nodded.

"Please understand, I have only told you this because of Tobias' behaviour. I do not like my personal life being discussed by all and sundry. My husband has an important job to do and I will not have this incident undermine him. He deserves better than that, especially as Tobias' accusations were untrue, but people like salacious gossip and truth often does not matter. Maxentius knows that Tobias is alive, as does Marcus Aelianus and, while I cannot prevent anyone from spreading rumours, I hope I can rely on your discretion." Tullius nodded emphatically saying that he would also tell the guards to have a care.

"I think they respect you, Hannah Valerius, even though you do not behave in a way they would expect of a woman; for you treat them with respect, they see the dignity with which you care for one who is a prisoner and that you enter these walls without fear. Then today it appears that you handled this man's insubordination with forbearance; I do not think they would wish you to be humiliated further. Also your husband is the commander of the garrison and although they are assigned here as my guards, ultimately they are under his authority. They would not wish to incur his displeasure." I smiled with relief and exhaled a breath I hadn't realised I was holding.

"Thank you, Tullius Rufinus, I am indebted to you."

"As long as you continue to treat my gladiators while ensuring my household staff are not slack in their duties, there is no debt." He grinned back at me. Our talk then moved on to mundane matters involving the upkeep of the living quarters. Tullius had begun to implement my proposals in the few days since I had been here and, the men under his protection had agreed to assist with the cleaning of their rooms, once a decent enough carrot had been dangled!

Hopefully, once this became part of their routine, they would not even question it. After thanking Tullius, and telling him that I would be back in two days to stitch Darius' wound, we left him to his work. Petronius was very quiet on our walk back and I did not disturb his thoughts; simply huddled inside my cloak and tried to avoid the puddles.

Petronius saw me to my door and then with a quick bow, went on his way, still without saying anything. Sighing, I brooded over whether he would ask to be relieved of his duty, but didn't spend too much time on it. I had plenty of things to do to distract me. Going into one of the smaller rooms, which I had commandeered for my medicines, I began to mix up herbs and oils into balms and salves. I had discovered that some of them would last for quite a long time owing to the preservative qualities of their ingredients, so I liked to have a good stock of them.

I made up several bottles, ensuring that they were stoppered securely and into a blob of wax I had poured onto the side of each one I scratched a mark. Different marks represented particular mixtures and I had listed every type on a tablet, which was stored on a high shelf out of the way of small children, who might be inclined to use it as a toy. I was quite proud of my efforts; it had taken a long time to set up but it made my life so much easier and I didn't have to keep taking the stoppers out to smell the contents of my bottles.

Once that was done, I tidied up and refilled my bag in case I was called out. Any old cloths or bandages were either washed or, if beyond saving, burnt. Satisfied that I was up to date with all matters medical, I prepared some food and enjoyed the quiet of my home. We had a two-storey house normally the upper floor would be allocated to another family, but this had been given to Maxentius as Garrison Commander, so we had the whole of it. We had offered the upper level to Aliza, giving her somewhere to retreat to that was her own private space away from the rest of us. She was not young and the children could be tiresome.

We had the lower floor, which was very spacious. The oecus, or main hall, was also the largest room and one, which Maxentius had explained, would normally be used for banquets. Unlikely to be having lavish feasts, we had turned it into our living area and it also gave the children a place to play when it was wet outside. There were two tables, a large one for our meals and a smaller one tucked into an alcove, which the children used for their lessons and anything else requiring a flat surface.

Most of the internal walls were covered in exquisite frescoes in shades of red, green and yellow and we had the usual domestic rooms. I did find the layout rather confusing but I was getting used to it. A small peristyle courtyard led off the atrium, but we had a much larger garden at the rear of the house. In the vestibulum or entrance hall, Maxentius had carved 'Welcome' into one of the walls, then underneath that, 'go in peace and return in peace' in both Hebrew and Latin, in recognition of both of our heritages.

While I had been busy, the clouds had lifted and the sun was trying to shine, so I decided to spend a little time pulling weeds from the courtyard garden; they always came up much more easily after rain. As I worked in the quiet of the afternoon, I heard the same strange rumble that had woken me a week or so previously. I went out into the street and glanced around, but saw nothing to indicate what had caused it. Then I raised my eyes, staring over the top of the pines towards the mountain and saw tendrils of smoke rising from its lofty peak, which seemed rather odd. I would have to ask Maxentius what that meant.

Something pulled at the back of my mind; it felt like a warning but I couldn't hold on to it. I thought of the woman in the white room. Was it her? She had helped me before when danger loomed. Was something going to happen that meant I needed her? I pondered this for a little while, but nothing else came, so I tucked it away, to be brought out again if necessary.

Soon the rest of my family were home. Aliza had bought some fish for the main meal, which she was cooking in a sauce with vegetables. Flat bread accompanied it and we had a large flagon of wine on the table. I had discovered recently that some considered it inappropriate for Roman women to drink wine. I assumed it meant drinking to excess, for I had seen women enjoying a goblet or two. I decided, however, that since I was also a Hebrew and wine was good for the digestion, I would pretend it didn't apply to me. The men managed to make it home early too; seemingly the riotous masses didn't like the rain, so Maxentius and Marcus had the chance to relax over a meal for once.

The children loved it when their father and uncle were home before they went to bed and after the meal, dragged them into silly games, the five of them romping around the house 'til they were all exhausted. After having been so listless over the last few days, it was lovely to see them bouncing around again. Finally they calmed down and I managed to get them to bed, at which point they begged me for a story. Happy to oblige, I made up some fluff about a horse and a dog having adventures together. It was quite ridiculous, but they didn't care and were spellbound as the tale unfolded.

After promising to tell them more of the same the next time, I kissed them goodnight and doused all but one of the oil lamps. Closing the door, I went back to the living area, where my two Romans were discussing their day. I knew I would have to tell them what had happened at the Gladiators' School, for I did not want them to hear it elsewhere.

I let their conversations waft over me until Maxentius asked me what I'd been up to. Taking a deep breath, I told them what had happened and what I had said. I was careful not to gloss over anything, because if somebody did start spreading rumours, I didn't want Maxentius to be caught unaware.

"I'm sorry, I probably should have ignored him, but I was so furious. I didn't feel scared, or sick, I just felt angry, so angry that I could have easily boxed his ears," which, as I am not very tall, drew an amused grin from Marcus and a rumble of laughter from Maxentius.

Then I told them what Tullius had said,

"...and I hope he means it, I don't want to embarrass you."

"You could never embarrass me, my Hannah." Maxentius said gently. "This man caused you great distress, harming both your body and your soul. I would not have worried if you'd taken his sword and run it through him." I gazed at my husband, relieved that he understood and that he didn't seem overly worried.

"The names he called me, could they be used against you? What if someone wanted to undermine your position or blacken your name?"

"Hannah, I was a prisoner of the Zealots. Any Roman worth their salt would know I would not have been in a position to behave in that manner..." — blithely ignoring the fact that we had kissed many times before the night that Tobias had attacked me — "...and if they choose to believe spurious tittle-tattle, I have no desire to be in their company. Marcus can vouch for us; he was there too remember." Marcus chuckled.

"Do not fret, Hannah, he should not take up a moment more of your thoughts. How happy do you think he would be if he knew you were worried about what he said? Do not give him that satisfaction." I smiled at him, the man who had taken the place of my brother in my heart. I was so lucky to have met these two who had changed my life in ways I could never have imagined.

Our conversation drifted into more mundane matters when I suddenly remembered —

"Oh, I forgot, did you hear the rumble this afternoon? It was late in the day and I saw smoke rising from Vesuvius. Is this something we should be worried about?"

"I'm not sure, we heard it also, but most said it was normal behaviour for the mountain. It's as though it is having a bad dream."

"Hmmm, bad dreams can become nightmares and this mountain seems restless."

"I know that there are mountains which explode, fire comes spewing out and it can be very dangerous, but they are bubbling all the time, Vesuvius is not like that. I think we are at greater risk of another earthquake." I knew I wasn't going to persuade him, so I gave in but was not convinced. I hoped that if the other woman in my head knew something, that she could somehow get the information through to me.

Chapter Eleven

Nearly two millennia away, we were making real progress in our little corner of Pompeii. By the beginning of the third day on-site, we had worked our way right around the insulae and only had three more dwellings to investigate. There were actually five left, but another group that had been involved in some of the original excavating had done the last two the previous week. We were quite pleased as it allowed us to take more time with the remaining buildings. It was a cooler day, the weather had turned drizzly overnight, the damp air was heavy with scent from the tall umbrella pines surrounding the site and the clouds were low over Vesuvius, shrouding its menace.

The first one we entered had never been allocated a name; nothing had been uncovered to identify who had lived there, although two Egyptian-style herms — a kind of bust — had been found during the early excavations. It was of modest size with a small garden and some areas were showing signs of weather damage. There was a beautiful niche Lararium, or shrine, in one of the walls that surrounded the garden and, hints of the frescoes that had adorned the interior, could still be seen.

We added to any information already recorded, noting any change and as far as we could tell, this house had not been undergoing any repair work at the time of the eruption. It may have been abandoned after the earthquake of AD62, its owners never returning, or it may not have been damaged at all. All that was left to do there was to bring in the technical equipment to see whether anything was beneath this level.

The next house was much larger and as we went in Nate read from his notes that this had been designated Casa del Cherem or House of the Hebrew, because of an inscription in the vestibulum, or entrance hall. I felt an icy trickle run down my spine and was unable to prevent a shiver.

"Someone walk over your grave, Hannah?" asked Sebastian, noticing. Oh, Sebastian, I thought, if only you knew. I grinned at him and shoved him in the shoulder

"There are so many ghosts here Sebastian, it would not surprise me if they were sitting with a cuppa watching us work." He raised his hands in mock horror and we both laughed, but I was wary now. The House of the Hebrew — no, it couldn't be, it seemed too easy. Nate pointed out the inscription; it was faded but still legible. It was in Latin, which I understood and Hebrew, which I didn't. Slowly tracing whatever remained I worked out that it said, *Welcome, go in peace and return in peace*.

Under my fingers, the stone felt warm and, as I translated the text, images flooded my mind like the echo of another's life — pictures of a family enjoying a meal; children chasing through the rooms; laughter and fun; and most of all, a lot of love. This had been a happy home. As the faces became clearer, I was aware that Nate was asking me something but I couldn't hear him properly.

Maxentius and Marcus were sitting down next to a low table, holding goblets, a sound made them turn and look in my direction. Had I made that sound or was it her? The world receded and there was a roaring in my ears. No, I refused to let this thing take me. I needed to stay here. The pull was stronger — but you need to tell them, Hannah, you need to warn them. Fighting it now — no, I can do it in my dreams; she knows I'm in her dreams. Maxentius suddenly started to move towards me.

I felt a hand on my shoulder, someone asking if I was okay. I couldn't see who it was but I heard myself speaking, the words coming from a long way away.

"Get Max, please get Max." Then I pitched forward into darkness.

"Hannah, are you alright? Did you hurt yourself?" Of course I didn't, I only slipped. Still on my knees, I looked at my hands, which I expected to be gritty and scuffed from the damp dirty ground, only to find that they were clean, just a bit red. A wooden tray was on the tiled floor in front of me; how did that get there? I hadn't been carrying anything other than a notebook. I shook my head, feeling rather odd. An arm lifted me gently off the floor and sat me down in a chair. Funny, I don't remember there being any chairs in these houses.

I looked around but my vision was cloudy. Where were Nate and Sebastian? Why were these people dressed so strangely? My mind couldn't process what I was seeing and then a voice broke through the fog —

"Hannah, my love, what's wrong? You look most perplexed. Are you sure you are unhurt?" A little girl ran up and leant on my knee.

"Mama, do you need me to kiss it better?" The words were familiar, words my mother would have said to me when I was hurt, heard and repeated by a child, but I didn't have any children. The girl looked into my face and squeezing my cheeks in her little hands, kissed me squarely on the lips. Satisfied that she had done her bit to help me, she ran back to wherever she had come from.

Bewildered, I blinked; images swirled, refusing to come into focus. I put trembling hands to my head. Had I banged it — again? A pair of strong arms lifted me out of the chair and carried me through to another room. I panicked and began to struggle, but the same voice calmed me.

"Relax, Hannah, you are safe. Maybe you hit your head, though I'm unsure what on. Rest for a few moments, it is quiet here." He laid me on a very comfortable bed; it was cool in this room, which looked vaguely familiar.

"Don't leave me, please don't leave me." My voice rose in my anxiety.

"I am here, my Hannah." 'My Hannah.' That phrase, that voice, I knew both. I was desperately trying to pin down what was going on, when I felt a large hand take hold of one of mine and a thumb start rubbing my palm. The images converged and the picture froze. I remembered.

"Maxentius?" I whispered, "Maxentius is that you?"

"Of course it is. Who else do you think...?" He stopped mid sentence, "...wait, we've had this conversation before, many years ago." He looked at me for a long moment and I gazed back at him, willing him to understand. "Is she...are you here again?" I nodded, sighing.

"It seems that way. I am sorry and I hoped it wouldn't come to this, but I have been seeing you in my dreams lately and Hannah, your Hannah, seems to need me. I thought you were still on Masada. I had no idea you had come here to Pompeii and at first I was confused by what I was seeing. I only really worked it out a few days ago, in my time and I think I know why we have re-connected. Then this morning, I was entering your...this house and I touched the inscription at the doorway, now I'm here."

Our conversation was nonsensical; I was still his Hannah, it just that there were two of us in her head now. My voice was her voice, but it was like she had suddenly gained an extra sense. I hesitated, debating whether this was too much. He had understood the last time and the knowledge I had shared with my ancestor had saved his life, but I wasn't sure that he could handle it again, not that there was a whole lot I could do about it.

"I had hoped I would be able to share what I know through our dreams, but looks like that plan has been ruined." I tried to smile, but was unsure of his reaction. He noticed my apprehension and squeezed my hand.

"Do not worry; it will just take a little while to adjust to the change. I have never forgotten what you did for us but I knew you were no longer part of our lives. You — Hannah — stopped talking about things that would happen many years in the future. When did you go?"

"The day you rescued me — her, from the cistern. I, she..." oh this was confusing, "...needed to rest. Just before you fell asleep you told her you had made it and I knew she was safe. I knew you had kept your promise and the next thing I woke up in my world." He smiled, remembering that day, the horror and the joy.

"We remained on Masada for over four years, helping with the repair and rebuilding. It is a shame you didn't wait around, you would have been very impressed." He winked at me and I felt my heart flip-flop, torn between the two men in my life. "Then recently I was recalled to Rome and posted here to quash the recurring riots." He hesitated for a moment. "How is it you are here in Pompeii? Are you able to share this knowledge that we need?"

"Max, my other Max, and I came for a holiday. Well, actually we went to Rome and met up with some of the archaeologists we knew from our time at Masada. They invited us to join them here for a week. We have been investigating some of the insulae, whether they were undergoing repair at the time of the eruption and whether there are any layers underneath that level which can provide further information on the history of the city." Listen to yourself explaining this Hannah — good job he knows you.

"Eruption? What eruption?" Concerned now.

"The mountain behind this city, Vesuvius, it is going to erupt, killing nearly everyone here and burying everything within a forty mile radius. It will happen in less than a year, I think. Please, you must make sure that you have all left before this happens. Pompeii will be completely covered in volcanic ash and will disappear from history for nearly seventeen hundred years. There will be very little chance of escape if you are in this town when the mountain explodes. Please, believe me..." my voice trailed away and very quietly thinking it unlikely that he would hear, I added, "...I couldn't bear it if anything happened to you," words I had whispered many years ago when we had first met and I was treating his wounds.

He did hear, as he always heard and gently lifting me off the bed gathered me to him, enfolding me in his arms. Sighing, I leaned into him and, curving his hand round my neck, Maxentius tilted my head and kissed me. His lips were firm and cool, but loaded with promise. I kissed him back, feeling a slow burn begin in the centre of my body. Involuntarily, my arms went around him; his body felt strange, yet so familiar. I murmured his name and he hugged me close; this man whose life I had saved, this man with whom I had fallen in love and had married, this man with whom I had borne a child, yet although the Hannah from this world had never left, I had lost them and had thought never to see them again. This was like coming home.

"I realise I should know, but, until my head catches up, am I supposed to be doing something other than this right now," I whispered against his lips, "like running a household?" I felt him chuckle.

"Yes, but I'm sure they can spare you for a little while. In fact, just a minute." He laid me back on the bed and left the room. I felt bereft, yet struggled to understand why. He was the other 'me's' husband and I loved Max. All I could think was that, as before, we had become one in this life — her love was my love, her passion mine.

Seconds ticked by; I lay on the bed musing over what had happened. Had they found Max, my Max? Did he know that I was here? And if so, how would he get me back? More to the point, was I still lying on a damp and muddy floor in this same house only two thousand years in the future? My head really did not want to deal with it and the dizziness returned. I breathed deeply trying to banish it, but it persisted. Coming back into the room and after making sure he had closed the door, Maxentius came over to the bed, looking somewhat anxious.

"You're still rather pale," sitting next to me.

"It's nothing," shyly, "just a little dizziness, too much thinking about how I got here." He pulled me against him, my back nestling against his chest. I could feel his heartbeat; it soothed me, calming the panic, which was still circling the edge of my senses.

"Are you going to be okay with this?" I asked tentatively, tracing the backs of his hands with my fingers, noticing callouses and scars from minor injuries, which I had treated so many years ago.

"I've managed before and, strange as it sounds, having someone who knows what's going to happen can be comforting." I twisted in his arms and stared up at him. His eyes, green as a forest, twinkled down at me.

"I don't know how long I'll be here, but I guess, if Masada is anything to go by, it will be until the eruption at least." Unable to stop myself, I lifted my hands and ran them through his hair, removing the leather strip that held it back. The green eyes darkened and I had to blink to make sure I was still here; they were so much like Max's eyes.

"Where did you go just now?" I asked, distracting myself momentarily.

"Just asking Marcus and Aliza if they could keep an eye on the children for a while. I said that you were a little woozy and

I wanted to sit with you to make sure you had not hurt yourself, something I feel I should check," beginning a slow exploration of my body.

"What did I do?" trying to maintain my breathing, like I really cared at this point.

"It looked as though you tripped over the rug, or your own feet, but in an effort not to drop the tray you were carrying you came down with a bit of a crash. Then you had that funny turn and we thought you might have banged your head. On what we had no idea, although now I know that was most unlikely." His fingers slid underneath my clothes, teasing across my flesh.

"No, I didn't bang my head, I just slipped through time," baldly, then bit my lip. Maybe that was too much. I felt a giggle bubble up; my life was so ridiculously complicated. Maxentius halted his delicious progress up my body to lean back and look at me properly, raising an eyebrow at my expression. "Well honestly, do you hear me? I sound crackers."

"Yes I hear you, it's a good job I'm used to you. Now shut up." He, most effectively, shut me up, his lips plundering mine. Heat flared along my veins as he kissed me nearly senseless, for a long time. The slow burn was curling around my stomach and part of me continued to muse over how I could feel like this, but trying to rationalise it was making me woozy again, so I gave up. I was powerless in his hands anyway; it was easier just to let it go for now and sink into the sensations that Maxentius' fingers were creating along my body.

Somewhat later as we lay curled up together enjoying the peace, my mind still battled with the emotions that this reunion, of sorts had brought to the fore. It was so odd, as though I had to catch up on six years, even though I hadn't been anywhere. I snuggled closer.

"I'm not ready to face the world yet," I murmured, "can we stay here a little longer?"

"I'm pretty sure Marcus has everything under control," Maxentius replied, kissing me gently.

"Sometimes I wish it was just you and me, back on Masada," I said, a little wistfully, "no-one else to worry about, nothing else to keep us away from each other. I know that's selfish and I love our family, but I miss being able to do this when we want, like we could before." He nuzzled my hair, kissing my neck, sending shivers of delight down my spine.

"I miss it too, my work here keeps me away from you for more hours than I am comfortable with, especially as you might be called out to the Palaestra or the Gladiators' School at any time. I would prefer to accompany you than send Petronius. I miss being able to pop across a courtyard and talk to you, or hold you or..." wiggling his eyebrows wickedly, he let that hang, "...I would like to think we might find that freedom again one day."

"Yeah, but most likely by then, we'll be old and grey and have no energy for this." I smiled

"I cannot imagine ever not wanting or being able to do this," he grinned, "it is part of life, like breathing and eating. We just might have to take it more slowly." I giggled at the image that his words created in my head and then gasped as Maxentius began playing his fingers over my back. Sighing, I stretched along his body, fitting myself to his shape, as each touch, each caress seemed to bring me back into his world; a world I realised I had missed.

Eventually, we decided we should probably attend to whatever it was we'd abandoned when I'd fallen over. I had to familiarise myself with this house and those in it, as well as the town. Not being sure how long I would be part of this world, I did what I had done when on Masada — just let instinct guide me. Hannah knew what she was doing; I was just here for the ride. The only control I had was over their future and I hoped that I could save them one more time.

Chapter Twelve

I saw that it was late afternoon, so my working day, if I'd had one, was over. It was close to the time of our evening meal and I could smell the food Aliza was cooking, making me realise how hungry I was. Marcus and the children had been in the garden and, at Aliza's call, trooped in, all of them requiring a wash before we sat down.

Poor Marcus looked as though he had been rolling in the veggie patches and, sheepishly, he excused himself, returning to his own apartment to clean up. He was back within a few minutes, explaining that he had been giving the children piggybacks and had forgotten that their feet and hands were coated in mud. His description made us all laugh and the small fry were chortling with glee over their antics. While this was going on, I suddenly became aware that my head had adjusted and I was simply Hannah — just with a little extra knowledge.

"It's a good job Uncle Marcus is so patient," Maxentius smiled. "I may not have been happy if you had covered me in mud." They looked at him, unsure whether he was serious or joking, finally deciding that he was joking, for surely no-one could dislike being muddy and, applied themselves to their meal with gusto. We chatted over the food, keeping it light while the children were within hearing.

They were excited about the possibility of having chickens in the larger garden at the back of the house. Marcus had said he would make an enclosure to keep them off the planted area and the three of them wanted to help, so the conversation centred around the design of the hen house, some ideas of which were outlandish in the extreme. Still, it was entertaining.

After they had gone to bed, dragging Aliza along with them for a story, the three of us relaxed in the living area. It was a peaceful time of day; the fire crackled in the grate, which along with the light from the oil lamps scattered around the room, cast shadows over the walls, highlighting details in the frescoes decorating them. It was a very pleasing room, this one; the furniture was functional yet well made and the chairs were for comfort, not for a display of status. We had no-one to show off to anyway. Marcus and Maxentius talked about the gangs; it was becoming a regular topic of conversation between us in the evenings. They were at a loss to know how to stop them and they were gathering momentum. I listened to them for a while and then butted into their discussion.

"It will probably come to a head in one huge fracas and, hopefully, you'll be able to quash it at that point. The problem is there are so many small protests happening all over the place that you cannot possibly deal with them all. This could be their plan; divide and conquer. Don't let them suck you into trying to disperse those brawls; just monitor them and make sure they don't get out of hand. You need to be prepared for the big one. That will be the one that they join forces for, in the hope that you have spread yourselves too thinly across the city to get back in time to subdue it." Absently, my fingers tapped out a tune on the goblet I was holding and I continued.

"Mind you, I think that you need to let them believe you are struggling to manage the problem. Get your men to discuss the lack of soldiers seconded to quell the protests; let them do this while they patrol the streets. They will be heard and their grievances passed on to those organising the riots who will assume that you have no power to stop them. They will think they can get away with a larger disturbance. Sometimes, you need to lose a battle to win the war." I winked at them as I wound up, noticing that they were both looking at me as though I'd fallen out of a tree.

"How on earth do you know so much about these gangs, Hannah?" Marcus asked.

"By listening to you two talk about it every night. Also, you do remember that I lived with a bunch of Zealots who spent hours plotting the downfall of Rome? Eventually some of it sticks. This is all you talk about. I know how much it frustrates you but you have to think like an agitator, not like the law-abiding citizens that you are. They do not give this..." I clicked my fingers together "...about the law, yet you have to abide by it and uphold it. You are the ones with restrictions; just think outside the square." Then I realised that my last phrase may well not be used for several hundred years, if not two thousand years. Oh dear, I needed to watch myself — again — I could get away with it when I was with my two Romans, but others would not be as understanding.

"I think you may be right," Maxentius said, mulling over my words. "I had not thought about it in those terms. We will have a meeting in the morning before we go out on patrol and discuss how we can spread the word without seeming to." They discussed this for a bit longer until Marcus, yawning prodigiously, took his leave.

"You shouldn't let those children run you ragged," I smiled at him, "they have way more energy than the three of us put together."

"Yes, but it's fun," he grinned. I shook my head in disbelief.

"You are a glutton for punishment, that's all I have to say; oh, except thank you, we do appreciate how much time you spend with them." He gave me a quick hug and, nodding to Maxentius, left.

We tidied up, secured the house and went to bed.

"It doesn't seem like five minutes since I got out of this bed," I said.

"Well, it isn't all that long," Maxentius, grinned wickedly.

"Haha, very funny, you know what I mean," batting him on the arm, as we undressed.

"Hmm, not sure I do," he replied, coming around to help me with my tunic.

"I'm quite capable of undressing myself," shivering as the cold air stung my skin.

"Maybe so, but this way is so much more fun," tossing my clothes in the corner.

"Hey, that's my..." the rest was cut off as his mouth descended on mine and we continued where we had left off just a few hours earlier.

I woke later in the night. It was raining heavily outside, thunder rolled around the bay. I checked the children in case they had been disturbed, but they were fast asleep. I pulled their blankets right up, making sure they were properly covered, for the weather had cooled considerably. I watched the storm for a while — the lightening illuminated the sky, flash after flash — and listened to the downpour clattering on the tiles. I was due to visit Darius the next day and I knew this rain would make the going very muddy — ugh.

I'm not sure how long I stood there, but suddenly Maxentius was beside me.

"What are you doing, my Hannah? It is still night."

"The storm woke me and I wanted to check on the children."

"Come back to bed. You will get cold standing here in your bare feet." He put his arm around me, the heat from his body warming me and I realised I was shivering. I was falling asleep and by the time we reached our room, he was virtually carrying me.

"Sorry," I said drowsily, "I can't seem to stand up." Maxentius chuckled as he lifted me onto the bed.

"If I had a denarius for every time you've said that to me, I'd be a rich man." I tried to open my eyes, but they were so heavy and the last thing I felt was him lying down next to me, pulling me into his chest.

When I woke again, it was morning and it was still raining, although the storm seemed to have passed. Maxentius was already up and gone. He had left me to sleep, bless his heart. I washed and, placing the clothes that Maxentius had so blithely dumped on the floor in the basket of laundry, rooted out clean ones from my cupboard; then, once dressed went to see what everyone else was up to. The weather meant that they would probably need to stay at home; although I knew Aliza had things she needed to do without three excitable children hanging off her arms.

"If you can wait 'til after the sixth hour, I can take the children once I return from the Gladiators' School." Aliza nodded with relief. Our day organised, I ate my breakfast, gathered all my medications together and waited for Petronius.

As usual he was prompt and we made our way along the muddy paths to the school. It was very cold and I needed my warm cloak this morning, which was held closed with my beautiful clasp, the red stone standing out against the deep grey of the material. Petronius commented on it and I told him when and why Maxentius had given it to me. It still felt like a talisman and I always made sure it was securely fastened. I would be devastated if I lost it.

We arrived without incident, by which I mean that I didn't fall in the mud and Tullius met us at the entrance.

"The Dacian seems much better today. I think he will be able to begin light training by the end of this week."

"I hope so. His wound looked to be healing well the last time I was here. I will report on his progress after I have seen him"

"We have moved the Jew to another room. You need not worry about having contact with him while you are here." I smiled at the gruff old soldier and patted his arm.

"Thank you my friend, you are most thoughtful." He nodded and left us to our task.

We made our way along the corridors to the Dacian's room, the inevitable guards following in our wake. The door was standing ajar and the room looked clean and tidy. The air was not stuffy, nor did it smell of sickness. This was a good sign. Darius was sitting on his bed, apparently waiting for me. I smiled and said good morning; he nodded in response and I opened my bag, removing everything I would need.

I asked him to lie down, motioning to him so he knew what I meant. Covering his lower half with a sheet, I lifted his tunic. The bandage was still relatively clean, another good sign. Unwinding it carefully, I removed it and then peeled back the swatch of material covering the wound itself. It was ten days since I had stitched the wound and every time I had come to check on Darius it had looked better. It was still clean, there was no infection and there was definite healing. The honey I had rubbed along the line of stitches and over the scabbing had kept the skin soft and I hoped, less itchy.

The stitches would need to come out soon, but I would leave them for two more days, just to be certain that the skin had knitted properly. Cleaning any residual salve and honey off the injury, I pressed gently around the edges, watching Darius to see whether it was painful. His face remained impassive, but I could not detect any underlying discomfort. No clenching of the jaw or narrowing of the eyes.

Breathing a sigh of relief, I smiled and squeezed his hand. His eyes widened at my actions. It was obvious no one had touched him with anything other than enmity for a long time and his face reddened with confusion.

"I think you will be able to train again soon. I want to be sure your skin has closed fully before you do and I will come in two more days to check. If everything looks good, I will remove the stitches then."

I finished wiping over the gash and applied fresh salve, massaging it in with careful fingers. Placing a fresh piece of cloth across the wound, I covered it with a new bandage, making sure it was securely fastened. I offered him a drink of the poppy juice, but he smiled shyly and shook his head.

"I do not need," he said haltingly. I grinned back at him, tidying my things. As we were about to leave he motioned to Petronius and asked him something. Petronius glanced at me and then nodded his head. Darius grunted in what sounded like disapproval, but I did not feel it appropriate to ask. I said goodbye and that I would see him in two days; he acknowledged my comment and we left.

There were four other men with minor cuts and scrapes, that I needed to check on, but I didn't want them to become worse through lack of proper care. We found them all in their respective rooms and it didn't take me long to clean and re-bandage their injuries. As we headed back to Tullius' office, I asked Petronius what the Dacian had asked him.

"He wanted to know whether it was true that the Jew had insulted you. I confirmed that he had."

"Oh," was all I could think of in response. I did not know why he even cared? Odd. We chatted with Tullius for a little while and I told him that I would be back in a couple of days, barring any accident that required my attention prior to that!

Petronius walked with me back to my home and asked whether I would need him again that day. I assured him I would be fine that I intended to take a walk with the children in the afternoon, but we shouldn't need an escort.

"Just be careful, Hannah, these rioters are everywhere."

"I promise; thank you for worrying about me." He grinned and waved his goodbye, disappearing into the headquarters building.

Entering our home, I realised that there was no-one in; Aliza must still be out with the three littlies. I set about preparing something for our midday meal; we had some cold meat left from the night before to which I added bread, cucumbers and cheese. It should be enough to see us through until the evening. About half an hour later the four of them came in. Efraim, Liora and Claudia were very excited to see me; it was unusual for me to be home at this time. We enjoyed our meal and then Aliza left for the afternoon.

She had met some women at the market who liked to sew and, as she was a very good seamstress, they had asked her along to their meetings. I think it was really just an excuse to get together and gossip. Still, it gave her something to do away from this house; she was becoming quite well known to many of the people who worked in the local markets and shops. It was lovely that she had this; we had taken her away from everything that was familiar to her and it could not have been easy.

I tidied up the table and washed the food platters. We played for a little while and then I suggested we go for a walk. The sun was coming out and, even though the paths would still be muddy, it would do us good to stretch our legs and get some fresh air! Wrapping up warmly, for it was still chilly, we all wore the strongest footwear we owned, which were leather boots lined with felt and laced up. I wasn't sure whether women were supposed to wear them, but I was not walking out in my sandals. My boots were still damp from my excursion of the morning, but they would be enough to protect my feet from the mud.

Stepping out into the weak afternoon sunlight, we made our way along the main street, towards the Forum. Things were always happening there and, hopefully the children would be distracted for a while. We spent a lovely couple of hours meandering around. Efraim dragged me to the chicken stands at the market to show me the types he thought we needed to get. To be fair, he was looking at colour not whether they were egg-layers, but his heart was in the right place. I bought each of them a sweet bread, laughing as they tried to stop the honey filling from dribbling down their chin. The afternoon was waning as we turned for home. I knew they would sleep well; their cheeks were rosy from the chill air and their exertions.

We weren't far from home when I became aware of a loud noise in the distance. I took no notice for such things were not unusual. We carried on walking briskly, singing a children's ditty and swinging our arms. Claudia was holding my hand and the other two were dancing about in front. The noise got louder and I turned to see a large group of men behind.

Anxious now, I hurried the children along, but they couldn't walk fast enough. Before we had gone a few more yards, the horde was on us. They seemed to be running from something else and I could see mounted soldiers behind them.

More than a little scared now for the safety of the children, I tried to push them out of harm's way, up into the doorway of one of the houses. I have no idea how it happened, but suddenly the throng of people was sweeping me along. My hand was wrenched from Claudia's and I could hear her wailing. I was pushed and pulled, then I was falling into the roadway there was mud everywhere.

The clatter of hooves came closer and I covered my head, realising that there was every likelihood that I was going to be trampled to death in front of my children. There was yelling and bawling and still the sound of the horses. I lifted my head and screamed at the top of my lungs for the children to go and find Papa. As I looked up, a horse reared over me, so I did the most logical thing and fainted.

Chapter Thirteen

Someone was shaking me, I could hear screaming and wanted them to shut up, what an infernal racket, why would anyone need to be doing that? So rude. I shrugged the hand off me and the screaming continued. Whoever it was, was really upset. The arm was back shaking me and calling my name. Why wouldn't they leave me alone? I wasn't bothering them. I put my hands out to push them away, and the person shaking me grabbed them.

"Hannah, Hannah, HANNAH!" The voice was very loud. I tried to open my mouth to tell them to get off me when I realised my mouth was already open — well that was weird. So I clamped it shut — and the screaming stopped. Oh good grief, was I the one screaming? What on earth for? My mind was whirling. I remembered mud and horses and people running.

The voice tried again, quieter this time, but no less insistent.

"Hannah, come on baby." Where was I? I struggled to open my eyes. At least that would be a start. The effort was nearly too much. I felt shivery, as though I was coming down with a cold and my eyes were so heavy. "Hannah, you need to open your eyes." Okay, okay, I thought grumpily, you should try, its not easy. I grumbled at whoever was talking, my voice sounded hoarse, that would be from all the screaming no doubt.

"What do you want?" I muttered.

"I want you to open your eyes and look at me."

"Uhhhh...no, it's too hard. Can't you let me be?"

"No, come on. Please, honey just for me." Oh well, if it's just for you, whoever you are, sure. I tried to turn away, but the owner of the voice wouldn't let me, turning me back over.

"Oh, please, please leave me alone."

"I can't. C'mon Sunshine." 'Sunshine', I knew who said that, didn't I? I searched my mind for who it was. Someone tall, with green eyes — wait — green eyes! Suddenly mine flew open. Meeting those green eyes, which were looking back at me full of alarm, "Hey there sweetheart, thought we'd lost you for a moment." He smiled at me and I remembered that smile, it made my heart thud.

"Max?"

"Who else?" Well, you know that's a silly question. "What happened honey?"

"I have no clue; where am I?"

"In the admin building by the entrance to the ruin, we carried you here after you fainted. They let us use this room." I stared at him, trying to recall fainting, but couldn't.

"Where did I faint?"

"In the house you were working in. Sebastian said you were laughing and joking about ghosts, then suddenly you asked them to get me and passed out. That was a good half an hour ago." Half an hour, was that all? I'd lived through two days. I remembered that the same thing had happened when we were at Masada; time didn't work the same way.

I forced my brain to think backwards. Snapshots of what I thought had been my day flashed up, horses, children, gladiator, Maxentius, suddenly —

"It was the inscription."

"What inscription?"

"The one in the vestibulum, it was in Hebrew and Latin. It was their home. I was in their home. Oh Max! I need to go back! The children. I fell and there were horses and the children were with me and I don't know what happened." I knew I was gabbling as panic coursed through me and I tried to get up, but found that my body didn't want to play. I looked down at myself, expecting to be coated in mud, but I was fine, although the knees of my jeans were a bit grubby.

"Hannah, there's nothing you can do now, they'll be ok, someone will find them. Just rest for a moment. You need to tell me what happened."

I sat back, gazing at Max who was quite pale.

"I'm sorry, I didn't mean to scare you."

"It was the screaming that scared me! It came out of nowhere and it was really loud."

"I know, I hadn't realised it was me and I really wanted them to shut up." I chuckled weakly. "Ok, this probably won't make any sense, but here goes. I was translating the inscription and suddenly I could see people, but sort of faded images, you know; it was Maxentius and Marcus. Then Maxentius turned towards me as though I'd spoken to him, but I knew I hadn't. Someone touched my shoulder and I asked them to find you, the next thing I was back there. I'd fallen over a rug or something and dropped a tray."

I continued with my story, telling Max exactly what had occurred and that we had been walking back from the Forum when I had been mown down by a mob of men.

"I was screaming at the children to go and find Maxentius and the last thing I remember was a horse rearing over me." I shuddered at the memory, fear bubbling up again. Max moved to sit next to me on the sofa where they had lain me and hugged me to him, kissing the top of my head.

"It's okay, sweetheart, we'll work it out." The quiet of the room enveloped us and my fear began to subside. Logically I knew there was nothing I could do, but since not much in my life was logical, I still wanted to try.

"Can we go home, Max? Well, not home home, I mean to the villa? I don't want to be here anymore today. Will they mind? They probably think I'm a liability anyway. First Masada, now Pompeii ... honestly." Max chuckled.

"I think after your little floor show they'll be fine with you going home." He grinned. "Do you feel up to walking yet?"

"Not quite, my legs feel wobbly, I think I need a bit longer." He nodded, saying that he'd go and find me a cup of coffee. After he'd gone, I lay back on the sofa, trying to get my head around the last few hours. I felt out of sync. Not surprising really and although when this had happened before I hadn't wanted to go back, now I did. I was desperate to know whether those three children were safe.

It was several minutes before Max returned with my coffee, but it was worth the wait, being steaming hot and delicious. Its heady aroma and caffeinated goodness fired along my synapses, making me feel much less woozy. We sat for maybe another half an hour before I felt ready to walk home. I glanced at my watch; it wasn't even lunchtime. Goodness, I thought, smiling to myself, I certainly know how to fill in a couple of hours. Max raised an eyebrow at my expression and I explained why I was smiling.

"It seems so bizarre, we've only been out of the villa about three hours, yet I've fitted in nearly twenty four." I chuckled. "Good job nobody's listening to this, they'd think I'd lost the plot!" Max laughed and our mood lightened. "C'mon, let's go, I think I can make it now." We gathered up our belongings — someone must have brought mine — and walked slowly back to Geoff's villa. The cloud was still low, but it wasn't raining and it didn't take us long to get home.

Once there, Max took my bag from me and pushed me gently into the living room.

"Go and take a load off, Sunshine, I'll put these away. I might need to pop back in a little while just for half an hour or so, to let them know what's happening and where I got to, but I won't be out for long." I wasn't sure I wanted him to leave me or whether if I was going to 'go back,' it would be better if I was on my own. I put the kettle on for a hot drink and while it boiled, plonked myself on the sofa. I still felt shivery and wondered again whether I was coming down with a cold. My throat hurt, but I was pretty sure that was from the screaming rather than from anything else.

Max came into the room just as the kettle boiled and brewed two mugs of tea, bringing them over and placing them on the little table in front of where I was sitting. Scooching me up, he sat down, pulling me into his arms. It was a huge couch, big plump cushions and wide seats and was so long Max could lie right out on it. Made it a very comfortable place to snuggle. There was a colourful blanket or throw lying along the back of it, which I pulled over us — well me mostly.

"Are you cold, Hannah?" as Max watched me arrange the rug.

"I can't seem to get warm. Was I lying on the ground or something?"

"As far as I know you landed on your knees and didn't fall any further, you weren't damp when they carried you to the admin office."

"Maybe I've caught a bit of a chill." I shivered again and Max looked thoughtfully at me.

"Maybe it's shock. Sounds like you had one heck of a day." He winked at me and I smiled back. I suddenly realised that I felt very tired.

"If you need to go back, it's okay, I think I might go to bed. That might warm me up and I feel ever so sleepy."

"Only if you're sure, I don't really like leaving you, but I think I should at least let them know how you are and check on what else I should be doing."

"Seriously, hon, it's okay...I'll finish this tea, then go have a nap." He hugged me close, kissing me gently.

"I know, but I worry about you, Sunshine, I don't want to lose you again. Last time was bad enough." I leaned into him, returning his kiss and for long moments we lost ourselves in each other's embrace.

"I don't want to lose you either, but I'm afraid I can't promise anything. Although I'm here with you now, which suggests I must come back, even if I go again." I said realising how convoluted that sounded. I grinned. "Just go, I'll be fine." One more lingering kiss and, reluctantly, he got to his feet.

"I won't be long, I'll lock the door on my way out, I've got the keys. Have a nice kip."

He left and I heard the lock click. Finishing my tea and standing both cups in the sink to soak, I walked through to our bedroom. Even on a day as dull as today, the room felt bright and welcoming. I shrugged out of my clothes and decided to take a long, hot shower before I lay down. The fierce jets massaged my body, but I felt no warmer.

Wrapping myself in one of the enormous fluffy towels, I went back along to the bedroom, drawing the blinds and turning on the bedside lamp. Draping the towel over the beautifully ornate towel rack, I rooted around in the chest of drawers until I found one of Max's T-shirts. Pulling it over my head, I slipped between the sheets, dragging the thick comforter up to my shoulders. Turning out the lamp, I curled up and almost immediately fell asleep.

The stench was appalling, a combination of human sweat and waste; it was making my eyes water and I tried to breathe through my mouth. I was sitting on a cold and dirty floor and, looking around, I made out at least three other people in this dank and tiny room, which if I wasn't much mistaken was a cell. Shaking my head, I tried to remember how I'd got here. My last conscious thought until a few minutes ago was the horse, rearing up over me. I felt bruised and sore, but as I flexed my arms and legs, I didn't think anything was broken. The horse must have missed me.

I was very cold and realised that my cloak was missing. A flare of panic ran through me. My clasp! Oh please don't let me have lost the clasp, my most treasured possession. Not that I could do anything about it. On top of that, I noticed that somehow my clothes were torn and my boots had gone. What on earth had happened to me? The other people in this room with me were all men; they were talking amongst themselves and glancing over at me. I knew how vulnerable I was; I doubted anyone would come to my aid if they decided I was fair game.

One of them came over to me. I pushed myself up against the wall, wrapping my arms around my chest. He knelt down next to me and quietly asked me if I was hurt. I gazed at him in astonishment. What did he care? He smiled ruefully.

"I saw what happened to you, I know you shouldn't be here, you were not part of the protest."

"My children," I whispered hoarsely, "did you see my children?"

"I think they are safe; the soldiers certainly didn't run them down or grab them like they did you."

"Why did they grab me? I was just walking along the street, 'til your mob, at least I assume they were your mob, flattened me into the mud."

"I think it was just because you were there, they rounded up everyone in the vicinity, but I fear you are the only one who should not be here. I am pretty sure the rest of us were all involved."

"What will happen?" I asked anxiously.

"They will bring us before the magistrate who will decide our fate. Usually it's just a fine, but as there have been many fights lately, he may not chose to be lenient."

"How bad could it be?" I asked, almost inaudibly, dreading his answer. He thought for a moment.

"Well, usually just a fine, but could be incarceration; or worst case, I guess they could behead us." I blanched and tried to stem the terror that threatened to overwhelm me.

"Surely not; I was just walking with my children."

"I know that, as do several other people here, but I doubt they will listen to us and, who knows whether the magistrate will believe you? Unfortunately they often don't much care for the truth."

I could not believe this was happening to me; what if I ended up in the arena? No, Hannah, don't be ridiculous; someone would see who I was before then. Surely someone would listen to me. Why hadn't the soldiers who brought me here recognised me? I tried to get a grip, knowing my thoughts were borne of panic not common sense. Then I looked down at myself and realised that if my face was anything like the rest of me, I would be unrecognisable. I was completely coated in mud and goodness knows what else. I also remembered that I was wearing my preferred attire, which looked more Hebrew than Roman and I wasn't wearing any jewellery; they would think me a slave. In an attempt to make myself look more presentable, I used the hem of my over-tunic to wipe my face, but probably made it worse.

"How long have we been here?" I asked my cellmate.

"Several hours, we could be here for days, they caught a lot of us." I nodded distractedly, my thoughts turning to my family. Had the children made their way home? We hadn't been far away; hopefully they would remember how to find it. Would Maxentius think to look for me here? Wherever 'here' was. I could feel the cold from the floor seeping into my bones; I shivered and got up in an attempt to warm my muscles. Everything ached. Had we been beaten? I asked the men if this was the case and they said that they had, so it was most likely I had too.

"They beat women, even one already unconscious?"

"If you're an agitator, they beat you; doesn't matter whether you're a man or a woman, conscious or otherwise, makes no difference to them." I recalled the conversation I'd had with Maxentius and Marcus the night before; surely they hadn't implemented their ideas already? No, they wouldn't have had time; this couldn't be the big one they were worried about. If it wasn't, I did not want to think about how awful the outcome could be when it did happen.

Sighing, I swung my arms round me; I was so cold and even though the mud had almost dried, what was left of my tunic remained damp. I knew the risks of wearing wet clothing for too long. Still, if they were going to behead me, it wouldn't matter whether I had a cold. I felt an hysterical giggle rise in my throat and forced it back; it would not do to lose control in front of these men.

I asked whether I could sit with them, hoping the warmth generated by all our bodies would stave off the chill. Darkness had fallen and I knew nothing would happen now until the next morning. We talked most of that night. The men, whose names I had discovered were Priscus Regulus, Caelius Quintillus and Septimus Laurentinus, were not of lowly status, nor troubled by lack of food or bad housing. They were men of rank who held positions of authority. They just hated Vespasian — no, maybe not hated — but they had wanted the other guy to win and now they were letting the administration know that another challenge for power was never far away. Crimes against the Emperor were punishable by death and I feared for these men, but they knew what they had done and believed in their cause. How many times had I heard that in my life?

When it came to me telling them who I was, I hesitated, concerned about how it might affect Maxentius, but could not really see any point in hiding it; doubtless they would find out soon enough. So I told them. Initially they were disbelieving, knowing the regulations surrounding serving members of the Roman army and marriage. However after I explained, briefly, the circumstances, they understood. When I went on to tell them of my work as one of the medici at the Gladiators' School and to those who trained at the Palaestra, opposite the amphitheatre, they seemed quite impressed.

"So, if you ever need a physician, you can call for me, although I hope it won't be necessary." They grinned at me, saying that the way things were going, my services might be needed sooner than I thought. Our confinement had created an alliance of sorts, the noise from the rooms around us was not as loud now and I presumed most were trying to sleep, but we kept talking. I listened as they discussed the political situation, trying to store it all up so I could tell Maxentius, if I ever got out of here. Not that I wanted to cause any more problems for these men, but I needed to understand both sides. There had to be a better way than this constant rioting.

Eventually, I must have fallen asleep, for suddenly it was daylight and I worked out that I must have been in this cell for at least eighteen hours. I was hungry enough to eat a horse and felt quite lightheaded with fatigue and cold. My cellmates were fast asleep, snoring loudly. The smell was much worse. With all these people using the floor as a toilet, my teeth seemed to be permanently clenched to prevent myself from throwing up. It was an absolute nightmare and I still had no idea about my children.

The hours ticked by slowly. Soldiers or guards came and took people away; I don't think any of them came back. There didn't seem to be a particular method behind whom they took, but it felt as though we were being left until last. I was so cold that I had trouble stopping my teeth from chattering and started to think I would never be warm again. I was very sleepy too. I knew that hypothermia was now a real possibility and that I had to keep awake or risk dying from cold. My skin was taking on a blue tinge and my thought processes were becoming sluggish.

Trying to fight it, I walked around the room, taking care to avoid anything that looked questionable. I tried to work up some emotion about all this, but the effort was too much. I needed to get angry, because if I didn't, by the time I was in front of the magistrate I would seem like a gibbering wreck. Forcing my brain to work, I practised what I would say. I thought about the children and my husband and the time I had been in this hellhole. I thought of my other Max, my other life and the reason I was here in the first place. I needed to get through this because of the eruption that would devastate the town.

After a while, I felt a little better. Either that or I was actually worse — my body lulling me into a false sense of security. Finally, as the light seemed to be fading at the end of another day, two guards came to our cell. Opening the door, one of them stood guard, while the other one came in and took hold of me, yanking me along with him. I managed a quick goodbye to my new friends as my legs struggled to keep up with the man holding my arm. He manhandled me along several corridors and up a short flight of steps into a large room. There were soldiers stationed around the walls and seated at a huge desk was the magistrate.

Chapter Fourteen

My anger began to bubble. By my reckoning, I had been held for around twenty four hours and it seemed as though I was the only woman, yet I had been left until almost last to be questioned. I was cold, tired and hungry and knew that there was a fair chance that I was going to be ill after this little venture. I was covered in mud and goodness knows what else and, someone had taken my boots and my cloak. I remembered that I was the wife of the Garrison Commander and that I was absolutely furious.

I focused on the floor in front of me, trying to get myself under control. The man at the desk spoke ponderously and yes, he seemed to think I was part of the riot. I listened to him droning on for a while, then bored with his pontificating and determined to cut this short, I lifted my head, my eyes flashing green fire. One of the soldiers gasped and went pale. I assumed that, despite my bedraggled appearance, someone had recognised me, finally. He nudged the soldier next to him and muttered something under his breath; they both looked horrified. Ignoring them, I held up my hand. The magistrate stopped speaking and looked at me questioningly.

"Excuse me, honoured Sir, am I permitted to speak?"

"All in good time woman. I am reading the charges against you."

"Charges! I fear you are mistaken; there should be no charges. In fact I think I deserve an apology." He raised his eyebrows. "I was walking home from the Forum, with my three children when I was flattened by a mob, nearly trampled on by a horse and dragged in here unconscious. I have no idea whether my children were hurt and I do not think my husband will be very pleased."

"If you have broken the law, I imagine he will be very upset with you."

"Not with me, Sir..." I paused, "...with you."

The magistrate studied me for a long moment and made no comment, but I wasn't about to shut up. If he was going to lock me up again, I was going to give him a real reason. It took nearly all of my strength, but I drew myself up.

"If any of these..." I paused and looked around the room and said the next word with thinly veiled sarcasm, "...men had bothered to check, they would have discovered that my name is Hannah Valerius and I am a Roman citizen, not a slave. I am also a medica at both the Gladiators' School and the Palaestra..." I waited until I knew he had understood me, then I dropped the only name I thought might help, "...and my husband is General Lucius Maxentius Valerius, the commander of the garrison here in Pompeii, assigned to the position by the Emperor himself."

One of the soldiers left the room and another walked over to the desk and whispered something to the magistrate, who looked at me, then back at the soldier nodding. It was getting harder to keep my anger burning. I was so cold now that my brain wasn't functioning properly and I was struggling to remain upright, but I had no intention of letting this man see how weak I felt. The tension in the room mounted and I didn't know what we were waiting for. Minutes ticked by; no one spoke. My knees began to buckle. The soldier standing behind me grabbed my arm and yanked me upright, hurting my arm. I yelped and glared at him. If I'd had the energy, I would have cried, but I had nothing left.

Suddenly there was the sound of running feet and there was a collective gasp as Maxentius — like an avenging angel — in full armour, his cloak billowing out behind him, burst through the door. He thumped his fist down on the desk demanding an explanation. The magistrate stuttered something about my being part of a mob. The soldier holding my arm let go and I dropped to the floor. Chaos reigned all around me but I didn't care. Maxentius had found me.

The next little while was a blur. I heard my husband raging at the magistrate, something about children and their mother and not asking me who I was; the magistrate claiming that they thought I was a slave who was part of the protest, which enraged Maxentius even more. The soldiers who had been guarding the cells came in for their fair share of recriminations too. They should have taken more care, checked me properly, given me a cloak at least. They didn't reply. It didn't do your army career a lot of good if you answered your commander back, especially when it was about said commander's wife.

The cold was overtaking me. I knew I was losing my grip on reality and tried to get Maxentius' attention, but my voice couldn't be heard over the racket. I tried again.

"Please, Maxentius, please." Nothing. Nobody was even looking at me. The soldiers had moved away from me, anxious not to be connected to what had happened and no-one was close enough for me to reach out to. I was unable to stand; there were tremors running through me; my vision was clouding and my concentration fading. I started to bang my hand on the floor, which was tiled, so it didn't make much sound, but I kept banging and banging, hoping someone heard.

Finally, the noise around me quietened down, but still I kept banging, unable to stop now. There was a strange silence and I realised they were all staring at me. All I wanted was for my husband to remember that I had been locked up for twenty-four hours without food, water or warmth and wanted him to take me home. He could shout at the magistrate and his soldiers later. Suddenly he was there, scooping me up into his arms — it's a good job I'm so small — and he was so lovely and warm that my teeth started chattering again. He pulled his cloak off his shoulders and wrapped me in it.

"Oh my Hannah, I am sorry, I thought I had lost you, I have been out of my mind with worry. Then when I find you, I am so busy being angry at everyone who did this that I leave you on the floor."

"Please just take me home..." then, "... oh no, your cloak will get all muddy."

"Pah, it is nothing, we'll be there momentarily, we're not far."

"I can walk, you know." I felt his chest rumble with laughter.

"I know you can, my love, but let me carry you, just this once."

"If you must." I sighed and leaned against his shoulder. The rhythm of his stride was soporific and was lulling me to sleep. My body still wouldn't warm up, but at least I was safe.

The next time I opened my eyes I was in my own bed. I hoped I was clean otherwise all the bedding would need washing. The tremors continued to ripple through me, but my teeth weren't chattering anymore and I was able to focus again.

My chest felt tight and my breathing was not normal and I knew I needed to get these things sorted out or I might become very ill. I tried to get up, but a gentle hand pushed me back against the pillow.

"Rest, my Hannah."

"Maxentius." I had to whisper; it was too hard to talk normally. He was sitting next to me on the bed and leaned in to hear me. "Please, will you and Aliza help me? I need Aliza to mix up something to prevent this sickness from getting worse and I need you to find one of the large cooking pots, fill it with water and hang it over the fire. You will need to add some mentha, to help my breathing." Gasping a little with the effort, I stopped speaking and looked up at my husband to make sure he had understood me. He nodded and, patting my arm, left the room.

Trying to stay awake long enough to see that my instructions were carried out, I pushed myself up on the pillows, thinking about our children. I assumed that Claudia, Liora and Efraim were safe, but I hadn't seen them yet and, in my confused state, worried that there was something Maxentius wasn't telling me. After several minutes, Maxentius returned with the pot, hanging it over the fire, which we were lucky enough to have in our bedroom, the warmth from it already circulating through the room. Aliza came in with a great handful of jars and I pointed to the mentha. Maxentius poured some into the pot, the heady scent suffusing the air. Immediately my breathing felt easier.

Then I pointed at three other jars and asked her to pour five drops of each into a pitcher of water or wine, I didn't much care which. She went to do as I asked, coming back with the pitcher and a small drinking cup. Maxentius poured some of the potion into the cup and held it for me to drink. It smelt terrible and tasted worse, but I hoped it would do the trick. I could not get sick. I pulled a face, shuddering as I drank it down, making Maxentius smile, something he hadn't done since he found me at the magistrate's office.

"You should rest now, my love." I grabbed his hand.

"Our children, are our children safe?"

"Of course they are, my Hannah. They came to tell me horses and soldiers were trampling you. Efraim even brought your cloak, which must have been pulled off you somehow."

"My cloak? You have my cloak and my clasp?" I gazed at him in hope.

"It is over there on the top of your clothing cupboard." I started to cry then, racking sobs that hurt my throat and my chest, but I couldn't help it.

Maxentius gathered me close rocking me like he would one of the children.

"Hush, my Hannah, hush now, you will make yourself feel worse." Didn't think that was possible actually, but after a few minutes, I made a huge effort and drew a tremulous breath.

"Sorry — don't know what came over me, I am such a mess." Maxentius chuckled.

"Yes, but you're my mess and for that I am eternally thankful." He kissed the top of my head and kept rocking me. The warm room, the scent of mentha and his arms finally worked their magic and I slept.

I awoke, cocooned in warmth, my limbs felt heavy and my head was pounding. That'll teach you to fall asleep with the fire lit, Hannah, I admonished myself. As I turned my head, I realised that there was no fire; the warmth was due to a thick comforter and several blankets. Confused, I raised my head and looked around, then fell back against the pillows. This wasn't Pompeii — well it was, but it was the villa not my/her home. Movement caught my eye; Max was standing looking out through the French window, so I was me again.

I was finding it difficult to breathe and my throat was prickling. I had felt unwell earlier. Was that why I had felt so cold? Had I been aware that she was falling ill? Were we sharing the same sickness, or was it pure coincidence? Sensing that I was awake, Max turned from the window came over to the bed and sat down.

"Hey there, Sunshine, how're you feeling?" I tried to speak but my voice was raspy.

"Not brilliant." I croaked. "What time is it?"

"Just after two," he replied, stroking the hair off my hot face. "I think you might have caught a cold." Understatement, I thought. "I've boiled the kettle. Do you want one of those hot lemony drinks?" Walking towards the door, I nodded.

"I'll be back in two ticks," he threw over his shoulder as he disappeared along the hallway.

I lay against the pillows, feeling as though I should get up, but really couldn't be bothered; it was so comfortable. I mulled over what had happened. The riots were a worry, but I was still more troubled over the eruption, even though it wouldn't happen for several months. Maxentius was the one who would need to be persuaded to leave. His priority would be the safety of Pompeii, not necessarily his wife and family. I had to think of a way to make it impossible for him to stay once the danger was imminent. Thankfully, I had a little while to work on it and, hopefully, at some point I would get to go back where I would be of more use than through dreams alone.

Max came back in with my hot lemon. I tried to sit up, but found I had no strength. Pathetic, Hannah, quite pathetic.

"Please help me," I whispered hoarsely, "I can't seem to do anything today." He grinned, lifting me into a sitting position and sorting out the pillows behind me so that I didn't slump back down again. "Thanks, hon." I smiled. "Was everything okay at the site?"

"They'll manage. I could do with going in for a couple of hours tomorrow, but that'll depend on how you're feeling. I don't like leaving you when you're ill, who knows what might happen."

"I'll be better tomorrow, I'll be able to come with you." Max chuckled

"Oh, I don't think so, sweetheart. Possibly the day after next but definitely not tomorrow. Your skin is on fire, you're flushed, you can hardly talk and I imagine you are struggling to breathe." I would have blushed if my cheeks hadn't already been so red.

"I'm sorry, that was idiotic of me, but I hate being sick and I'm missing out on all the fun."

"I know, Sunshine, but one day here or there won't make much difference. If I do go in, it won't be for long, I'd rather be here with you anyway."

"What, when I'm in this state! You should be running for the hills, you don't want to risk catching it." I tried to laugh, but it turned into a bout of coughing, tearing at my throat and chest 'til my eyes watered. "I mean, look at me, I'm a wreck." Max gently pulled me to him.

"Hey, shush, it's ok. C'mon, sip this drink. It's cool enough now and might stop that awful cough." I drained the mug, the hot lemony flavour was soothing and I was feeling sleepy again.

"Max?"

"Yes, sweetheart."

"Will you sit with me little while?" I knew I sounded forlorn, but I couldn't help it. I felt utterly miserable and the thought of him leaving me alone with my misery was too much right then.

"I'm not going anywhere, Sunshine, just let me..." He settled himself on the bed and gathered me back against his chest, rocking me in a strangely familiar fashion. I felt the medicine in the drink start to take effect and relaxed into Max's arms.

Chapter Fifteen

I tossed and turned, unable to get comfortable, as the fever raced through me. If I lay on my back I coughed, if I lay on my side my chest hurt. The only way I seemed to be able to relax was sitting upright and that didn't feel very restful. One minute I was hot, the next cold; and when I did manage to get some sleep, my dreams were tortured: I was covered in filth and squalor, magistrates with bulbous heads leered at me, soldiers pointed, ridiculing my clothes and my hair. I was begging them for a cloak to warm me, but they just cackled with raucous laughter.

I was vaguely aware of someone cooling my forehead with a damp cloth and removing the covers when I was burning up, only to drag them back over me minutes later when I started shivering with cold. The persistent cough kept wracking my body and my breathing was laboured from the infection in my chest. I had no idea where or who I was; my dual worlds melded and entwined. I saw both Maxentius and Max but didn't know whether it was in my dreams or in reality.

I know I cried out for them and I hoped I cried for the right man in the right world, but I was too ill to care. At one point I became aware that someone else was in the room with me, someone other than whichever of my men had been looking after me. He stuck something cold in my mouth and I felt the sting of a needle. Oh, I thought, dazedly, that must be the modern me; I don't think we have hypodermic syringes in ancient Pompeii. Whatever he gave me knocked me out — no more nightmares, no more confusion, just blessed, dreamless oblivion.

I must have slept for hours, for when I finally woke it was daylight again. My head wasn't pounding quite as badly and my breathing seemed less laboured. I was almost fearful of opening my eyes, unsure of which world I had woken in, so I decided to keep them shut a little longer. Good one Hannah, 'coz that's going to help. I sensed movement near me; a hand grasped mine and a deep voice asked —

"My Hannah, are you awake?" I was back with Maxentius and in this world was probably suffering from bronchitis or even pneumonia. I hoped they had kept the fire going with that mentha pot.

I tried to reply but there was nothing, not a croak, not even a whisper. I knew I had no choice now. I felt the familiar rub of my husband's thumb on my palm; it was so comforting. Finally I gave in to the inevitable and opened my eyes. He was gazing down at me, his eyes full of worry and I hated being its cause. I tried again — still nothing. It was so frustrating; I needed to know what they had been dosing me with, if anything and, how long I'd been there. I suddenly remembered that I was supposed to take Darius' stitches out. Had anyone informed Tullius that I was sick?

I pointed to my mouth and my throat, then shook my head, hoping Maxentius was able to work out what I meant.

"You don't want food?" No, I shook my head; that wasn't right. Desperately I tried to speak again and managed a throaty rasping sound, then shook my head again, holding his arm and gazing at him beseechingly. "You have no voice?" I nodded. "Well we know that. Does your throat hurt?" I nodded again. "What about your chest?" Another nod. "Right, more mentha in the pot and you can have another dose of that foul-smelling stuff you asked Aliza to mix up." I nodded one more time, smiling rather wanly. The effort just to get that sorted had exhausted me.

"You'll be better soon, my love. You just need to rest and let us care for you." I felt a tear run down my cheek. Geez Hannah, you are rubbish. Maxentius caught it with his finger and leant in to kiss where it had stopped. His lips were cool against my fevered skin and another tear followed the same trail. I felt so helpless, this was not who I was. I was the wife, the mother, the healer — not the bedridden, snivelling wreck lying under these oh so comfortable covers. "Oh, my Hannah, don't cry. I'm here." Maxentius cupped my face and kissed my tears away. "Come on, my love, crying will make you cough and that will hurt your throat even more." I sighed and leaned into him, needing to feel his arms around me, knowing I could draw strength from his touch.

He wrapped his arms around me, holding me close. I breathed in his scent and relaxed against him. The mentha began to permeate the air and my chest started to feel less constricted. Aliza came in with a goblet of the medicine and I drank it quickly trying not to taste it at all.

"Would you like to change into a fresh night slip?" she asked. "It might help." I nodded, smiling my thanks at her. While they helped me change, I noticed that my body was badly bruised; presumably from the battering I'd taken when the mob had flattened me and maybe from the guards. I looked up at my husband who grimaced.

"It was much worse when we first got you home. Luckily, I remembered about arnica and massaged it over the bruising. He winked at me, no doubt recalling the times I had needed to use it on him when he was first on Masada. He was so proud of himself and grasping his hand, I turned it to kiss his palm and then pressed it to my heart. He smiled down at me, his eyes full of love, which in itself was enough to make anyone feel better. Finally, changed into a clean night slip, I was ushered back into bed. Aliza had changed the sheets quickly and the bed felt cool against my skin.

The draft I had taken was working and I knew a proper sleep would work wonders. Sliding down between the sheets, I snuggled up to Maxentius, who was sitting alongside me, his feet up on the coverlet and hoped he would stay. He held my hand, resuming that gentle rubbing of my palm with his thumb; the familiar motion finishing what the medicine had started. I slept.

I have no idea how long I was asleep, but it was dark when I next woke. I realised I was still in the world of ancient Pompeii when I noticed the oil lamp burning on the little shelf by the door. I was on my own. Where was Maxentius sleeping? I hoped it wasn't on the sofa in the living area; he would never be comfortable on that. The fire was crackling in the grate, casting interesting shadows across the ceiling and walls, making the images in the frescoes look as if they were dancing. The air was heavy with mentha, but it was definitely easing my chest and I found swallowing was a lot less painful.

I pushed the covers back and made an effort to get up. My legs were rather wobbly, but I thought I could make it through to the main room, if I used the walls for support. Pulling a blanket around my shoulders and sliding my feet into warm house slippers, I staggered through to where I thought Maxentius would be resting. It took me quite a while; I was pathetically weak and needed to stop once or twice to get my breath. Honestly, Hannah, I thought to myself, you do get yourself into some pickles.

I made it to the living area in one piece, Maxentius was stretched out along the sofa, snoring gently, looking as tired as I felt, making me worry about just how long I had been unwell. His face, in repose, looked so vulnerable that my heart swelled and it was all I could do to stop myself from stroking his cheek. The fire in this room had died down and the air was chill. The blanket covering him was rather thin and I could not do with him becoming sick as well.

Navigating around him and taking care not to bang into his feet, which were hanging off the end of the sofa, I cautiously edged my way to the hearth. There were several logs stacked in a basket. I lifted the top one and shoved it onto the embers, then added another for good measure, standing for a moment while the flames began to curl around the wood. Satisfied that they had caught, I turned to go back to bed. Knowing I'd be under very warm covers in a minute or two, I pulled the blanket from my shoulders and laid it gently over my sleeping husband, hoping that it would be enough to keep him warm. Unable to resist, I touched his cheek and brushed his hair with a light kiss, smiling as the firelight illuminated his craggy features.

Slowly, I made my way back to bed, spotting the disgusting medicine on the bench as I passed. Tipping the flagon, I drank straight from it, not bothering to pour it into a goblet first; as only I was drinking it, it didn't matter. By the time I was back in bed, I was drained; clearly I was not close to being fit again quite yet. The bedding had cooled, but the fire was still blazing merrily away, keeping the room warm.

Sliding between the sheets, I pulled the covers right up to my neck and lay looking at the fire; conjuring pictures in flames, letting the potion work its way into my system. I wondered what the other 'me' was doing — was she, I, unwell still too? What about Max? I wished I could tell him I was ok. My thoughts became jumbled. I couldn't focus on any one thing and so I gave up trying and was suddenly asleep.

Daylight was filtering through the shutters and I could hear the sounds of my family when next I coaxed my eyes open, but I had no idea of the time. I really should be helping them, I thought; it's not fair that I am lolling about in bed. I'd managed to get up during the night; maybe I could do more after such a good sleep. I swung my feet out of bed and was about to stand up when I heard footsteps in the hallway and turned to see who was coming. I felt like a naughty child being caught out as I met Maxentius' eyes.

"Where precisely do you think you're going, Hannah?"

"Well, I thought I might get up so I could help," I croaked. At least I had something resembling a voice. He burst out laughing and I looked quite affronted — really, how rude was that?

"Oh no you don't; hop back in there, we can manage a little longer without you," he grinned, "although its nice to see you trying to get up."

"Well, I managed in the night, I could sit in the room and clean vegetables, or do the mending." At least that's what I tried to say; not all the words were very clear. He gazed at me in exasperation.

"So that's how the fire stayed lit? And how I ended up with one of your blankets?" I nodded. "Hannah, thank you my love, but you could have got chilled doing that."

"The room was cold and you looked so tired, I only had to get back to bed." I sounded sad as I said this, remembering his face. He was at my side, hugging me to him.

"Don't worry about me, Hannah, I'm as tough as old boots."

"No, you're tired from working long hours and having to care for me, it's not fair." My voice caught as I finished speaking and I doubled over in a paroxysm of coughing. Eyes streaming, I gasped, trying to breathe as my body was wracked by the outburst.

"And you think you're fit enough to be out of bed?" Maxentius queried gently, as the bout finally stopped.

"Okay, maybe not." My heartbeat was rapid and my head was pounding. I realised that I had to give in and let them look after me. So much for feeling better. "I'm sorry to be such a burden." I knew I sounded as I looked, woebegone and I hated showing that I was weak, but I couldn't help it. Maxentius held me tightly, before helping me back into bed, adjusting my pillows, so I could sit upright for a while.

"Stop worrying about it, we'll be fine. Now, do you think you can cope with seeing the children just for a minute, they've missed you." I smiled up at him, my eyes shining.

"Oh, could I really? I've missed them too, it seems like forever since I last saw them, which I s'pose it could be, as I don't have a clue how long I've been ill."

"This will be the fourth morning since I brought you home." I stared at him in consternation — four days? Added to that, there was the time I was in the cell. This would never do.

"Oh Maxentius, I had no idea! I really must get up." Starting to get back out of bed, I was forestalled by a large hand.

"No, my Hannah, you must rest. How many times did you tell Marcus and me that this was the best medicine; that if we tried to do too much too soon, we would make ourselves worse? You should learn to follow your own advice." He was frowning at me in mock severity making me blush sheepishly. Giving in, I let Maxentius tuck the bedding back around me. To be honest, I really didn't feel up to it, but that didn't stop me wanting to try.

"Ready? This will just be a very quick hello."

"They should not come close, in case I am contagious." He raised his eyebrows. "In case they also get what I have." I explained, forgetting that some words may not be used yet. He nodded and disappeared out of the room, returning almost immediately with three very excited children. At the door, he bent down and explained that Mama was still sick, so they needed to be quiet and not jump on me. I smiled as I watched them nodding earnestly that they understood.

They came over to the side of the bed, looking a little scared, truth be told. I smiled at them.

"I'm nearly better, sweethearts, I've just got a very nasty cold and I don't want you to catch it." My voice was so raspy and as they just stared back at me, I couldn't tell whether they understood. I could see Claudia's bottom lip trembling and took her little hand in mine. "Why so sad, my Claudia?" She just stared at me and shook her head. I looked up at Maxentius who, also at a loss, shrugged his shoulders. I glanced at the other two. "Efraim?" Gently cajoling. "Tell me." Efraim drew a deep breath.

"We thought you were deaded in the road. You screamed a lot, then you were gone and we didn't know who had tooken you." Recalling his panic Efraim reverted to childish vocabulary and I bit my lip so as not to smile at his words.

"Surely Papa, Uncle Maxentius, told you he rescued me?"

"Yes, but that was after ages. I found your cloak, but not you. The girls cried." I glanced at the two girls; Liora looked as upset as Claudia. I knew they would have been terrified, but had hoped this would have faded once they knew I was safe.

"My darling children, I am so sorry I scared you, but you were brave and ran to tell Uncle Maxentius, right?" They all nodded. "Then he found me and brought me home. I have been very sick, because I was covered in mud, lost my cloak and got very cold, but I'll be better soon. I don't want you to worry about me anymore."

"Mama?" This was Efraim and it took all I had not to glance up at Maxentius. This was a new development; I'd always been 'Aunt Hannah.' I smiled at him.

"Yes, my Efraim?"

"Please don't ever leave us again." I felt my heart crack. These poor children, two of them had already lost one set of parents and they feared they'd lost me too. Determined not to cry, I put my hand out and grasped his. I shook it and said in a voice, already croaky, now full of tears —

"I promise, I will never leave any of you again; well except to go to work and do the shopping. Can I do that?" I winked at him and he grinned back nodding, happy now. Liora and Claudia demanded to have their hands shaken as well and after more shaking and promising, Maxentius said that Mama needed to rest and ushered them out.

Chapter Sixteen

It was several minutes before Maxentius came back to me, for which I was rather thankful, as I was trying to stem the flood of tears that Efraim's demand had caused. Contrary to current evidence, I have no patience with weeping women, but his little face when he spoke had been so serious and he had called me 'Mama.' I ask you, what's a girl to do? Crying seemed the obvious answer, but, it's okay, I'd blame my illness — good one, Hannah. Maxentius peeped at me from the doorway.

"Safe to enter, my love?" he smiled at me and I smiled back, albeit it rather damply. I scrubbed away the last of the tears with my fists, then with the edge of the sheet.

"Those children," I whispered, hoarsely, "what on earth...?"

"I hadn't realised they were still so frightened. I told them you were safe, but had to stay in bed. They only saw you for a minute when I brought you home and you were fast asleep. Maybe they thought I had found you, but you were actually dead and I was hiding it from them."

"Bless their little hearts, they'll be better now. Did you hear Efraim?" Maxentius nodded.

"When you told them to come and find me, they came hurtling into headquarters, passed all the other soldiers straight to me, even ignored Marcus. Efraim was yelling 'Papa, Papa' all the way through the building. It took me a full minute to work out that it was him calling for me, it sounded so odd.

"Are you happy with them calling you Papa? It changes your relationship with them once you are no longer just Uncle."

"I think we've been Mama and Papa to them since we lost Aharon and Raizel, my Hannah. This way though, they have made the change naturally, we haven't made them do it to suit ourselves. They are as much our children as is Claudia."

"Oh Maxentius, I do love you." Sighing, I reached out for him, pulling him closer and snuggling into his arms. "Do you have to go to work?"

"For a little while, but first I'm going to build this fire up, refill the water in the pot and add some more mentha. Then you can take another dose of that foul drink and sleep some more. I'll be home before you know it." He kissed the top of my head, before suiting his words to actions and soon the house was quiet again. Everyone had left to attend to their various tasks and I was alone.

During the next couple of days, I slept more than I was awake. By the third day — and something like nine days since I had been taken to the cells — I was sick of being in bed and decided, in complete disregard of Maxentius' instructions, to get up and have a wash. My husband, in deference to me, had fashioned a large tub in the space I had allocated as a laundry room. We already had one huge sink, which we used solely for washing clothes, but this was smaller and on a slightly raised platform. We were able to bathe the children in it and it was big enough for us adults to have a proper wash, without having to use one of the bathhouses. I had never become used to the communal toilet and bathing rituals so loved by the Romans.

Hanging a fresh pot of water to boil over the fire in the living area — the one in our room was still steaming with mentha — I retrieved some clean clothes. Once the water was hot enough, I carried it carefully through to the washroom and dumped the whole lot in the tub; then refilled it, hanging it back over the fire. Stripping off my night slip and using a cleanser I had made up from oil, salt and lavender, I enjoyed my first proper wash since I don't know how long. I made sure that any vestiges of mud were rinsed clean and, by dint of sitting on the edge of the tub, was able to soak my feet properly.

It was bliss, I could take my time, as no one needed me and it was a good job, because everything seemed to take twice as long as normal. Once satisfied that my body was clean, I wrapped myself in a blanket and turned my attention to my hair, which was like a bird's nest. Using a small bowl, I scooped up water from the freshly heated pot and hanging my head over the tub, rinsed then washed my hair, using the same lavender mixture minus the salt. Eventually I was done and rubbing myself dry, dressed in a day tunic rather than another night slip and went into the main living area.

I was curled up on the rug in front of the fire, a thick blanket wrapped around me, combing through my long dark locks in a vain attempt to untangle them, when I heard the door open. Feeling guilty for being there and knowing I had ignored Maxentius' request that I stay in bed, I felt hectic colour flood my cheeks as, turning, I saw my husband stroll into the room. He stopped short when he saw me.

"Hannah, I thought I said you should stay in bed." His brow furrowed.

"We...ll, I felt sticky and uncomfortable, so I had a bath. Then I washed my hair, because it was disgusting," appealing to him.

"If you'd waited, I could have helped. How long did it take you?"

"Errr... a bit longer than normal."

"So you've been standing around naked in this chilly weather while you are still sick?" He sounded rather angry and I supposed I understood why, but I hadn't coughed once since earlier, a fact of which, I immediately and quite proudly, apprised him. He came over and sat on the floor next to me, touching my skin to see whether I was cold.

"I'm sorry Max..." I whispered, using the diminutive in the hope of diffusing his ire, "...I was desperate to feel clean and, since no one was around I could take my time but I didn't let myself get cold. Please don't be angry with me." My voice even, when whispering, was still hoarse, making me sound very forlorn.

Sighing, he shifted so that he was sitting behind me and pulled me into his chest. I wriggled until I was comfortable, wrapping my arms over his and holding his hands.

"My love, you need to have a care, I did not ask you to stay in bed for my sake. You have been very sick. The last time I saw anybody so ill he..." Maxentius stopped speaking and I tried to turn so I could see his face.

"He what? Max?"

"Nothing, it doesn't matter, just please do as I ask." His voice was tight; I still wasn't forgiven. He picked up the comb I had dropped at his entrance and started running it, not very gently, through my hair. I mulled over his words until with a jolt I worked out whom he had been talking about. Squirming around, I stared at him, removing the comb from his hand and cupping both of mine round his face.

"Oh my love, you meant Sergius?" He looked at me for a long moment. "It's not the same thing, I just had a fever from being so cold for so long. His was a devastating infection from an injury that no amount of care would ever heal." I gazed into his eyes, willing him to believe me, as I realised that they had all thought I was going to die. "Did you honestly fear that I might die?" He nodded again, unable to speak, his eyes haunted by the memory of the last week.

"Efraim thought you dead when they came to get me, they thought the horse had crushed you, then we couldn't find you. I had men searching everywhere; it was as though you had disappeared into thin air. Finally, after more than twenty four hours of looking, a soldier from the courts came running in, telling me about a woman who looked like you brought in front of the magistrate. He wasn't sure as she was filthy, but she had green eyes and was telling the magistrate off." He paused and I squeezed his hand.

Shuddering, he went on.

"I ran...I ran all the way, then when I opened the door and saw that you had to be held upright by the guard, I couldn't believe it. Who did they think they were to be treating you this way? Your clothes were torn, you were blue with cold, there was not one single inch of you that was not coated in mud, I'm not surprised that no-one realised it was you. But your eyes, your eyes were so full of fury, even if everything else was unrecognisable, I would know those eyes anywhere."

"Well, I'd decided that if they were going to throw me back into that cell, I would give them a real reason." I muttered darkly. His lips twitched, but he was not about to let me off so lightly and continued.

"When I picked you up from the floor, you were like ice and we couldn't warm you up. No amount of blankets, no matter what we did, your body seemed frozen. Hours of trying to get heat into you, then suddenly you were too hot, your skin burned with a fire that we could not break and this went on for nearly four days. You were obviously having nightmares and you called out for me, but even though I was right there, I couldn't reach you, the fever's grip was too strong. Then you had no voice and I don't know which was worse, listening to your rasping cries, or not hearing you at all. Hannah, I have never been so afraid in my life. So when I ask you to stay in bed, I'd be most appreciative if you would follow my instructions."

By the end of his tirade, Maxentius' voice had lost its hard edge, but clearly he was still very annoyed with me. It was so rare that we fought; in fact I don't think I could ever remember him being this angry with me and I hated it, I didn't know how to deal with it. My heart clenched in my chest and my stomach knotted, but I couldn't find the words to make him understand that I hadn't known, that I was sorry, that I never intended to cause so much worry. I bowed my head, my still damp hair falling over my face, hiding the pesky tears I was determined would not fall.

I moved to get up, deciding that it was probably better to leave him while he was still so upset. I'd go back to bed, maybe that would help. I had been up too long anyway. I felt weak and my limbs were trembling from the effort not only from my exertions of the day, but also from all the emotions his words had stirred up.

"Now where are you going?" Maxentius held my arm preventing me from standing up, his frustration clear.

"Away from you." My tone was flat, my voice empty, biting back tears. I shrugged his hand off and tried to stand. It took nearly everything I had not to fall, but I forced myself and had nearly made it, when suddenly Maxentius reached up and pulled me back against him.

"You are quite the most exasperating woman I have ever known, my Hannah." He held me close, nuzzling his face into my hair, gently kissing my neck. His actions undid me; I finally gave up trying to be brave and burst into tears.

"I'm sorry, I'm so sorry. I didn't know. How could I know? You weren't the only one who was afraid. It wasn't like I was enjoying a holiday at the beach. I was terrified that you'd never find me. I thought the children had been hurt or killed and then I ended up in a cell with three men who hate the Emperor. I thought that they would throw me back in gaol, or decide to behead me, or make me fight in the arena. I didn't mean to get sick or scare you and now you're angry with me." There was no rhyme or reason behind my words, which just tumbled out and I was sobbing so hard that I was barely coherent.

"Oh Hannah, hush, hush my love, I'm here, you're safe. I wasn't angry with you, just very worried." As he had done the night he brought me home, Maxentius rocked me like a baby, but I could not gain control of myself. This had been building up since those idiotic rioters had mown me down. My own terror had had no outlet, I had been too ill. Nightmares had not been soothed away, as I had not woken enough to tell anyone of them. Maxentius cradled me in his arms, keeping up a flow of quiet chatter, but it was a long time before his words began to calm my shattered nerves.

Eventually, the storm passed, but it left me feeling like an old dishrag, my breath coming in shuddering gasps. I knew I should probably go back to bed, but I didn't want to move, the fire was warm and my husband's arms so comforting. I could feel myself falling asleep and as I couldn't think of anywhere better to be right then, snuggled into Maxentius' chest.

"Tired my love?" I nodded. "I should get you back to bed."

"No, not yet, it's so cosy here by the fire...with you. Can you stay, or are you supposed to be at work now?"

"They can manage, I think a quiet afternoon with you might be good for both of us." Sighing contentedly, I rested my head against his shoulder and he re-adjusted the blanket so that it wrapped around both of us. The warmth from the fire, which was still crackling merrily, enveloped the room and all was peaceful.

I dozed for a while and when I woke, felt a little better. Maxentius got up and made me a drink of hot water squeezing some fresh lemon into it, which was both soothing and refreshing. As we settled back against the bench, we started talking, going over what had happened from both of our perspectives. Maxentius had no idea what I'd gone through and he was aghast, not only at how they had treated me, but also at the appalling conditions of the rooms we had been held in. I told him about the three men I had shared a cell with and what they'd been discussing.

"I don't know if it's pertinent, but they could be worth meeting with. Who knows what information you might be able to get out of them. That's if they ever made it out of that revolting cell."

"I'll get a couple of the men to locate them, it might prove very fruitful. Thank you my Hannah." I pretended to curtsey, not easy when you're curled up on someone's knee.

"My pleasure, good Sir," grinning up at him. He leaned down and kissed my nose. I tilted my chin and brushed my lips to his. I felt Maxentius inhale sharply and he held me tighter.

"I know I'm not really up to where this might lead, but I don't think a few kisses could do any harm, do you?" Sliding one hand up his back, the other trailing along his arm.

"Hannah, you are a minx. Not an hour ago you were falling asleep; now look at you." He cupped my face, kissing me tenderly.

"I can't help it, it's all your fault," I murmured against his mouth.

"My fault? How d'you work that out?"

"Well, if you weren't so handsome..." running my fingers through his hair, "...and irresistible..." then down his back, finding the gaps in his tunic and teasing his warm skin, "...I wouldn't have any desire to do this." His breathing quickened as my fingers played over his body.

"Hannah," in a voice that was not quite steady, "much as I could very happily give into this, you are definitely not well enough."

"Sure?" Tracing lazy circles.

"No, I'm not sure, but I think bed would be a better place for you, regardless of what you have in mind. You have been up for far too long and this fire is dying down."

He lifted me carefully, carrying me through to our room, ignoring my protests that I could manage and lay me on the bed. Drawing the covers up over me, he put another log on the fire and topped up the water in the pot, the mentha infused steam still percolating the air. To be fair, I was feeling rather weary and although in my mind, I was perfectly capable of seducing my husband, my body had other ideas.

"Sorry, I don't think I can..." I yawned and before I'd finished the sentence had fallen fast asleep — unaware that Maxentius stood for long moments, just watching me, making sure I was breathing easily; unaware that he leaned over and kissed me, brushing the hair off my face; and completely unaware that he stroked my cheek and whispered his love for me. I was lost in dreams.

Chapter Seventeen

The light playing over my eyelids seemed too bright; it would hurt my eyes if I opened them. So I elected not to bother. Trying to turn over, I was halted by a hand on my shoulder.

"Hannah, you need to let the doctor check your eyes." No, I didn't; nothing wrong with my eyes. I put one hand over my face, cutting out the light and batted at the person holding my shoulder with the other. "Hannah, come on, just two ticks, then you can go back to sleep." The voice was familiar, but I was too tired to place it. The hand was pulling at me and again I pushed it away. "Hannah, you must wake up; please baby, just for me."

"Oh for heaven's sake, why can't you leave me alone? One minute you want me to sleep, the next you want me to wake up; make your mind up." I knew I sounded crotchety.

"What? I haven't said you need to sleep. You haven't woken up yet." Well of course I had, several times in fact and been told off into the bargain. As I was thinking this, a faint memory stirred; was I back in my own time? Sighing, I gave in to the insistent hand and opened my eyes. Staring back at me was my other Max and behind him a tall man with a stethoscope around his neck.

"Hannah! Finally — you were well out of it. That shot you had last night certainly did the trick." I vaguely recalled feeling a needle, but that seemed like ages ago, not just the previous night. I shook my head in confusion.

"What shot?"

"The doctor here..." nodding his head towards the other man, "...gave you an injection of antibiotics to try to knock this infection on its head, before it took hold." I looked beyond Max to the man with the stethoscope.

"What infection?"

"Seems like you have the flu or maybe bronchitis, but it's a severe bout and you spiked a high fever. I had to call the doctor in the early evening, because you were delirious and I couldn't wake you up. Bed rest for a couple more days, but he reckons you'll be okay by then." A couple more days, no way, that'd be the end of our time in Pompeii and I'd have missed everything at the site. I struggled to sit up, my limbs heavy, Max helped, propping me against the pillows.

"I can't stay in bed any longer, I've already been here five days," I hesitated, "no, it must be more like a week. I'm missing everything." Both Max and the doctor looked puzzled and I stared back at them. "What?"

"Well, you've only been in bed since yesterday lunchtime, honey. I think you might be a little confused." I bit my lip, feeling colour wash up my cheeks, as I realised what I'd said and why I'd said it. I kept forgetting that when I was in the past, time often moved at a different pace and I had been there and back a few times lately — confusion was the least of my worries. Oh boy, I needed to get a grip on this.

"Sorry," I muttered, "just seems longer, I guess." The doctor smiled sympathetically and motioned that he wanted to examine me. I nodded and he was quick but very thorough. My chest was wheezy and when I breathed out even I could hear the crackles. He suggested a second injection, as he wasn't happy with my progress and I nodded again. Seemed easier than arguing and, if nothing else, I knew it would put me back to sleep. He administered the needle almost painlessly, for which I was very thankful, then after a short conversation with Max, said his goodbyes.

Max left the room with the doctor, presumably to show him out, then came back and sat next to me on the bed.

"Now, Sunshine, I think you owe me an explanation."

"For what?"

"For whatever's been happening to you. I know you were delirious, but some of what you were muttering about was more than just the fever talking. I was pretty sure you'd been, or were still, back..." he paused, "...there and, your comment about how many days you've been asleep just convinced me."

"You sure you want to know?"

"Of course I'm sure, I need to understand this. It's different this time; you seem to be going back more frequently, but for shorter lengths of time. I'm just worried that something will keep you there."

"I'll always want to be here with you," I said shyly, reaching for his hand. "This is where my life is, it's just sometimes I'm needed there." He squeezed my hand and sat next to me on the bed, making sure the bedclothes were snugly around me and then draped his arm around my shoulders, drawing me close. "Be warned, though, I'll likely fall asleep in the middle of this, since that doctor just jabbed me with his magic knock-out juice." Max grinned.

"I'll make a note of where you get to." I grinned back and nestling against his chest, began to tell him what had gone on in my other world. It's a very good job walls don't have ears, because it would have sounded totally implausible. Halfway through, I could feel the medication take hold, my words began to slur, I could feel myself sliding down the pillows and I had to force my eyes to stay open. I grasped Max's hand and started to say —

"I think the rest might have to..." but I never finished speaking, the magic juice had indeed knocked me out.

I knew I had slipped between worlds before I even opened my eyes, for I could smell the mentha in the air. Truthfully, I wanted to be here, I missed Max, but there was work for me to do in this life and I was afraid that I might not get to do it. I couldn't let my family perish in the eruption and I felt there was also more that called for my attention, most especially the gladiators at the school. I stretched luxuriously under the warm covers and suddenly realised that I didn't feel quite as ill. My chest wasn't tight and it was much easier to swallow.

Turning over, I looked towards the window, guessing, by the angle of the sun that it was probably about nine in the morning. The house was quiet. Where was everyone? What day was it? I hadn't been in my own world for many hours, but that could be two or three days in this one. Carefully, I lifted the covers and swung my legs onto the floor. My house shoes were next to the bed and I slipped my feet into them, pulling a blanket off the bed to wrap around me.

Cautiously, I walked along to the main room, no sign of anyone, but there was a platter on the table and a goblet of some tepid drink. I sniffed it. It smelled like calda, the spicy wine drink, popular at this time of the year. It needed to be warmer, oh for a microwave I wished, giggling a little at the thought of trying to explain that one. I found the pot, filled it with water from the pitcher standing near the platter and hung it over the fire. Wandering over to the window, while I waited for it to boil, I noticed that there was frost on the ground. Winter had us well and truly in its grip and I was very thankful that our home, which was not small, was warm and cosy.

I drifted through the house, checking to see that it was tidy. The children's room was a bit chaotic, but that was to be expected and didn't bother me. The rest of the house was spick and span. Aliza must have been cracking the whip while I'd been out of action; cleaning was normally my domain. Bless her heart. I sent up a prayer of thanks to whichever god it was that sent her to me the night of the massacre.

Returning to the living area, I sat on the sofa in front of the fire, watching the flames dancing in the hearth, pondering my next move. I needed to get back to the gladiators; I hoped one of the other doctors had removed Darius' stitches. I had a feeling that the first games of the season were due soon and that would create work for me. I also wanted to check around at the Palaestra to see how the young men were going with their training. I felt a proprietary interest in both of these places, despite my opinion about using men for blood sports and I missed visiting them. I realised that I was feeling much better, I hadn't felt this motivated in days. This was a good sign; this was a very good sign.

The water bubbled in the pot and I scooped some out to pour into the goblet. Curling up on the chair, I warmed my hands around the cup, inhaling the spices. I felt a draft through the room as the front door opened and turned to see Aliza and my children come in. Claudia, Liora and Efraim, ran over, demanding cuddles and kisses and then shoved each other to see who could get on my knee first. Aliza tried to calm them down, but I waved her away, smiling delightedly at this welcome.

"Thank you, Aliza, let them have their moment, I'm feeling much better and it's lovely to hear them so happy." She smiled back at me and went to put away the food she had brought in.

"Do you need some help?" I asked, but she shook her head.

"I'm fine, you just play with the children, they've missed you."

"I've missed them too and you, it's an age since we have talked. Thank you for looking after this house and me so well. I do not know what I would do without you." She shook her head.

"It was nothing." Blushing furiously, she turned back to sorting out her purchases.

My babies chattered away about their day, I watched them and thought how big they had grown, no longer babies, not even close. Efraim was twelve years old now. He needed more to challenge his mind than the short lessons we gave him at home, spending afternoons at the Forum or playing in one of the parks. Maybe we could hire a proper tutor for them all, even the girls would benefit. I did not want them to grow up without some formal education. We had taught them how to read and write, but there was so much more they could learn. I made a mental note to talk to Maxentius about it, but for now I enjoyed the simple pleasure of spending time with them.

I shooed the children to their room to change their footwear into house shoes and suggested that they might like to tidy up a bit, before going into my own bedroom to dress properly. I had a quick wash, brushed my hair, tying it into a loose plait, then dug out some warm clothes — long sleeved light woollen under shift in deep rose and an over dress in a paler shade, also light wool. I was unsure how warm I would be, having spent so long in bed, so I also found one of my mantles; I could wrap myself in that rather than a blanket if I felt cool during the day.

Sliding my feet back into my house shoes, I returned to the living room. I felt rather at a loss, used to being busy during the day; I now had time on my hands. It was too cold to do anything in the garden and there was obviously nothing to do in the house. The children were happily making more mess under the guise of tidying up, Aliza was pottering about preparing the midday meal and the men were at work. I didn't think it would be a good idea to go out, but I wondered if I could ask one of the soldiers to take a message for me.

Quickly changing into my outdoor footwear, I would need to replace those lovely boots that had disappeared; I told Aliza

I was just going around to the headquarters. She frowned at me and told me not to be long, but didn't stop me.

"I'll only be a few minutes, Aliza." I promised and hurried through the connecting walkway to the administration building. It was quiet here, they must all be out. I made my way along the corridor to Maxentius' office and knocked quietly.

He called a 'come in' and was astonished when I poked my head around the door.

"Hannah, what are you doing here, shouldn't you be in bed?"

"Actually, I feel much better thank you, my love; look I've even managed to get dressed." I gave him a quick twirl, noticing his mouth twitch as he tried to suppress a smile.

"Well I'm rather glad you didn't come over here in your night things, you impossible woman." I beamed at him and winked. "What brings you over here?"

"Is Petronius around? I'd like to get a message to Tullius at the Gladiators' School. I was due to take stitches out of one of the men two days after I was taken to the cells — oh dear, I sound like a real vagabond — and they probably have no idea why I haven't been back." Maxentius chuckled at my expression.

"Do not fret, my Hannah, Tullius knows what happened. The school was one of the places we looked when we couldn't find you and he had some of his guards help in the search. They think highly of you over there." I felt my cheeks grow hot.

"I haven't done much, just stitched up a prisoner of war and dealt with minor wounds on a few others."

"Well, for whatever reason, they were all worried. Tullius said he would ask one of the other medici to check on the Dacian, he's the one you meant, yes?" I nodded. "Petronius is out at the moment, I will send him with your message, when he returns. What do you wish to tell him?" I picked up one of the tablets and scratched my note for Tullius, placing it at the edge of Maxentius' desk.

"How busy are you?" I asked wistfully. "Will you be home on time tonight?"

"Pretty busy, my love. We have found the three men, finally, with whom you shared a cell and they have agreed to come in and talk to me. It will be a very useful discussion I think, but likely a very long one." I sighed. "Bored are you?" he asked, knowing me well. I nodded again, walking around to stand behind him. I rested my hands on his shoulders and bent to kiss the top of his head. He leaned back against me. "You are a tease, my Hannah, you distract me when I should be attending to my work." I ran my fingers along the top of his tunic, letting them slide between the material and his skin.

"I don't really care," I said kissing the back of his neck and along his jaw line. He inhaled sharply and pushing his chair back, reached around to pull me onto his knee.

"Well that's perfectly obvious, but I refuse to take you here on this desk; anybody could walk in."

"Mmmm...so they could," I murmured against his mouth as I kissed him into partial submission. He groaned, his lips responding, plundering my mouth with all the built up passion of what felt like too long since we'd been together. I twisted so that I was sitting facing him, my body pressed against his; I could feel his desire for me and knew if I carried on he would not be able to stop. I wasn't being fair so, drawing a shuddering breath and being the one who had started this, reluctantly I pulled away.

His eyes were as dazed as I knew mine must be.

"Oh, my love, I'm sorry, that was unfair of me, but I find I need you quite badly and temptation was getting the better of me." He looked at me, his expression very comical.

"So now after doing that to me, you're going to up and leave?" I kissed him again.

"If anybody came in..." I let the sentence hang. He nodded ruefully.

"True enough."

"Although, if you can take a break later..." getting off his knee and leaning in for another kiss, "...you know where I'll be." I winked, turned and, blowing him a last kiss, fled before my heart talked me out of it.

Chapter Eighteen

I hurried back home through the chill air. Aliza had put the food out and the children had finished whatever they'd been doing in their bedroom, which was something I did not want to think about. Over the meal, Aliza mentioned that she had seen posters all over the town advertising games to be held the following dies Saturni. I ran my knowledge of Latin through my head, working out that this would be a week on Saturday. Problem was I had no idea what day today was; I would have to ask Maxentius.

The children wanted to know whether they could attend, but I shook my head.

"It's not a place for children, even children as grown-up as you Efraim," noting the frown appearing on his little face. He was torn now between wanting to be thought of as an adult, yet still liked the cosseting he received as a child. The next few years would be interesting. "I will ask whether there are any events for youngsters. Maybe they have chariot racing or something similar"

"Will you go Mama?" asked Liora.

"No, my precious, it is mainly to entertain men, although women do watch. It is a long day and I may be required to look after those who injure themselves. So I will probably wait in the Palaestra, in case they need me. I do not like these types of games."

"Why not, Mama?" Claudia asked.

"Because people get hurt and I do not think that is fun. Now..." trying to change the subject, "...what are you doing this afternoon?"

"We are going to the house of Cornelius and Aemilia," said Liora importantly. They had met these two — twins who lived about ten minutes away — one day when they had been watching some children's entertainment near the Forum. They had formed a fast friendship and although the twins were closer to Liora's age than Efraim's they all, including Claudia, got on very well. They played nicely together and my children weren't discriminated against because of their different heritage; something that had worried me when we came here.

I had noticed that here in Pompeii, probably because it was such a trading hub, there appeared to be all manner of people from different creeds and cultures, rubbing shoulders with each other quite happily. It was quite the cosmopolitan city and generally all its citizens and visitors, seemed to mix without judgement on race; status yes, but that was the same everywhere.

"Well, I hope you have a lovely afternoon, please may I have a hug and a kiss to keep me going?" They giggled and did as I asked, before rushing off with Aliza chattering nineteen to the dozen. I smiled as I watched them go, trying to decide what I could do with myself for the next few hours.

I found a basket full of mending, which I started to tackle. We tried to repair as much as possible, especially for the children, as they were growing so quickly; otherwise we'd be spending all our income on clothes. I had worked out a way of altering my old tunics into dresses for Liora and Claudia, they liked the colours and it gave them a few more options for outfits. Even as young as they were, they loved fashion and it was very amusing watching them choose clothes when they dressed. I was absorbed in trying to sew up a tunic for Efraim, when I sensed movement behind me; I'd known my husband would come.

Maxentius rested his hands on my shoulders in much the same way I had done to him less than two hours previously. My heart had already quickened, as had my breathing, my body zinging at his touch. I rose and turned to face him, my sewing slithering to the floor. He stared at me with an expression of barely concealed hunger and my heart thudded. Neither of us spoke. I gazed back at him, drinking in his maleness, his broad shoulders, his muscular stature, his long legs. Shivers began rippling down my spine.

Kneeling on the bench, I reached for him; he leaned down and cupped his hand around the back of my neck with one hand, tilting my chin with the other. Dipping his head and sighing my name, he kissed me, his lips just brushing mine, the merest hint of a promise. Then just as his kiss seemed to deepen, he broke away and stood watching me, his breathing uneven. I slid off the bench and turned to face him, feeling electricity crackle between us.

"I am unable to stay long." His voice was ragged.

"Then don't make me wait." Without thinking, I stepped up onto the bench as he moved towards me, I was being very unladylike, but I was past caring. He lifted me over and I clung to him, burying myself in his kiss, a kiss that branded me as his as if there was ever any question. He carried me into our bedroom and the fire that had been smouldering since I'd been in his office earlier, in fact the fire that was always smouldering, burst into flame.

A most delectable while later, we came back to earth.

"How soon do you need to go back to work?" I murmured, running my fingers across his chest.

"Right about now, I should imagine," he muttered hoarsely, capturing my hands in his to prevent their downward progress.

"Are you sure?" I moved against him, smiling wickedly as I watched his eyes darken.

"Minx," was all he managed as the spark reignited pulling us back into a whirlpool of passion in which, I could quite happily have drowned.

Eventually, Maxentius said he would really have to go back to work while I, stretching like a cat, decided I might just stay in bed. I had nowhere to be and nothing to do. The children would be out for ages yet.

"Oh, I forgot to ask, Aliza mentioned that there are posters up for gladiatorial games next week. Is that right?" He nodded, answering me while he had a quick freshen up.

"Yes, an event the protestors might target. Huge crowds, lots of excitement, best place to create mayhem. This is one of the questions we'll be putting to your three cellmates. Now I really have to go." I knelt up on the bed, and lifted my face for his kiss, wrapping my arms around his neck, as he obliged.

"See you later, my love." I breathed against his lips. "Try not to be too late." He grinned down at me as he adjusted his cloak.

"Highly unlikely when I know you're waiting for me." He dropped one last kiss on the top of my head and quickly left the house.

I snuggled back under the covers, persuading myself that since I'd been unwell, an afternoon nap would not be unexpected. Tomorrow, I would get back to my work, but for now slumber called — just half an hour — and was instantly asleep. I dreamed of a pale yellow room with huge windows; it looked light and airy. A familiar figure was sitting in a chair that looked very comfortable, holding something in his hand, a memory tugged at me. It was a book. Oh I missed books. On the bed someone was sleeping. It was the woman; her cheeks seemed to be overly flushed compared with the rest of her skin, which was quite pale. Had she been sick like I was? I tried to hold the image, wanting to see more, but it faded.

The sound of children's laughter woke me, I looked out of the window and realised it was well into the afternoon; I had slept much longer than I'd intended. Having a quick wash to clear the cobwebs, I dressed quickly and went out into the living area to see the three children surrounded by all sorts of toys.

"My goodness, where did all this come from?" I asked smiling at their happy faces.

"Cornelius and Aemilia said we could borrow them and take them back next time we go," replied Efraim, waving what looked like a kite under my nose. "Please may we go and play with this now?"

I glanced out of the window, although the day was waning, there would be enough light for a little while.

"Come on then," I grinned, "let's see what we can do." They whooped with joy, pulling their cloaks back on, which they had dropped by the fire and ran outside. We went through the courtyard and along the walkway to the large plot at the rear of the house, half of which was given over to Marcus' veggie patch. This was where I hoped we might be able to have chickens, but we hadn't got around to it yet. I followed them carrying the kite, which looked to be of good quality. I hoped my three wouldn't damage it.

"So, do you know how to fly a kite?" I asked

"Cornelius showed us and we had a go, please may I try?" Efraim asked. I handed it over, keeping my eye on him. He lifted the kite carefully, holding it steady until the breeze caught under the material. Then he released the string gently, letting the kite find its own air current. He was very good and I was surprised at his patience, as he was not known for taking things slowly. For a small boy, he did remarkably well. His face was a study in excitement and the two girls were jumping around shouting in delight.

Suddenly a voice called my name and I turned to see Marcus standing at one of the windows on the upper floor of the headquarters building.

"He's good, isn't he?" he called down. I nodded and Efraim, hearing his uncle's voice, shouted up to him —

"Look at me, look at me, it's really flying."

"Hush, Efraim, we don't need to tell the whole town." I smiled as I spoke and he giggled sheepishly.

"Sorry, Mama, but it's so much fun." Marcus disappeared only to reappear a few minutes later in the garden.

"Nice to see you looking better, Hannah; you had us all worried." I blushed and thanked him for his concern, then said —

"You cannot keep away, can you? I thought you were supposed to be interviewing those three men." I grinned.

"No," he chuckled. "I need to check this out and they haven't arrived yet, so I have a few spare minutes. Where did Efraim get it?"

"One of their friends lent them it for a few days. I just hope we can take it back in one piece."

"Maybe I could make them one; it can't be that hard. Hey, Efraim..." calling to my son who bounced over, "...please may I take a look at your kite?" Efraim handed it over and so began a serious discussion about how to build one. The girls entered into it as well, although their contribution was more to do with colour of material, rather than the design or structural integrity of the kite itself. Still, we spent a happy hour or so working out what we could do.

The daylight was fading and I persuaded the children to come indoors. Marcus went back to his office saying he'd be over for dinner as usual and he didn't think they would be late. Sitting the three small fry in front of the fire, I gave them all a drink of warm milk. Romans considered milk to be an uncivilised beverage, using it for medicines or cheese and so rarely drank it, but I had grown up drinking goat's milk and knew it was good for bones and teeth. It was also very useful for settling down over-excited children and worked far more quickly than anything else.

Since we weren't entirely sure of the time the men would come home, Aliza and I sorted out the evening meal, feeding the children and ourselves. I really had no idea when my two Romans might be finished and, Aliza was meeting up with some of her sewing friends. One of them would come and escort her both ways so that she didn't have to walk there on her own. It was at moments like this that I felt guilty for bringing her here with us, for I knew she missed her home more than she admitted, but at least she had made some friends and enjoyed socialising with them.

It also made me reflect on whether we would ever see my homeland again. Strange as it seemed, I missed Masada and our life there, which had been far simpler than the one we had here in Pompeii.

Chapter Nineteen

After the meal, I bathed the children and then we sat by the fire while I told them stories and dried their hair. Both Claudia and Liora had long curly hair in rich chestnut brown, like mine, which was beautiful but took some combing through. Eventually, all the knots were out and once dry, I plaited both, tying bows of coloured ribbon around the ends. I spun them to face me smiling at how cute they looked.

As I smiled, a memory rose in my mind of a book I had read as a child and it made me think about my other world. What was happening? Did they find anything that we left here? Did we make it out before the ash fell? Surely we must have done, otherwise how could I be there and here? Dragging my thoughts back to my current life, I sent them to their bedroom, telling them I would be along in a few minutes.

Aliza went out with her friend and after I'd tucked the children up in bed, I curled up on the sofa and waited for the men to come home, musing over my complicated life. Then I wondered whether Maxentius had managed to get any useful information from Priscus Regulus and his two colleagues. I must have dozed, for the next thing I knew a deep voice was saying my name and a hand was shaking my shoulder.

"Hannah, wake up, it's late. You didn't need to wait up for us." I opened my eyes into a pair of deep green ones smiling down at me.

"Have you eaten?" I asked trying to come around, the warmth of the room making it difficult.

"I assumed the platters on the table were for us?" I nodded. "Good," dropping me a wink, "because that's what we ate." Handing me a goblet of wine, he sat down, drawing me into the circle of his arms, as Marcus chose the chair by the fire.

This way too comfortable; I would be asleep again in seconds. Shifting slightly so that I was actually sitting upright, I shook my head trying to clear it and had a quick sip of the wine.

"So, was the meeting fruitful?" I asked. They looked at each other and then both nodded.

"It was very interesting; we talked for a long time."

"So I noticed," I interjected dryly. They both grinned ruefully.

"I know it's late, but we didn't want to break their flow. If we'd stopped, they might not have been inclined to come back. You were right, my Hannah, they are men of rank and status, but they were not in support of Vespasian when he was persuaded to challenge Vitellius."

"But that's so long ago, why are they still so upset? From what I can work out, this man has stabilised the Empire, surely that is a good thing?"

"I think it was more to do with the civil war that followed the death of Nero with four men jockeying for power in one year and then, that the man who eventually won, while he had attained senatorial status, was not from one of the ancient patrician families."

"Well, that seems to be a bit of a ridiculous argument. I understand he had a distinguished career in the military and when he was proconsul, his skills as an administrator won him high praise. While I abhor what happened in Judaea, I can understand his motives, for his only objective was to quash a rebellion."

The two men looked at me in astonishment. How on earth did I know all this?

"Why are you looking at me like that? I keep telling you that I listen. I hear you two talking, I hear people discussing things in the street and around the Forum," not to mention that I had studied it at university nearly two thousand years in the future. Probably best keep that part to myself.

They accepted my words, although Maxentius did look at me a little longer, his brow creased and I imagined he was going to take me to task about it when we were on our own. Apparently, my erstwhile cellmates had confirmed that the upcoming games were too good an opportunity to miss and would be targeting any and all of the elected officials who turned up. Thankfully the Emperor wasn't attending this time.

"I suppose at an event like this, their actions would have much more of an impact than just small protests in the streets? I still don't really understand the point. What are they hoping to achieve?" I asked.

"I'm not even sure they know anymore," Marcus replied. "Maybe it's just to let the Imperial administration know that there are people out there who might gain enough followers to topple the Emperor, should the political climate or the balance of power change."

"But surely, they are at more risk of being imprisoned or worse if they keep this up."

"Yes, but if you attract enough followers, especially if any of them happen to be in the military, there will be too many to deal with and we'd end up with another civil war."

"I just hope they realise how many people could be seriously injured if they start something at the games. It could be more of a bloodbath than usual, only this time it will not be entertainment." The two men nodded their agreement.

"We'll have a lot of soldiers surrounding the amphitheatre; hopefully that will be enough of a deterrent." Maxentius said.

"Just you two make sure you keep safe. I don't want to have to spend weeks treating your wounds — been there, done that." I grinned at them and they chuckled, remembering those first weeks on Masada after the rebel ambush. "I'm sure I can find maggots though, if I have to." I continued, winking at Marcus who shuddered in disgust.

"No, no, no...never again," he said shaking his head. "Just thinking about it makes me feel queasy." Laughing we recalled those days, which seemed so long ago, when I first met my two Romans — those days that changed my life forever. I glanced up at Maxentius, who smiled at me, with eyes twinkling and knew exactly what he was thinking about.

Marcus left soon after, as it was now very late. Maxentius and I sat for a little longer, then secured the doors and went to bed. As I expected Maxentius was not going to let my comments from earlier pass without question.

"Right, Hannah, what was all that about the Emperor? You cannot possibly have learned all that from overhearing snatches of conversation." I finished undressing, pulled on my nightshift and slipped between the sheets before I answered him.

"I studied Roman history at university. The period from Augustus to Hadrian was my favourite and covers about one hundred and seventy years." I watched his face as he tried to process this.

"Who on earth is Hadrian and what is a university?"

"Are you sure you want me to tell you?"

"Try me." So, firstly I clarified what a university was. That took some doing for the concept was far beyond anything he could relate to in this era. Although education was available to the rich and some — men only — went on to rhetoric schools to become orators and the like, the idea of huge numbers of men and women attending a purpose-built educational establishment that taught hundreds of lessons was completely foreign to him.

Secondly, I explained who would follow Vespasian and when they would take power. As I was telling him, I added that Hadrian, who would commission the building of an incredible wall across the top of the Province of Britannia, had only recently been born. To give him his due, Maxentius accepted what I was telling him, which could not have been easy.

"So, Vespasian will die before the end of this year?"

"Yes, sad to say — for he was a good man — a couple of months before Vesuvius erupts," I tried to pin down the year, "which will happen in August of AD79, but I think you would say it was about 830 ab urbe condita. I get confused with the dating systems." He looked a bit puzzled, so I just shook my head. 'Don't worry about it; I think I'll know when we should leave. Suffice it to say that less than two months after the death of Vespasian, we will need to be out of here."

Maxentius finished getting undressed and got into bed, pulling me into his arms.

"I don't know how you do it, my Hannah."

"Do what?" I asked snuggling into his chest.

"Have all this floating around in your head, information from hundreds of years in the future, yet you continue with your life as if it is not there."

"I can't do anything to change the whole world my love, only our tiny little part of it, for I'm sure that is why this knowledge is given to me, why she's in my head. There can be no other reason than that she is here to save us."

The next morning I woke up at my usual hour. Maxentius had already gone, but everyone else was still at home. I washed and dressed, taking a little more care this morning, as I was going to be visiting the Gladiators' School. I was excited about having my routine back and seemed to be suffering no lasting effects from my illness. The five of us enjoyed the first meal together and I was able to make sure my bag had everything in it I would need, before Petronius came to collect me.

In general, the days were less cold. I hoped that spring was not far away, but this morning was damp and chilly and I was very pleased to have my heavy cloak, as well as the new boots Maxentius had somehow procured for me. Petronius was concerned for my health, fearing my being out in such weather, but I assured him I was fine.

"Maxentius would not have let me come, if he was at all worried Petronius, trust me, this is doing me the world of good." To distract him, I asked whether he would be attending the games. He thought that he would probably be on duty, but as he'd seen them previously, he wasn't bothered. He did tell me about them though, which kept us going all the way to the school.

We went to find Tullius first, so I could apologise for my absence; for regardless of the fact that it had been out of my hands, I disliked letting people down. He was at his desk and bestowed a huge smile on me as I knocked on his open door.

"Hannah, wife of Maxentius, it is a pleasure to see you again. I trust you are well?" I smiled back and nodded.

"Yes thank you, Tullius Rufinus. I am sorry that I have been unable to attend the school; hopefully my absence has not caused too great a strain on the other medici."

"Thankfully, there has been little need for their attendance. However, I expect you would like to check on the Dacian? He has had his stitches removed, but if you are anything like the other physicians, you will want to see for yourself."

"Thank you, my friend, that would be much appreciated." He nodded and signalled to the guard, who was waiting at the door, to escort us through the school.

"Is there anyone else you would like me to check while I'm here?" I asked. Tullius thought about it for a moment and then mentioned several men, also prisoners of war, who had shown symptoms of fever and he wanted to be sure they would be fit for the games. I confirmed that I would examine them and we took our leave.

We followed the guard along the chilly walkways. I hoped the living quarters were warmer than this; otherwise it would not surprise me if all the gladiators fell ill. We reached the room of the Dacian and found Darius sitting on his bed talking to his roommate, one of his countrymen, whose name I vaguely recalled was Mihai. Darius smiled when I entered, which surprised me, but I returned it, asking him how he felt.

"Good, I am good," he replied and lifted his tunic to show me the scar. I asked him to lie on the bed so I could check it properly and he willingly obliged. I examined the wound noting that it had healed well and that the scarring would not be too bad. Whoever had removed the stitches had done so with care.

I had brought a small pot of balm, which I knew was good for wounds such as these. It strengthened the damaged skin and reduced the chances of long-term scarring. I handed it to Darius, explaining that he needed to rub a small amount in every day, demonstrating what I meant and checking to be sure he understood. He nodded and I asked the guard whether it was acceptable that I leave the jar with Darius, as it was for his use only. He nodded his agreement and I packed everything else back into my bag.

"I am glad you are well, Darius. Try not to do this again." I winked at him; he grinned sheepishly and then said something about the games. I asked Petronius what he meant. The two of them had a short conversation and then Petronius told me that Darius was excited because he had been chosen to fight.

My heart sank. Even though gladiators were considered an expensive commodity, these men were prisoners of war and probably only one rank up from the condemned. I knew that it might be a case of kill or be killed, unless the audience granted clemency. However I could not dampen his enthusiasm, he had just as much chance of winning as his opponent, so I smiled and said I was very happy for him and wished him luck. He grinned back, he and Mihai launching into a very cheerful song. Chuckling at my expression, Petronius explained that soldiers used to sing this the night before they went into battle. Amused, I nodded my approval and waving a goodbye, left them to it.

We carried on to check on the other men whom Tullius had mentioned. Bearing in mind I had been unwell, I took pains to cover my nose and mouth with a cloth before entering their rooms. I had no desire to fall ill again. One or two definitely showed signs of a raised temperature, but their breathing sounded clear and none of them had a sore throat or cough. There was no fire in these rooms to remove the chill and they were rather draughty, causing me to consider that this might be the cause of the problem. Circulating air was a good thing, but not if it was making the rooms cold and damp.

I dispensed some of the same foul-tasting medicine I had taken when I was sick and said I would be back the next day to examine them again. There were four Hebrew men and two more Dacians, all prisoners of war, all supposed to fight in the upcoming games. I speculated over whether there was even any point in my doing anything if they were going to lose their lives in a matter of days. As with Darius, I knew they had a chance. If they had trained hard and had good strength, they may win their bout. Sadly, I realised that they would probably be fighting each other, so one out of every two might die.

I could not let myself think about it — these men who had fought bravely for their own countries, only to be captured, paraded as prisoners, then chosen to be gladiators and they were the lucky ones. I knew that when we were on Masada, had Maxentius and Marcus been unable to persuade Silva of my worth, the fate of some of them might have befallen me. It was too close. I shook my head trying to dispel the images that rose in my mind and, quickly tidying my things, left the last of the rooms.

Walking slowly back to where Tullius' was ensconced, I ruminated over the problem of warmth, realising that they would not risk a fire in the rooms in case the men decided to burn the place down. Would extra blankets be available, or warmer clothes? Was there a hypocaustum, or underfloor heating system, beneath the building? If so, that would warm both levels, but even if they did have one, I imagined it would not be inexpensive to run.

On reaching Tullius' office, I asked him about this. He confirmed that no, they didn't have a hypocaustum, but would consider providing extra blankets.

"I know that this is costly, Tullius, but these men will get sick again and again if their rooms are cold and damp. It wouldn't be for long, as the weather should warm up soon, but it will help next winter — conveniently forgetting that Pompeii wouldn't be here next winter.

"Would it be possible to hang some heavy material across the doors and windows at night during colder weather to keep out the draft? If you can find a merchant who has some for a good price, I know people who could make them up for you." He thought about this and said he would discuss it further and let me know. I knew I had done all I could do and thanked him, saying I would be back the next day to see how those with suspected fever were faring.

As I was about to leave, he stood and rather awkwardly said he was sorry about what had happened to me and was glad that I was again well enough to attend the school. I smiled at him and without thinking, went over to him and gave him a quick hug.

"You are very kind," I said and, before he could respond, slipped out through the door. Petronius was chuckling as we walked away.

"I don't know how you do it, Hannah, but before long you will have him wrapped around your little finger." I grinned at him,

"I know; this will work out very well, I think." We walked home chatting about this and that and I asked whether he would be able to go with me the next day. I was sure I would be fine on my own, but Maxentius was still concerned about the protestors and I certainly did not want a repeat of my last encounter with them.

Chapter Twenty

The next two weeks were filled with visits to the Gladiators' School and the sports ground. The young men who trained at the Palaestra would be putting on an exhibition of their sporting prowess and, as such, quite a few of them had become rather overexcited and therefore careless; mostly small lacerations and bad bruising, but a few had managed to give themselves quite deep gashes, requiring further attention. One even had a broken wrist, but was determined not to miss out, such was the credit given to participants. I doubted his chances, but no one could doubt his resolve. They kept me very busy and I loved it.

Some of the more senior and trusted gladiators were also training in the Palaestra as there was much more space. They needed to familiarise themselves with the amount of room they would have during their bouts and, while the yard at the school was suitable for general fitness training, this was much closer to the size of the arena. Much as I hated the idea of the fights, their dedication and skill astounded me. In my time, these men would be seen as the cream of their sport, paid a fortune and treated like gods. I understood why they amassed such a huge following.

I was beginning to gain respect amongst the rest of the medici also, for which I was truly grateful. It meant that we could work alongside each other, without them feeling as though I was treading on their toes. Tullius had asked that I be present at the games and, although I really had no desire to be there, he assured me I could stay where the gladiators gathered. This was at the Palaestra, where those chosen to fight waited their turn and meant that I would not have to watch the games. The children had been told they could watch the chariot races, which were being organised especially for the youngsters, but then Aliza would take them home. Claudia was not sure she even wanted to do that but the other two really did, so she gave in.

Whatever ailment had caused the six prisoners to be unwell cleared up quickly and, I was sure this was more to do with the days becoming warmer and less damp than anything else. Still,

I kept my eye on conditions at the school, worrying that it could recur if ignored. Tullius had agreed to get the material for the drapes and I had asked Aliza whether her group might be interested in making them up, adding that they would be paid for their time.

Maxentius and his garrison prepared too, making sure that there were enough soldiers to guard the amphitheatre as well as keep watch around the town. It was an arduous task, but it was something they were very good at and I hoped there wouldn't be any trouble. It was the first games of the year, so excitement would be at fever pitch. It would be a shame if a bunch of rude protestors spoiled it.

Finally, it was the day of the games and it dawned bright and sunny, albeit rather cool as spring was only just making its presence known. I suddenly realised that I had missed Christmas, and that in this time they didn't celebrate it; strangely I hadn't even noticed. It was weeks since I had seen my other Max, but I knew that the passage of time wasn't the same and since I was unable to get myself back, I tried not to worry about it.

The Gladiatorial Games were an all-day affair, starting with a parade in which everyone who was involved would take part. I did not need to be in position until the games themselves were underway so I took the children to watch the procession. The sponsor of the games, who in this case happened to be the magistrate in front of whom I had been dragged, led it. I wondered, rather sardonically, whether he would recognise me now that I was clean.

Efraim, Liora and Claudia were fascinated and shouted along with everyone else, cheering them on. Musicians played, while acrobats danced, juggled and turned cartwheels, all accompanying the contenders as they marched towards the arena. I watched in silence, still unable to cull this entertainment. We followed the procession as it entered the amphitheatre through the Porta Triumphalis — the main gate — and then the children stayed, along with hundreds of others to enjoy the chariot races, while the main events were set up.

Normally, these types of races would be held in the circus, but as there wasn't one at Pompeii and as all the participants were youngsters riding small chariots, they held them in the amphitheatre. Thankfully, none of the contestants fell out or was hurt, but I was relieved when it was over and Aliza could take my three back home. A crowd of attendants came out to rake the sand smooth again and very quickly the arena was ready for the main action.

The first proper event was the display by the men from the Palaestra. They were very agile and the crowd loved them. Many, of course, would be relatives, as most of these young men were from families of high status, but they also had a strong following amongst the other youngsters. Even the young man with the broken wrist managed to compete, but came out of the amphitheatre looking very white and accepted a draft of my poppy juice gratefully, once I'd re-bandaged his poor arm. I was happy enough to watch their demonstrations and was able to do so from one of the tunnels connecting the backstage of the amphitheatre to the main arena.

Following this display, mock fights using wooden weapons were staged, some of which were very funny. The combatants made the audience howl with laughter at their antics. Their skill could not be denied, but it wasn't supposed to be taken seriously. So far I had enjoyed the morning, surprising myself into the bargain. However, I refused to watch the next event, which involved animals being forced to fight each other. It was hard enough to listen to the sounds of them screaming in pain from the sports ground where I waited for it to be over. Neither did I have any intention of returning until any and all blood had been removed.

Maxentius had told me that during the lunchtime break, condemned criminals were executed. Firstly I'd decided that anyone who could watch that kind of thing during a *lunch* break needed their head read...ugh and, secondly I prayed that there were none to be executed this day. It was hard enough knowing that those gladiators who were prisoners of war would be fighting. I remained where I was, sitting under a tree by the swimming pool, where Maxentius and Marcus found me not long before the afternoon's entertainment was due to start. They looked quite formidable in their full armour, but that didn't stop my heart from doing its usual flip-flop as I watched my husband walking towards me.

"Hannah, you cannot enjoy the games from over here." Maxentius smiled as he kissed me.

"I'm very happy to stay here until I'm needed, thank you very much. I have no desire to see animals ripped to shreds and I didn't know whether there were any executions, so I wasn't going back 'til the actual combat starts. In fact, quite honestly, I'd be happy to stay here for the rest of the afternoon, but I s'pose I should show willing."

They both chuckled, aware of my feeling about the games. "What will you be doing?"

"We're watching the perimeter of the amphitheatre, along with about a hundred other soldiers. The rest of the garrison is spread through the main areas of the town," Marcus replied. "So far it's been a typical day at the games. Some silly nonsense from those who have already had too much to drink, but no violence. Let's hope it stays that way."

"Come on, we'll walk you over," Maxentius said, pulling me up from the bench. Reluctantly, I accompanied them. While I knew my medical skills might be required, it didn't mean I wanted to stand and watch the reason for them. My two Romans waved a goodbye as they went off to attend to their own duties and I carried on to the tunnel through which the gladiators would enter the arena. The first few groups were already waiting, dressed for combat, but their clothing, armour and weapons differed substantially.

I knew that there were several types of gladiators, both heavily and lightly armed and that within each of these groups their weapons were quite diverse. Similarly armed opponents fought each other to prove their superior skills within those rankings, but this was infrequent. It tended to be heavily armed gladiators, such as the Murmillones; recognisable by the stylised fish on their crested helmets, pitted against lightly armed participants, such as the Retiarii, whose weapons were a fuscina or trident, a pugio or small dagger and a weighted net — much like a fishing net.

The armour — a metal greave on the lower left leg and leather guard on the right arm and wrist — helmet, shield and gladius (sword) of the Murmillo offered some protection, but also restricted his movements; whereas the lack of armour on his opponent gave him the advantage of agility and speed. It all came down to skill. Most gladiators, even those considered 'heavily armed' wore only a loincloth, their bare chests demonstrating their masculinity. As I waited for the combat to begin, I studied their weapons. There was such an array — swords, nets, lassos and spears — that I shuddered at the damage I knew just one of these could inflict.

The first to compete would be the Equites, or horsemen, who fought only against each other. They fought in pairs and the general idea was to enter the arena on horseback and throw carefully aimed spears at their opponents, trying to unseat them before eventually dismounting and continuing their fight on foot using either a gladius or a long sword called a spatha. Very lightly armoured, as they needed freedom of movement, their skill both on the beautiful horses and on the ground was incredible and I was fascinated by how nimble they were. Three pairs fought at once, spread out over the arena, giving the audience a great spectacle.

I breathed a sigh of relief, when at the end of the bout they and especially their horses, were all still alive. The 'losing' gladiators had been wounded, but nothing particularly serious and they had fought well; the audience seemed to be benevolent this day and spared them. Tullius had told me that it was rare for the higher-ranking gladiators to be put to death if they lost, especially if they had fought bravely and with prowess. Their entertainment value was more important than their deaths; something I was extremely thankful for. Along with another medicus, we cleaned and bound their injuries and they went back to the school in the company of their trainers.

The competitions went on all afternoon. I was amazed that the audience could be bothered to watch for such a long time, but they lived for these events. It was at the top of the social calendar; even women attended and to those living in Pompeii, the amphitheatre was at least as important as the Forum, if not more so. A vast, circular construction, sunk deep into the earth, a reminder of times when these arena were in natural hollows, the amphitheatre could seat up to twenty thousand people — almost the whole population of the town.

Far simpler in design than later arenas, I knew that by my time, it was acknowledged to be the oldest surviving Roman amphitheatre and probably the blueprint for subsequent buildings of this nature. Its internal layout also provided a microcosm of Roman society, being separated into three distinct areas. Separated by a low barrier, the elite sat in the sections closest to the action, with the middle level allocated to the general populace. Women and slaves were consigned to the upper level, farthest from the show. There was no roof, but velaria, or large sails, which were swung out from the top of the structure, did offer decent shade. Food and drink were available all day, vendors setting up stalls outside the amphitheatre or carrying trays along the walkways. It was very well organised.

I did not have the stomach to watch any more of this spectacle of violence. Many of the combatants came off bleeding heavily and I was kept busy dealing with their injuries. One or two would need watching as their wounds were very deep, but I did not think I would lose any of those under my care. All the medici were similarly occupied and before long we were all hot, tired and spattered with blood. Towards the end of the afternoon, Darius appeared along with several other prisoners of war. My heart sank; I knew that these bouts would more than likely end in the death of one or more.

Their trainers had decided that they would fight in two teams, which today meant that it was Dacians against Hebrews. There were six on each side and all were lightly armed. They did have leather wristbands, but no helmets or greaves. They were all barefoot and all loosely shackled. To my mind it was utterly barbaric, but this was what the crowd had been waiting for. This was when their bloodlust would be satiated. These men were nothing to them, enemies of their Empire, their lives worthless.

Darius nodded to me as he walked to the arena's entrance. I smiled back, hoping that he would survive. His team gathered round him, it seemed he had been designated their leader. The Hebrew prisoners followed, several feet behind. Among them was Tobias and as they marched past where I was standing, he deliberately shoved into me, nearly knocking me over, glaring at me with that all-consuming hatred. Darius noticed the kerfuffle and narrowed his eyes, muttering something to Mihai who glanced my way. The guards pushed Tobias back into line, one of them apologising to me as they passed. I nodded, still rather unnerved. I had been close enough for him to cause me serious injury; his weapon was a short sword.

The audience was howling for the fight to start. There were men in the arena whose job it was to incite the crowd and they were whipping them into a frenzy. I turned away, walking back along the tunnel, so that I could not see into the stadium. I knew when the gladiators entered, for the noise reached a cacophony. I stood with another medicus, whose name I knew to be Publius Gallus Blandinus and one of the trainers, keeping my back to the arena's entrance. The fight seemed to go on for hours. I had no idea whose side the crowd was on, but the ebb and flow of sound was a good indicator of how well each 'team' was doing.

A long groan meant that there was a man down; a rousing cheer meant there had been a well-fought bout. There were the sounds of men grunting with the effort, the scrape of metal against metal or, worse, metal against flesh and still the overwhelming roar from the crowd. It brought back memories of Masada, the night of the massacre, increasing my agitation. I had to get away from this din, just for a few minutes. Yelling over the noise, I told Gallus Blandinus that I needed fresh air and almost ran out of the amphitheatre. It wasn't much quieter at this side of the wall, but at least the noise didn't echo here like it did along the tunnels.

I hurried back over to the Palaestra, slipping in through the student entrance and returning to my seat near the pool, letting the cool air waft over my face. How long had they been fighting? Regardless of anything else, they would be exhausted, restricted by their ankle shackles, making every movement twice as hard as without. They also knew that they were there to die; that having been saved once, their sole purpose was to die for the enjoyment of a crowd. I just hoped that if and when any of them was killed, it would be quick.

While I was sitting there, I stared up at the dark mass that was Vesuvius, noticing again that tendrils of mist or smoke were curling up from its peak. At least those who died today would not be buried under tons of burning ash, their breath sucked out of them by the hot wind that preceded it. It made the violence going on in the arena seem almost inconsequential, but this would not be entertainment.

For no apparent reason, thinking of Vesuvius made me think of Max. I missed him and ruminated over what might be happening to me in my own time. I knew that no major head injury was involved this time, so how was it that I was still here? Was it because I needed to be? I mulled it over for several minutes, failing to come up with an answer for, in the end, whatever the reason, there was nothing I could do about it.

Shrugging my fanciful thoughts aside, I made my way back over to the amphitheatre. The fight was continuing, although some were already off the field. Two of Darius' compatriots, Mihai and Gavril were talking to their trainer, blood running from several cuts, but their wounds appeared relatively superficial. I glanced along the tunnel and could see men lying in the sand. Were they dead, or just too injured to move? Who was still fighting?

Tullius appeared next to me.

"What is happening?" I asked him. "Who's still out there and how many are dead?"

"At least four may be dead, or at the very least severely injured, but we cannot enter the arena until this fight is over. Darius is fighting Tobias. They are the only two still standing," he replied, hesitating a moment before he continued. "I think it might actually be for your honour." I gazed at him horror-struck.

"What do you mean?"

"Darius was angry that Tobias insulted you. His compatriots must have told him about it, for he was still injured and abed when it happened." I vaguely recalled Petronius saying something about it.

"Surely it was not enough for this level of animosity?"

"They will use anything to feed their anger; they need it to fight. You treated Darius with dignity, despite his being a prisoner of war and he has decided that Tobias's words were disrespectful and degrading."

"Oh by all the gods, they cannot do this! They will not stop until one is dead and the other dying."

"This is the nature of gladiatorial combat, Hannah, wife of Maxentius; you cannot interfere." I had to stop myself from running into the arena to tear them off each other, but now I knew I had to watch the fight. I could not turn from it if there was a chance that they were fighting over me, however misguided and idiotic that might be. I forced myself to walk along the passageway to the combatants' entrance.

I watched them battling each other; they were both tiring now, for they had been fighting for a long time. Well matched, both were tall and muscular, both had been soldiers — their military training had come to the fore — and both were very, very angry. Blood was running from various wounds, but neither was prepared to concede. They circled and jabbed, circled and jabbed. Then one would hurl himself at the other, fists and knees connecting with chins and ribs. Then back to the circling, somehow avoiding the bodies of their teammates spread around the arena.

The crowd was in uproar; they loved it. These two men had given them the fight of the day and it was still going on. They would talk about this for weeks, whatever the outcome. Tobias struck out at Darius, slicing him along his arm, while at the same time Darius swung away catching Tobias' upper thigh. Sweat was pouring off them and their bodies were covered in blood, which was mingling with the sand kicked up by their feet. I really wanted it to stop. Was there any way it could be stopped? I went back along the passage to find Tullius.

"How long will you let this continue? Can you decide to call a halt if it looks as though neither man will prevail?"

"If it goes on much longer, I will consider it. The audience will still be able to choose a winner. There is a chance that they will allow both to live, since they have provided excellent entertainment, but do not get your hopes up." He looked at me curiously. "Why do you care, Hannah? Tobias attacked you many years ago and recently insulted you while in my school. Do you not wish him dead?"

"I do not wish anyone dead for fun, Tullius Rufinus. If they are killed in battle or executed for their actions, that is quite different from having a crowd of hysterical people baying for blood to top off their day's entertainment. If you don't put a stop to it soon, I may have to go out there and do it myself."

He looked at me, assessing whether I was serious. I stared back unflinching. I knew my words were merely bravado, but surely he could see that to allow the fight to continue was inhumane, regardless of the combatants' status. Then sighing, I said —

"They are so tired, Tullius, if they are such good entertainment, wouldn't it be better to let them live for another day, another fight?" He knew the sense of my words, especially now as the sun was beginning to set. The games had been on for well over six hours, excluding all the pre-game events and processions. People would start to think about setting out for home. It would be better to finish the day on a high note, by telling the crowd that these two would fight in the next games.

Minutes ticked by. Then making a decision, Tullius walked out into the arena, just as both men looked to be failing. The crowd was still roaring its support for their favourite, but as Tullius reached the centre, he held his hand up and within seconds the noise had stopped — the sudden silence almost as deafening. He waited, motioning Tobias and Darius to him. They staggered to the centre of the arena. Tullius began to speak, his voice modulated, yet his words reached every spectator.

"Honourable guests, these men have fought a brave fight. They are well matched and have shown great courage. Although now prisoners, they were once men of war and displayed this same resolve on the battlefield. Did you enjoy their struggle?" There was a unanimous 'yes' from the crowd. Tullius continued. "Would you like to see them fight again?" Another 'yes.' He waited until they had settled down. "The choice is yours. We can let them continue today and one of them will surely die, or we can look forward to another great battle at the next games. What say you?"

Chapter Twenty One

I looked around the arena from my vantage point in the passageway, holding my breath. There was no sound at all and everyone seemed to be twisting or clenching their fists. I had no idea what this meant; it definitely wasn't the thumbs up or thumbs down action, which for long enough had been the generally accepted gesture for the kill/spare decision in my time. A whisper began to ripple through the crowd, it grew louder and louder, but I couldn't understand what they were shouting. By the time it reached me it was like thunder.

"Spare them! Spare them! Spare them!" Was I hearing this right, the crowd wanted to spare *both* of them? Tullius bowed to them, giving them their head for a few minutes, then raised his hands for silence. They responded immediately.

"By your decree they are spared." He bellowed the words and the crowd went wild. Taking a hand of each of the men, he lifted their arms to the audience, turning them so that everyone got to see them. They were both trembling with fatigue and I did not know how they were still standing. The three men bowed and Tullius escorted them out of the arena to the exultant cheers of the crowd.

I released a breath I hadn't known I was holding. Tullius hurried the men along the tunnel and handed them over to their guards and trainers. He nodded to me and left to finish his duties for the day. I walked towards the small group; Gallus Blandinus was also there ready to treat one of the combatants. I motioned that I would take Darius; Gallus nodded and, accompanied by a guard, led Tobias away gently.

Although I examined Darius quickly in the dim light, I knew that all the dirt and blood had to be washed off him before I had any chance of working out how many wounds he had. The guards told me that none of those lying in the arena had survived and that they would be carried out through the Porta Libitinensis, the exit for the dead and then back to the School. Knowing that at least two of them were Hebrew, I made a mental note to ask Tullius if there was any ritual he required me to prepare.

I asked the guards to take Darius over to the changing rooms in the Palaestra and help him to clean up. They did as I bid them and I followed slowly; it would take them several minutes to remove all that muck. I met them in the changing rooms, noticing that Tobias was there also. Despite their exhaustion, the antagonism between the two men hadn't subsided one jot. They were staring at each other like caged tigers.

Checking Darius' wounds, I was thankful that the one I had recently treated had not been re-opened, but he had a few very nasty gashes. I set about cleaning them out. I knew it stung for he flinched several times, but I was as gentle as I could be. Rubbing my salve into the wounds, I bandaged him up and offered him a sip of the poppy juice. He shook his head and I smiled at him.

"I'm glad you are not dead," I said quietly, unsure whether he understood. He nodded, grunting an acknowledgement.

Seated at the other end of the room, Tobias was glaring in my direction. I looked at him; his injuries were similar to those he had inflicted on Darius. Tullius was right, they were well matched. I walked along the room to where Gallus was packing up his bags, and asked him about Tobias.

"He will live, he will be very sore and those wounds will give him some pain for several days, but he seems tough." I agreed, saying that Darius seemed about the same, adding that we would need to make sure no infection set in from all the dirt and blood that had been caught in the wounds as they fought.

"Tullius said you asked him to stop the fight," Gallus said. "Why?" I repeated the same words I had spoken to the lanista. "It was a brave request, Hannah, wife of Maxentius, not many would have dared."

"I had to say something and Tullius did not have to listen to my suggestion, it was his choice. It had gone on too long. A quick kill in the heat of the fight is one thing, but killing your opponent because he is exhausted is not sportsmanlike. That is not a fight, it is an execution." Gallus smiled and patted my hand.

"After a while, you don't even notice. I hope you never lose your convictions." I smiled back and said I would see him the next day at the Gladiators' School.

I was about to leave when I heard Tobias speak. Slowly I turned back to face him. The guards were prepared, but I knew Tobias did not have the strength to hurt me at this moment.

"What?"

"You asked the lanista to stop the fight?" I nodded. "Why?"

"You heard what I told the medicus. Neither of you deserved to die today."

"You believe that? Truly?" I nodded again. My words confounded him. "Even though you know I hate you?"

"Even though I know you hate me, Tobias, son of Reuven. Despite everything you did to me, however badly you hurt me, even then I never wished you dead. I just wished never to see you again."

Gathering my bag, I walked out into the fading sunlight.

I trudged home feeling unutterably weary; thankful that our house was only a few streets away from the amphitheatre. It was lovely to walk into its quiet haven, away from the noisy crowds wending their way home in various stages of inebriation. The children were having their evening meal and Aliza was setting food out for the rest of us. They clamoured for all the gossip of the games, but I said I needed to go and clean up before I told them. As my tunic was coated in grime, blood and dust, they were happy to let me go.

Walking along to the washroom, I stripped completely, dumping my dirty clothes into the large sink before washing myself thoroughly in the smaller one. I rinsed my hair also, which felt gritty from all the dust. Once finished, I wrapped a large sheet around myself and slipped into our bedroom, digging some clean fresh clothes out of my cupboard. By the time I was dressed, I felt much better and combed my hair through, trying to untangle my unruly locks. I was so engrossed in this task, that I didn't hear footsteps along the corridor, or my husband entering the room.

Suddenly a hand removed the comb from mine and continued drawing it through my hair, steady sure stokes, carefully working through all the knots. It was lovely having him do this, very relaxing and so intimate. When he had finished, he kissed the back of my neck and handed the comb back. I smiled at him, catching my hair ready to twist it into its usual plait.

"Leave it loose, Hannah, just for once." Quietly.

"But it gets in the way." Plaintively.

"For me." I gazed at him for a long moment, before nodding my acquiescence. He grinned at me and winked. I watched as he changed and even though he had left his armour in the headquarters along with his sword, he still looked every inch the military general.

"My mother has sent word that she would like us to visit," his words interrupting my reverie.

"Oh," I said a little warily, "when?" He thought about it for a moment.

"I think she would like us to arrive in five days, she is having a house party, or some such thing for several guests and wants us to attend." I gaped at him.

"Several guests, like how many?"

"Probably twenty five or so, that seems to be her usual number. That'll include my sister and her family though."

"Twenty five?" I squeaked. "Are you kidding me?" I had, despite my best efforts, introduced the use of some questionable colloquialisms.

"No, why would I kid?"

"Twenty five people, all of whom I don't know; oh Max, this is a bad idea."

"Why?"

"Well, I'm not a Roman woman of status and we have children who are not all ours."

"Adopting children in Roman society is quite normal, many families do it, often to carry on the family name, it must be said, but they are usually treated well."

"I know but even though they were granted citizenship, our children are still Hebrew, how will your mother's friends take that?"

"It will be fine and the children will love it, all that space and fresh air and green grass."

I was flustered by this plan. I had met Maxentius' mother, Claudia, our daughter's namesake, when we were in Rome and she seemed very kind. She was tall, like her son and the epitome of elegant sophistication — the complete opposite of me in fact. We had not seen her since our arrival in Pompeii as she had stayed on in Rome over the winter. I had never met his sister, Antonia, who was married to someone in the government, but what he did or what his name was, I could not tell you. They had two children, who were a little older than ours.

Claudia, the elder, lived in a large villa outside of Pompeii along the Bay of Naples, one of many villas along this stretch of coast owned by wealthy families. Luxurious retreats from Rome, these holiday homes offered an escape from the city when it was too hot, too cold or too crowded.

"How long would she expect us to stay?"

"Oh, about a week I would think?"

"A week?" If anything, my voice went up another octave. "We can't be away for a week! I have responsibilities, you have a job and we have an Aliza and a Marcus." Maxentius chuckled.

"Well, they're invited of course and, I'm sure Tullius and Ennius can spare you for one week."

"Yes, but it's not that long since I was sick and I couldn't work then and I..." Maxentius shut me up, quite effectively by the simple method of kissing me. I struggled against him for a few seconds before giving in, enjoying the moment. The minute he stopped, I started to speak again desperately trying to come up with reasons why we couldn't go.

He put his finger on my lips.

"What are you so afraid of, my Hannah?" His eyes searched mine. Sighing, I tried to explain.

"I am not a woman of Rome. I have no airs and graces. I have no experience of how to behave in polite society and although I am educated, it was a very unusual education. I cannot play a musical instrument or quote from the Greek philosophers. I have lived with rebels; I treat gladiators and young sportsmen. I do not want to let you down."

He pulled me across the bed into his arms.

"You could never let me down, my love."

"Oh, I think we both know that's not true," I muttered against his chest. "I do not have the fancy words that high-born ladies use and do not understand the dance that they do with expressions and innuendo. What if they've heard about Tobias?

What if they've heard about my being dragged before the magistrate? This would do you no good at all."

"Hannah, I do not care about these societal expectations. I am a soldier and I love you. That is all there is to it, there is no more. We will attend this gathering, but if at any point it becomes uncomfortable, we shall leave. My mother knows me well; she will understand." I knew he had decided, so I capitulated but could not quite control the niggle of anxiety playing at the back of my mind.

We went through to the living area and told the children all about the games, leaving out the gory details. Maxentius said that there had been no trouble at all. Maybe the high profile of the soldiers put them off; maybe my three cellmates had decided this was not the event at which to cause mayhem. For whatever reason, the protestors had decided to give the games a miss. He was very relieved, but realised that it probably meant they had something else in the pipeline.

Marcus arrived and after sorting out the children for bed, I joined them for our usual evening meal; even Aliza sat with us for a change. I told her about the trip, but she said that she would prefer to stay here in Pompeii; she had many things planned and was not about to miss out on any of them. I respected her choice; it would not be easy for her to be in that kind of company. It also meant we didn't have to close up this house while we were away.

Surprised and delighted at being included in the invitation, Marcus was looking forward to staying at the villa. Apparently there were orchards and planted gardens; he couldn't wait to check them out, always on the lookout for new ideas. He plied Maxentius with questions about what was grown, did they change the planting cycle and how large were the grounds. Maxentius chuckled, holding his hands up in mock surrender, saying it was no use asking him since he really didn't have a clue and, diverted the conversation to the chicken coop that Marcus and Efraim were going to build. The two of them had spent hours designing the enclosure and had even started collecting wood.

Remembering Maxentius' talents on Masada, I asked whether he was going to help. He winked at me.

"I think I may prefer to observe from a distance; I know what those two are like once they get going. I do not want to interfere with genius." The thought of Maxentius being able to keep his nose out made us all laugh. He was the one with the talent where creating things from wood were concerned. We didn't need a palace, just a regular old coop would suffice, but I knew that's not what we would end up with. They would be very spoilt chickens.

Long after Marcus had left and long after Maxentius and I had gone to bed, I was still wide awake, despite the long day we'd had. I could not get my mind to shut down, so eventually I gave up and let it drift. I thought about the upcoming house party and began to plan what we would need to take. I knew we'd have to hire a wagon and horses, for although we three adults were used to riding, it would not be possible with three children and a lot of luggage.

Turning over I tried to settle. Maxentius, who was fast asleep by now, seemed to be aware of my wakefulness and pulled me to him. I snuggled against him, feeling his heartbeat against my back and hearing his steady breathing. Normally that would be enough to soothe me to sleep, but not this night. I could not understand my agitation; as far as I knew nothing catastrophic was due to happen for several months and this would just be a gathering of people. Okay, so they were probably all people of very high status, except me, all well versed in the ways of society, except me and all ready to judge me.

My thoughts stopped. Was that it? Did I expect to be judged and be found wanting? My background, life and behaviour were well outside Roman mores and I knew I didn't fit neatly into the category for women of the era. Was I worried for me, or for Maxentius? Just as I tried to fathom it out, exhaustion overtook my brain — finally and I fell asleep.

I was in the yellow room again. The woman was tossing in her sleep; she seemed very distressed and was muttering words that I could not understand. The tall man, who looked worried but not sad, was standing talking to another who was holding a slender clear instrument with a sharp point on one end. It reminded me of the needles I used to stitch wounds, only much finer. He leaned over and pushed the pointed end into the woman's arm. She shuddered but did not wake up and, as I watched, she stopped tossing. The tall man sat next to her on the bed and in a hauntingly familiar gesture, pulled her into his arms, cradling her head and rocking her as she settled.

Chapter Twenty Two

I bolted awake. It was still dark although it seemed less inky black suggesting that dawn was not far away. I could not understand what had woken me and, listening for a moment, thinking one of the children might be having a nightmare, but there was no sound; the house was silent. Shaking my head and assuming it must have been in my dreams, I lay back down, only to hear it again. A long, low rumbling, like distant thunder and I knew it was the mountain.

Getting out of bed carefully so as not to disturb Maxentius and throwing my mantel over my shoulders, I tiptoed through the house and out into the garden. Through the lightening sky, I could just make out Vesuvius. Smoke was drifting up from the peak, a little more than I'd noticed the day before, during the games, but nothing much. As I stood, a mild tremor ran under my bare feet, only discernible because everywhere was so still. If this had happened during the day, no one would have noticed.

How many people did I dare tell of this and when? It could only be a select few, for I could not change history, but neither could I deliberately abandon those closest to me to their fate without some warning. I would have to pick my time with care. Sighing, I retraced my footsteps, going back along to the bedroom. Maxentius stirred as I slipped back under the covers.

"Ooof, your feet are like ice; where have you been?"

"Just outside for a moment; I heard the mountain." He came awake then and I was aware that he was looking at me in the darkness.

"It was rumbling?" I nodded, then realised he probably couldn't tell.

"Yes and there was an earth tremor, but it is quiet again now. Go back to sleep, it is still early."

"Not sure I can now you've stuck your cold feet on my legs...brrrr" He shivered then caught me to him, kissing my nose.

"Gracious, Hannah, your face is cold too, how long were you out there?"

"Maybe five minutes, the rest of me is warm...oh 'cept my hands." Taking wicked delight in running my very chilly fingers down his warm chest.

"Oh it's like that, is it? Come here, minx." He wrapped his arms around me and proceeded to demonstrate a very effective method of warming me up, after which we slept and for me this time there were no dreams.

I knew the next few days would be busy, what with preparing for the trip to the country and making sure I did not neglect my usual duties. The day after the games, I went to the Gladiators' School to find out whether they needed me to help with those men who had died and to check on the injured combatants. I was directed to a long room, adjacent to the domestic quarters. Through the open door, I could see several long stone benches standing side by side, on top of which lay the bodies of the deceased. I took a deep breath and entered the room. Two of the other medici were already there, Gallus Blandinus and his colleague whose name I learned was Decimus Florianus Camillus. We greeted each other formally and then, in undertones, discussed who would do what; it seemed disrespectful to speak otherwise.

I asked whether either of them knew of the religious or cultural persuasions of the men on the slabs, but they both shook their head. I would be able to determine whether any one of them was Jewish, but beyond that I had nothing either. I knew, however, that if any one of these men was a Jew, custom dictated that they needed to be buried soon, within a day of their death; although I suddenly realised that such traditions were unlikely to apply to prisoners of war. I carried with me ritual ointments, myrrh and rosemary, as well as aloes, a sacred oil distilled from the resin of the Aloes wood tree, which although had medicinal properties, was used mainly in the burial ritual. However, it was a costly oil so I was sparing with it.

We carefully washed the bodies, removing all traces of blood and dirt. Their injuries were devastating and even if any one of them had survived the initial fight, he could not have lived. I was appalled all over again by the damage that one man could inflict on another for the amusement of a crowd. I noticed that three of the five who had died were Jewish and asked the two men whether they would allow me to cleanse and wrap their bodies according to tradition. They agreed and carried on preparing the remaining two.

They looked so young and I could not help but be reminded of Sergius. They had fought to save my country from the might of the Roman Empire and, having failed, were brought here to fight on a whole other level. What a waste! As I sprinkled the burial oils over the linen sheets in which we would encase their shattered bodies, I began quietly to croon the same lament I had sung the day we farewelled Sergius — a lament for the death of a soldier. Suddenly I realised that Gallus and Florianus had joined in. How did they know this eulogy? Our hushed voices harmonised and washed over the silence in the room, hopefully giving peace to the torn souls of these brave men.

Finally it was over and the bodies were wrapped in shrouds. I had no idea whether they would be buried or cremated; that was beyond my purview. I tucked a spring of rosemary into the folds of each shroud, placing my hand on each head as I did so. This was all we could do; the rest was up to Tullius. Coming out of the dim room into the bright sunlight made me blink and we three medici walked slowly over to where Petronius was waiting for me.

"How did you know of that lament?" I asked the two men as we made our way across the training yard — empty this morning while the men rested.

"We have heard it many times on the battlefield, Hannah, wife of Maxentius. It cannot be forgotten."

"You are military doctors?" I asked diffidently. They nodded, saying that on retirement from the army, they did not want to lose their skills, so had joined the Gladiators' School, making sure that those who lived and trained there had the best care.

I knew these men would have seen far worse than anything these gladiatorial fights could throw at them and I was in awe.

"Yet you have accepted me, a woman, into your circle. You have no idea how honoured I feel."

"This works both ways, my dear. You bring new skills and techniques and have introduced treatments and practices that we have not heard of. It is knowledge we should always share."

"I would like that very much." I smiled shyly and we all nodded our agreement.

The two older men left through the main door, but I still had patients to check on. One of the guards escorted me to Darius' cell, as both he and Mihai would need their injuries examining. I found them in cheerful mood — they had survived to fight another day. I spent quite some time cleaning their wounds, then rubbed salve into the deeper ones and any of the lacerations that bothered me. Once satisfied that I had checked every gash and cut, I re-bandaged those that needed it and said I would be back to check on them in two days. They both smiled and thanked me. A cordial relationship was growing between us and I had begun to feel very protective of these prisoners whose only crime was to be from a conquered nation.

I repeated my actions with all of those whose wounds I had treated the previous day. Some were in worse shape than others and I made sure their injuries were properly dealt with, but I did not think any of them would die. That was my hope anyway. Once my rounds were completed, I made my way back to the lanista's office to apprise him of my plans.

First, though, I told him that we had finished preparing the bodies of his deceased gladiators. He seemed genuinely saddened by their deaths and confirmed they would be dealt with that day. Regardless of custom, it was not healthy to have five bodies left for too long. Then I advised him that although I would be back in two days, after that I had to go away to a family villa. His amusement at my reluctance to attend the gathering was obvious, but he merely wished us an enjoyable time. I glared at him and possibly harrumphed, but he shook his head, laughter twitching at his lips and shooed me out.

Petronius and I walked back along the quiet pathways, chatting about the games. Despite his previous enthusiasm, I think he felt much like I did, as he muttered that once you had seen it in real life on a battlefield, it lost its entertainment value. I thanked him for escorting me home and said that I would see him the day after next. He smiled and went back to his regular responsibilities. I entered the house trying to work out which I should deal with first, adults or children.

I went with children; it seemed to be the easier. As they were out, I was able to go through their clothes unsupervised. If Claudia or Liora had been there, it would have taken me twice as long, although Efraim didn't much care about what he wore as long as it fitted him. I made three piles of clothes. Before we left Masada I'd had Maxentius fashion several large boxes out of wood, which were secured with long leather straps. They weren't the most practical of pieces but you could fit much more in them than the leather satchels or rolls that seemed to be the only other style of waterproof luggage. We would be able to fit everything into two of the smaller boxes, which I dragged in from one of the storerooms.

Once I'd sorted the children's clothes, I did the same for Maxentius and myself. Hauling all my dresses out of the cupboard, I sifted through until I had found the best ones. I intended to wear my usual tunic and undershift for the most part, but conceded that I should take several of my more fashionable outfits as well. The current trend seemed to be either cream or white, which I had shunned in favour of a mix of pastels and vibrant shades. I preferred colour in my life and since I neither knew nor cared about the current fashions, I wore what I liked, not what society decided I should wear. I just hoped my choices would not cause embarrassment for Maxentius' family.

Maxentius was easy: his tunics were pretty much all the same and I lifted out most of them, adding a couple of togas. To this growing pile of clothes, I added underthings, cloaks, boots, sandals and house slippers. I had no idea what the weather would be like so I covered all the possibilities.

Halfway through this task my husband came home to tell me he had finished for the day and asked me would I like to take a walk with him? He guffawed when he saw the pile of things I had started to pack into the first box.

"How long do you think we are going for, my Hannah?" He laughed. "It looks like we'll be away for a year." How rude, I thought, after all my hard work. I glowered at him and pointedly turned my back, while I continued to place clothes neatly into the box. He came around the bed and picked me up, carrying me out of the room and dumping me unceremoniously at the front door.

176

"Hey, I was busy." Trying to retain a modicum of control.

"It'll still be there when we get back." He chuckled, kissing me soundly. "Come on, woman, the day is wasting." Giving up, I grabbed my cloak and followed him out into the street.

It was still mild, the bright blue of the sky taking on a paler hue as the afternoon wore on. The tall pines rustled in the breeze and the air was full of birds singing and insects buzzing, heralding warmer days. I couldn't remember the last time just the two us were together like this; it seemed long ago. Maxentius held my hand as we strolled down the road towards the Forum and we chatted about this and that; nothing important just the everyday conversation of two people whose lives were bound together. Should we take some kind of gift with us to his mother's villa? From where would we hire the wagon and horses? Had Claudia stopped sucking her thumb? How did we persuade Efraim that spiders do not make good pets? You know, this and that.

The Forum, when we reached it, was not as busy now at the end of the afternoon, but the food stalls were still there and we bought some sweet rolls filled with honey and nuts. They were delicious and we walked along eating them, the honey making us very sticky. Thankfully, at regular intervals along the pathways were water fountains, where we could rinse our hands. I felt as though all my responsibilities had been taken away. I forgot about children and house parties and gladiators and erupting mountains. This time was just for us, cherished moments together.

We walked as far as the entrance to the port. It was bustling, even at this time of day; a continuous trail of merchants bringing their wares up the long steep path either by donkey or cart. The sun sparkled on the water, the bay spread out before us, dotted with boats of all sizes. The Roman naval fleet, based at Misenum about thirty miles along the coast, sat at anchor towering over the merchant vessels coming in and out of the port. It was all colour and movement and noise. We watched for a long time, Maxentius with his arm around my shoulders keeping me close to his side. It was a magical afternoon.

Eventually, reality invaded our idyll and we turned for home. We didn't hurry though; it was not evening yet and the sun was still making its way towards the horizon to set in a ball of flaming glory out over the sea. By the time we got back, everyone else was already there. Marcus and Aliza were sorting out the meal and the children were playing in the larger garden at the back of the house. Marcus and Efraim had finished the kite, so I fancied there might have been some testing underway.

"Well, hello you two; knew as soon as food was being laid out you would appear," Marcus said laughingly.

"Of all the cheek." I grinned, shoving Marcus in the shoulder — well upper arm actually, he being tall like my husband. "We should have stayed out for the evening, Maxentius; it seems we are most predictable. After all, there was plenty of tasty food to choose from near the Forum."

"They're only jealous, my love. We have had a lovely afternoon with no cares while Marcus had to do reports." I giggled at Marcus' expression and went to hang up my cloak, changing into my house shoes while I was at it.

We had an uproarious evening, for no reason that I could think of, except that it seemed everyone was in a holiday mood, despite the fact that it was still four days before we would set off. We finally banished the children a good two hours after their normal bedtime and sank into the chairs in front of the fire, which we still needed in the cool of the evenings. I breathed a sigh of relief.

"Peace and quiet at last. What on earth has got into them tonight? Crackers."

"Just happy, my love," smiled Maxentius, passing me a goblet of warm calda. I grinned back, wrapping my hands around the beaker and inhaling the spicy aroma.

"I need this." The two men chuckled as I sipped, letting it trickle down my throat, warming me right down to my stomach. "Oh and it is very good."

We made more plans for the upcoming trip. Marcus had already organised the wagon and two horses. There was a stable about two blocks along from our house and he had come to an arrangement with the owner. We would set out in the early morning, hopefully arriving by mid-afternoon. It was not a great distance to the villa and the roads were excellent, but travel took time, especially with children and we had set aside the day so that we could enjoy it. Marcus had hired a rheda carucca, a covered wagon, which had bench seats and space for the luggage. It meant that the small fry might be able to sleep for some of the journey — if that was possible over the rattling and the noise.

Plans made as far as we could, we said our goodnights. I had some free time the next day, but I hoped to visit the young men over at the Palaestra to see how well they had recovered after the games, especially the one with the broken wrist. I quickly packed my satchel, a beautiful leather bag that Maxentius had presented me with after I had been unwell. It had lots of space for my ointments and bandages and, very importantly, was waterproof. It was so much better than the cloth bag I had been using and I was very proud of it.

Finishing my preparations, I blew out the lamps in the main room and joined Maxentius in the bedroom. He had cleared us a space to sleep by dint of shoving all my nice neat piles of clothes onto the floor. I looked at the mess and glared at him knowing I should tidy it all up, but was too tired to bother. He did not appear to be repentant at all; simply grinned at my expression and carried on undressing. The fire was dying down but neither one of us felt the need to add another log; the room was comfortable and our bedcovers were made of thick materials. I changed into my night slip and snuggled between the sheets.

"What a lovely day. You should sneak away from work more often. I could get very used to it."

"Wish I could, my love, but it was a rare gift this afternoon and more precious for it." He kissed me very satisfactorily before blowing out our lamp. The glow from the fire sent shadows flickering around the room. I turned over, curling my back against Maxentius' chest. He wrapped his arms around me, resting his chin on my head. Safe and warm, we slept.

Chapter Twenty Three

The following few days were a blur, the students at the Palaestra had recovered well from their exertions at the games. The young man with the broken wrist was still in great discomfort and I told him it would be several weeks before it was properly healed. To ease his pain, I fashioned a splint for him to immobilise the joint, strapping it snugly with bandages, showing Ennius Balbinus, the trainer, how to do it in case it needed replacing while we were away.

Of the remainder, some needed bruise ointment and one or two had grazes and scratches that required attention, but nothing serious. They were all such fit and healthy young men and their trainer looked after them well. Of course it helped that they were part of the elite, so had the best of everything, but they were good kids and seemed to get a lot out of their training sessions. The injured gladiators were on the road to recovery and the few we were worried about would be watched over by the other medici. I felt able to leave them with a clear conscience.

At home, I washed everything that wasn't nailed down, dried and packed them, then re-packed, because I just had to check everything twice more and the house had been cleaned within an inch of its life. Finally, by the morning of the fifth day after the games, we were ready. Intending to set out before the sun rose, we had said goodbye to Aliza the previous night, so we didn't have to disturb her when we left. Dawn had just broken as we put the luggage in and we had packed food so that we could eat on the journey rather than try to persuade the children to have breakfast so early.

We had moved the bench seats in the wagon so that they faced each other, pushing them together to form a makeshift bed. Laying a thick comforter over the seats, we coaxed the children into the wagon and once they were lying alongside each other, covered them with a couple of blankets. Warm and snug, they were asleep again in minutes. Marcus rode the second horse and I sat next to Maxentius while he drove.

It was a lovely morning, the sky was clear, the sun was coming up and we were on our way. It took us a little while to leave the conglomeration that was Pompeii and its outskirts, but soon we were in the countryside, just the birds and us. There was very little traffic at this time and most of that was made up of people travelling on foot. We made good time and stopped for food after about two hours. Maxentius reckoned it should take us about five or six hours to reach his mother's villa, road conditions and small children's requirements permitting.

The day was rather fun actually. I persuaded Marcus to let me ride the second horse for some of the journey. I loved the feeling of flying over the grass. I was careful not to tire the creature but she was a beautiful ride. The children stayed awake after their first meal and I taught them how to play 'I spy,' which kept them going for ages. As the day wore on, though, fed up with being confined to the wagon, they began to get rather fractious; so I told them they could run alongside.

We were travelling much faster than their small legs could go, but Maxentius was happy to slow the horse down to a walk and let his children tire themselves out trying to keep up. Claudia gave up first, begging for a piggyback, which I provided, then Liora demanded that Marcus let her ride the horse. Efraim was determined not to stop, but even he conceded defeat after a good hour of exercise. He was absolutely exhausted when we lifted him back into the wagon and the three of them soon nodded off as we began to last stage of our journey.

It was mid-afternoon and the day was still warm when we pulled up to a very long driveway.

"Well ... this is it," said Maxentius, making it sound like he was showing us a bread roll, not his family estate. He turned the horse into the drive and we trotted along gazing at the splendidly manicured grounds. I knew that these villas were large but I'd had no idea how large. Marcus was waxing lyrical about the gardens we were passing, but I was dumbstruck — a very unusual occurrence, let me tell you.

Finally, we reached the front of the house, which seemed quite unprepossessing after what we'd just driven through, but even that would surprise us. I lifted three very tired children out of the wagon. Claudia wouldn't let me put her down, shyness making her cling to me. She was a tall child for her age and heavy; I couldn't carry her for very long. Two grooms appeared, one taking the reins of the second horse, while the other hopped up onto the wagon and began to drive it around the side of the villa. I wasn't really sure what we should do, but Maxentius just sauntered through the doorway, shouting for his mother.

We followed him into an enormous atrium, whose impluvium, or rainwater catchment pool, was bigger than our bedroom. There was so much light and space. I waited with the children, Claudia still hanging on like a limpet. Marcus offered to take her from me, but she wouldn't even go to him and I was struggling to hold her. Maxentius had disappeared through the opening at the far end of the atrium from where we could hear sounds of conversation and laughter and suddenly a rush of people came towards us.

Liora and Efraim hid behind Marcus and me as the group approached us. Maxentius' mother, her face wreathed in smiles, enveloped Claudia and me in a hug, then swung her namesake out of my arms crooning to her and telling her about all the fun they were going to have. I was astonished; Claudia just went off with her grandmother, without so much as a backward glance. I stood there gaping as Maxentius came up to me with his sister and her husband. My husband grinned at my expression and, without giving me chance to catch my breath, introduced me to Antonia, his sister and her husband, Julius.

They seemed like lovely people, welcoming us all with smiles and hugs. Antonia's children, Julia and Antonius, came running through and dragged Liora and Efraim with them to join in whatever games they had been playing. I was rather overwhelmed but in a nice way. We were swept through the atrium into a large room, which opened onto a stunning balcony, or exedra. The mosaic floor was exquisite and my classical history art and architecture seminars popped into my head as I was admiring it. My lecturer would have loved this. I really wished I had my camera with me — and quite how would you explain that, Hannah? I admonished myself. The wall paintings were just as beautiful giving the whole space the feeling that we were in a lush garden.

The view was spectacular; the villa was cut into the slope of a hill, which ran all the way down to the bay. There were three levels in total, each one jutting a little further out giving the impression of deep steps and a very unusual design for the period. The lower level held all the bedrooms, the middle was where the family normally lived and the upper level, where we were standing, was for entertaining. There was a bathhouse, a swimming pool, a peristyle courtyard and the domestic quarters. Surrounding all this were the gardens and Maxentius told me that the estate stretched as far as the eye could see. It was vast.

Marcus was totally enamoured; he was already deep in conversation with Maxentius' mother about what they grew, the seasonal changes and whether he could meet the gardeners. Claudia, as she had asked us to call her, laughed and, like her son said she had no idea but he was welcome to spend as much time in the gardens as he liked. Marcus grinned and thanked her, turning to admire the view laid out in front of us.

After a very pleasant interlude when we had all manner of refreshments pressed on us, I realised that it would be a good idea to change and unpack. Also I was very weary and Maxentius, glancing across the room, must have noticed how tired I looked. He murmured something to his mother who also looked over and nodded. He came over and, grasping my hands, pulled me up out of the chair, placing his arm around my waist.

"Mother has told me which rooms we have been allocated. Would you like to freshen up?" I smiled gratefully at him.

"I really would," I whispered, still rather dazed by everything. He smiled down at me and asked whether the children wanted to come and see where they would be sleeping. Julia and Antonius wanted to show them too, so the seven of us made our way along numerous corridors and down several flights of stairs to the bedrooms. I didn't think I'd ever work out this maze of a house.

Julia opened a door halfway along one of the hallways into a lovely room containing three beds, saying that this was for our children and that Maxentius and I were in the adjoining room. They all tumbled in, choosing which bed they wanted and checking out what else was in the room. We left them to it and carried on to the next door. Our room was huge, nearly as big as the quarters we'd had on Masada. A large bed sat on a raised platform at one end of the room, with a couch and table at the other end near the large picture window. The fresh air was ruffling the curtains and the view was as incredible as the one from two floors above us. The sun was beginning to set now, a golden ball sinking into the sea, its fiery rays kissing the earth. I was captivated.

"Oh Maxentius, you are so lucky to have grown up in this place. How did you ever find it in yourself to leave?" He grinned.

"I was a young man who wanted to see more of the world than this corner and the army seemed like the best way to do that."

"But you're in it forever, virtually. Wouldn't the life of a merchant have been better?"

"I was not interested in being a merchant and as the son of an equestrian family, politics or the army was the only real option and if I hadn't joined the army, we would never have met, my Hannah." He smiled his slow toe-curling smile. I walked over to where he was leaning against the couch and hugged him close.

"Which would have been a travesty," I said as I kissed him and nestled into his chest.

His arms enveloped me and we stood together, enjoying the last of the daylight. Shadows were lengthening, the colours mutating from vibrant greens to quiet greys and it was so peaceful. We were used to a bustling city, which was generally noisy for most of the evening. Here, all was hushed, nothing but the breeze rustling through the trees. Sighing I moved to start unpacking, even if all I managed was to find something fresh to change into for the evening. Maxentius went to find the children before they could destroy that beautiful bedroom and brought them along for a wash.

There was a large washbowl and pitchers of cool water on a stand in a little alcove. I cleaned the children's face and hands and persuaded them to change into clothes rather less dusty than the ones they were wearing; then sent them to find Julia and Antonius, who apparently had the room at the other end of the hallway. Then I stripped off my travelling dress and treated myself to a thorough wash, rubbing sweet oil scented with rose over my skin and through my hair.

Rooting around in one of the trunks, I found one of my new dresses. It was a deep emerald green undershift with sleeves that fell to my elbows complemented by a pale lime green sleeveless over tunic. The silky material was almost translucent, the colours dissolving into one another and I loved it. I tidied my hair into a plait, but in deference to Maxentius' mother, piled it up on my head, leaving a few loose strands to curl around my face.

There was a polished metal mirror in this room and I was quite pleased with my efforts. Maxentius' expression when he came around to where I was dressing was enough to tell me he liked it.

"My beautiful Hannah, do we really need to go and be sociable? I would be delighted to stay here and slowly remove all this finery." I grinned at him, batting him away.

"Oh, and after all my efforts; plenty of time for that later; it would be most unfair on your mother if we failed to show up for the meal." He sighed dramatically and changed into a fresh tunic while I sat on one of the chairs and waited for him, unwilling to try to find my way back to the main part of the house on my own.

The evening was very enjoyable; there was no awkwardness amongst us, even though I had never met most of them until this day. The food was delicious and it just kept coming; I lost count of the variety and number of dishes. There was wine, which I was informed was from their own vines, something that attracted Marcus' attention again. As the evening wore on, however, I could see that the children were flagging. Several times I had noticed Claudia droop into her platter; it wouldn't be long before she was fast asleep.

As soon as it seemed appropriate, I quietly asked Claudia, the elder, whether she would mind if I took the children to bed. She smiled and assented. Julia and Antonius looked just as tired, Antonia motioning that she would come with me and we could get them all settled. With as little disturbance as possible, bearing in mind my three had to kiss everybody before they departed, we hustled them away to the bedrooms. It was a good job Antonia came with me, for there is no doubt I would have become lost.

As we reached the lower level, I realised that there was a serious discussion going on between the five cousins. Then Antonius turned back to his mother and me, asking whether it would be possible for Efraim to share his room and for Julia to go in with Liora and Claudia? Antonia and I looked at each other. I murmured under my breath that it was fine with me, but I understood if she would prefer to keep her children to their usual night-time routine. Antonia grinned and said she thought it was a fine idea; it would do Antonius good to have a male friend to talk to and play with, away from his sister who tended to boss him around.

We nodded at the small fry and they whooped their way to the bedrooms, Julia running into hers and grabbing everything she thought she might need, while Efraim did the same in his room. There was a chaotic few moments while all the children did their best to trip each other up in their haste to sort their sleeping out arrangements but finally they were settled. I got my three into their night things before washing their face and hands. I also made sure they had rubbed their teeth with the salt and mentha mixture I had created for this purpose.

It was something I had first made while on Masada. I was used to brushing my teeth but back in this era there was no toothpaste or toothbrushes. Despite the very healthy diet we adhered to, I still worried about the risk of bad teeth, so had come up with this as a method of keeping teeth and gums healthy. It seemed to work and the mentha was an excellent way to freshen up the mouth.

Antonia was intrigued, so I explained what it was and she asked whether I would mind if she tried some on her children. I was more than happy and scooped out an amount for her to keep in their wash area. Since Julia and Antonius wanted to do everything my three did, they happily complied with their mother's wish. Eventually they were all in their respective rooms and tucked in, although how long that would last I wasn't sure. They did look quite tired though and I hoped it wouldn't be too long before they were fast asleep.

Chapter Twenty Four

Antonia and I made our way back to the others who had spread out around the exedra. We sat for a little longer, chatting about our lives. Claudia knew of my work with the Gladiators' School and wanted to know how I was faring there. Antonia was fascinated that I was a physician and demanded to know all the gory details of wound treatments. I guessed Maxentius must have told his family something of my history, for they seemed rather well informed. The men talked about whatever it is men discuss, presumably politics, the latest uprising requiring the military to subdue it, problems within Pompeii and Rome.

Claudia also told me the plans for the rest of the week. Each day would bring more guests, some staying here, some already staying in neighbouring villas and on the last day, there would be a large party for everyone. I must have looked rather anxious, for she assured me that all her friends were quite lovely and dying to meet me. I didn't believe that for one minute, but it was nice to hear.

I caught Maxentius' eye and he knew I needed my bed. It was very late and our day had started before dawn. We made our excuses and I thanked them all for making us so welcome, then strolled back to our bedroom. I leant against the window for a long time, gazing at the stars. Here we could see them almost as well as we had been able to on Masada. The night sky was full of them.

Dragging myself away, I tried to tidy the room so I wouldn't have much to do the next day, but found I was too tired to concentrate. Maxentius eventually removed the dress I had folded and refolded several times, laid it on the storage cupboard and drew me over to the bed. Pulling my clothes over my head, he gently laid me down, drawing the exquisitely made sheets and thick quilt up over me. I didn't even feel his kiss on my cheek slumber had already claimed me.

Surprisingly, I enjoyed the next few days. The friends that Claudia had invited were, for the most part, delightful. There was more food and wine than I had ever seen and the meals went on for hours. Maxentius and I managed to escape the formalities now and again, either to enjoy a walk through the estate, or to take the horses on long rides. I'm sure some of the guests thought we were crazy, but it was exhilarating galloping over the fields. We even found a way down to the water's edge and rode along the beach. Those few hours of private time were what kept me sane.

Marcus, as expected, spent every spare moment in the gardens, hassling the staff about what they were planting, how to treat them, when to prune. However, he could not avoid the evening meals and was always surrounded by a gaggle of women, who flirted outrageously with him. He was a good looking man, his hair and eyes a rich dark brown, nearly as tall as Maxentius and with the very slightly rough edge all soldiers seemed to have. He bore the attention with unfailing good humour and treated all of his admirers with the utmost respect.

I had discovered that some of the men were to be avoided once they had imbibed more than they should have done, but I soon worked out who had wandering hands when tipsy. There also seemed to be a tacit agreement that whatever went on in dark corners was acceptable regardless of marital status. I was perplexed at this kind of behaviour. If Maxentius chased any women, never mind someone's wife, I'd have punched his lights out and as a wife I would be mortified if my husband thought it acceptable to pursue another's partner.

We discussed it one evening as we were dressing, me fearing I might lose my temper and break the bounds of acceptable behaviour. He told me that it was quite normal in certain circles, at which point I was very clear about what would happen to him if he dared follow suit.

"I have quite enough on my hands with you, my Hannah, I have no desire to be caught up with any of these other females."

"Good, I'd hate to bruise my knuckles." I grinned at him. He chuckled, kissing me soundly.

I had decided I should wear one of my more fashionable outfits. The under tunic was in deep peacock blue, with an ice blue stola or sleeveless tunic caught at the shoulders by very thin straps. The stola was made overly long and had to be hooked up under a belt, the folds forming what looked like another layer of material. It was quite an annoying outfit in all honesty, but I felt I should conform at some point during the festivities. I had tried, without much success, to style my hair, but Maxentius asked me to wear it loose, so I just caught up the long strands at the side of my face, twisting and pinning them onto the top of my head. Securing the twists in place with a long thin curved band made of some kind of gold effect metal; the remainder cascaded in dark curls down my back.

"I'm not sure this is a good idea my love, it will get very untidy." I smiled, as Maxentius ran his fingers through it, entwining them in the curls and trapping me against him.

"Oh, I think this is a very good idea," he almost purred, "I will have fun untangling it later."

"Hey..." I said, disengaging myself, "...behaviour like that will not get us to this evening's entertainment." I winked at him.

"More's the pity." He sighed. We were both finding the endless parties and socialising quite enervating, this lifestyle being very much outside of our comfort zone.

"Only a couple of days left, then we can go home to our quiet, boring lives."

This soiree was the last one to be held in the evening, the next day would be the big finale, an all-day extravaganza, just the thought of which gave me a headache. How did these people afford such luxurious affairs? It was during this visit that I realised how big the gap was between those with money and those without and I understood a little more about why those without felt so powerless.

We made our way to the upper level; the huge room with its glorious exedra looked very sumptuous. Women in beautiful dresses wafted around the room, chatting in small groups, or lounging on the sofas. Most of the men had chosen to wear togas over their tunics and were leaning against the walls, or fireplaces, or the edge of the balcony; their languid attitudes creating a picture of sophisticated gentility. The noise was muted; not much wine had been drunk yet. Food was carried around on platters, so that guests could try a bit of everything without having to move. There was also a long table laden with food at one end of the room, if one desired more than just a bite.

I gripped Maxentius' hand.

"Don't you dare leave me until Antonia comes," I muttered. "I cannot face these people on my own." Maxentius looked down at me and smiled, lifting my hand and kissing my palm. I stared into his eyes and for a split second there was just the two of us. Then the moment was broken as a flurry of people gathered us up into their group, demanding to know everything about us.

Uncomfortable sharing my private life with people I have never met, I stood quietly next to my husband letting him take charge of the conversation and it seemed that he knew some of these people rather well. After a little while, I began to relax, especially when Antonia came in and swept me away from Maxentius into a group of younger women, all of whom she knew and all of whom had children of similar ages to ours. The party was going very well, food and wine were flowing and the room was full of light and noise.

Sometime around the middle of the evening, I went downstairs to check on the children, who had not been included in this party. They were all in the room next to ours, happily playing what looked like a very complicated game. I sat with them for a little while and then having kissed them all, told them not to be too long before getting into bed and left them to it. They had been very good these last few days: playing outside, getting under the feet of all the garden staff and learning to ride horses. This was the first evening they had even been awake after their regular bedtime.

Slowly making my way back to the party I met up with Marcus who was taking a break from the crowd in the atrium.

"Escaping, are we?" I grinned at him. He rolled his eyes at me.

"It's all just a bit exhausting," he chuckled. "Worse than being on a battle field." I laughed at his rueful expression. We sat chatting for a time; it was a lovely cool space, only dimly lit compared with the main rooms. The wind had picked up and I could see clouds scudding across the sky through the large opening in the roof. Thunder rumbled in the distance and I made a mental note to check on the children if it got closer.

Just as I was about to rejoin the guests, I heard my name and, thinking someone wanted me, turned in the direction of their voice. My footsteps were halted as I heard her next words.

"I cannot believe Claudia allows her in the house. She is a Jewess, one of those Zealots from Jerusalem. She should be a slave, or better still dead, not the wife of an army general." I looked back at Marcus in shock; he grimaced and, standing, moved towards me. Who was this woman and how did she know so much about me? My first instinct was to confront whoever was speaking; she obviously did not care who heard her, as her voice was not hushed. I heard a murmured reply, but could not make it out.

Determined to put a stop to it, I began walking towards the speaker, but her discontented tone made me pause again as she began to reveal her version of my life, her words echoing back to me through the atrium. Yet again I was being called a whore, only this time in front of genteel company. She knew about the incident in the cell and the death of my brother; still she kept talking. I couldn't believe what I was hearing. Who on earth was this woman and from whom had she gleaned her information? I was thankful that Maxentius' family knew all about me and that our children were in bed out of earshot. I turned to speak to Marcus about it, but he'd gone. I felt panic rising. What should I do?

Just as I was thinking this, the woman started talking about Maxentius and how I had ruined his life, that he should divorce me and find a proper Roman wife, one who could provide him with a son and heir. It was becoming harder to hear her. The approaching storm was drowning out some of her words, which felt like blows and unconsciously I lifted my hands to ward them off. Someone else started to speak, a calm measured voice and whatever that person was saying caused a hush to fall over the room.

I didn't want to hear; all I wanted was to get away but there were so many people. I couldn't walk through to the exedra; I would have to pass them all. Thinking I would find a quiet place on one of the other floors, I turned, stumbling a little in my hurry to escape. Raising my head to see where I was going, my eyes locked with those of my husband who was coming in from the far side of the room, Marcus at his side. I smiled rather sadly at him and slipped away.

I didn't know where to go or what to do and realising the closest door would take me outside, took it. I stood in the darkness, buffeted by the wind, which howled through the pines, tugging at my dress and tearing at my hair. There was no moon, but the lightning illuminated the pathways. The maelstrom bore down on me, bringing with it a cloudburst. I lifted my face hoping the rain would wash away her invective, which was still whirling around my head. My life on Masada, my work as a healer and my unusual status, how did that become twisted into my being a harlot who had tricked a Roman soldier into marriage, ruining his life into the bargain.

Just as I found the path that would lead down to the bay, the cloudburst became a deluge and I heard Maxentius call my name. Turning, I saw him and Marcus coming towards me. As they did so, I felt the earth tremble; my vision began to recede and the world to spin. I could feel everything fading away and instinctively I reached for my husband, but my fingers touched another's face, similarly featured. A tall man in a room full of soft light and I fell towards him.

Someone was holding my hand, it felt comforting, safe and I was warm and cosy. I was out of the storm — that was something. I concentrated on trying to work out where I was. The last thing I remembered was touching a man's face, but whose? I was almost afraid, would I be looking into Maxentius' face? Or would it be Max? And if so, how long had I been away?

If it was my Max, I knew it likely that I would be back with him for only a short while; the ties binding me to ancient Pompeii were not ready to be loosened yet. There was no help for it — I opened my eyes. I was indeed back in my own time and I was still in bed — good grief! — how long had I been ill? Max was sitting on a wicker chair next to the bed, holding my hand. He looked to be snoozing, but as I turned my head he opened his eyes and I squeezed his hand gently. He smiled his toe-curling smile and my heart thudded in response.

"Morning, Sunshine. About time you woke up. Whatever that doctor gave you certainly knocked you out." I gazed at him for a long moment, drinking him in. It was months, in my head, since I had slipped between worlds and I worried that I'd forgotten what he looked like. I was pleased to note that I hadn't and that all my usual feelings rushed back in to warm my heart.

"Hey there," I whispered, "I've missed you." He stared back at me and I willed him to understand what I meant.

"How long were you...have you...did you...?" He struggled to finish the sentence.

"Around six months, I think. How long, was I...have I been...the time...?" I had the same problem; I wasn't sure either of us wanted to know.

He seemed hesitant, so I tightened my grip on his hand and pulled him towards me. He sat on the edge of the bed, searching my face, looking for answers hidden beneath the surface. I smiled pensively.

"It's okay love, I can tell you what's been happening, but I'm pretty sure it's not over yet." I wanted him next to me, his arms around me, anchoring me to him. My head was still in both worlds and I was finding it hard to separate the two. I pushed myself up on the abundance of pillows and waited until Max had made himself comfortable, then I snuggled into his arms.

"So, how long was I out of it?"

"Two days." I stared at him in astonishment.

"Are you sure?"

"Well 'course I'm sure, it's only Thursday morning, you fell ill on Tuesday."

"How many times did the doctor come?"

"Three. We could not get the fever to come down. He'll be around again in an hour or so to check on you, although I think you're on the mend." He smiled down at me hugging me close

"Only two days; that seems so weird. So much has happened and I've missed out on all the fun at the site." My voice was still rather husky.

"Oh, they've extended the work for another two weeks and we're welcome to stay on here if we want. Geoff seems keen to include us, if you think you're going to be up for it."

"It's just a cold Max, I'm sure I'll be fine."

"It's not just a cold, sweetheart, the doctor said you'd caught a nasty chest infection, which is why you ran a fever."

"Have you managed to get to the site?" I asked. He shook his head.

"No, I didn't want to leave you, but that's okay, if we're here a bit longer there'll still be plenty for me to do. They've been keeping me updated with texts. Like I said, it's only been two days." Two days, that did not seem possible, although I remembered that my six years on Masada had equated to about four weeks in this world. Time ran altogether differently.

I sighed a monumental sigh, realising once again how complicated my life was. Max turned my face to his and gazed down at me, his green eyes darkening with an emotion I could not read. I stared back, feeling my heart quicken. He leaned towards me, tilting my head ever so slightly and brushing my lips with his. He pulled away and a quiver rippled through me as I continued to stare at him.

"Tell me," he muttered, running his thumb along my throat.

"All of it?" I questioned, as he kissed me again, feather-light.

"All of it." I still refused to break eye contact and I could feel Max's heartbeat increasing.

"Right now? Or is there something more important? Something that can't wait?" I whispered against his mouth, feeling him tremble as I kissed him back.

"Maybe give it a minute." His mouth descended on mine, capturing it, possessing it. My response was immediate; I leaned into him, winding my hands around his neck and pulling him closer. I needed to feel this passion; it would be my lifeline when my other world drew me back. Max slid down to lie full length on the bed, moulding me to him, as best he could with all the blankets between us.

Just as I thought I might drown in his kiss, he drew back with a shuddering breath. Kissing my nose, he pushed errant strands of hair off my face.

"You have been sick, my love; I cannot in all conscience let this go any further."

"I know, but it was so lovely. Just hold me then; surely that must be allowed. I'm pretty certain it's in the rule book for convalescents." He chuckled, obliging me.

"You are a minx, Hannah," his words so familiar. Another face swam over my vision. I pushed it away; not yet; it would be soon but not quite yet.

Chapter Twenty Five

A little while later the doctor came and examined me, pronouncing himself much happier with my progress, but would pop around again in the evening just to be on the safe side. Telling me to keep warm and drink lots of fluids, he patted my hand in an avuncular manner and left, after a quick word with Max. All of a sudden I was tired again, but was really fed up with being in bed. I asked Max whether it would be okay, if I went through and lay on the sofa for a while, that I'd take the comforter and pillow and that it would just be nice to look at a different set of walls.

Max couldn't see it being a problem and carried everything through, coming back to help me. I was sure I'd be fine, but as I went to stand, found that my legs were a tad wobbly. He guided me through to the lounge and settled me onto the couch, making sure I was well wrapped up. The fire was lit, throwing warmth throughout the room. It was a dull day, but just being able to look straight out at the garden made me feel brighter.

Max made me a hot lemon drink and then sat next to me, shifting my pillows so I could nestle against him.

"Okay love, before you drop off again, do you think you can tell me some of what's been happening?" I nodded and began to describe the events that had shaped my days. I explained that I had been very sick in my other world and that maybe somehow this infection was connected. It sounded nonsensical as I said it, but normal was measured on a whole other scale in my life. I told him about the gladiatorial games, the fight between Darius and Tobias, the deaths of the prisoners and then finally about the house party.

I hesitated as I was telling him about this, as it was still very close; in fact, as far as I was aware still going on in my other world — oh you know what I mean. I explained about the woman and her comments, about how I'd run out of the villa into a storm, but I couldn't finish the story.

"I just needed to try to clear my head. No, not quite true. In reality I was running away, although I have no idea where to. Her words were like poison, dripping into the ears of all those listening. How was I supposed to respond? She was destroying everything and I didn't even know her." My voice, still croaky, was rising in my anxiety, making me cough. Max hugged me, waiting until the bout stopped.

"Hush, my love, it will work itself out. How could she destroy everything? It's not like Maxentius doesn't already know everything about you...her...Hannah." He searched my face. "What are you afraid of, that some nasty piece of work could split them up? Hannah, sweetheart, have some faith in him, he fought against all the odds to have her, to marry her, do you think he would ever allow anything to ruin what they have?" I knew he was right and as I nestled back against Max's chest, feeling the steady beat of his heart, my anxiety began to subside.

I spent the rest of the day resting on the sofa, watching some television, which was most strange after living without this kind of technology for what, in my life, had seemed like months. I tried to read my book, but couldn't focus on the words, so I gave that up. It was nice just relaxing, not having to concentrate on anything and having Max there with me. We talked and while I snoozed, he read; it was a peaceful sort of a day, one for healing.

Even so, by the evening I was feeling rather the worse for wear; my head was pounding and my chest wheezing. When the doctor came back, he was more than a little concerned and suggested one more injection. Whatever he had been giving me previously had ensured a settled night without me tossing and turning so, reluctantly, I agreed biting my lip as he administered the medication. He had a few more words with Max, then said he'd be back the following evening.

After he had gone, I went back to bed, knowing that the injection would knock me out sooner rather than later. Max helped me get settled and then curled up next to me with his book.

"Where have you been sleeping?" I asked curiously.

"Right here."

"What, in the chair or in the bed?"

"The chair, silly; why?"

"You can't keep doing that, you need to get a decent night's sleep. Surely there's a bed in the spare room?"

"Yes but you might..."

"Never mind 'yes but,' you'll get sick. Then where will we be, other than up the proverbial creek?" He grinned, hugging me.

"Don't worry about me, Sunshine, I'll be fine. I'm well practised at this remember." He winked and settled me against him. I was just about to say something else when the injection found its way into my system and I was asleep.

I was lovely and warm; I stretched and snuggled further under the covers. This was blissful. I must have slept very well. I realised I was naked, which was weird as I'd been wearing one of Max's T-shirts when I went to bed. Maybe I'd become hot in the night and thrown it off. I sensed movement near me and was tempted to open my eyes, but found I couldn't be bothered. Somebody sat on the bed, lifting the hair from my face.

"I thought I said sleeping in a chair was bad for you," I muttered grasping the hand and kissing its palm. I heard quiet laughter.

"Please don't ever change, my Hannah." My eyes flew open at this; I was back in my other world. I'd known it would be quick, but hadn't realised it would be this quick. I stared up into eyes, green as a forest, searching his face. Refusing to relinquish my hand, he began the familiar slow circling action with his thumb against my palm. For some reason that made me want to cry; it was such a loving gesture.

"I'm sorry you felt you had to run."

"I'm sorry I ran." Speaking in unison.

"Hannah." His voice was warm, like dark chocolate, smooth and irresistible. "Hannah, my only love, why did you not wait for me?" I drew a ragged breath —

"Oh Maxentius, I wasn't thinking, I just needed to get away, that woman, her words..." my voice trailed away. He made an inarticulate sound and drew me to his chest, pulling the blanket up over my bare shoulders.

"Do not think of them, she is just an unpleasant woman with a penchant for scurrilous gossip, uncaring about who she hurts."

He was quiet for several moments and then suddenly I felt his chest heave with more laughter. I looked up at him, trying to work out what on earth he found so funny in all of this. He saw my expression and explained, his eyes twinkling with amusement.

"Oh, my love I'm not laughing at you, but you should have waited to hear my mother on the subject."

"Oh no!" I said miserably. "Now I definitely have to leave. It was bad enough knowing that all those guests believe I'm some kind of whore, but I really thought your mother had accepted me." Maxentius looked at me in astonishment.

"No, you goose; she wiped the floor with her." I stared up at him.

"What?"

"She quite calmly told them how we had met; how you had saved my life and that of Marcus; that you are a trained physician, not a prostitute; how you rescued your brother's children because you could not bear them to be killed and that we married because I am hopelessly in love with you."

"She did not say that last bit." I giggled, hope flickering.

"Actually she did, but as I was following you at the time, I wasn't there to be teased about it. Antonia told me. Apparently my mother squashed Hortensia like a bug."

"Are you?" I asked shyly, suddenly needing reassurance. He looked down at me. I was snuggled up against him, my hair, still damp from the rain, a complete mess — I knew leaving it loose was a mistake — curling over his arms. His eyes darkened with the intensity of his feelings.

"Have been since the moment I first saw you." My breath caught and my heart thudded. Twisting so that I was facing him, my arms went around his neck, my hands sliding up into his hair, removing the leather strip that held it back and pulling his head down to mine.

"Please kiss me," I whispered. He willingly obliged.

A good while later he lifted his head and by now the inevitable slow burn had begun its slow curl through my stomach.

198

"How did you get me back here?" I asked, twisting his hair in my fingers.

"Carried you. It's not the first time, 'course you were thoroughly drenched by then." That explained my lack of clothing. He winked at me. "You seemed to faint, but it was almost as though you had disappeared." Letting his hands trail along my skin.

"Well I kind of did, disappear I mean." I looked up at my husband, hoping he would understand.

"Ah." His hands stilled. "It was like that was it?" I nodded, "...and?"

"I was only back for a little while. I've been unwell in that world too." Then I told him what Max had said. Maxentius listened and I knew it would have to be weird for him to hear words from a man who also loved me — only two thousand years away.

As I finished he was quiet for a moment, absorbing what I'd told him, along with the events of the evening. His hands resumed their journey making it hard for me to concentrate.

"So this other man, it seems he knows us very well."

"Well you are very alike and apparently you have fallen in love with an impossible woman. One whose behaviour frustrates, exasperates and confounds you."

"Yes, but she also bewitches, captivates and enchants me. I find I am unable to extricate myself from her; we are bound." He smiled down at me, his lips descending to brush against mine. "I am sorry, my Hannah," he whispered against my mouth, "I can never let you go."

"Oh well, if you say so." I tried for nonchalance, failing dismally as a huge grin spread across my face and my eyes shone with green fire. Maxentius drew a sharp breath and gave in to his desires. The world fell away as we lost ourselves in each other.

The next morning dawned bright and sunny; spring was well and truly upon us. The gardens were covered in blossoms and the sound of birds filled the air as they flew to and fro searching for nesting materials. As I admired the beautiful view, I recalled that in the not too distant future all this would be gone, inundated by ash and volcanic debris and my heart ached. Bringing my mind back to the present, I rejoiced in the fact that it was the last day of our week here in the country. I missed our relatively quiet life back in Pompeii. I still, however, had to face everyone who had been there the night before, as well as apologise to Maxentius' mother. I just had to get through this long day of partying. I really wished I could have avoided it, but that was not polite.

By the time Claudia appeared, I had been up for ages helping the children with their breakfast before sending them outside to play. All five of them were having a whale of a time chasing butterflies, climbing trees and generally running amok. My three would miss this beautiful garden. I had been standing watching them from the balcony, making sure they didn't cause too much damage or wake the rest of the household with their noisy games, when Maxentius' mother joined me.

I started to apologise for my discourteous behaviour the previous night, but barely had I got my first words out when she rested her hand on my arm hushing me gently.

"Hannah, my dear girl, it is not you who should apologise but Hortensia. She was the one who felt it necessary to denigrate you, the wife of my only son, in my home in front of my guests. I am horrified that someone I considered a friend could be so vulgar and I am sorry that her words made you feel you had to leave. Many years ago, she hoped my son would marry her daughter, but of course he chose the army and her dreams were shattered. My home should always be a haven for you and your family, not somewhere that makes you feel uncomfortable."

I stared at her, not quite sure what to say. She smiled then, a warm and loving smile, the smile of a mother and continued.

"Hannah, if it wasn't for you, I would not have my beloved son and three more grandchildren. For as Antonia is the daughter of my body, you are the daughter of my heart." I blushed to the roots of my hair. I had no idea she felt this way and was completely lost for words. Impulsively, I hugged her and although I think this surprised her, she returned the hug, squeezing my shoulder as we drew apart. Aware of my husband's approach, I turned, his face telling me that he had heard most of our conversation.

"Thank you, my mother." She returned his smile, their affection for each other clear. I felt myself relax; maybe I could get through the rest of this relatively unscathed.

"Now, let's get this party started," she grinned and, disappeared toward the domestic quarters in a flurry of white silk.

We stood together for a moment, my husband and I enjoying the quiet.

"I'm going to have to tell her, you know," I said, "and Antonia; I do not want you to lose them." He knew what I was talking about and he nodded.

"Yes, but when?"

"Soon. Maybe I will tell them that much as they hate staying in Rome during the heat of the summer, this year there will be a reason not to leave. There will be all the celebrations when Titus becomes Emperor; hopefully that will be enough to persuade them. We just need to make sure they are not here. This villa will be buried, along with most of the others along this stretch of coast."

I hesitated for a moment and then said — "Will she be here today? Will I have to face her? Were you really going to marry her daughter?" Maxentius knew to whom I referred, but could not help me.

"I never wanted to marry anyone until I met you, my love, so she would have had a long wait. Hortensia may decide to turn up, to see what havoc she has wrought. We'll just have to show how little we care for her opinions." He winked at me, dropping a kiss on my forehead. I hugged him tight.

"Just stay close."

"Don't worry, my Hannah, I'll be right next to you."

The morning flew by, as preparations ran full tilt. The meal would go on all day and into the evening, involving tens of courses, interspersed with entertainment or short breaks to stretch your legs or simply relax away from the formalities. Apparently it was acceptable to change between courses, if you so chose. I failed to understand the enjoyment behind putting on such lavish celebrations. It was utterly exhausting.

I managed to excuse myself for a little while by saying I was going to check on the children in the garden. We played hide and seek, a game all of them were good at. The spacious grounds provided plenty of hiding places and soon the sound of laughter could be heard rippling around the estate. Marcus and Maxentius joined us, as did Antonia and her husband, Julius, who it turned out was a charming man and easily persuaded into silly games. Like Maxentius and me, theirs was a love match and Julius adored his family. Whatever the risk, I had to save them.

The ten of us played for a good, long time, the hiding places becoming more and more ridiculous the more tired we became. Eventually, panting from so much running around, I threw up my hands in surrender and called a halt, saying that it was time to go and get ready for the party. We trooped into the villa, going to our various bedrooms to freshen up and change. I called my three to me, wanting to wash them in our room, so that I would know that they had been cleaned as thoroughly as possible. Satisfied that they were presentable, I told them to go and change into their best outfits. Efraim grumbled a bit as he did not like to dress up as he called it, but once I told him that Antonius would have to do the same, he gave in.

Reluctantly, I began my own preparations, washing thoroughly and searching out another of my new outfits. I had decided, after last night, that I would prefer to be comfortable rather than fashionable and chose a dress of my own design. The undershift was in dark gold silk, the same shade as the metal on my clasp. The sleeves fell nearly to my wrists but each had two long slits, one just below each shoulder and the other below each elbow. A tiny red stone was sown at either end of these slits, their facets catching the light as I moved. The over-tunic was in the palest gold, trimmed at the neck and hem with a thin red band and was gossamer fine, the darker shade of my undershift glimmering through.

I plaited my hair and then piled it up into a long twist, securing it with my cloak clasp, as if wearing my beautiful talisman would somehow protect me. I had discovered a way of threading another pin through the fastening, which I could then twist into my hair. The result was that the clasp nestled firmly into the centre of the twist, the red stone glowing in the dark mass of my hair, complemented by the red jewel-like stones on my tunic. I had a pair of gold sandals, which I was slipping my feet into just as Maxentius entered the room.

Chapter Twenty Six

As I stood up, his jaw dropped.

"By all the gods, Hannah, you undo me." I grinned at him, very pleased with his reaction.

"So this outfit is acceptable then?" He carried on staring at me.

"You will knock their eyes out, my love."

"Oh good, exactly what I was hoping for, maybe it will make them forget what happened last night. Are you going to change or do you intend to stand there and stare at me all day?" He informed me that there was nothing he'd like better, but did move to wash. He dressed in a white tunic, throwing a toga around his shoulders. Leather sandals completed his outfit and we were ready.

We entered the main room, just as several other guests arrived. I gripped Maxentius' hand, and felt his thumb rub my palm, the familiar gesture soothing me and, I felt my heart calm its fluttering. Moving into the exedra, we leaned against the balcony, Maxentius handing me a goblet of wine, which I gulped down in a most unladylike fashion. Antonia came over and complimented me on my choice of outfit. I grinned, saying that it was like soldier's armour, that I needed this in case of any verbal battles that may occur during the day. Claudia, the elder, also commented on my attire, especially the clasp I had in my hair.

"Maxentius' father brought that stone back from Lusitania Hispania where he had been procurator. I gave it to Maxentius when he joined the army, asking the goldsmith to fashion the metal surround after a soldier's helmet." I knew that she had given the clasp to Maxentius, but I looked at her curiously. Maxentius never talked about his father; who had died several years earlier, something I mentioned now. Claudia sighed rather sadly, "The two of them were very close when the children were growing up," she said, "but when Max decided to join the army rather than follow his father into politics, they drifted apart. Antonius was a quiet and bookish man, who could not understand why Max preferred to put himself in danger rather than choose the safety of a government position."

"Surely there is no such thing as a safe government position?" I questioned. "The machinations of those jockeying for power make it equally, if not more, dangerous than being in the army. At least there you know who and where your enemy is." Claudia stared at me, as if suddenly aware that I knew more than most women should know about current affairs. I grimaced inwardly and clarified, "I listen to Maxentius and Marcus when they are discussing politics and I lived under a volatile situation in Jerusalem before my brother took me to Masada." Claudia seemed to accept this explanation and, after saying that she was pleased Maxentius had gifted me the clasp, went to welcome arriving guests.

So it began. It was one of the longest days of my life and was, in some respects, worse than sitting in a cold cistern waiting for the Romans to breach the walls at Masada. At least I'd had some idea of what was going to happen that day; of this I had no preparation, not helped by my apprehension over whether Hortensia would put in an appearance.

Strangely, no one mentioned her name to me, which was a relief; maybe this was how polite society worked. I asked and answered, chatted and listened. I smiled at jokes that were not funny and laughed outright at those that were, answered numerous questions and asked some of my own. By the time the afternoon stared to fade, my jaw hurt. I looked around the room for my husband who was deep in conversation with a man I did not know. I had no desire to intrude, so I waited. Sensing my presence, even from the other side of the room, Maxentius looked up and winked. I smiled back and he motioned me over. The man he was talking to excused himself and Maxentius joined me on one of the seats in the exedra for a few minutes of peace and quiet before going to fetch some food.

Marcus sauntered through, having spent the last couple of hours surrounded by women, both single and married, who apparently found him irresistible.

I giggled at his expression; he looked completely flustered.

"Oh dear, becoming rather daunting, is it?" He laughed, nodding his agreement.

"I don't know why they have attached themselves to me."

"Well, you are the youngest single man here, bar the children and you are considered quite the catch." He stared at me, dumbfounded. "You are Marcus! The fact that you are soldier and technically unable to marry makes you all the more attractive. You are like forbidden fruit."

His face was a picture; it was obvious he had never even considered this. He groaned, just as Maxentius came back with a large and very delicious looking platter, which he placed on the table between us.

"What on earth?" Looking at Marcus' pained expression. I picked up a few pieces of food and explained.

"I'm just telling Marcus that he's so attractive because he's off-limits." Maxentius guffawed, telling me to stop winding up his second in command, it wasn't fair. I grinned, saying that I'd merely clarified the situation for him.

We moved on to other topics of conversation, chatting desultorily about our return journey. We would be leaving the next morning and although for the most part I had enjoyed the visit, I wanted to get back to our home and our normal lives. While we are talking, I suddenly overheard the less than dulcet tones of Hortensia, who must have decided to make an appearance. I looked at the two men, feeling my stomach clench. Maxentius held my hand and smiled.

"Do not let her upset you, my love, for then she will have won." I knew he was right, but that didn't stop the flicker of panic that ran through me. I gave him a tight smile; he pulled me close and kissed me. "It will be fine," he whispered. I leant against him drawing strength from his body; and then, refusing to appear cowed, I straightened my shoulders. I had nothing to be ashamed of; who did she think she was, this woman and her insults?

"Do I look all right?" I murmured. Both men looked at me in astonishment.

"You look incredible, my Hannah, why do you ask?"

"Because I intend to flatten the bug your mother has already squashed."

I stood up, all five feet of me and shook out my gown letting the material flow around me. I picked up a goblet and after checking my hair in its shiny surface, gulped down its contents. I then looked at my two Romans, my eyebrow raised.

"In order?" They both nodded. "Right then, let's do this." I walked slowly into the main room and to my chagrin a hush fell over those diners reclining around the long table. I'd rather hoped they wouldn't notice me, but I was determined and squared my shoulders. Hortensia was holding court at one end and it took her a moment to realise that all around her conversations had dwindled. I drifted along the room so slowly that I was almost floating, forcing my face to remain expressionless. When I reached her, Hortensia looked up at me, without recognition. She didn't even know what I looked like. All that vitriol and she had no clue who I was. I felt a deep anger stir within me, but kept it at bay.

I smiled at her and spoke, my voice calm, measured.

"I'm so sorry, I'm afraid we haven't met. You are?" She looked flustered. This was not how it was done; the hostess made the introductions. I stared at her, my eyes limpid, inviting her trust. I could see Claudia and Antonia watching with interest and, Maxentius and Marcus with barely suppressed glee. The room had fallen completely silent.

"My name is Hortensia Aquilinus, I am a neighbour of Claudia Valerius. And you?"

"Oh, but I thought you already knew who I am; after all you spent much of yesterday evening discussing me." I smiled sweetly. "No mind, I am Hannah Valerius, wife of your hostess' son." She stared in consternation and started to splutter, but I had no intention of stopping there and forcing a note of boredom into my voice, continued.

"I could easily refute all the aspersions you so kindly cast against me last night, but I have no desire to lower myself to your level and it would be unkind to my husband's mother. I would simply like to ask why?"

"What do you mean why?" Haughtily.

"Why you felt the need to say what you said?" I asked lightly. "I find I am quite interested. Is it maybe that you are still angry that Maxentius chose the army rather than to wed one of your daughters? Then had the audacity to marry me, a prostitute from Judaea?" She flushed, ugly colour washing up her cheeks. "Was there someone else you had in mind whom you consider to be a more acceptable marriage partner? For, I'm sure that if you introduced her to me, I could decide how adequate she would be as my husband's next wife." A ripple of suppressed laughter threaded through the room.

"Of course, because you consider me a whore, there is a whole other level of training that any prospective wife would be required to undertake before being able to satisfy my husband..." turning, I winked at the other guests who were chuckling openly now, "...he is rather a handful..." I paused, "...but I'd be happy to help. Please, do get in touch." I smiled beatifically at my nemesis touching her shoulder in a gesture of complicity; noticing that Maxentius and Marcus were biting their lips, so as not to laugh. Hortensia glared at me, but I appeared unruffled and with a swish of gold, turned, gliding down the length of the room towards the balcony.

Once I reached the comparative seclusion of the exedra, I collapsed onto one of the sofas, trembling all over. So much for dignity and poise, Hannah, I thought to myself — if Hortensia could see you now she'd have a good laugh. Maxentius and Marcus followed me in, chuckling to themselves. I glanced up at my husband, my expression remorseful.

"I'm so sorry, Maxentius, I know that was uncalled for and cruel of me, but I was suddenly very angry and that seemed better than punching her lights out."

"I think you have silenced her, a very commendable achievement and, made everyone else respect you into the bargain." I must have looked bewildered, for he continued. "You made it sound funny, taking the heat from her accusations and making them humorous. It is a rare person who can turn an insult into a compliment." They started chuckling all over again, as Claudia and Antonia joined us.

"Bravo, Hannah," smiled Antonia. "That was perfect. What did you say to me about having no understanding of the nuances of the upper class? I rather think you could teach them a thing or two." I looked up at my hostess and smiled a little ruefully.

"I am sorry, Claudia, regardless of what you said this morning, that was not polite when a guest in your home. I'm afraid my anger got the better of me." She grinned back at me, not looking the least perturbed.

"Hannah, my dear, the aim of putting on a house party such as this is to be the centre of gossip for quite some time afterwards. I do believe we have achieved our goal and I, for one, am thrilled. Now, I must check on the next course," with which she swept out of the exedra and through to where the food was being assembled. I leaned back against the sofa, unwilling to rejoin the guests.

"I think I'll hide here for the rest of the evening," I muttered, to the amusement of the other three. "Give me bad-tempered gladiators and riotous mobs any day over high society." Laughing, Maxentius handed me a goblet of wine and, sitting down next to me, pulled me to his side, his arm slung over the back of the sofa and across my shoulders. I leaned into him and started to relax. "I'm so glad we're going home tomorrow," I whispered for his ears only. He grinned down at me and kissed my nose, not caring who saw.

Incredibly, my husband was right: throughout the remainder of the evening several of the guests complimented me on how I had handled the situation with Hortensia and even thought I had downplayed it. I was just relieved that I hadn't exacerbated the situation. Still, I was very glad when the last guest left and we could finally get to bed. I had begun packing earlier in the day and there wasn't much left to do, however; I was too tired. I merely traipsed back and forth, picking up things to put in the boxes, then placing them anywhere but. In the end Maxentius removed from my fingers whichever piece of clothing I was holding, laid it on the box and pulled me to the bed.

"I think you need to rest, my Hannah," he said, his eyes twinkling down at me. I stared at him, so tired that I could barely comprehend him. He lifted me onto the bed, slid my clothes off and I was asleep before he'd drawn the covers up.

I dreamed of the woman in the bed again. She seemed much better. The colour in her cheeks looked normal and her breathing easier. No longer watching from the chair, this time the man lay alongside, his arms wrapped around her in much the same way as Maxentius held me. I guessed that whatever had been wrong with her had passed. I knew she was still with me, so there must be more she needed to share, but I worried about her other life and how could she be in two places at once. I wanted to tell her that we would be fine, that I took her warning about the volcano seriously and would save anyone I could, that it was okay for her to stay in her own world. Even as I was thinking these things, the dream started to fade, the picture dissolved and I lost the connection.

Chapter Twenty Seven

I woke suddenly, unsure about what had disturbed me, other than my dreams. I lay for several minutes listening. The night was quiet, the room still. Through the huge window, which we had left un-shuttered I could see the stars. It must have been the dream. As I was contemplating this, I heard an ominous rumble; the mountain was growling, sending little shock waves through the ground. The villa trembled on its foundations, but it was a minor quake and as soon as it began, it was over. It was getting nearer. These earth tremors would continue with increasing frequency over the next few months until the pressure became too much and the mountain would blow its top. I didn't have long.

Shivering a little, more from knowing what was to come than from the cool air, I snuggled back under the covers. Maxentius, attuned to me even in slumber, gathered me close, the warmth of his arms comforting me as I drifted back to sleep. The next time I awoke it was full daylight and I had slept longer than I had intended. We had so much to do before we could leave and here was I lying around in bed. Puzzled as to why Maxentius hadn't woken me and frustrated with myself, I rushed through my morning ablutions. Dressing with more haste than care, I hurried through the house to the room where breakfast was served.

My husband was helping the children with their meal as I fell, rather than walked into the room. I halted abruptly, noting his patience with them, feeling a warm glow around my heart as I watched them together. He looked up at my ungainly entrance and smiled slowly, his face lighting up.

"We thought you needed a lie-in before our journey. We have nearly finished, then we will go and finish sorting everything out," he said, pushing a platter towards an empty place at the table. I sank into the chair gratefully and began to demolish the food, which was delicious.

"I'm not sure I should let you four loose with the packing," I grinned between mouthfuls. "I would like to get our things home in as neat a fashion as possible."

"Pah...we four make a great team, don't we?" He looked at our children who nodded enthusiastically. "Have no fear, my Hannah, it will be done just as you like it. Now relax and enjoy your meal." He gathered them up and they trailed after him, chattering about who would be the best packer. Sighing and knowing it was most likely that I would have to re-pack everything, I gave in and left them to it. Since most of our clothes would have to be washed anyway, it didn't really matter.

Once finished and taking care to thank the slave who had served the food, I made my way back to the bedrooms. To my surprise, they had done a fairly creditable job and, although I was itching to make sure everything was tidy underneath the layers I could see, I forced myself to leave things just as they were. Maxentius chuckled at my expression, knowing exactly what I was thinking.

Thanking the small fry for their hard work, I told them to go outside and find their cousins. I checked our room and the two bedrooms our children had been in, making sure we hadn't left anything behind. I did find the odd shoe and toy in the most peculiar of places — how they had ended up there was beyond me — but eventually we were ready.

Marcus had been up very early and had helped the grooms prepare the wagon and horses. He lifted our boxes onto the back of the wagon alongside his and then there was nothing left but to thank our hostess. They were all there — Claudia, Antonia, Julius and their two children. I thanked them all, especially Claudia for making us so welcome, feeling quite tearful as we hugged our goodbyes. We had settled the children into the wagon, Marcus had mounted the second horse and we were about to set off when I slid out of my seat and walked back over to my new family.

"This may sound very strange, but there is something I must tell you and I hope you will believe me." I paused, taking a deep breath. "In a few months a great sadness will come to the people of Rome and its Empire. I think you will already be in the city when it happens and I beg that you remain there. Please do not think of returning here even if you desire it most dearly. A terrible catastrophe is looming and I cannot bear the thought of any of you being caught in its horror. I would ask that you close your houses, taking your staff and slaves with you. I know this is unusual, but I would not request this if it were not imperative." I could see confusion in each face, but I continued, reaching my hands towards them, beseeching them to understand.

"I know how this sounds, but I implore you, please trust me, I would have you out of danger, for if you remain here, you will surely perish." I grasped Claudia's slim fingers in mine and kissed them quickly, before climbing back up onto the wagon. Maxentius smiled at me and looked at his mother.

"Believe her, my mother, her words are the truth; please, do not ignore her warning. To lose you would break my heart." I watched as his mother absorbed her son's words. I could only hope that she believed us. Nodding, he clicked the reins and the horse began the long journey home.

We waved for a long time, the children hanging out of the back of the wagon, yelling goodbye to their cousins. Then we persuaded them to settle down and enjoy the ride. Meanwhile, Marcus was looking rather disturbed. He had heard my entreaty and I could tell that he wanted to ask me about it. More than that, he was mulling over my words and I wondered whether he remembered a similar conversation many years ago one evening sitting in an exquisite palace on a remote plateau near the Dead Sea.

We had been travelling for about an hour when he wheeled his horse around and came to trot alongside the wagon. The children were playing 'I spy,' so would not have been listening to us. He studied me for a long while and I knew what was coming.

"Are you going to explain Hannah?" he asked rather abruptly. I glanced at his face, which was shadowed.

"That depends," I replied.

"On what?"

"Whether you are prepared to listen, actually listen, or whether you are just going to ride along next to me being angry," I retorted and then made an effort to soften my tone. "I am not prepared to bare my soul to someone who has no desire to hear me. I certainly don't want to talk about it while we are travelling. There are too many small ears about, but if you think you can wait 'til this evening, I will tell you then." I reached out across the gap between the wagon and his horse and touched his hand. "You will understand when you hear what I have to say. Please trust me." He stared at me, searching my face, as he seemed to fight some internal battle.

"I trust you, Hannah. I will wait." I smiled at him and we left it there — me hoping he meant it and Marcus still looking rather tense. I glanced at Maxentius who winked at me and squeezed my leg.

"It'll be okay my Hannah," he said in an undertone, "I will be with you, we will tell him together." I smiled rather wearily.

"Sometimes its just a bit much, all this knowledge," I muttered."

"Yes, but you want to save them, don't you? You can't have it both ways, my love." I knew he was right, but I feared the reaction of those I needed to tell. I had only ever told Maxentius and by some miracle, he had understood. I may not be as lucky with Marcus.

The journey home was almost as enjoyable as our journey to the villa, except that I was anxious about my upcoming conversation with Marcus. He was as important to me, in some ways, as Maxentius. He had taken the place of Aharon in my heart and I would be devastated if I lost his friendship, but I could see no way around it. He would have to be told.

The children were very good; they slept quite a lot of the way and we reached the outskirts of Pompeii by late afternoon. The town seemed noisy after those few days surrounded by such peace, but I welcomed it. They were familiar sounds, sounds of our home. I glanced up at the dark mass that was Vesuvius; no smoke today, but I felt its destructive menace lurking just beneath the surface. Not wanting to deal with the horror I knew would be loosed, I turned away, focusing my attention on getting three very tired children out of the wagon and into the house.

I didn't really want to wake them, but it was too early to put them straight to bed and they needed to eat. Thankfully, Aliza was home, so she and I carried the girls in while Maxentius brought Efraim. By the time we'd perched them on the chairs in front of the fire, they'd started to come around and the smell of the evening meal coaxed them into wakefulness. Marcus unloaded the boxes and then returned the wagon to the hostler, calling that he'd be back as soon as possible.

We sorted the children out with their food, leaving them to enjoy it while we began the Herculean task of unpacking yet again. Much needed washing, so I just dumped those items in the laundry sink; I would worry about fine-tuning it the next day. By the time we'd done as much as we could, the children were finished, so with a quick wash I sent them to their room asking that they change for bed, but that they could play for a little while. They went off happily, excited to play with their own toys again. Marcus reappeared shortly thereafter and we four adults enjoyed a normal, one-course, properly filling meal. It was so relaxing not to have to worry about wading through several courses, while talking to lots of people we didn't know.

A little later, after we had persuaded the children into bed and tucked them in and, after Aliza had gone to one of her evening groups, the three of us sat around the fire with a goblet of warm calda. The atmosphere was tense and I was very nervous. It was a big risk this telling, this sharing of a part of me that I had hidden from everyone except my husband. I mean honestly, I'm about to tell someone that I have another woman in my head who lives two thousand years in the future and gives me knowledge of something catastrophic so that I can save the lives of those closest to me! Utterly ludicrous!

I looked at Maxentius who grasped my hand, his thumb rubbing my palm, calming me. Taking a deep breath, I began to talk. I explained everything to Marcus in exactly the same way as I had to Maxentius more than decade ago and, to my other Max, in my other world eighteen months previously. You see...even that sounds crazy. I looked him in the eye and spoke in quiet, reasoned tones, telling him everything right up to why she was here now.

I showed him the clasp, explaining that this whole thing began because the other Hannah had been given it as a gift; that it had been handed down through hundreds of generations of women in our family, each having been told to guard it well and that I believed it was this clasp, my talisman, which connected us. I was trembling by the time I had finished, partly from fear over Marcus' reaction and partly because it had brought back so many emotions.

I dropped my gaze, gripping Maxentius' hand like a lifeline, hardly daring to breathe. I would understand if Marcus did not believe me. Why should he? I just hoped that, with everything we'd been through, he trusted me enough to know I had no reason to lie. The room was almost silent; the only sound was the fire crackling in the hearth, although I was sure my two Romans must have heard the thud of my heart.

Moments passed — nothing. Marcus was staring into the fire, his face impassive. I looked at my husband despairingly. The same fears that had plagued me while I was telling Maxentius flooded back. I considered whether I should leave the room and let him talk it over with his commander and loosened Maxentius' hand. My husband looked down at me and I motioned towards our bedroom, indicating my intention. Imperceptibly, he shook his head and pulled me to him.

After what seemed like a lifetime, Marcus turned back to me, his tone curious.

"This was how you knew that the Romans would breach the wall and about the massacre?" I nodded, adding that until we arrived in Pompeii, I hadn't felt any connection to my other self since the day he and Maxentius rescued us from the cistern.

"It's as though she knows when I'm in danger and somehow is able to merge with me, providing me with what I can only describe as an extra sense; an awareness of what will happen, but trusting that I will not change the course of history, just adapting the knowledge she can share with me to save those I love." I sighed. "Marcus, I know this is a lot to comprehend and I understand if you think I am completely bonkers. I would have preferred not to burden you with it, but you asked and..." I trailed off, unable to read my friend's expression. He sat like a stone.

I thought of all we had been through together, of the weeks I had spent treating his wounds, of the years we had lived and worked alongside each other. Was I about to lose him? I didn't think I could bear it. I leaned into Maxentius, who tightened his arm around me. I was still trembling and inexplicably, I could feel tears forming. Shaking my head, I pulled out of my husband's embrace and stood.

"I'm sorry, Marcus." My voice was full of sorrow. "I will leave you to your thoughts. Maybe it is better if I am not here. I will answer any of your questions, if and when you chose to ask them, but I'm not sure I have the strength to wait for your decision." I moved towards our bedroom, fighting not to cry, weariness from the long day and a glut of emotional baggage threatening to overwhelm me.

"Hannah!" His voice arrested me and I half turned, expecting the worst. "Hannah, why did you not trust me enough to tell me sooner?"

"Marcus, I trust you with my life, but this is far more complicated than anything you have ever had to face. I am asking you to believe that I am two people in one body, one of whom is from nearly two thousand years in the future. I hoped I would never have to tell you, for I feared that it would be too much to deal with and you would no longer want to share your life with us. I have already lost one brother; to lose another would break my heart. What if it had been the other way around? What if you were the one with this knowledge? Would you have wanted to share it?"

Tears were running down my face now. Maxentius moved towards me, but Marcus got there first. He wrapped his arms around me, holding me close, his hand cupping the back of my head drawing me against his chest. There was nothing remotely lover-like in his embrace; it was the way I remembered Aharon hugging me when I was a child after we had lost our parents. Hope flared as I sobbed wretchedly in his arms.

"I believe you, Hannah, I believe you; please don't cry." I don't think Marcus had ever seen me cry, not once in all the years we'd known each other, which is quite impressive when I think of the number of times Maxentius has been treated to one of my meltdowns.

Just as when I had told Maxentius, regardless of Marcus' reaction, my relief at being able to tell the second most important man in my life — well in this life — was palpable. A relief that made it hard for me to stem my tears, but realising that hysteria borne of fatigue tickled at the edge of my senses, I made a determined effort to control myself. Drawing a shuddering breath, I waited for the trembling to subside. As I started to calm down, Marcus gently handed me over to my husband, who lifted me onto his knees, hugging me against his body, cradling my head into his shoulder.

Marcus refilled our goblets and we sat quietly for a little while letting our emotions settle. I desperately wanted my bed, but I would not sleep until I knew everything was right between us. Marcus started to ask questions, questions about the other Hannah, questions about what she/I knew, what she had shared with me. Then he wanted to know more about the eruption that would soon devastate this town and many others around us. I told him all that I knew, which took some time, but I think eventually we pretty much covered everything.

Then, in a question hauntingly familiar to one Maxentius had asked me recently, Marcus said —

"How do you do it Hannah? How do you have this floating around in your head, knowing you cannot share it?"

"Knowing that everyone would think me stark raving mad is one reason," I smiled. "The other is that she shares this knowledge, trusting that I will try to save only those whose lives are bound to mine."

I leaned forward and grasped his hands. "You have to promise me that you will do the same, that regardless of what I have told you, you will not try to change anything. The mountain will erupt, it will bury everything and Pompeii will disappear out of history for centuries. We cannot change this; only how we deal with it before it happens. You and Maxentius are the only people who know who and what I am. It is not something I wish to broadcast, especially after everything else that has happened to me recently."

Marcus squeezed my fingers.

"I promise, Hannah, thank you for trusting me."

"I have always trusted you, Marcus, since the very first time I remember treating you." I winked at him, my allusion to what I thought was our first meeting making both of my Romans chuckle and lightening the mood. "See, when you ask me stuff, I can always pretend I had no clue because I wasn't here when it happened." I grinned.

"Not sure you'll get away with that very often, my Hannah," said Maxentius, his eyes twinkling. "Now, it is very late and we all have a call on our time in the morning. Maybe we should retire and revisit this tomorrow, if we need to." He raised his eyebrows in question to Marcus who agreed and made ready to return to his rooms.

Needing to be sure, I asked tentatively —

"Marcus, are we okay?" I looked up searching his face, trying to read whether he was saying one thing, yet meaning another. He looked down at me, his expression open and untroubled.

"We are as we have always been, Hannah. You are the sister of my heart and nothing will ever change that." He hugged me again, then nodded to Maxentius and slipped out through the connecting corridor at the back of our home.

I released a huge sigh and sat back down, resting my head on my hands, thankful that the conversation was over and thankful that I had told Marcus. I had not enjoyed keeping this part of me a secret from him, even though I had felt it necessary. I was bone tired, not even sure I could drag myself to bed. It was after midnight and I was due at the Gladiators' School the next afternoon. I was quite happy to sleep where I was and felt myself sliding down on the sofa.

Maxentius shook my shoulder, trying to wake me up enough to get to bed, but I was too far gone, so he scooped me up, carrying me through to our room. I had no idea that he had undressed me, had drawn the covers up over me and had moulded me to him as he had lain next to me. My other world had reached out for me and in my exhausted state, I slipped through.

Chapter Twenty Eight

We were back on-site. I had thrown off my cold or chest infection, or whatever it was and felt much better. Max had made me take the rest of the weekend to recover properly — worried that the turn in the weather might cause a relapse — but I knew it was just precautionary. I was excited to be back at the ruins. There were places I wanted to see and I needed to go back to the House of the Hebrew and wander through its layout, to see whether anything was familiar. I also wanted to visit the Gladiators' School for the same reason.

Max had said we would go in a little later and meet up with the others at morning tea. We had agreed to stay on for the extra two weeks; both of us had so many days holiday due that we'd booked six weeks in total. No one was expecting us back yet. Max had emailed Edward to let him know of our plans and had mentioned that we'd left a suitcase in the spare room of his apartment, since initially we intended returning to Rome at the beginning of our third week away. Edward had replied saying if that were the case, would we mind if he stayed another two weeks in Max's flat? He'd met up with some university friends during the conference and they had invited him to do some sightseeing with them — fortuitous for all of us.

I had asked Max if he would be with me this first day back. If I was going to explore buildings or ruins that I had lived and worked in, in my other life, I wanted him next to me holding me in this world. I think his response went along the lines of, 'I don't think I'll ever be able to let you out of my sight again.' So I guess he was okay with my plans. I had returned to this life two days earlier and had presumed, all things considered, that it would not be for very long. It was as though there was a slender thread holding me to my ancient world, extremely delicate yet unbreakable, which unwound just far enough for me to think I was here to stay and then without warning drew me back.

I had filled Max in on the few days since I had last been here and although he seemed resigned to my disappearing again, I know he hoped it wouldn't happen. We arrived on-site to meet the others at the café, all indulging in strong coffee. I faced a barrage of questions about how I was and managed to fend them off good-humouredly. It seemed that they had all been worried, especially those who knew what had happened at Masada.

Nate had obtained permission for Max and me to go into the House of the Hebrew, for it was still off-limits to the general public. He would come along with us to unlock the protective gate and then meet up with us at the Gladiators' School. He was obviously perplexed about why I wanted to revisit this house, but I said it was because I hadn't had the chance to see right through it and was intrigued by the story behind it, especially after so recently visiting Masada. I'm not sure I convinced him, but he was happy enough to let us in.

After asking Max to secure the very large padlock when we left, Nate pottered back to the Gladiators' School. I walked slowly through what would have been the vestibulum and into the atrium. I could see how it should look as clearly as though I was back there. I could hear echoes of my life, as though the stones had absorbed my memories, holding them safe until I needed them again. Max was right behind me and I asked whether he wanted to know about this place. He nodded and, in exactly the same way as I had woven him a picture of my life at Masada, I began to describe this home in my other world.

I wandered through the ruins pointing out the main living area where the beautiful frescoes could still be seen on the walls, barely faded over time. I ran my hands across them tracing the designs with my fingers, remembering how much I — well she — loved them. I showed him how the furniture was arranged around the fireplace and, where the kitchen, the bedrooms and the laundry were located. Then I went outside through the small courtyard into the larger garden beyond, explaining that this was where we'd planted vegetables and had a chicken coop. Some damaged amphorae lay haphazardly against one of the walls and I realised, with a jolt, that they were ours, ones that had held wine or oil. I lifted one or two of the pieces, turning them in my hand, confused as to why they were out here in the garden and not in the storeroom.

The stairs up to what had been Aliza's rooms were still intact, though the upper level was long gone. I couldn't see anything of the connecting pathway to what had been the garrison headquarters but the building remained. In my mind's eye I could see Marcus calling down from the first floor, asking Efraim about his kite.

As I talked, building an image of my life here, I could feel my worlds colliding and melding: voices calling to me, children playing with their toys, Aliza telling me about her day while cooking a meal and my two Romans chatting over a glass of warm calda. Much as I loved Max, the more I talked, the more I realised that I missed this world; it was as much a part of me as breathing. I would never be free of it and even though she may not always need me, I was forever connected to my ancient counterpart. Had she ever seen my world? Then I remembered that she had. When I had been on Masada, I had dreamed of myself in the medical centre without realising it was me. Oh, that sounds rather convoluted, Hannah concentrate on one job at a time.

My voice trailed away as I leaned against a ruined section of wall, looking along the remains of the peristyle courtyard. The sun was breaking through, its rays catching the colours in the frescoes. At this point, I had no other information to share; I did not know what had happened, except that this house had been eventually covered in ash. According to the archaeologists, no skeletons were found here, but that didn't mean we had all survived.

I gazed across at Max, who was sitting at the bottom of the stairs watching me with an odd expression on his face

"You miss them don't you?" he asked, his voice wistful. I couldn't lie to him, but I needed him to understand.

"Yes, in a way I do," I replied, walking over and kneeling on the bottom step in front of him, "but a part of me has lived this other life, okay, not physically, more subconsciously, or subliminally. You know that I don't actually go into the past, more like there's an extra sensory connection. The hardest part for me is the strange way that time passes. A few hours or a couple of days here can sometimes equate to the same in my other life, but more often than not its months, even years. It means that I appear to have experienced more with them, than I have with you and that makes me so sad. I'd far rather it was the other way around."

I tentatively touched his hand, feeling suddenly shy with this man who, in this world, was my whole life. He looked down at my hand, then back up into my face, staring into my eyes and reading the truth of my words, his own eyes darkening with some deep emotion.

"Max, I..." I never finished my sentence; he leaned forward and kissed me, lightly, like the touch of a dragonfly's wing. Sighing, I leaned towards him. We were alone here, just the two of us, no interruptions. Drawing a ragged breath, he wrapped his arms around me and pulled me to him. His lips descended on mine with a fervour I wasn't quite expecting, but welcomed anyway. The slow burn ignited, sending heat licking along my veins.

The world slowed, all I could hear was my heartbeat, all I could feel was desire, as Max continued to kiss me almost senseless. One arm held me to him, while the other began a slow exploration of my body, his cool fingers grazing my skin, causing frissons of delight to ripple down my back. Unsure what had prompted this, but luxuriating in the sensations coursing through me, I simply let go. It was like the first time he had kissed me, that incredible night under a million stars at the bottom of a desolate outcrop of rock in the middle of the Judaean desert. Now, as then, I wished this would go on forever.

Now, as then, Max drew away and the cool air cut between our faces. Still holding me close, he ran a trembling hand through my hair, pushing back my fringe, which always seemed to need trimming.

"Don't stop, please don't stop," I murmured. Max kissed the tip of my nose.

"We have work to do, Sunshine, otherwise I would have no hesitation in taking you right here on these stairs."

"Would've been fine by me," I responded dazedly, waiting for my heart to resume its regular rhythm. Chuckling, he helped me up, brushing the dust off my jeans and steadying me, as my legs didn't seem to want to hold me.

"I love you, Max." I wanted to say more; I wanted to wipe away the anxiety that seemed to be haunting him but I didn't know how. I couldn't stop what was happening to me, but I needed him to understand that he was my lifeline. My eyes held his, green on green, willing him to believe.

"I love you too, Hannah, I just hope its enough." There was something in his tone as he set off to walk back through the house. Puzzled, I grabbed his arm and turned him back towards me.

"Enough for what?" I said, searching his face.

"Enough to hold you here, to me, to this world." Frustrated that he still didn't seem to get it, I felt a flick of anger.

"What, so suddenly, after everything we've been through, after everything we've talked about, it's all becoming too hard for you; is that what you mean?" Remembering what he'd said when we were in Rome, I flung his words back at him. "What happened to 'I'm never letting you go, I've waited too long,' or that you wanted to be the one protecting me? Max, I can't help who I am! I thought we'd been through all this. Don't you get it? The only thing that keeps me sane, the only thing that keeps me anchored here is you. If it weren't for you, I think it would be very easy for my soul to separate from my body and never come back, leaving me forever lost out of time." Fear and distress sharpened my voice. Was I losing him?

"I don't choose to go back, I have no control over it, but I know I need to save them, they are part of me, they will always be part of me. Neither do I want to lose you...I can't lose you...oh God, I can't lose you." No, this could not be happening to me. Tears were pouring down my face now. Oh good grief, Hannah, more with the waterworks! Abruptly, I sat back down on the step and curled in on myself, wrapping my arms around my knees, rocking back and forth in my agitation. Darkness touched the edge of my vision. I didn't want to fall, but I could feel the pull of my other world.

Panicked now, I tried to shake it, desperate for Max to tell me everything was okay. My breathing came quick and sharp and the cold air caught the back of my throat. I started to cough, a residue from my illness. It was a nasty flare-up and I couldn't catch my breath; every time I tried, it set me off again. The lack of air in my lungs was making me feel faint and spots danced before my eyes.

Then he was there. He lifted me up from the step and held me tight, running his hands down my back in long soothing movements. Eventually, the bout ceased and I was able to breathe again, but I was trembling all over from the force of the attack and the fear that I was going to slip away in the middle of an argument. Shuddering, I rested my head on his shoulder, feeling the strong steady beat of his heart. He continued to stroke my back, talking quietly about everything and nothing and, although I have no idea what he said, his voice, as always, calmed me. After a little while, he said —

"I'm sorry Hannah, I didn't mean that it was all too much. I meant that I hoped my love was strong enough for you to hold onto, that the memory of it while you're..." hesitating, "...there in your other life, is enough to draw you back to me." He tilted my chin, so that he could look into my eyes. There was something else there, a hint of fear, something he hadn't said. This was weird; it was usually me who needed reassuring.

"What else Max? What are you afraid of?" Something flickered in his eyes and for a moment I thought he might not tell me. Then, with a deep breath —

"If you must know, I'm afraid that the other man in your life holds more of your heart than I do. In your own words you have spent longer with him than with me. You married him and had a child with him. How do I compete with that?" I stared back at him in astonishment. This was what he was worried about? This is what haunted him?

"Oh Max, surely, you don't, you can't..." I stopped speaking, realising that he did and he could. How could I make him believe? "I didn't fall in love with him, or marry him or have a child with him." He looked at me sceptically. "Well okay, in a way I did, but through the other Hannah, they were her emotions, not mine. While she and I may share some of the same characteristics, Maxentius doesn't even know what I look like or how I behave. He doesn't know how I think or feel. He only knows her, but he understands that she and I are connected, that occasionally I'm a part of their lives so that I can share my knowledge. He knows that it's the only way I am able to help them, to save them." I gazed up at him, willing him with every fibre of my being, to believe me.

"All I can tell you is that I love you with all of my heart, not just a piece of it. You are my other half. Without you I think I would simply cease to exist. You waited for me last year, you came back to me this year and while I know that there was a time before I loved you, I can't remember it, I feel as though we've been part of each other forever. My life began when you told me you loved me, the night you first kissed me under those millions of stars at Masada; that's when I became whole." I stopped, not knowing whether I'd even come close to persuading him, but I couldn't find any more words.

Suddenly I remembered the clasp, which was in my backpack. I leaned down and rummaging through the bag, found it and pulling it out of its pouch, I handed it to Max, murmuring —

"This talisman was given to my ancestor by your ancestor. Yes okay, her love is my love, but we are both in love with you, just in different lives. You and I have been connected throughout the ages, our lives are entwined, our love is timeless and we are forever bound." I knew that my words sounded old fashioned and I stopped speaking abruptly, hoping I'd said enough. He rolled the clasp around in his palm, staring into its ruby depths, its facets sparkling red flame in the sunshine. You could be forgiven for thinking it had a life force, for it seemed to pulse with some hidden energy. He lifted his head to look at me and as I gazed back, I saw the fear fade and vanish from his eyes, to be replaced by a new, more profound emotion.

"Oh, my love," he sighed my name and, running his hands through my hair, drew me to him, resuming the kiss we had so reluctantly broken off just a short time ago. We stood for what seemed like hours, but was really only a few minutes, oblivious to the world around us, descending deeper and deeper into each other. It was a very good job we were the only people in this building. Soon, too soon, reality stepped in. We had to get on with our day and if we stayed much longer who knew where it would lead? Well, actually, we both knew exactly where it would lead, which was why we stopped.

Reluctantly, we gathered our things together and I made sure the clasp was safe in the inside pocket of my backpack. Slowly, we walked back through the home of my — no our — ancestors. I knew it was unlikely that I would get to see this place again, so I wanted to soak it all in. I stood in the atrium, looking though the main living area and out to the garden.

Max came up behind me, wrapping his arms round me and resting his chin on my head.

"You okay to leave, or do you need a few more minutes?" I shook my head, turning round in his embrace.

"No, I think I'm done. I just want to see that inscription at the entrance."

"The one that made you 'go back'?" I sensed his unease.

"It'll be okay, Max, you're here, just hold my hand." He nodded and we moved towards the doorway. I traced the words, both Hebrew and Latin, feeling the same emotions that my ancient counterpart felt when Maxentius showed her them millennia ago; but that was all. The past stayed quiet and for a little longer, I was just me.

Max secured the padlock and we made our way along the Via dell'Abbondanza to the Gladiators' School where we would meet up with Nate and Sebastian. As we were walking Max took my hand, squeezing it gently and rubbing his thumb along my fingers. The action was so familiar that I had to look at him twice to make sure I hadn't suddenly gone back without realising it. There was no way I was going to tell him that mind you — not after the deep and meaningful of the last hour or so — but it warmed me, making me feel safe.

By the time we arrived, the others were well into their work. Max would be involved in the excavations and I said I'd log anything they needed, then photograph what they were doing. Although there had been a lot of work done in this area, there were still small pockets that needed recording before they brought in the equipment that could see below the AD79 layer. I was rather nervous entering this area, bearing in mind what I knew of it. It had sustained quite a bit of damage, the upper floor was completely gone, but the wide staircase up to the second level was intact; as were the much narrower ones on the east and west sides that I had preferred to use on those few occasions I had needed to go to the upper level. Much however, had been protected under the ash and was easily recognisable, to me anyway.

The Doric columns surrounding the training ground stood like ageing sentries, some broken, others managing to remain upright. In antiquity, the fluted sections had been painted, alternately red and yellow with two blue ones in the centre of each side of the yard and the lower, non-fluted section was always red. I remembered the cool of the pathway that ran between these and the main building; and where the gladiators entered the space. I knew which room had been the lanista's office and where those who had been condemned were housed. Unbidden, I thought of Petronius and Tullius. Did they survive? Had I dared warn them?

I could have told Nate and Sebastian all about the domestic areas, such as where the medical quarters were, including the long dim room where I had helped prepare the bodies of the dead for their journey to whichever afterlife they believed in. In fact, it was all I could do not to spill it out; to me the memory was very close, it was only days since I'd last been here. I knew in which room Darius and Mihai had lived as well as those of their Dacian comrades and, where Tobias had been sitting when he saw me through his open doorway. I could even hear the sounds of their shackles as they walked. Images and sounds swirled through my head, making it hard for me to concentrate.

By sheer force of will, I pushed it all to the back of my mind and began photographing the section they were working in, stopping occasionally to log finds or draw the layers. By lunchtime we had made good progress. Nate reckoned we would only need one more day to finish recording this layer and then we could bring in the ground-penetrating equipment. We walked down to the café at the centre of the site for lunch, relaxing over pizza and coffee, discussing the ruins. I really wanted to see some of the other villas, especially the House of the Vettii, the House of the Faun and the Villa of the Mysteries, this last one is actually outside the main walls but apparently worth the extra walk.

A short while later, I was standing in the doorway waiting for Max, letting the chatter of the tourists coming and going for their lunches wash over me as I looked out across the ruins. I could see my other life superimposed over them; the way the buildings had looked, the people walking to the Forum, soldiers leaning against a wall watching for trouble while eating a honey-filled roll. Suddenly I realised I was slipping through; the images were stabilising and sharpening. Panicking, I turned to grab Max's hand, but it was too late, I was already there.

Chapter Twenty Nine

"Whoa, Hannah, careful, you don't want to drop anything." Bewildered, I glanced up at the person who'd spoken, his hand steadying me. Deep green eyes were smiling down at me, apparently amused at my clumsiness, which to be fair, is well known. Shaking my head to quell the roaring in my ears, I tried a smile. "What's wrong, Hannah?" Concerned now.

I couldn't make my voice work, words refused to form, my mouth felt as though it was full of cotton wool. The hand pulled me to a body, one that felt familiar and slowly the roaring quieted. "Hannah? What's going on?" Still unable to speak, I just leaned against him, drawing deep breaths, willing the world to stop spinning. He sat me down on something cold — it felt like a stone bench — and removed whatever had been in my other hand.

In a determined effort to stop the dizziness, I dropped my head between my knees, continuing to draw lungsful of air. Eventually, it cleared and I was able to sit upright.

"Where am I? What happened?" I muttered, confusion still clouding my brain.

"Near the Forum, you just seemed to miss your footing on the pathway." Maxentius — yes, I'd worked it out — replied. "Hannah...?" He was studying my face, disquiet etched on his.

"Ohhhhh..." I drew a shuddering breath, accepting the transition, but unsure of how much time had passed since I'd been away. "... I'm sorry, I know this is a strange question, but how many days is it since I told Marcus?"

"I'm not certain, maybe a month. Hannah, what's going on?"

It took me a few more minutes to get my bearings. It was a beautiful day, everything was fresh and green; flowers and blossoms making the town look like a colourful painting. The umbrella pines were rustling in the warm breeze and the sky was full of birds, searching for bugs no doubt. I guessed it was probably late April or May. I had around three months to come up with a plan to save this man who looked at me with such anxiety.

"I've been...she's...I can't..." gathering myself I tried again. "I've been away and now I'm back and I can't remember the last month, well not yet at least. It might come back to me, it usually does, although..." I let that hang, thinking that I had no real recollection of my childhood, or youth; not much of anything 'til I was caring for three Roman soldiers at Masada. Maxentius held my hand, accepting my confusion as being quite normal.

"It's okay, my love, I can fill you in." As we sat there, he proceeded to tell me what had been going on over the past few weeks. I'd been kept busy at the Gladiators' School, as the next games were due in three days. There had been a couple of brawls and along with the other medici, I'd been treating several badly bruised men. Thankfully, only fists had been used, which although had done plenty of damage, was mostly superficial. One or two had cracked ribs or a broken nose, but they were on the mend. The boys at the Palaestra had been unusually careful and, other than the odd massage for tight muscles, there had been no injuries. I noticed that there were posters here and there on walls of shops; the battle between Darius and Tobias was the headliner. My heart sank; oh no, here we go again.

My family were well. Finally, a tutor had been engaged and the children had lessons three mornings a week. Efraim was soaking up everything he could and although the girls were less inclined to concentrate on their work, they did try. Marcus had taken everything on board and although he had asked Maxentius a few questions, had carried on as if nothing had changed, for which I was truly grateful. As my husband finished his wrap up, he asked about the other me. I explained about my last few days, even telling him about what Max and I had been doing up to the moment I slipped back through time. I wondered what had happened to me in my own world and how long I'd be away this time.

"So, much of this town survives?" Maxentius queried.

"An incredible amount. The ash preserved the buildings, as well as many everyday objects — tools, silverware, jewellery, wagons, weapons, even bodies. Without the frescoes from Pompeii we would know very little of Roman wall painting. Archaeologists even found jars of preserved fruit and loaves of bread. The government and an international heritage organisation protect this site. It's visited by millions of people every year." Maxentius looked astonished.

"Really, this little town?"

"Maxentius." I pressed his hand. "Along with Herculaneum and Oplontis, Pompeii provides a snapshot, sorry..." as he looked at me askance, "...an image, or picture, of the Roman world in AD79. In the calendar of my time, that is this year, the one we are now living through. The sites are incomparable, their worth inestimable. How does it feel to be a part of it?" My husband sat back, trying to take it in. Remembering what Max had said, I realised how hard it must be for Maxentius, knowing that I was living two lives, yet he would never be part of one of them. While he mulled over my words, there was a rumble and the earth quivered. I looked up at the mountain; it looked quiet today but it would not last.

We sat a little longer until I felt able to walk without my legs giving way underneath me. Maxentius said he'd had some free time, so we'd decided to take a walk and I'd found some herbs and oils at the market, which explained the bag. It was early afternoon and he needed to get back to headquarters; there had been some bad clashes with rioters over the last couple of weeks and he needed to coordinate the garrison's ongoing response.

Apparently I was a free agent, having visited the Gladiators' School that morning and, as Maxentius told me this, an odd sensation ran through me, bearing in mind that was where I'd been before falling through time. The children were playing with Aemilia and Cornelius and, Aliza was meeting with her friends. It gave me time to get my head around which world I was in and, by the time we reached our home, I felt quite normal again, if that is a state I am ever able to achieve. Maxentius kissed me, hugging me close, before heading back to work. I took my purchases into the little room where I stored all my tinctures and sorted them out into their respective jars or pots. Some of the herbs needed drying, so I tied their stalks together with twine and hung them upside down from one of the beams, their scent permeating the small space.

It took me quite a while to sort everything out, but I enjoyed it. I liked working with the different oils and balms, testing new mixtures for their efficacy. It always amazed me that even though I had to readjust when I slipped between my worlds, I never forgot all the knowledge I had built up about healing. To be fair, sometimes I had to rely on instinct, but it had never let me down. Aware that it was only three days until the next games, I made sure that I had plenty of clean bandages and cloths and that I had a good supply of the ointments and salves I used for cleaning wounds.

I went out to the storeroom to draw some poppy juice from the large amphora in which I kept it. The pot was stacked, along with several others against the back wall of the room, out of the reach of inquisitive children. As I did so, a picture popped into my head of a woman in strange clothes finding my jars in the garden. How odd; how did they get there? Another followed and then another, images flickering through my mind until the final one, when they suddenly slowed. I recognised the woman; it was the other 'me'. She was facing the tall man — the one who had held her hand in the white bed — and was giving him my clasp, which seemed to be glowing, her expression one of entreaty. Even though I had only been back a couple of hours and that I should know the reason, I couldn't grasp it.

Trying to work it out made me feel dizzy all over again, so I gave up, dragging my concentration back to the job in hand. I finished topping up the pitcher with the poppy juice and, after securing the storeroom door, replaced the jar in my medicine room. Satisfied that I had done everything I could there, I checked my leather bag to ensure it included all I required for the next day. Going through to the kitchen, I poured myself a goblet of water and decided to drink it in the courtyard. As I sat in the quiet, the image of the other 'me' still hovered at the edge of my consciousness, demanding attention, but try as I might I could not pin down why.

My family arrived home soon after; the children were full of their afternoon with Aemilia and Cornelius. Aliza had much gossip from her friends, which she said she would share after the small fry had gone to bed. We prepared the evening meal and my two Romans appeared, as if on cue, just as we were serving it. It was unusual for us all to be together for a meal, so it made a lovely change. Eventually, we persuaded the three children to go to bed, once their father and Marcus had played in the garden with them for a short while, allowing Aliza and me to tidy up.

A little later we four adults were enjoying a goblet of warm calda in the living area, the children finally settled. Now, Aliza could share her gossip. It seems that she had been told by a reliable source — one of her friends — that the Emperor was expected at the upcoming games. I glanced across at Maxentius, who nodded imperceptibly. I grimaced, knowing what this meant; it was too good an opportunity to resist. The protestors would jump at the chance to cause mayhem and it could get very ugly. Unaware, Aliza was quite excited about the chance to see an Emperor, which was strange, as she had no reason to like Vespasian and said she might go along with her friends.

We chatted about the games for a little longer, then Aliza excused herself; she had things to do in her own rooms and wanted an early night. After she had gone, the three of us fell silent, caught up in our own thoughts. I was mulling over the logistics of treating injured gladiators as well as injured spectators and rioters, while my two Romans were no doubt worrying about how to employ the garrison to greatest effect. The Emperor would have his own guard with him and Maxentius' men would augment them, but how would they keep the rioters at bay? Three days' notice seemed unusually short, something I commented on.

"It's often a last minute decision," said Maxentius. "That way, anyone with ill intent shouldn't have time to carry out their plans, although in this case I'm not sure it will make any difference. These protestors have been ready for months, they are always prepared." He sighed. "It will be a very long day." Marcus nodded.

"I'm sorry Hannah, I fear you and your fellow medici will be very busy." I smiled ruefully, noting that I had just that afternoon made sure my stocks were well supplied. Marcus looked at me as though he wanted to ask me something, but wasn't sure whether he wanted to hear the answer.

"What is it, Marcus?" I asked him gently.

"Is this...will he...do they?" Hesitating. "Is this when we lose Vespasian?"

"No, he is not killed by rioters. He dies from a sickness and I think he is with us for another month or two yet," I reassured him. "Whatever happens at the games, the Emperor is not hurt." The relief on Marcus' face was almost comical. I grinned and collected the goblets to refill them. Our talk turned to mundane matters and about an hour later Marcus went over to his own quarters.

Maxentius and I sat for a little while longer, enjoying the peace, before turning in. Just before I blew out the lamp, I looked my husband in the eye.

"Please stay safe, Max. There are things that I fear have been set in motion which we cannot control and I could not bear it if you were hurt."

"Trust me, my love, I do not deliberately place myself in harm's way and I will take every care, but I am a soldier and I have a job to do." It wasn't enough but it would have to do. He pulled me close, soothing my fears the best way he knew how and, for a little while it worked.

The day of the games dawned warm and sunny. There was an air of anticipation, for what was always a spectacle would today have the added bonus of the Emperor's presence. Over the previous few days, Maxentius and his men had searched out as many of the protestors as they could find and removed them from the city's boundaries, temporarily incarcerating them in the barracks outside the walls. Some they had been unable to locate, but they hoped that they had reduced the risk to the general public.

As the Emperor was attending, there would be several executions during the lunch break. I did not know who the condemned were, but chewed over whether I would have the chance to slip them some poppy juice just before they were dragged into the arena; it would make their death less traumatic. My three would go to the procession, as they had the last time, but then they would spend the rest of the day with Aemilia and Cornelius. It was the twins' birthday and they were having a party for several of their friends. It would keep them well away from the amphitheatre and, by extension trouble all day.

Maxentius left just after first light and I got up soon after, slipping out of the house to the Gladiators' School not long after the second hour for one last check on the men who would be fighting this day. They all seemed as ready as they could be; Darius and Mihai were champing at the bit. I did not check on Tobias, but Tullius told me he was also raring to go. I hoped their battle would have the same outcome as the previous one, but logic told me it was more likely one of them would die, or lose and be condemned by the crowd.

I met with the other medici, noticing that my two army doctors, Gallus Blandinus and Florianus Camillus, were among them and we chatted for a while discussing the fitness of some of the gladiators. None was happy about the planned executions, as wild animals would likely be used. Whatever the crimes of those condemned, men of healing dislike such torture to be inflicted on human beings for someone else's pleasure. After making sure we were ready for whatever the day threw at us, I returned home and got my family ready. Aliza was coming along with us to the procession, but still hadn't made up her mind whether she was going to attend the main event. I had said my piece; it was her choice.

By the fourth hour we were in position along the route, Efraim, Liora and Claudia jumping up and down in excitement. We were hard pushed to stop them from running off, but by threatening them with bed instead of the party, I managed to control their antics. Soon, we could hear the roar of the crowd as the parade wound its way towards the amphitheatre. The sponsor had initially been Caelinus Aetius, the town's other magistrate, but he had deferred this honour to his Emperor — an expected decision — and Vespasian headed the procession.

It was a surreal moment for me, bearing in mind I had studied this man and how he ruled the Empire, in my other life nearly two thousand years hence and, now here I was seeing him in the flesh. He was very imposing and, although he exuded power and authority, he had a kindly face. I remembered that, along with his military expertise, he was admired for his humour and affable nature. These qualities had marked him, by modern historians, as one of the 'good Emperors'. His countenance reflected this, but I felt that he looked unwell; his face seemed rather pale and his posture that of someone in discomfort. Maybe it was the beginning of his last illness.

Shaking off my dark thoughts, I enjoyed the rest of the procession, except for the march of the condemned, who were shackled by their ankles and wrists, then chained to each other by throat manacles. I shuddered when I saw them: utterly defeated, their heads bowed, the crowd booing its distaste. Even accepting that their crimes might have been heinous and that by executing them in such a public manner would act as a deterrent to other would-be criminals, didn't mean I had to enjoy their hopelessness.

As the last athlete cartwheeled his way down the road, I whisked the children to the twins' home, leaving them in the capable hands of Flavia, their mother. She said she would keep them until either Maxentius or I could collect them at the end of the day. Thanking her, I waved to my three, making sure they remembered to give the twins their gifts and made my way to the Palaestra.

The games followed their usual programme and I was kept very busy tending to minor wounds until the lunch break. There would be no scheduled animal fights today, but the condemned would face being torn limb from limb by large beasts that had been starved for the past forty-eight hours. The men had no hope of survival. They would be left shackled and most would either bleed to death or die from shock. I had been unable to give any of them some of my poppy draft for they were kept well away from the gladiators; so I stayed over at the Palaestra until I was sure it was all over. It was harrowing enough hearing their screams as they died.

I hadn't seen Maxentius or Marcus at all and they did not appear during the lunch break, which surprised me, but I assumed they would be very busy trying to ensure that no protestor got close to the Emperor. By late afternoon, when the bout between Darius and Tobias was due to start, I was hot and tired. My tunic was smeared with blood and dirt and my hair was falling out of its plait. The crowd of spectators were ready; they had been waiting for this all day and their excitement had reached an hysterical level. Tullius introduced the two men, who had been excused from the team battle, to save their strength for this final one. Reluctantly, I made my way to the tunnel at the back of the amphitheatre and waited with the other medici.

The bout started. Darius and Tobias circled each other, getting a feel for his opponent's fitness. Their trainers had done a good job for they looked well prepared. The circling went on for several minutes until, suddenly, they hurled themselves at each other, their fists and feet making contact with bone and flesh. Blood spurted as Darius landed a well-timed punch to Tobias' face, who just as quickly swung an uppercut to his opponent's chin. They had no other weapons at this stage and I wasn't sure whether they would be given any as the bout drew on. The way they were going with their fists, it was unlikely any other weapon would be needed.

I retired to the back of the amphitheatre, unable to watch. Standing at the participants' entrance, I stared up at the mountain. It looked so benign in the sunlight; it's thick forests near the top, opening on to fertile fields along the lower slopes. Although, from this distance all still looked lush and green, recently, there had been reports of crops dying and vines withering for no apparent reason. I knew this was related to the volcanic activity, but I doubted anyone would believe me, so I kept quiet. There was nothing anyone could do about it anyway. It was hard to believe that soon the peak would blow and that beautiful vista would be obliterated in a matter of minutes.

Turning away, I decided to try to freshen up and walked over to the Palaestra where I could use the sinks. Enjoying the cool of the changing rooms, I washed my hands, running damp fingers through my tousled hair in an attempt to tame the curls. I managed to re-plait it into some semblance of tidiness and brushed as much as I could of the dust and dirt off my tunic as I could.

The roar of the spectators could still be heard, so I knew the fight continued. It must have been going on for at least an hour. I walked over to the bench by the swimming pool and sat under the shade of a tree. I hadn't been there for very long, when suddenly everything went quiet. Startled, I glanced towards the amphitheatre, but obviously couldn't see anything. Heart in my mouth, I hurried back, slipping along the tunnel so I could see into the arena. One of the men was down, but I couldn't work out which one. He was moving, but looked to be in agony. The crowd was hushed, waiting to see what would happen. Would the other man finish him? It was all I could do not to run into the arena and help the injured prisoner, but I knew I had to stay put.

As the wounded man tried to stand, I knew he was probably doomed, as even from where I was standing I could see that his leg was broken. He must have fallen from one of the mounds of rocks or wooden structures that had been set up around the arena to make the fights more interesting. The bone was sticking out through his skin and blood was pouring down into the sand pooling dark red. He would die from blood loss if he weren't treated soon. Desperately, I looked around for Tullius, who was coming along the tunnel towards me.

"Please, Tullius..." I whispered, "...I don't know which one of them is hurt, but please don't let him die like this." I grasped his hand in my agitation. "They have given the crowd an excellent afternoon's entertainment, can you ask them if they will spare both again?" Tullius gazed at me for a long moment.

"I will try, Hannah, wife of Maxentius, but I cannot expect a second reprieve. Do you wish me to do this even if the injured man is Tobias?" I nodded.

"The man's leg is sticking out through his flesh, he is bleeding to death. Even if he is reprieved, I doubt that I, or any of my colleagues will be able to save him, but he cannot be left in such agony for long. It is inhuman and makes us worse than the criminals who were executed today."

Tullius entered the arena to the roar of the crowd of spectators; they knew why he was there. He quieted them and made his plea. The now familiar twisting of the hands began and their chant rippled through the seats. "Spare them, spare them, spare them!" The ripple of sound reached a crescendo; it was deafening. They wished to spare them? I shuddered with relief; these two men had fought so well that the audience wanted to keep them both alive, at least for now. Tullius acknowledged their decision, but waited until the Emperor approved it; he had the final say. I held my breath, crossing my fingers and closing my eyes. Then, realising I needed to know which way the decision went, opened them again.

The crowd went wild. It appeared that Vespasian had approved the choice and the two men were spared. Immediately, two auxiliaries ran onto the sand with a sort of stretcher made of wood and carefully lifted the injured man onto it. I watched as he saluted the crowed — who cheered again — then he fell back against the pallet. He was carried through the tunnel and straight across to the Palaestra, I followed them, my bag already open, asking one of the trainers to get a lot of water and a large bowl. His bearers laid him on the ground and I fell onto my knees next to him. At Gallus' insistence, the trainer removed the shackles. We could not do our job while they were still in place and it wasn't as though the prisoner would be able to run away.

Without even stopping to see who it was, I began my examination, talking to myself as I assessed his injuries. Gallus knelt at his other side and we worked together, cleaning the dirt away before trying to do anything else. Blood was pouring from the wound and the break was horrendous. It needed to be set; the bones had to be rejoined or he had no chance at all. Even if we could do that successfully, his chances were slim, but we needed to try. While we worked, Gallus told me that wounds such as this were typical in men who had fallen from their horse or from a great height.

Finally, the wound was as clean as we could get it. The next step was putting the bone back. We would need to stretch the leg and then try to click the broken pieces together. Acting as fast as I could, I removed the splinters that were shattered beyond hope, then washed the whole area again with water, in which I had dissolved salt and vinegar. I still had no idea whether it was Darius or Tobias; all my concentration had been on the injury. Glancing up at the trainers who were standing close by, I asked one of them to hold the man's shoulders so that he could not move. I found my little jar of poppy juice and offered some to the prone man and for the first time, I looked into his face.

Chapter Thirty

It was Tobias. For a split second I faltered, unsure whether I could continue treating this man who had hurt me so many years ago. Then my training kicked in and I lifted his head, encouraging him to sip the draft. Speaking to him in Hebrew, so he would understand, I told him that this juice would dull the pain, which I could see was unbearable.

Whatever my feelings towards this man, I couldn't stand by and watch this level of suffering. Absently, I contemplated whether this was what had drawn me to the gladiators. Was it all so that I would be able to face my tormentor and be free of the terror? I had no time to ponder this; we had work to do.

Waiting for a moment for the draft to take effect, we readied ourselves. This had to be quick and we only had one chance to get it right. The trainer held Tobias' shoulders while I placed a twist of cloth in his mouth to bite down on. Two of the other medici held the top of his leg, while Gallus and I positioned ourselves near his ankle, hands over hands for a steady grip. Gritting my teeth, I counted down from three.

On one, we all pulled and Gallus twisted the bone so it slotted back into position. There was a grinding sound as the bones clicked together and Tobias, unable to stop himself, screamed in agony and fainted. The fifth medici, who I noticed was Florianus, ran his hands along the joint, feeling the connection and after a long and very tense moment, nodded his satisfaction.

We released our grip carefully, allowing the leg to settle and the skin to relax. Blood still pooled under the torn flesh but not as fast. Tobias' toes, which had been turning blue from lack of a blood supply, began very slowly to return to their proper colour. He had a long way to go, but we may well have saved his leg and thus, his life.

I was trembling with the effort and both Gallus and I were splattered in blood. Gently washing the wound, I made sure that as far as I could see there was no splinter of bone or dirt lodged within, before covering the gash with my salve, adding extra honey and myrrh. Finally bandaging the leg in a way that restricted any movement but allowed blood flow to his feet, we could do no more. Now it was a matter of time.

He needed to be where he could be observed full time and, with a sinking heart I realised that my house was the closest place. We could put him in the headquarters; there were spare rooms on the ground floor and he could be guarded round the clock. Sighing with the irony of it all, I indicated that this was probably the best plan. By this time Tullius had joined us, and he looked at me, disquiet etched on his face.

"Are you sure, Hannah? This man of all men does not deserve such care from the person he treated so badly."

"I cannot in all conscience do otherwise, Tullius," I replied. "He needs constant care and I do not see how he can be carried all the way back to the school just yet. If he is lodged in the headquarters, he can be guarded and if someone is willing to help me, we can share the load."

Florianus said that he would; he just needed to collect some things from his home and would be back within the hour. Wearily, I nodded, knowing that we would be in for a long night, but that there was no help for it.

"As soon as he can be moved, I will make arrangements for him to be taken back to the school," Tullius said, realising that my mind was made up. Bearing the wounded man, the two auxiliaries followed me along the narrow pathways to the headquarters, where we knocked. Amazingly it was Petronius who admitted us, looking at me and then at the man on the pallet in astonishment.

"Don't ask, Petronius," I said. "I'll tell you in a minute. Which is the closest unused room?" He took us along the corridor to a room near the back of the building. This was advantageous, being close to the domestic space and two doors along from the connecting walkway to my home.

The men laid the pallet down gently and I left them for a moment to collect some bedding from next door. Maxentius still wasn't home, which bothered me. Where was he? I needed to tell him about this as soon as possible, as he was likely to protest. Gathering the sheets and blankets, I went back along the walkway and into the headquarters. Tobias looked terrible; he had come round with the movement of the pallet, his skin was clammy and his face was as white as the sheets I was laying over him, he needed to sleep. I thanked the auxiliaries, who bowed, telling me they'd report to Tullius.

Gallus had walked the short distance with us and stayed with me until Florianus arrived. Petronius was rather anxious about the proceedings, so I explained why we had brought the prisoner here.

"We need to find guards who can watch him round the clock, Petronius," I said. "He is still a prisoner of war even though he can't even stand and I know Maxentius will want a sentry posted. Do you know where he is, by the way?" Petronius shook his head.

"The last I saw of him he, Marcus and a contingent from the garrison were dealing with a large mob of protestors who were trying to storm the Emperor's box in the amphitheatre." I stared at him, my worry increasing. Surely they should be done by now?

While I was ruminating over this, Florianus appeared in the doorway. I asked whether he would be able to take first watch, as I needed to attend to my family. He was happy to, so after filling Petronius in on the rest of our intentions, I returned to my home. The house was quiet. Where was everyone? I had just begun to feel rather panicked — it was quite late now and they should all be here — when suddenly the door burst open and the rest of my family came in.

Then I remembered the twins' party. Oh my goodness, I'd forgotten to collect my children from Flavia's house and realised that must be where Maxentius had gone. What a terrible mother! I was so relieved that I sank into the chair, feeling rather wobbly. The children ran over talking nineteen to the dozen about the party and I answered them as best I could, but my mind wouldn't focus. Maxentius noticed my distraction and called them to go and get ready for bed. He came over to me, sitting close and giving me a hug.

"I was worried about you," I said, leaning into him. "I heard there was a problem late in the day."

"We had to forcibly remove some protestors from the amphitheatre, they were rather fired up and it took some doing. Then once we'd taken them into custody, I left Marcus to finish up and went to collect the children. What's wrong?" I looked at him and taking a deep breath, told him what had happened at the arena.

"And this man is lying on a pallet next door?" I could hear the anger in his tone.

"There was nothing else I could do, my love." He made a reflexive movement; I placed my hand on his leg. "Please, let me finish." I explained my reasons, especially that having him so close meant that I would have protection while I was treating him. "All your guards are there, I'd be safer next door than anywhere else."

"You didn't need to treat him; any of the other medici could have treated him." I knew what was bothering him and I understood his anxiety, but I needed him to understand my actions.

"Maxentius, this is the only way I know. Yes, any of the other medici could have treated him, but I cannot allow them to shoulder all the burden; we need to work together to have any chance at all. I didn't think I'd be able to help him, but I had to. Instinct took over and it was more important to take away his pain than worry about what he did to me. I will never forget that, but if I want to call myself a healer, I cannot let such things interfere with my work. In any case, he may not even live; his injury was devastating, but we had to try."

I held my husband's gaze, willing him to trust my judgement. He wrapped his arms around me, pulling me to his chest.

"I love you, my Hannah and I love your passion for your work, but I will not sit back and let anything happen to you. I will have two guards posted around the clock and you shall never be alone with that man." I smiled up at him, nodding my agreement.

"I love you too, Max, more than life itself. Now, stop fretting and kiss me." He obliged.

Much later, after I had washed and changed, settled the children into bed and enjoyed a meal with Maxentius and Aliza, I went back along to the headquarters building. Maxentius came with me, the children were safe under Aliza's watch for a little while. Maxentius would sit with me tonight and Petronius had agreed to stay as well. Florianus had administered some more of the poppy juice in the hope of giving Tobias a restful night. I thanked him and told him to get some sleep; he would take over from me in the early hours. Petronius had set up a bed in the room next door for my fellow medicus, who took himself off looking as tired as I felt.

I studied my patient's face. Seemingly, he was resting but his skin was still clammy and his breathing erratic. Infection was a real possibility bearing in mind the way in which he received his injury. I undid the bandage. Maxentius gasped when he saw the damaged limb.

"See, this is what man is forced to do to man for the sake of sport. It is barbaric. A quick death would be much more acceptable."

"Even incapacitated, I still don't trust him near you, my Hannah."

"I know, and I love you for it, my husband." I smiled over Tobias' inert body at Maxentius.

Turning my attention to the task at hand, I checked the wound, allowing the air to circulate around it for a few minutes. Very carefully, I ran my fingers over the leg, gently pressing the flesh, checking for swelling and bad circulation. There was no sign of infection so far, but that didn't mean it wasn't lurking deep within. I washed it, taking care to let the water run in as far as it could go, then patted it gently with a soft cloth. Once satisfied that it was clean and dry, I reapplied the salve and bandaged the damaged area. I knew that the torn skin would need debriding eventually, if he survived long enough to need it, but for now it was enough to protect the wound. Finished for the moment, I sat on the floor, wearily resting my head against the wall.

Petronius had found a couple of chairs and was sitting in one of them, but Maxentius came and sat next to me. Taking my hand, he began to rub his thumb on my palm and I leaned my head against his shoulder.

"You know we could use those chairs, don't you?" He grinned down at me.

"Oh, this is so much better," I whispered. "You, me, the floor, a critically injured patient." He chuckled and kissed the top of my head. We chatted quietly and I must have dozed, for I suddenly felt someone shaking me.

"Hannah, quickly, something's wrong." I came awake immediately; Tobias was tossing and writhing on the pallet. So much for no sign of infection! Maxentius grabbed my bag, as I tried to unwrap the bandages.

"Please can you hold his shoulders? I need to get this off and he's tossing too much." Petronius came over and helped, the two men pinning Tobias down as firmly as possible without hurting him.

Finally I got the bandage off and I could smell the infection, even before I could see it. Frustrated, I motioned for a lamp, which one of them handed to me. Holding the light over the injured leg, I could just see the telltale signs of poison. Despite all our care, there must have been some filth lodged deep inside the wound. I asked Petronius to bring me the bowl and pitcher of water, which I had placed on a cupboard near the door. Filling the bowl with water, I quickly washed my hands and then discarding that, refilled it adding salt and a few drops of frankincense.

Very gently, I tried to wash out the infection, but it was impossible to see whether I was reaching it all. The damage was so great, not only to the bone, but also to the surrounding tissue. Splinters of bone had torn muscle and flesh and I knew that there might be minute shards embedded where we couldn't see. Oh what I wouldn't do for an X-ray machine, I thought. Not helpful, Hannah. Pushing thoughts of modern-day, sterile hospitals to the back of my mind, I concentrated on what I could do. I worked for a long time, hoping I had caught the rot before it had set in too deeply.

No doubt owing to the pain, Tobias regained consciousness while I was ministering to him, but I don't think he knew who any of us were. I gave him some poppy juice, which helped him back to sleep, but then he fell into delirium. In his torment, he muttered and cried out and, from what I could make out, he thought he was a young man, back in Jerusalem. In spite of everything he had done to me, I felt very sad, remembering tiny snippets of my life when we were children playing in the neighbourhood, without cares or worries. How had he changed so much? Had I? I had so little recollection of anything before I met my two Romans.

No time to ponder such things, as the fever I knew would come took hold and one moment Tobias' skin burned with a heat I could not cool; the next he shivered with cold. The last time I had to deal with anyone so badly wounded was Sergius, over a decade ago on Masada. Memories from those weeks ran through my head. Was there anything I could do? Could I save this man, or would he die, like his hated enemy, in a land far, far from his own?

It was a very long night, I told Maxentius not to wake Florianus — he could sit with him the next day. He had worked just as hard as I had during the games and was considerably older. I was in a rhythm now and tired as I was, it was easier for me to keep going than to try to explain what was going on. If I could get Tobias through the night, maybe he had a chance. My two guardians helped me by bringing fresh water, sheets and cloths, as I needed them.

At some point Marcus joined us and I managed to persuade my husband to go and get some rest; one of us needed to be able to deal with three children the next day. Since I had Marcus and Petronius, Maxentius reluctantly acquiesced and went home, his shoulders drooping with fatigue. The three of us chatted about this and that while Tobias was more settled and I asked what had happened to the protestors. Marcus said that they had been taken to the garrison, outside of the city's walls, where they would await sentencing. My three acquaintances from the cells had been involved and now they all faced serious charges. You couldn't storm the Emperor's box and get away with a rap on the knuckles!

"Is there any chance that I could visit them while they're out there?" I asked Marcus.

"Maybe; you'll need to check with Maxentius but I don't see it being a problem. Why would you want to?" Curiously.

"They were kind to me in their way, I would like to return the favour, even if it's just for a few minutes. Were any of them hurt?"

"Probably. We weren't exactly worrying about their comfort when we were dragging them out of the amphitheatre."

"How did they even get in?"

"They must have gone in separately and managed to join up once they were inside. It's very difficult to tell an antagonist from a spectator. It's not as though they wear a banner on their chests with 'I am a protestor' blazoned across." I grinned at Marcus, picturing such an image in my head.

Just as Marcus finished telling us, Tobias started tossing in his sleep, the fever spiking again. Quickly, I soaked a cloth in cold water and placed it on his forehead, then did the same with a sheet. Wringing the sheet out, I laid it over Tobias trying to cool his skin, which felt like it was on fire. While waiting for his temperature to drop, I undid the bandage, the wound was now oozing yellowish-green pus and it smelt terrible. The two men with me backed away, appalled at the smell and the state of the injured leg.

"By all the gods, Hannah, how can you heal that?" Marcus whispered, his face pale.

"I'm not sure we can, we just try. I have to keep cleaning it, then covering it with balms and salves, then bandage it to protect it from further damage in the hope that I can kill the infection." I sighed. "This is a ghastly wound though, I'm not sure whether we can save him. Surely you have seen worse on the battlefield?"

"Yes, but they were already dead," Petronius interjected, with macabre humour. Fair point, I thought.

"Sergius' wound was almost as bad as this, but it was to his abdomen and there was no shattered bone," I said. Marcus looked at me in shock.

"I had no idea. I don't remember much about those first few days and by the time I was aware of what was going on, he was bandaged up." All the while we were talking, I was treating the wound, washing out the pus and squeezing my water, salt and frankincense mix as far as I could into the leg. It was running all over the floor, but I couldn't tell how much good I was doing.

Leaving the wound to dry naturally, I checked Tobias' pulse. It was very fast and irregular, as was his breathing. His skin was cooling and, as I expected, he started shivering as the heat fled from his body. Tremors were running along his frame and he was still tossing. I tried to get him to sip some of the poppy juice, but his teeth were chattering so hard that it was impossible.

I was very glad that I had Marcus and Petronius with me, for I think I would have panicked had I been on my own. It was over twelve hours since Tobias had been injured and he was getting worse, not better. Also, in the back of my mind were the other injured gladiators that we had treated throughout the games. How were they? On top of all of this, I really wanted to sleep.

I noticed that Tobias had stopped shivering, so I tried to get him to drink the draft; this time I managed to get a little passed his lips. The effect was almost immediate; he calmed down and his breathing steadied. I reapplied the salve to the wound and bandaged it firmly, knowing that I would have to repeat it all over again very soon.

Just as I finished, I reached out to check Tobias' temperature. Even though he was calmer, he was still muttering — nothing that made any sense and all of it in Hebrew. I don't think he had any clue where he was or why he was hurt, or even that he was hurt. He was lost deep with himself. As I touched his forehead with the back of my hand, he grabbed my wrist, twisting it and making me gasp with sudden pain. Marcus was on him in an instant; angrily peeling back the fingers that had gripped me so tightly that I could already see bruises forming.

"Wait, Marcus, look at him. He's not seeing us, he's seeing something else, something that scares him."

"He need be scared," said Marcus. "After what he did to you, he should be terrified."

"Yes, I know, but he's muttering about a life a long time ago, before he was on Masada, I think. He doesn't even know who I am." Marcus wasn't convinced, but returned to his seat, watching Tobias carefully.

Unable to do any more for my patient at the moment, I went across to the laundry. I washed the bowl thoroughly and refilled the pitcher with fresh water, then I dropped the dirty cloths and bandages into a bucket; I would burn them later. Taking the bowl and pitcher with me, I replaced them on the top of the cupboard then nipped back into my house, Firstly, finding the arnica to rub over my bruised wrist, hoping Maxentius wouldn't notice; and secondly collecting a flagon of calda and three goblets. Apologising that it was cold, I poured it out, passing the goblets round. Thanking me, the two men drank deeply while I just sipped mine, as following suit would not have been the best idea.

I scrutinised Tobias, looking for signs of change. His breathing was still erratic and his cheeks were flushed with hectic colour but he wasn't tossing, which was something. I realised that the light in the room was not too dark; dawn was breaking, the world outside was beginning a new day and I hoped that Tobias would live through it. Florianus appeared in the doorway, looking well slept and asked why we hadn't woken him. I explained my reasoning to which he nodded, understanding perfectly.

By the time I had briefed him on Tobias' condition, the sun was above the horizon, its rays sending long fingers through the window. It was time for me to get some sleep. Two more soldiers entered the room, the next shift. I greeted them, but left Florianus to tell them why they were needed. Thanking Marcus and Petronius, saying that I hoped they'd be able to get some rest, knowing it was highly likely that they would be needed later in the day at the garrison, I made my way along the connecting path to my home.

No sound yet; everyone was still deep in slumber. I stripped off my clothes and dumped them in the laundry sink, tiptoeing quickly along to our bedroom; Maxentius was fast asleep, snoring gently. Not bothering with my night shift, I slipped between the sheets and, unable to stop myself, kissed him gently on the cheek. He stirred enough to pull me to his chest, kissing the back of my neck. I snuggled against him and was asleep immediately.

The sun was high overhead when I woke up and the house was quiet, which was strange as I assumed the children would be here. Slowly, I stretched, feeling my joints crack as they realigned themselves. I ached from my hard work of the day before and a long night spent leaning over my patient. I washed and dressed, then wandered into the main room to see what I could find to eat. Aliza had left a platter of bread, cheese and fruit for me, which I devoured, suddenly realising how hungry I was.

I would be busy today, I wanted to check on Tobias and see how Florianus was holding up, and then I should really pop along to the school to check on the other injured men. Mentally dot-pointing what I needed to do, I gathered my things and went along to the temporary sick room next door. Florianus was dozing in a chair and Tobias was fast asleep. They both looked peaceful so I didn't disturb them. I knocked on Maxentius' door, but there was no answer. Peeping my head around, I noticed a pile of wax tablets on the desk. I scratched a short note to my husband, telling him that I was going to the Gladiators' School if anybody needed me.

Chapter Thirty One

Petronius wasn't in the headquarters, so I asked one of the other soldiers to accompany me. While I doubted that I was at risk from the protesters at that moment since they seemed to be incarcerated at the garrison, I didn't want to upset Maxentius. The young man was happy to oblige; it gave him something different to do. His name was Nonus Julius Germanus and we chatted about his life in the army as we walked along. Not yet jaded by long years of war, Julius was still enamoured of the military and made an enthusiastic companion. Arriving at the school, the guard escorted us to the lanista's office, where Julius waited outside.

"How is the Hebrew?" asked Tullius. I waggled my hand.

"So, so," I replied. "I fear we may lose him yet. There is severe infection in his wound and I do not know whether we can clear it. The damage was terrible." I knew that even if Tobias lived, he would likely lose his leg, but as an amputation was the last thing I wanted to consider, I left it for now. "How are the other gladiators, those who were injured?"

"Most seem comfortable. Gallus Blandinus is already here and I think he went to where the dead are laid out." I nodded, saying I would go and assist him, then check on Darius, if that was acceptable. Tullius agreed so, confirming I'd see him before I left, went to find Gallus in the long medical room. Julius said he would wait in the quadrangle, I think he probably knew one or two of the guards and it was good excuse to chat.

There were several bodies this time; some were the condemned and others had died during their fight. They were already laid out in a neat row and Gallus had begun the difficult task of cleaning them. Wrapping an old sheet around my waist to protect my tunic, I joined him. We worked together in silence; words just didn't seem appropriate, for the bodies of the dead were a ghastly sight. Those who had faced the wild animals had been torn apart, some were even missing limbs and those who had lost their bout in the arena were not much better.

It took us a long time, but eventually all were cleaned and wrapped in shrouds, ready for their next journey. I found it peculiar that a society, while happy to allow men to be destroyed for sport, still wanted their remains to be cared for and I meditated over whether some had families who wished to claim their loved one. As a final gesture, I placed a sprig of rosemary on the top of each body and we left them in the cool dimness, hoping their souls would find repose.

Gallus asked how Tobias was faring and I gave him an update, saying I would be checking on him after I'd finished at the school. He nodded and said he might try to relieve us later in the day. I squeezed his hand gratefully; we needed as much help as we could get. Then I made my way to Darius' room where he was resting on his bed. Mihai was not there and I wondered whether he was already back at training. Darius smiled when I entered, but I could tell he was in some discomfort. Tobias had managed to get in some serious blows of his own; Darius had severe bruising all over his chest and back, a split lip and a very black eye.

I told the guard I would need to rub ointment onto the prisoner's body to relieve the bruising so he called for another guard and, the pair of them stood close while I applied arnica over the damaged skin, grinning at Darius' expression as the pungent aroma from the balm filled the room.

"It will help," I told him, but he didn't seem convinced. I checked his eye, pressing the area around the socket gently; as far as I could tell it wasn't broken but it was so swollen I couldn't be sure. I had some ointment that I thought might help and rubbed it in carefully. As I finished up, I patted his shoulder and said I would be back to check on him in two days. As I rose to leave, he caught my hand.

"The Hebrew, does he live?" I nodded.

"Yes, for now at least, but his leg is badly broken." I stopped unsure of how much Darius would understand. He grunted an acknowledgement but I couldn't tell whether the news pleased or disappointed him. Maybe I would ask Petronius to talk to him when I was next there.

The guards escorted me back to the lanista's domain and I told him we had finished preparing the dead and that I would be back in two days. He nodded, asking that I keep him advised of Tobias' condition. Agreeing, I left meeting up with Julius who was waiting for me at the main entrance and we meandered slowly back to the headquarters. As we were walking, the ground trembled and involuntarily I looked up at Vesuvius. I could see smoke above the peak and a shiver ran down my spine. Julius noticed my reaction and followed my gaze.

"The mountain is unhappy," he said. I looked at him, waiting for him to elaborate, but he continued walking.

"What do you mean, Julius?" I asked.

"The mountain has been growling for many moons; soon the growl will become a roar and we shall feel its wrath."

"I fear you are right; we would be wise to take every care." I left it at that. Julius was the first person I'd talked to who seemed to have some awareness of what would happen. Hopefully he would recognise the signs and get out before it was too late.

The rest of our walk was without incident and he left me at the door of the sick room. Florianus was working on the patient's wound. Kneeling next to him, I asked how Tobias was doing.

"Not well, Hannah; the poison is deep and although I have cleaned the area several times today, I don't seem to be able to stem it."

"This was what I feared last night. I think there must be dirt so far inside that we would have to open the leg up to get to it and I do not think he would survive such an operation." We agreed that we had to keep doing what we were doing and hope — that was all we could do. I told Florianus that I would be back within the hour to give him a break and went along the walkway to my home.

As I walked in, I heard a gaggle of voices and saw what appeared to be a multitude of people. It took me a few moments to realise that it was Maxentius' mother, sister and family. I gaped, what on earth were they doing here? Where would I put them? We didn't have enough room and, most importantly, was the house tidy? On top of this, despite wearing a sheet while I was cleaning the dead, I knew I was filthy. My clothes were covered in grime and blood, both they and I needing a good scrub. I must have looked like a wreck before these elegant women in their beautiful travelling clothes.

Before I had a chance to slip away and clean up, Claudia spotted me and swept along the room to hug me. I put my hands out to stop her saying that I needed to change before we greeted each other as I was covered in filth. She ignored me completely and caught me to her in a warm embrace, before Antonia did the same. I shook my head at them in exasperation.

"You are both as bad as Maxentius; he never listens to a word I say. How is it you are here and where is he by the way? Did he know you were coming?"

"We found him at the garrison and he accompanied us here," said Antonia, sidestepping my last question very neatly. "He had to go back but said he would be home before the last hour. We are on our way to Rome." I pricked up my ears, Rome — please let them stay there until the danger had passed. "We were hoping you might agree to our taking the children with us. Julia and Antonius have been begging to spend more time with their cousins and we thought this could be a wonderful opportunity."

I stared at her, thoughts tumbling through my head. Did I want to be without them? We had never been apart, not even for one night, but if they were in Rome and if they stayed there for the summer, they would be safe and I wouldn't have to worry about getting them away from here. What about their lessons? I must have looked bewildered for Claudia came to my rescue and said we would talk about it later over a meal. I nodded distractedly and excused myself, going along to my bedroom to change. Oh, I hoped Maxentius would be home on time; I couldn't decide this one on my own.

After freshening up, I sat on the edge of our bed for a few minutes enjoying the quiet thinking about whether my children were home. Was Aliza with them? I hadn't seen any of them but the room had seemed very full, so maybe they had been there. Dear me, my mind was all over the place at the moment — get a hold of yourself, Hannah. I had to get back to the sick room; all this would have to wait until later. Making my way back to the others, I noticed that Aliza was there handing out wine and sweetmeats and then I spotted my three playing with their cousins at one end of the main room. I smiled at her, mouthing a thank you; again blessing whichever god had brought her to me. I explained that I was needed elsewhere, but that I would be back as soon as possible and left before anyone could stop me.

I knew I was being cowardly; I didn't want to have to face such a huge decision, even though I knew it would probably save their lives. The thought of not seeing them every day hurt my heart. Pushing it to the back of my mind, I returned to the sick room. Florianus looked exhausted and I suggested he have a break to get some food and rest. He agreed, telling me what he had been doing for Tobias during the day, then left me to it. The patient looked deathly ill; his skin was ashen and I could see that it was still clammy. His breathing was laboured and his pulse, as I checked it, erratic. Florianus had only just re-dressed the wound, so I left it well alone for now, but persuaded Tobias to drink some of the poppy juice, hoping it would calm him. He seemed to respond, his chest settling into a more even rhythm, but I didn't expect it would last.

I had been watching my patient for maybe an hour when Maxentius came into the room to check on how I was faring. I went into his arms, not caring that there were two guards stationed in the room with me.

"Hey, my love, what's all this?" He tilted my chin so he could look down into my eyes.

"Your mother, how did you...she wants to...they thought it would be nice if ... I don't know whether I can..." I couldn't seem to complete my sentences and I felt my husband's chest rumble with laughter at my incoherence.

"Oh Hannah, come here, what's got you so worked up?" Sitting down on one of the chairs, he pulled me onto his knee, oblivious to his subordinates' astonishment.

"Your mother, she's here, in our house, where will she — will they — all stay? We don't have enough room. Did you know she was coming? They want to take our children to Rome." Words tumbled out of my mouth with little regard for intelligibility. Thankfully, my husband is used to me and managed to make sense of it.

"No, I didn't know they were coming, but yes I let them into the house. I have no idea where they will stay and yes, I think it might be a good idea to let the children go with them." I stared at him for a long moment. "Hannah, if what you told me is true, then we need them to be safe and away from here, this is their chance."

"I don't think I am able..." I had to stop as I felt tears forming and had no intention of crying in front of these guards. "We've never been apart," I whispered. Maxentius held me close.

"I know, my love, but I think we must let them go, they will be fine, we will see them soon enough. You do not want them in danger, do you?" He murmured the last part close to my ear, so that his soldiers would not hear. I knew he was right, but it was so hard.

"I can't tell them, you'll have to do it, you can make it sound like an adventure, I'll just cry." He grinned and agreed, telling me he'd see me later. Dropping another kiss on my head, he went back to his office, leaving me with Tobias and the two guards.

I had noticed during the last few minutes that my patient's temperature was spiking again. Washing my hands, I carefully peeled back the bandages. The injury was no better; in fact it looked worse. The skin surrounding the gash was red and swollen, but the area inside the leg where we had tried to re-align the bones was pale and a large amount of yellow pus continued to seep through. Sighing in frustration, I filled the bowl with the salt and frankincense solution and tried to rinse away as much as I could.

Tobias was tossing and muttering in his delirium, making it hard for me to work. I asked the guards to hold him still while I desperately tried to squeeze the mixture into the wound, but it kept spilling out. Even though I knew that touching the injured area would be excruciating, I realised I had no choice. Placing one hand firmly on his leg just above the torn skin, I pressed down holding the limb still while I poured the contents of the bowl into the wound with the other. Tobias cried out in agony, but I'd done it; the yellow pus washed clear. Trembling with the effort, I thanked the two guards who stepped back to their posts, nodding in acknowledgement, happy to move away from the stench of poison and that awful wound.

Tobias had, unsurprisingly, regained consciousness during my ministrations and was staring at me through pain-filled eyes. I held his gaze for a long moment and then turned my attention back to his leg. Pushing the salve in as far as I could, then laying a cloth soaked in the same mixture over the wound, I bound the limb once more. Tears were rolling down Tobias' face and, without thinking, I grasped his hand.

"What is it, Tobias?" I asked gently.

"Why?"

"Why what?"

"Why do you help me?

"Because you need me to." Simple truth.

"But I hurt you so badly. I wish I hadn't hurt you. I was so angry with you for loving that Roman and not me."

"I know and it was a terrible thing you did to me, but I survived and my Roman still loves me. You are the one who lost everything. Was it worth it?" My quiet tones softening the words. I sensed movement behind me and knew, without turning, that Maxentius had returned and was listening at the doorway.

"No, I was young and foolish and look where it got me: a captive used for sport." His voice caught as another tremor ran through him, hot colour flushing up his face. I laid a cool wet cloth over his forehead and used another to wipe him down, trying to break the heat. The fever was dragging him back into a dark place, his words becoming nonsensical. I soaked another sheet in the cool water, wringing it out and laying it right over him, watching for the chills I knew would follow.

Maxentius came right into the room with a curious expression on his face.

"How do you do this?" I glanced at him, knowing exactly what he was referring to and wondering how many times I would get asked this same question.

"I have to. You know that I cannot let my personal feelings affect the way I treat someone. I said the same thing to Tobias many years ago when he told me you and Marcus should be killed. When you become a physician, it is the injury that you must deal with, not the person; although, in all honesty, I never thought I would be able to be in the same room as Tobias after what he did, let alone treat him, but he is in desperate need. If I turned my back on him, or anyone, I would not be the person you married."

My husband looked down into my eyes, remembering those first weeks on Masada, not knowing whether he or Marcus would be allowed to live. I shivered at the recollection, I had already fallen in love with my Roman and the fear that I might have lost him still had the power to haunt me. Taking my hand and drawing me into the corridor, away from interested observers, Maxentius pulled me to his chest, covering my face with gentle kisses.

I giggled, batting at him ineffectually, when suddenly he changed tack, cupping my head and kissing me soundly on the lips. I savoured it, letting all the emotions of the past thirty-six hours or so drain away, as his kiss went deeper and deeper. My arms went around his neck, my fingers entwined themselves through his hair and I abandoned myself to him, uncaring that we were standing in the main corridor of his headquarters, or that I had a patient to whom I should be attending.

It was several minutes before we came back to earth. I smiled rather hazily as, reluctantly, Maxentius broke away. He grinned down at me and winked.

"Go on, my little temptress, get back to what you were doing before we get carried away or my soldiers come across us." He pushed me gently back into the room and strolled along the connecting walkway, presumably going to see what the rest of his family were up to. I watched until he disappeared, then returned to Tobias, who was calm for the moment. His skin was cooling, but as yet he wasn't shivering. I rested the back of my hand on his forehead. It didn't feel overly hot, but his skin, rather than being clammy, was now dry.

Frustrated, I sat back on my heels, trying to work out why we couldn't slow the infection. I didn't want to risk poking around anymore than I had to, but I speculated over the possibility that it was just the result of some small splinters and whether they could be removed without causing more damage. As I was pondering this, Gallus appeared in the doorway. I smiled gratefully at him and, as he sat down in one of the chairs, I shared my fears about Tobias.

He too had been mulling it over, coming up with the same answer as I had. There was nothing for it, we had to take another look deep inside the wound. This room did not have enough light; the only place we had a chance was in the open air, with all the dust and airborne things that might contaminate further the already infected injury. We had no other choice. I asked the soldiers whether there was anything we could lay the patient on, something like a high table or bench. One of them went to look, while we prepared ourselves.

I went along to my house; thankfully Maxentius was still there, chatting with his mother and sister. They looked up as I entered and I motioned my husband over. Explaining quietly to him what we intended to do, I asked if he would keep his and our family away from the rear garden; it would not be pleasant and there might well be screaming. He nodded his understanding and said that he would send Marcus over as soon as he returned from the garrison. Florianus had been sleeping, but we needed him, so I woke him gently, apprising him of our plans. He was worried about the risks, but knew it was our last chance to try to help the wounded man. He wasn't the only one; this would be as close as we dared get to an amputation.

The soldier had found a long trestle-like table, which he and his comrade carried out into the rear garden. I scrubbed it down thoroughly and then scrubbed it again, just to be sure. Laying two old but clean sheets over it, we waited as the same two soldiers carried Tobias out of the headquarters building. Word had obviously gone around, as several of the garrison who happened to be in Pompeii today came along hoping to watch the proceedings. Knowing we could not really prevent them, we agreed that they could, but that they had to stay well back, or go and stand up on the upper walkway. None of us could afford any more cross-contamination than there already would be.

We all washed our hands and arms and I'd found more old sheets that we could tie around our waist, protecting our clothes as much as possible. Gallus and Florianus readied their instruments and I made sure we had plenty of cloths and bandages, water, poppy juice and salves. Tobias had come round again, so I told him what we needed to do. He blanched when I explained that we had to dig into his leg for slivers of bone, but I reassured him that we'd be as fast as possible. I had some mandragora, which I said we would slather over the wound, hopefully numbing the pain somewhat and we gave him a good draft of the poppy juice.

As ready as we could be, we began. I unwound the bandages carefully and removed the pus-soaked cloth from the gash. We rinsed the wound several times trying to wash out as much of the infection as possible. It was a mess, the flesh inside the leg was necrotic and the smell was appalling. I dribbled some of the mandragora over the injury and we started our search.

We took it in turns, as we had to hold our breath while leaning over the wound; the stench was so bad. Between each search, we checked Tobias to make sure, firstly that he was still alive; and secondly whether he needed any more poppy juice. It was obviously excruciatingly painful; the prodding and poking of the instruments made him scream but we did find several tiny shards. Eventually Tobias passed out, which meant we were able to dig a little deeper, but soon we realised that if there were any more slivers, we would not find them. Rinsing the wound several times more, then coating it with salve, we re-bandaged the limb. That was all we could do; the rest was up to Tobias and his own strength.

None of us felt very confident but at least we had tried. We were covered in blood and pus. The sheets we had used as aprons would have to be burnt, along with the pile of cloths and sheets we had used during the operation. Those watching clapped as we finished, but it was nothing to celebrate. Poor Tobias had slipped into a deep stupor and now we had the added worry of the potential for shock.

My two willing soldiers carried the pallet back to the temporary sick room and I pulled the two sheets off the table, adding them to the pile I would burn. Exhausted, we sat in the sun soaking up the afternoon's warmth for a few moments, while everything was reorganised around us. Maxentius came out with some food and water, which we fell on. I'd forgotten that I hadn't eaten since my late breakfast. Gallus said he would sit with the patient until either Florianus or I could relieve him. I said I'd be happy to do the overnight shift again, if Florianus could take over from Gallus. This seemed to suit everyone and, the two elderly medici walked back to the sick room together while I gathered up the platters and carried them into the house.

Claudia and Antonia were on the edge of their seat, obviously desperate to hear what had happened, but I was too tired and needed to clean up. Telling them I'd be back shortly, I went along to the laundry room and shrugged out of my filthy, blood-spattered clothes, dumping them in the large sink before indulging in a thorough, albeit cold, wash. I rinsed my hair while I was at it, rubbing sweet oil on my skin and through my hair in an attempt to banish the smell of poison from my nose. Wrapping up in a large blanket, I hurried through to our bedroom and dug out a fresh tunic.

Once dressed and looking as close to presentable as I could manage, I sat on the edge of the bed trying to slow down my thoughts. I had so much going on. If my children were going to Rome, I needed to get them ready, packing clothes, buying them things that would be more suitable for the big city. Where were Maxentius' family members going to sleep? Then there was Tobias. How long would he need to be next door and would he survive?

Sighing, I pushed all these thoughts aside and walked through to the main room. Everyone was there, save Marcus and Maxentius. The children were happily playing, while Claudia and Antonia were deep in conversation with Aliza who seemed very comfortable with these Roman women. Joining them, I let their chatter waft over me, soothing my weary mind. I knew I would fall asleep if I wasn't careful, but I didn't think I was able to stay awake. I curled up in the chair, hoping Maxentius wouldn't be long; we needed to discuss this visit to Rome. My eyes drooped and hard as I fought it, sleep won.

"Its okay, I've got you." A warm voice enveloped me, as the hand stayed me. Bewildered, I turned around to see who was speaking and why they were worried. I was in the chair; no one needed to 'get me.' A tall man was smiling down at me. I blinked in confusion. He seemed familiar, but his clothes weren't right. His smiled faltered as I just stared at him.

"Hannah? Hey, It's okay, Sunshine, I'm here. No need to panic." Who was panicking? Not me, I thought I was snoozing.

The hand pulled me close and I smelt a familiar scent. What was that? I felt I should know. It was intoxicating, stirring something in my senses and I wanted to breathe it in. I could feel the man's heartbeat. He leaned down and before I could stop him, he kissed my nose. Well that was...wait...kissing my nose! I knew who did that. I remembered that the scent was aftershave; I lifted my head and looked the man straight in the eye. Recognition flooded back: Max!

I drew a shuddering breath and looked around me; it seemed as though time hadn't moved at all. I was still standing near the doorway to the café. No way...surely even a couple of hours must have passed? It had been days in my other world.

"I need to sit a moment, please," I whispered. Max manoeuvred me to a bench nearby, where no-one else was sitting. He sat next to me, his arm draped casually along the back of the bench, his fingers just touching my arm.

"What happened, Hannah?"

"I've been...no, that's not possible, I can't have been...but I'm sure I was..." again with incoherence, Hannah I thought. Seriously — I'm surprised anyone ever understands you. I bit my lip and started again. "Is it still the same day? Have we just been talking?"

"Of course it's the same day..." there's no 'of course' about it, I thought, "...and no, you just grabbed my hand and hung on for dear life. Mind you, even though you were holding my hand, you were staring at me as though you didn't know who I was. We've probably been standing like that for about ten minutes. I just moved you away from the doorway and said you felt dizzy. Then, just now you let go." Impossible. I struggled to come to terms with the time shift, it was so weird, I'd been 'gone' for something like five days.

I turned my head and gazed at him, drinking him in; he was so handsome. He smiled a slow, lazy smile and my heart flip-flopped. I was still waiting for my head to catch up with my eyes, but I started to relax. Max let his fingers play gently along my upper arm, the light touch making me tingle all over. Sighing, I leaned against his shoulder and he rested his cheek against my hair.

"Want to tell me, sweetheart?" So, while we were sitting, looking out over the ruined town, the sunlight flickering through the tall umbrella pines, I told him. He was quiet when I finished. I didn't move, unsure of his reaction to my latest instalment, but his fingers continued to play their tune on my arm.

Just as I was thinking this, they stilled and then moved to my back, trailing along my spine. I wasn't even sure whether Max knew he was doing it; it seemed an absent minded action. I waited, the moments ticked by, then...

"How do you do it, Hannah?" This same question, the one everyone kept asking me.

"Which 'it' do you mean?"

"Dealing with Tobias, after..." I turned to face him. His expression was troubled, but whether it was to do with my coming and going so often or it was just Tobias, I couldn't tell. I shrugged.

"I, well really she, just has to; it's who she is. Regardless of what Tobias did to her and, by extension, me, she couldn't let him suffer such agony without at least trying to help. You'd think less of me if I ignored someone in so much distress, wouldn't you?" I squeezed his leg in my need for him to understand.

"Ye...es," he drew out the word, "...but, I'd've thought she'd prefer to let the other doctors deal with him."

"Would you?" I questioned him. He glanced down at me. I tried to read his face, but couldn't.

"After what he did, I'm not sure I could," he whispered. "He might have..." Unable to finish his sentence Max dropped his gaze. I squirmed on the bench so that I was facing him properly and looked him in the eyes.

"I'm okay, Max. She's okay. He was stopped and in her world it was many years ago. In my world it never happened. Tobias was the loser in all this. Hannah still has her Roman and I still have you." Max lifted his arm, which had been drawing lazy circles over my back and drew me to him planting a light kiss on my cheek. I turned my head as he did so, catching his lips with mine. Green fire flared in his eyes and I smiled against his mouth.

"Just love me, Max, that's all I ask."

"Always, Sunshine, always." I nestled against him.

"Can we stay here a few more minutes? This is so nice, just us two." He tightened his arm around me and nodded.

"Sounds perfectly okay to me." I watched the flicker of light and shade across the ruins; I smelt the coffee brewing in the café behind us and listened to the sounds of life all around us. I felt warm and safe and I rested my head back on his shoulder. I tried to keep my eyes open, but I was so comfortable and my eyelids felt so heavy...just a minute or two.

Chapter Thirty Two

"Hey there, Hannah, are you going to snooze the day away?" I woke to someone shaking my shoulder and I looked up into a pair of green eyes, but they didn't belong to Max. Groaning inwardly, I realised I'd returned to my other world. Geez, I was barely allowed to catch a breath at the moment. Not surprising I was dizzy. My eyes drooped again, as a large hand stroked my cheek, the thumb running over my bottom lip. "Hannah!" More insistent now. Lifting my own hands to my face, I batted the large hand away, but it came back immediately. Giving in, I opened my eyes again, feeling a tad groggy, either from dozing in the chair or sliding through time. I was going with both.

"I'm so sorry, I didn't mean to fall asleep, how very impolite of me." I shook my head trying to clear my brain of the sluggishness that was clouding it. Maxentius was standing in front of me, amused at my apparent sleepiness.

"C'mon, the meal is out and we have things to discuss." That cleared the haze away faster than anything else could have done. I ran my fingers over my hair, making sure it was tidy and, stumbling a little in my haste, went to freshen up with splash of water. Maxentius followed me, asking whether I was okay. He knew me too well.

"Hmmm...I will be, just needed a moment." Smiling over at him. He grinned back and winked.

"Not sure I can do this, Maxentius," I said. Aware of what I was referring to, he came over to me.

"It'll be all right, my Hannah, leave it to me. I can be quite diplomatic you know." He kissed my cheek, a gesture so familiar I nearly gasped aloud. I shook my head to stop the buzzing that filled my ears. The world spun and then righted itself. I was still here in ancient Pompeii but that was an odd reaction. I hoped I would be able to deal with these short bursts without making a complete idiot of myself.

"How is Tobias?" I asked, distracting both of us.

"He lives." Expressionless. "Florianus is with him."

"I will need to take the watch tonight, I fear. Gallus was with him earlier; I cannot let them take all the load."

Maxentius nodded, tight-lipped. Sighing, I squeezed his hand. "They'll be able to move him soon, my love." My husband nodded again. I started to leave the room when he caught my hand, pulling me back in.

"Please be careful, my Hannah, please." I leaned into him, wrapping my arms around him and tilting my head up. His head came down to mine and he plundered my mouth with his lips. Heat scorched along my veins and my legs buckled. He held me tightly, refusing to let me fall, his kiss deepening. I struggled, we had guests, but he continued, holding my hands to prevent me from pushing him away. Then, just as suddenly as he began, he stopped; the evening air wafting through the window flowed between us cooling our faces. I was breathing hard and my heart was racing. Staring up at him, I knew my eyes reflected the passion burning in his.

"What was the why of that?" I asked rather dazedly.

"I found I couldn't help myself. By all the gods, Hannah, I wish we were alone." Raggedly.

"Me too, good Sir. Maybe later?" I dangled the question, winking at him and pouting. He chuckled and held me for a moment longer, allowing our hearts to settle. "Come on, we have a meal waiting."

We went back into the main room, everyone was there, even Marcus had arrived. We adults sat around the long table, while the five children were happier sitting at the smaller one, where they normally had lessons. Inevitably, the chatter turned to Claudia and Antonia's proposal. I listened to their plan and knew I could not refuse the children this chance. They would have a marvellous time and they'd be safe. At some point during the discussion, I caught my husband's eye and nodded imperceptibly. Sitting across from me, he pressed his foot gently over mine acknowledging my tacit approval.

A few minutes later, as their enthusiastic descriptions wound down Maxentius said —

"We have talked about this and if the children wish to accompany you, we have no objection." His words seemed stilted, but he smiled as he said them, softening their formality. "When do you want to tell them?"

"No time like the present," Claudia replied and I could see how pleased she was with our decision. I glanced at Antonia, who was beaming like a Cheshire cat. As this simile from my other life crept in, I grinned to myself thinking I'd better be careful not to voice it. Maxentius raised his eyebrows, but I shook my head; I'd tell him later. We called all the small fry over and settled them around the table, one on each knee, except Maxentius who stood to explain what was happening. I buried my face into my daughter's curly hair, holding her close, determined to maintain my self-control.

They barely gave their father time to finish what he was saying before my three bounced off whosoever knee they were on and jumped around the room. So excited to be able to spend time with their cousins, they didn't even stop to think about leaving us. For this I was thankful; well, mostly thankful. Okay, I was devastated that they didn't seem to be at all worried about going away without us, but I wasn't going to let them see it. Antonius and Julia joined the shenanigans and for a little while the house was in uproar. Maxentius came to sit next to me and draped his arm casually over my shoulder, squeezing it now and again in a gesture of comfort.

Eventually, they calmed down, after being threatened with no trip after all, and started asking questions. Claudia and Antonia would be leaving Pompeii the day after next and wanted to take the children with them. It was a sensible move; they had brought staff with them, so there would be plenty of adult supervision and they were hoping to persuade our children's tutor to go also. It was just happening very fast. Bit like removing a Band-Aid I thought ruefully, painful but over quickly.

It took some doing, but we finally worked everything out. My suggestion about buying new clothes for my three was vetoed by Claudia, who said that she would buy them anything they needed while they were in Rome, saying that if she couldn't spoil her grandchildren, what was the point in having them? Then we had to work out who was sleeping where. The cousins informed me that they were all going to share my children's room, which for two nights didn't worry me. We did have spare rooms, but they were unfurnished, so I was at a loss for what to do with Maxentius' mother and sister. They told me, however, that they had organised rooms in the town, which was a huge relief.

The evening was drawing on and I needed to get back to my patient so, as the discussion continued, I slipped away, out along the connecting path to the sick room. Florianus was there and Tobias was sleeping, his colour no better than it had been when I had last seen him earlier in the day.

"How is he?" I whispered.

"Not so good; the infection does not seem to have abated at all and his delirium is becoming prolonged." I remembered Sergius and his last hours. The same changes were manifesting in Tobias. Suddenly, I realised two things: the first was that he would die, that I would lose him, no matter what we did; and the second was that this made me sad. He had been a childhood friend and, despite his actions on Masada, he didn't deserve this.

"So all we can do is make him comfortable?" I asked and my colleague nodded.

"I'm afraid so. I think it will happen sooner rather than later." I bowed my head, unsure whether I had the strength to watch another die, but knowing I had no choice.

Florianus patted my head in an avuncular manner and said he would be back shortly.

"I do not want to leave you to bear this alone, Hannah. We will support each other. Losing a patient is never easy and we have tried very hard to save this man." Without thinking, I rose to my feet and gave him a quick hug. He smiled and left the room. I sat back on the chair, staring with unseeing eyes at Tobias. Unbidden, memories from my childhood I thought lost, rose in my mind: Tobias and Aharon messing about in the street outside our home, playing with the other boys, chasing each other and laughing at ridiculous nonsense, pulling my hair, teasing me, the way boys do.

Forcing my thoughts back to the present, I turned my attention to my patient. The fever was running through him still and I could see blood seeping through the bandage. Carefully, I unwrapped the bindings, peeling back the last piece of cloth covering the gash. Florianus was right; this was so much worse. Had we caused this? Had our operation of earlier caused more harm than good? Should we have left well alone? In my heart of hearts I knew we had done the right thing, but the ruination of Tobias' leg still made me question our actions.

Tobias had awoken as I had been inspecting the injury. His eyes were full of pain and his face was ravaged. His breathing was shallow and his skin very dry. He gazed at me trying to speak. I glanced at him and talking softly told him to relax, that I would let him rest soon. He shook his head and tried again.

"Hannah, please Hannah." I stopped what I was doing and looked at him properly.

"What is it, Tobias?"

"Please Hannah, let me go. I know I am dying, please do not prolong it. What use am I now anyway? I will never be able to fight again." He stopped gasping for breath. I held his hand, running my cool fingers over his forehead. He was so hot.

"Don't you want to try, Tobias? You could help train the other gladiators."

"No, I couldn't, I am a prisoner and they would never trust me." I realised he spoke the truth, but I wanted him to fight for his life.

"I don't want you to die," I whispered. You are the last link to my childhood and my life before Masada." Again, I mused over whether this was what had brought me to the Gladiators' School — so that this man who had tried to break me would not die alone far from home and away from everyone he loved.

I heard movement behind me and turned to see Marcus standing in the doorway, his expression somewhat perturbed and I wondered how much he had heard.

"Marcus, please could you see whether Maxentius is free, I think I'm going to need him." He nodded and went in search of my husband. The fever spiked once more and Tobias began to toss, descending back into delirium. I laid a cold, wet sheet over him, hoping to break the heat coursing through him, but the fire refused to be doused. I had used three more sheets before I heard familiar footsteps and looked up to see my husband enter the room.

"What can I do, my Hannah?"

"Just stay with me. I have no idea what will happen when I lose him." I could see that Maxentius remembered the last time it had happened, so many years ago when we lost Sergius. I had fallen unconscious for several days, during which time I returned to my own world, or left this Hannah for a while at least. Bearing in mind the frequency with which I was going back and forth at the moment, I imagined it would not take much for me to slip away again.

Maxentius sat on the chair watching me work on Tobias. After what seemed like forever, his temperature finally began to cool, his mutterings ceased and his breathing settled, for now. I wanted to wake him up, to make him hang on, but I knew I would only be delaying the inevitable.

"So there is no chance for him?" My husband's quiet question broke through my anxiety.

"No, I don't think so. Florianus said as much to me before he left. He will be back soon." Wearily, I leaned my back against Maxentius' legs. He reached down and massaged the back of my neck trying to loosen the knots lodged there.

Almost immediately, Tobias began moaning again, the fever regaining control. I got him to sip a little of the poppy juice, but it didn't seem to make any difference. The tremors running through him were wracking his skeletal frame and I knew he didn't have any strength to combat them. Removing the damp sheet covering him, I found some balm infused with lavender and chamomile, both known for their soothing properties. I rubbed some into my hands and began smoothing it into Tobias' skin, along his arms and around his neck. As I was doing this, I crooned a lullaby, my actions bringing Sergius' last hours into sharp focus and I struggled with the similarities. Maxentius watched me, his eyes hooded, but I had no time to worry about why.

The scent from the balm permeated the air. It seemed to calm my patient and he stopped thrashing around. He came around one last time, looking straight into my face.

"Hannah." His voice was thready and I knew he was leaving this world.

"Yes, Tobias, what is it?" Taking his hand in mine and leaning close so that I could hear him.

"Thank you, Hannah, may your life be blessed." I smiled, squeezed his hand and, without thinking, kissed his forehead whispering that he had indeed learned to die with honour. Tobias smiled back, just a little and closing his eyes again, drew a long shuddering sigh and died. I just knelt there holding his hand, unable to move; too many emotions fighting for dominance. I wanted to scream my frustration at not being able to save him, cry for the loss of a one-time friend and rail at the system that brought him to this place. Most of all, I wanted to block it all out.

I checked his pulse to be absolutely sure; nothing, not even the faintest of beats. His eyes were closed, but unable to help myself, I ran my fingers over the lids, making sure they remained so. Then I placed the hand I had been holding across his chest and covered him with a clean sheet. Just as I was doing this, Florianus came back and when he saw what I was doing, his expression became sorrowful. The two guards hadn't moved during all of this and I glanced up at them, thanking them for their protection.

I couldn't look at my husband; I didn't want to see relief in his eyes, relief that the man who had hurt me so badly years ago was no longer a threat. Head bent, I left the room, making my way to the garden at the rear of our home where all was quiet. I looked up at the stars, millions of them twinkling in the vast heavens, making me feel utterly insignificant.

Maxentius came up behind me quietly, sensing my distress but unsure what to do. He put his arms around me, but I flung them off, stepping away from him.

"Go away, Maxentius. I know you are glad he is dead and no longer a threat, but I can't deal with that right now." My voice was harsh, but I couldn't help it. Ignoring me, he grasped my hand and pulled me close, his arms pinning me to him. Using my fists, I beat on his chest in a completely futile attempt to make him release me. "Let me go! Let me go!" Angrily, my eyes full of tears that would not fall.

"I'm not letting you go, my Hannah and I am not glad this man is dead. No-one deserves to die that way, whatever his crime." My fists slowed and I tilted my head to look into his face. His expression was open; he meant what he said.

"Oh God Maxentius, I lost him, I lost him." I crumpled in his arms, sobbing helplessly and would have ended up on the grass had he not been holding me so tightly.

"I've got you, my love, I've got you." He lifted me, carrying me into the house and along to our bedroom, away from the rest of the family who obviously knew something was wrong. He laid me on the bed, holding me until the storm abated, which took some time. Eventually, I cried myself out. He still held me, talking about anything that came into his head, just words, soothing me.

"I can't go back out there," I stuttered, hiccupping from the onslaught. "Not tonight, please make my excuses." Maxentius wiped my face with a cloth he found on the cupboard. He lifted my chin with his finger and stared down into my eyes.

"Rest, my Hannah, just rest, do not worry about my family, they are more than capable of sorting themselves out." He was stroking my hair, long calming strokes, I yawned, completely done in and before I knew it, I'd fallen asleep.

I had no idea how long I had slept. It felt like much longer than normal and, on waking, I felt stiff as though I'd been lying in an uncomfortable position. It seemed very light; I had definitely slept in. I stretched and felt someone take my hand. As I opened my eyes and looked around, I sat up in shock. I was still sitting on the bench outside the café with Max. Whaaaat? Bewildered, I turned my head. Max had his eyes closed, his head resting against the wall. It was still early afternoon, what on earth...?

Max opened his eyes and grinned at me. I just stared at him; my jaw may well have been somewhere near the floor. His grin faded and he sat up.

"Hannah, are you okay?" I just kept staring at him. My brain wouldn't form the words I needed to say and, inexplicably I felt tears pricking behind my eyelids. Before I could stop it, one ran down my cheek. "Hannah, hey baby, what's up? Don't cry." His arm which had been around my shoulder, tightened and he pulled me to him. "C'mon Sunshine, spill." I shook my head afraid that if I started to speak I would lose it and have a meltdown right here in the middle of Pompeii.

"Just a second," I whispered, my voice husky. "I can't..." taking a deep breath, I tried to control my tumbling senses. It was so unusual for me to come and go in the same day; it was making me feel very disorientated, but as my experience of this was relatively limited and of course I knew no one else to whom it happened, maybe this was normal. Max just held me close, stroking my back and after a few more minutes I felt able to speak with some coherence.

"He died, Max. I, she, couldn't save him. It was awful, it was so awful and despite what he had done to me — well her — she was so sad. I can feel her sorrow; my heart feels bruised." More tears followed the first one, trailing down my face and for the life of me I couldn't stop them falling. I didn't need to tell him who had died; he knew and, tried to rationalise it for me.

"She lost someone. It must be terrible, trying so hard to save a life, only for them to die and it's not like you've — or she's — had to deal with lots of people dying on you. The last one was that other soldier wasn't it? What was his name...Sergius? That was him yes?" I nodded. He was right, although I — or rather the other me — had dealt with many dead bodies; this was only the second person to die while I was caring for them. Our conversation, as with all of our conversations revolving around this topic, sounded absurd. Good job no one else was close enough to overhear. "For you it feels like these deaths happened close together, but in her world there's more than ten years between each loss. That's a long time, sweetheart." I gazed at him, my mind taking in that he had remembered everything I told him, even the name of the soldier I — okay she — had lost in those first weeks on Masada.

"Thank you, Max." Leaning in to kiss him on his cheek

"What for?" Turning, so my lips touched his and smiling slowly.

"For loving me enough to remember all this; you have no idea."

"Well, someone has to keep you grounded, Sunshine and I reckon I'm well qualified for the job." He kissed me, very satisfactorily, for a little longer and then squeezing my shoulder made to get up. "Sadly, we need to make a move; we've been sitting here for a good hour and we'll have been missed."

I didn't think I could go back to the Gladiators' School. I feared what would happen if I did and told Max this as we sorted out our backpacks.

"It's just that I feel like I'm stuck in a revolving door. I'm slipping between my worlds so quickly that the slightest thing seems to drag me through. The school is so familiar to me that I can picture it as it was before the eruption and I'm afraid that the longer I'm there, the clearer the picture will be. Then I'm gone. I don't want to keep letting people down or taking them away from their work, because I've 'disappeared' out of time. Let's face it; how could we explain that I keep falling asleep or fainting or whatever it is I do?" Max could see the sense in my argument, but his expression told me he was torn. I knew he wanted to go back to the excavations but didn't want to leave me either.

"It's okay love, just give me the keys, I'll walk home and have a quiet afternoon in the garden. Don't worry and, if by chance I do go I'll be safe. Just make sure you bring me back." I winked as I said the last bit, hoping to lift the mood. It worked, Max smiled and his shoulders relaxed.

"Only if you're sure, sweetheart."

"I'm sure. Now go on, you know you're itching to get back. I'll be fine, truly." We walked back to the School together where he hugged me very tightly for a long time, before kissing my nose and relinquishing his hold.

"Please be careful, Sunshine." He murmured in my ear, then turned into the gates and was gone.

I trudged back to the villa, feeling rather out of sorts. Too many sad things were crowding my memory. Tobias' death, the children leaving for Rome, my anxiety of the eruption and all the deaths it would cause. It wasn't as though they were really my problems; they were my ancestor's problem. But knowing we were still entwined meant that I was feeling all her emotions, even in my own world millennia away.

I made it home without incident, by which I mean I managed to stay in my own time and, letting myself in, dropped my backpack on the chair and opened the French doors onto the garden. The scent from the rosemary and lavender wafted through the room soothing my senses. I made myself a mug of tea and sat outside; it was still warm enough and the garden was so peaceful. Despite the autumn being well on us, the blossoms from the bougainvillea were still holding their own and the wisteria, a waterfall of soft purple, spilling off the roof of the pergola under which I was sitting. It felt like a sanctuary; I was safe here.

As the afternoon wore on, the temperature cooled enough for me to want to go back indoors. I left the doors open, however, allowing the gentle breeze to filter through the villa. I curled up on the sofa with my journal and began to fill in the gaps. I had managed to write down most of it but there were still some parts I needed to flesh out. I glanced through what I'd already written; even to me it seemed fantastical. As I read the pages, I could picture the days I was writing about, small; mundane things that make up a life, things you barely ever notice.

I added as much as I could but struggled to finish; my concentration kept skittering away. I was having difficulty focusing on one thing for any length of time and again questioned whether it was anything to do with my head injury. Or was it more to do with having to adjust to the rapid transitions I was experiencing? Like I've ever had the answer, I thought ruefully.

As I popped the journal back on the table, I noticed my clasp had fallen out of my backpack onto the floor. Picking it up, I intended to return it to the inside pocket where it would be safe when the light caught its facets, scattering red sparks over the cushions, like a tiny crystal chandelier. I stared into its depths. What was its secret? Was there even a secret at all? I swear it pulsed with a hidden energy, but there was no answer today. I rolled it in my palm and held it there, warm against my skin.

Resting my head back against the cushions, I pulled the rug over me and snuggled in, turning on the television hoping that the white noise would drown out the voices calling me back. It was strange that I rarely missed such modern conveniences when I was back in my ancient world and yet I'd always been puzzled about how people managed without them. Now I knew.

There was a man lying on a pallet, bleeding from gashes all over his body, begging me to help him, but I couldn't reach him. Every time I got close, he was pulled away. Why would they do that? Why wouldn't they let me help him? I was calling for them to stop and wait for me, but still they kept moving him. The blood was pouring all over the ground, leaving a long trail of dark red, his life force draining away. I needed to stop the flow. Desperately, I tried to reach him. I tried one last time and managed to grasp his arm, which came away in my hand. I screamed then and kept screaming, unable to stop my own torment and the agony on the face of the man whose arm I now held.

"Hannah, Hannah, **Hannah**! Wake up, it's just a dream, you're safe with me. Hannah!" I clung to whoever was holding me, shuddering in terror, becoming aware that this same person was running their large hands over my back trying to calm me down. I came awake slowly, confusion clouding my mind.

"His arm, where is his arm?"

"Whose arm, my love?"

"The man, his arm, it came away in my hand." Realising that my words were peculiar, I stopped talking and looked up. Maxentius was there, holding me, his hands soothing me. Then I knew it had been a nightmare. My world came into focus and there was no bleeding body, no detached arm in my hands. Relieved, I pushed into my husband's arms needing to feel warm and safe. He hugged me close, his hands still stroking my back.

"Sorry, so sorry." I shuddered again. Maxentius made me tell him what had happened. It was fading quickly now, but the fear was still there.

It was the same as always, the only thing that changed was the face of the man on the pallet. Sometimes it was Tobias, but more often than not it was Sergius. It was over a month since Tobias had died; yet the nightmares still came. With everything else that had happened since then, you would think the death of one man would have paled into insignificance. Yes, he was a man whom I had known as a child; the same man who had harmed me years later but still just a man and a prisoner of war to boot. Sergius, I had barely known, only a few short weeks and I had done everything in my power to save both of them. I could not understand why their deaths haunted me.

I dreaded the nights now; darkness became my tormentor instead of my friend and I rarely had enough rest. More often than not, I got up and wandered the house, or sat in the garden staring at nothing, my mind refusing to quieten. I had no appetite, which along with the lack of a decent night's sleep was making me pale and listless, but I couldn't seem to help it. Although I still attended the men at the Gladiators' School and the Palaestra, my heart wasn't really in it and I went about my days like an automaton, unable to find any enthusiasm for the work I had loved so much.

I had tried to help prepare Tobias' body before they moved him back to the School. I felt I owed him that much, but in the end I had found it too distressing, leaving Gallus to complete the ritual. Thankfully, he was sympathetic to my anguish. The children had gone to Rome two days after the death of Tobias. They were full of excitement and we had received word that they were loving every minute of their adventure. I, we both, missed them dreadfully, but were pleased that they were having so much fun. Not long after they left, the Emperor Vespasian had died leaving the Roman world in mourning. Vespasian's older son, Titus — yes, he who sacked Jerusalem — succeeded him and there were great festivities in celebration of his accession. I knew I had little time to come up with a way to get the rest of my loved ones out of this city.

That these things were not enough to override my nightmares confused me. I had tried to analyse myself, to get to the bottom of whatever it was that was preventing me from getting a dreamless sleep, but whatever it was refused to be uncovered.

Maxentius was still stroking me, running his fingers through my hair, his voice soothing me. My disturbed nights were not good for him either, for not only was he worried about me, but also my distress kept him awake. As we lay there I realised I'd had enough of this. It was totally unfair on both of us. I moved out of his embrace and got out of bed. My husband raised a quizzical eyebrow at me.

"I won't be a moment, my love; I can't do this anymore."

"What do you mean?" His voice followed me along the hallway, anxiety clear in his tone.

"This needs to stop. I've had enough. No more."

"How?"

"Poppy juice," I called back. I'd steered clear of using this draft to help me sleep. It had soporific properties, but it was a strong sedative and I knew users could become addicted to it. I had not wanted to risk such a thing; however, I had reached the end of my tether and needed to have my wits about me over the next couple of weeks.

I found the jar containing the opiate and poured three drops into a goblet of wine. Gulping it all down in one go, the peculiar flavour made me shudder. Hurrying back along to the bedroom, I slipped back under the covers and Maxentius pulled me to him.

"Are you sure that was wise, my Hannah?"

"I have to do something, Max. I will go mad if I don't get some sleep and you need a proper rest too. All I can say is that it's a good job we don't have three children to deal with at the moment." He grinned down at me kissing my nose; the familiar gesture tickling a memory at the edge of my mind, but I couldn't hold on to it.

Pushing it aside, I leaned up, brushing my husband's lips with mine. As ever, our touch sparked the slow burn in the centre of my being. He drew in a sharp breath.

"Hannah, you need to sleep." Caressing my body — well, doing that's not going to help me, I thought, feeling delicious ripples run down my spine.

"It will help," I murmured drowsily, the medicine already taking effect. I pressed my body against his feeling his immediate response and covered his chest in kisses, trailing my fingers over his muscles. I felt a tremor run through him and delighted in it.

"Oh Max, I do love you," I sighed and, without warning fell asleep. Maxentius chuckled and pulled me into his arms, tucking my head against his chest and soon joined me in slumber.

It was very late when I awoke. The day was almost over but I felt rather less ragged than I had the day before. My limbs were heavy though, which I assumed was a residue of the poppy juice and I knew I should really get up and shake it off, but I was very comfortable. There was a goblet full of what appeared to be water and lemon, next to the bed. I gulped it down, the cool mixture sliding over my throat refreshing me. I lay for a little while deciding what to do, when all of a sudden my thoughts became confused and I was asleep again.

I have absolutely no idea how long I slept but the next time I woke up, it was daylight; the pale sky suggested early morning not long after dawn. I realised that for the first time in weeks, I had slept without nightmares. Maxentius was snoring gently next to me. I raised myself up on one elbow and studied his face; his craggy features, so dear to me, that I was unable to prevent myself from touching them. I curved my hand around his cheek and brushed his lips with light fingers, following carefully with a kiss.

My husband's eyes flickered open and he stared at me, his green gaze so dark and deep I actually thought I might fall into it. Again, I remembered thinking that his eyes were like pools of night and I whispered it now, running my hand up from his cheek, where it had been resting, and through his hair while his eyes continued to hold me spellbound. His hands began their dance up my body, the delicate fabric of my nightclothes in no way hampering him. I shivered as heady sensations rippled through me and I leaned towards him needing his lips on mine, never breaking his gaze. He kissed me for a long time, letting the passion build.

While his mouth was seducing me, his hands caressed me tracing their way down my back, his tenderness melting my defences and sending heat scorching along my veins. I sank into his kiss tasting the soft velvet of his mouth, savouring the sweetness, which was like wine and honey. Maxentius trembled as his desire matched mine and I simply surrendered myself to his touch.

After what seemed like hours, the world re-formed around us and our hearts finally slowed. I couldn't let go, wanting more, but the intensity of our lovemaking had brought tears to my eyes and now I was unable to stop sobbing. It was a release of everything that had been haunting me for so many weeks and I felt a great burden rolling off me. Maxentius held me tightly, stroking my hair, letting me cry it out, murmuring my name and kissing my tears away.

Taking a deep breath, I tried to get my emotions in check.

"Oh, good grief, look at me; probably not the response you expected to your sublime ministrations." I tried a watery smile. Maxentius smiled back, his slow, toe-curling, heart-thumping smile. So familiar, another face merged with his, less craggy but no less dear. I shuddered feeling my worlds meld — not just yet, leave me here just a little longer.

"I'm just surprised it's taken you this long, you've shown no emotion about anything since the night Tobias died; not even when the children left and I expected you to bawl that day — nothing. I have been very worried. It's so unlike you not to be happy and cheerful and full of your day." I brushed his lips with mine.

"I'm sorry, my love, I don't think I knew I was doing it. I have been feeling so..." I hesitated, trying to find the right word to describe what I had been feeling, "...removed, lost almost. I'm sure it was more than anything to do with lack of sleep and recurring nightmares when I did sleep and I don't really know why I was having them, the dreams I mean."

"I imagine it is a combination of many things, not least that you ended up treating a man who had previously hurt you, had become a prisoner through no real fault of his own and had once been a friend."

"But that doesn't explain why I kept seeing Sergius. It was him I saw more than Tobias."

"Maybe it was simply because he was the only other man that you remember whom you have been unable to save." He made sense. I ruminated on it for a few moments, playing with the concept in my mind. It was as good an argument as any and, hopefully, I had broken my pattern of sleepless nights.

While these thoughts were running through my head, I became aware that my husband was beginning another exploration of my body, his fingers working their magic over my skin. Without caring that it was really time to be getting up, I abandoned myself to his mastery, letting his love wash away the last vestiges of my nightmares.

Chapter Thirty Three

Long summer days were upon us and, although the seasonal heat was lovely for a while, it began to pall rather quickly as we sweltered under a blazing sun day after day. Our only respite was the sea breeze, which blew in most afternoons. People rarely ventured out of their cool houses and tried to hug the shady pathways when they did. Smoke was rising from the mountain now, almost constantly; not a lot, just whispery threads, but it was enough to make me realise how close was the cataclysmic eruption.

The earth rumbled too, sometimes strongly enough to shake the buildings. I knew the two were connected, and tried to think of a way we could leave Pompeii without raising eyebrows. Then one day, to my surprise, Maxentius came home in the middle of the afternoon. He had news and I could tell by his expression that he wasn't happy about it.

"What is it, Max?"

"We have received word from Rome that we must accompany the prisoners there for trial." I knew which prisoners he meant; it was those who had tried to storm the Emperor's box at the last games. I was saddened, as this did not bode well for my three cellmates. They had been brought before the magistrate here in Pompeii, but no decision had been handed down. Since then, they had remained incarcerated at the garrison, along with several of their fellow protestors.

"Do they fear reprisals if they are sentenced here?" I asked.

"I think that's probably partially the reason, but also it was an attack against Vespasian and Titus may be using them as an example." I nodded, understanding why the new Emperor would see this as a good way to establish his credibility. There were many who feared, that with all his alleged vices Titus would be another Nero. I knew, however, from studying this man in my own time, that he would turn out to be a very effective ruler. I said as much to Maxentius and that I hoped Titus would be lenient.

Unfazed by my comments, Maxentius merely agreed, adding that they would be leaving for Rome in two days.

Marcus would accompany him, along with two centuries of his soldiers, the remainder staying in Pompeii to continue their regular duties. Dropping a kiss on my cheek, he went back over to his office, saying that both he and Marcus would be home for the evening meal.

Unable to do anything for them now, I sat for a while, thinking about the three men who had been kind to me when I had been in the cell with them. It seemed so long ago, yet it was only a few months. So much had happened since then. I had visited them a couple of times at the garrison and had managed to persuade the guards to let me treat the injuries they had sustained when Maxentius' soldiers had hauled them away from the Emperor. Now they just had to hope that Titus was feeling benevolent.

I began to plan what Maxentius would need. He said he should be away only about a week, but it was just a best guess. Who knew how long he would be gone? As I wandered into the laundry, checking to see whether he would require any of the clothes ready to be washed, I realised that we had never been apart — not even for one night, certainly not since we had married and even before then I saw him every day. I leaned against the wall reflecting on how I would manage, knowing that I was perfectly capable of looking after myself, but not actually wanting to.

At the back of my mind a thought tickled at me. As I let it roll around, I worked out that the eruption would be very soon, meaning that my two Romans would be far away from here. A wave of relief flooded through me. Was this how I saved them? Well let's face it, it wasn't anything to do with me, but if Titus' summons had done the trick, I might even change my mind as to who was my favourite Emperor! I could live for a little while without my husband if this unexpected separation saved his life.

Feeling much better about the whole thing, I finished what I was doing and collected a goodly pile of clothes ready to pack later. It would be very hot in the city, so I knew he wouldn't need any cloaks, but since everything would be destroyed very soon, I intended to include a few extras into the travelling box without him realising. The children had taken quite a lot of their clothes and toys, despite Claudia assuring me that she would buy them anything they needed, so I wasn't worried about them. I would be able to tell Marcus to add a few things to his pack, so that just left Aliza and myself.

I pondered on the logistics of getting us away from here. I had been very busy these last few weeks; there had been another games and there was one due in less than a week. The crowds had been very disappointed that their two favourite fighters would no longer do battle, but their loyalties were easily swayed, especially as Darius had won his last bout, killing his opponent, another prisoner. Within his category, that of prisoner of war, he was now one of the most popular gladiators and a big drawcard. I had seen him several times since Tobias' death. His injuries had healed well and he seemed genuinely saddened over the death of his fellow prisoner. I didn't know, however, whether it was because he had respected his opponent, or recognised that it could so easily, have been him.

More than anything, I had responsibilities and couldn't just walk away. We had a home filled with things that I would prefer not to lose; I had two jobs which kept me busy most days; and there were people I wanted to warn but couldn't until the last minute. I would ask Maxentius if there was some way I could send on our things to Rome, even if they were dispatched to his mother's city residence. I wandered into the garden and looked up at the mountain, dark and forbidding, a curl of vapour rising over its peak. So close; I just hoped I could time it right.

That evening the four of us discussed the impending trip to Rome. Trip! That made it sound like a holiday, not a large number of soldiers accompanying a group of agitators. Marcus was looking forward to it. He had loved the hustle and bustle of the big city when we had stayed there after our arrival in Roman Italy and, had been hankering for an excuse to visit again. Strange for a man who was happiest working in a garden tending plants. Aliza went over to her rooms quite early; she had been out all day with her friends and was tired. After she had gone, I spoke very seriously to my two Romans.

"I need to be able to send some things to Rome while you are there and you, Marcus, will need to do the same." They looked at me in astonishment.

"Why, my Hannah?" Maxentius questioned.

"Because, before you return this mountain will erupt and everything here will be destroyed. I would like to have as much as possible out of this house without it looking peculiar. Marcus, you will need to pack your clothes and anything else that you do not wish to lose. I assume you will be travelling in full armour?" They both nodded.

"What about you, Hannah?" Marcus asked. "How will you get away?"

"I'll think of something, don't worry. Once the games are over, I can say I'm coming to meet you and have some time in Rome. Now I just need to persuade Aliza to come with me."

"You think we won't be worried about you? How can I leave you knowing you are in danger?" My husband looked horrified.

"You have no choice; you have received your orders. Much as I hate the thought of you, of both of you, not being here, I would rather you were far away from here."

Even though they could see the sense in my argument, neither of them looked particularly happy, but their hands were tied. They could not disobey orders and I could not accompany them to Rome. I knew they were both remembering the last time I had told them to leave me, not knowing whether I would be able to avoid being killed by Eleazar and his band of merry Zealots on Masada.

"I think I must survive this. How else would I be able to pass down the clasp to Claudia? I have it with me here; therefore, I imagine somehow I get through this. I have to trust in the information the other Hannah has shared and, continues to share with me, to make my escape in good time." I watched the two men process this; incredibly they took it on board and seemed to accept that what I said was the truth. I leaned forward grasping a hand of each of them. "Have a little faith in me." I smiled and decided to change the subject, as they both looked troubled still.

"Now, there isn't much time to get organised, only one day really, so tomorrow I would like you, Maxentius, to find out to where I can send our things and if you, Marcus, wish to add anything to our packing boxes, bring them here as soon as you can." My practicality diverted them, as I knew it would and they launched into a discussion about what to take, what to leave and what I should send.

Later, after Marcus had gone to his rooms, Maxentius and I went out into the courtyard and sat for a while, enjoying the peace of the evening. I looked up at the sky. It was a little hazy, the heat dulling the edges of the night, but the stars were out in abundance. I leaned against my husband's shoulder and he draped an arm around me.

"I will miss you, my Hannah. We have never been apart." I smiled in the darkness, glad that he had also realised this.

"I will miss you too. The thought of not seeing you every day makes my heart ache, but we will manage, my love. Hopefully it will not be many days and just think of our reunion." I winked at him and ran my tongue over my lips. He chuckled.

"You are a tease. Come here." He pulled me onto his knee and kissed me until my senses danced with delight.

In what seemed like the blink of an eye, they were ready to leave. Obviously, as their charges were at the garrison, they would set out from there, so it was very early when they left the house. Marcus gave me a big hug, enveloping me in his arms.

"Take care, sweet sister, please take care." I smiled and nodded, squeezing his hand as he turned, leaving me alone for a moment with my husband. I stared at Maxentius, drinking him in, not trusting myself to speak. I didn't want to cry; he didn't need that on top of his other worries, but it was a struggle.

"I love you, my Hannah. Please, please do not leave it until the last minute before you escape this town. I fear that you will try to save too many and get caught in the destruction and I do not think I will be to live without you."

"I love you too, Max, more than you will ever know. I will see you soon." My words were whispered through a voice that was breaking. I held him close, kissing him as though my life depended on it and then released him. He turned to go, took three strides, then came back for one last embrace, before kissing the top of my head and vanishing into the early morning light.

I went back into our home, wandering through the rooms, seeing nothing. Forcing my tears back, I would not cry, I would see him soon. A cold trickle ran down my spine — well, I hoped I would see him soon. I knew my chances of escape were good if I managed to leave before the day of the eruption. I did have a vague recollection that it occurred the day after Volcanalia, celebrating Vulcan, the god of fire and forges — ironic really, but only I would see it. I thought the festival was quite soon, I just wasn't entirely sure when; I'd have to pray that luck would play a part.

Going into our bedroom, I picked up my clasp from the clothes cupboard and rolled it around my palm. Staring into its ruby depths, I fancied I saw the woman, lying on a strange yet very comfortable looking, chair, watching a flickering box. I knew her to be the other me, the woman who shared her knowledge and that she was also in my head. Surely, for her to be alive so far in the future, I, her ancestor, must survive. Ah, but your daughter is already away from here and safe, my subconscious cautioned. Yes, but she doesn't have the clasp; the clasp must be passed onto her. As I watched the image, it became misty and disappeared. Shivering a little, I replaced the clasp back on the cupboard and, pushing those unsettling thoughts to the back of my mind, went to make a start on the rest of the packing.

About an hour later, Aliza joined me and we had the first meal of the day together. She told me that she would be spending the day with her friends. This had become more than just an occasional appointment and I had thought there might be something more going on. Of late, she seemed much happier and she talked of a man named Levi more than you would someone who was just a friend. I kept my counsel. I was glad for her, however and knew she would tell me when she was ready.

After she had gone, I went out to the storeroom to find the travel boxes. They were at the back, behind the large amphorae, which held wine and oil. I dragged the huge pots out of the way, neatly stacking those that were nearly empty against the back wall of the garden. There was no point getting them refilled; they would be buried before I could use their contents. As I balanced the last one against the wall, a picture formed in my mind. The woman was in this garden, holding broken pieces of amphorae, turning them in her hand and looking puzzled, confused as to why they were outside. I wanted to tell her that it didn't matter, but the picture dissolved.

Sighing, I went back to the storeroom carrying the travel boxes one by one into the main living area and set about packing everything I couldn't bear to leave — children's clothes, the few toys they had left behind, everything Maxentius had not taken and some of my things. I would need a few garments for the next week or so, but most could be stored away. Once I had gone as far as I could with clothing, I walked into my medicine room, taking a mental inventory of all the ointments, balms and salves, the jars of solutions and essences.

I needed to save as many as possible; some of them were quite costly and to re-stock would take a very long time. I lifted my tablets down, those on which all the markings were listed. I definitely could not forget these and, placed them next to the bottles, where I knew they would not be missed. There were no small children looking for anything to draw pictures on, destroying all my hard work.

That done, I moved to the main room. I was not able to take furniture — that would be idiotic — and anyway, there was nothing here that I really wanted to take or would miss if I left it, except a piece of wood whittled by Maxentius into the shape of a pomegranate. He had done it years ago, not long after the massacre. As had been our habit, we would sit under the tree on our bench and he'd create wooden toys for the children. One day he presented me with this piece. It was so beautiful, carved to appear as though the pomegranate had burst open, its luscious seeds, sweet, plump and ready to be devoured. It was almost as precious to me as the clasp and there was no way I was leaving either behind.

By late morning, I had done as much as I could, so I gathered my bag and went along the walkway to see whether Petronius would be able to escort me to the Gladiators' School. He could and he did; we strolled along the pathways hugging the shade, chatting about this and that. He had not accompanied the protestors to Rome; Maxentius had appointed him second in command while Marcus was away. He was very proud of this opportunity and I knew he would carry out his responsibilities efficiently, being a conscientious young man.

There were no medical problems with the gladiators; they were all fit and healthy and those who had been injured in the previous games had recovered well. The upcoming event was unusual, for they normally went into hiatus during the summer months. It was too hot for them to be fighting, but these games were to be staged in honour of the new Emperor. The programme was rather shorter and there would be no executions but the risk to most of the gladiators was no different from the normal schedule; they would still be fighting, maybe to their deaths.

I chatted with Tullius for a few moments before I left and he told me that if I needed anything while Maxentius was away, I just had to ask. I thanked him, smiling gratefully. Finally, just as everything was about to go pear-shaped, I was part of this school, a member of the family of gladiators, the timing so typical of my luck. Never mind, I had a few days to enjoy it.

Petronius walked me home and then went back to file reports, or whatever it was seconds in command did. I entered the cool of my home, running my hand over the inscription that Maxentius had carved as I did. I wished I could take it with me, but imagined that if I tried to remove the section of wall it was carved on, the whole house would fall down around my ears. As my hand rested on the letters, I saw my modern counterpart do the same thing and found comfort in the knowledge that she would find this one day far into the future.

Aliza was home in time for the evening meal. It was so warm outside that we ate lightly: cold roasted vegetables drizzled with olive oil and breads with a little cold meat. After we had tidied everything away, we sat in the courtyard with a goblet of cool wine. I could see that there was something she wished to tell me, but seemed to be struggling to find the right words.

"What is it, Aliza?" I asked gently, touching her hand. She looked at me, blushing.

"It's that...well you see...Levi has asked..." she dried up and I smiled at her, suddenly guessing what her news was, but unwilling to take away her joy at telling me. I nodded encouragingly.

"Levi has asked me to marry him and go with him to Ostia where he has been able to buy a business." She took a breath. "I know I am too old for such nonsense, but it is nice to think someone cares enough to ask me to share their life."

"You are not too old, Aliza. I am so happy for you and I would love to meet this Levi."

"It is the gentleman who walks me to our sewing meetings. He is the brother of Leah, the lady who invited me to join them." I remembered a tall, kindly looking man with twinkly brown eyes, very polite. Now I thought about it properly, I recalled that those eyes lit up whenever he saw Aliza and he always smiled.

"When will you be married?" I asked, quietly, hoping against hope that they didn't want to wait.

"Well, we have been planning it for some time and it will take place the day after tomorrow," she replied, blushing even more than before. "I know it seems very sudden but Levi has to get to Ostia before next week is out to take over the business, a bakery. We had thought to marry when the days cooled, but he does not want to leave me here." And I do not want you to stay, I thought, thanking the gods of fortune that must have been smiling down on me lately.

I pressed her hand and kissed her cheek.

"I think that sounds perfect. Now tell me all about it." I sat back and listened to her chatter about what they had planned, realising with more than a little sadness that we had lost her. She would now be someone we only visited, no longer with us every day. Our lives were changing again. The evening wore on and although it was still early, Aliza, wanting to continue with her preparations, went up to her rooms. She told me that anything she left behind, I could dispose of as I saw fit. No need, I thought, the mountain will do that very nicely. I went to bed soon after. There was no-one and nothing to wait up for and the house was very quiet; even so it took me a long time to fall asleep.

I spent the following day going through the house from top to bottom, making sure I was as organised as I could be. I had packed as much as I could. There would be a few last-minute items but most of the boxes were now strapped closed. Then I went across to Marcus' rooms and checked to make sure he hadn't missed anything. Everything was very tidy; his military training clear in the neatness of the bedclothes and the positioning of his few pieces of furniture. A pile of wax tablets lay on his desk, the stylus placed alongside; nothing out of place, in anticipation of a return that would never happen. It reminded me of the rebels on Masada, tidying up their living quarters before they died. We humans must have an innate sense of order, unwilling to allow those who come after to find fault with how we lived our lives.

I walked through the headquarters, imprinting the rooms into my mind. I needed to remember this place. We had not been here very long, just over a year, yet it had been for the most part a very happy and fulfilling year. I peeped into Maxentius' office. Petronius was hard at work, but he took a break and we chatted for a little while. I asked whether they thought there were going to be any problems during Volcanalia, which he told me was eight days away. The festival was a good excuse for the over-indulgence of everything, especially alcohol. As was often the case on such days, the resulting hotheads kept the soldiers busy. He wasn't anticipating anything too serious, however, especially as most of those likely to cause riots had been taken to Rome. I left him to his work and returned home.

Aliza's wedding day was full of happiness; all of her friends were there to wish her well and the short ceremony was over almost before it began. Leah had put on a wedding feast for everyone and there was much merriment and, it was late afternoon before Aliza and Levi left. A wagon had been hired and all their worldly goods were stored securely inside. They were staying the night at a mansio, one of the roadside inns, for their journey even by fast carriage would take at least four days.

We had said our goodbyes and I promised her that we would visit Ostia as soon as it was feasible. I knew the children would miss her badly; they had barely known a time when she wasn't around and she was Efraim and Liora's grandmother. I admit to feeling very tearful as we waved them off on the first leg of their journey, but relieved that now I had to worry only about me.

Chapter Thirty Four

The days flew by and the games came and went, deemed to be very successful and, honoured the new Emperor in grand style. One or two of the gladiators were badly injured and required extensive treatment; their wounds would cause them pain for many days. I realised, with a jolt that they may well be dead before they healed anyway. As usual, there were a few deaths. I, along with Florianus and Gallus, tended to them the day after, in the long room at the School. As we finished and were walking back across the quadrangle, I asked if I might speak to them. It was quiet where we were; there were no guards. We stopped and to an idle observer would appear to be chatting about our patients.

"I just wanted to say thank you for being so kind and for welcoming me as one of the medici here at the school. I have enjoyed being part of this team very much."

"It has been a pleasure working with you, Hannah Valerius, but are you leaving us?" They looked puzzled. I took a deep breath.

"In a matter of days, the mountain behind this town will erupt, burying everything underneath it. You would do well to leave as soon as possible, taking all you hold dear with you. Don't ask how I know this, just please trust me. I am going to tell Tullius and let him decide how he wishes to handle the information, but in all conscience I cannot stand by and say nothing. You have become very important to me and I do not want you to die."

They both stared at me in astonishment, then looked up at Vesuvius, taking note of the smoke rising from its peak and surely recalling the earth tremors that were now a daily occurrence. As they turned their gaze back to me, I nodded.

"Please believe me," I whispered, and walked away. I could do no more.

Making my way to the lanista's office, I found Tullius hard at work. He looked up at my knock and invited me to sit.

"How are you, Hannah, wife of Maxentius?"

" I am well, thank you, Tullius Rufinus, and you?" Greetings over, I told him what we had been doing and then with yet another deep breath asked whether he trusted me. He looked at me for a long moment and then nodded his head.

"Why do you ask this, Hannah?"

"I am about to tell you something that will sound preposterous, but I must share it. What you do with the information is up to you." His expression changed to one of curiosity.

"I am listening." He steepled his fingers together resting them under his chin and leaned back in the chair. I told him what I had told Florianus and Gallus, what I had told Claudia and Antonia and what I had told my two Romans. As I finished speaking, the earth shook, adding weight to my entreaty.

He studied his desk for long moments and then raised his eyes to mine.

"Why did you decide to share this with me?"

"I think we have become more than acquaintances. I would like to think we are friends. The devastation will be horrific and I could not leave you to such a fate without giving you warning. You have men under your care who rely on you to protect them. How on earth do you think I would feel if I walked away and left you and them to your death?"

I was trembling with anxiety, my fingers twisting in my lap. "I realise I sound completely mad, but it is a risk I am willing to take. The eruption will happen very soon, I think in two days. When the smoke rising from the mountain thickens, there is little time left to escape." I walked around the desk, knelt down by his side and, squeezing his hand, repeated the three words I had spoke to the medici: "Please believe me." Standing, I bowed my head and walked out in the warm afternoon. I never saw him again.

Returning home, I looked around at the boxes I had filled. Even though two of the boxes were not small, there were only five in total and it seemed pathetic for a family of three adults and three children; Marcus included, for his things were there also. The wagon I had hired was due soon, so I had a last walk around, making sure everything I needed was packed away. I noticed the carved pomegranate nestling on my cloak next to my clasp. I would take it with me, as it would fit in my bag easily enough. Most of my medicines were stored in the trunks;

I intended to take only those few essentials that I did not like to travel without. I could leave any time I wanted; nothing held me here now.

The wagon drew up to the door in the late afternoon and the driver lifted the boxes into the back as though they weighed nothing. I gave him all the instructions he would need, including my mother-in-law's address and also where Maxentius was lodged. I paid him half; he would get the balance once he had delivered the trunks. Tipping his head, he thanked me for my business and rattled off over the cobbles towards the city gates.

I went back into the house; it seemed huge now, even though all the furniture remained scattered through the rooms. There was nothing left for me to do and I intended to leave the next day. I hoped to hire a horse from the same stables Marcus had hired the rheda carucca which had carried us to Claudia's villa. It was still early, but I had no reason to stay up, so, as had become my habit while Maxentius was away, I took a hot drink to bed, drinking it propped up against my pillows, watching the day fade, the light changing from blue to pink to grey. I was still awake when night fell and was entranced by the moonrise, its trek across the sky following a timeless path through the blanket of stars glistening in the heavens, their ethereal light providing a soft glow over a quiet little town nestling under a mountain.

The tremors were increasing. I was woken many times during the night, hoping the house would be able to withstand such grumblings, but by the morning, all was calm. Volcanalia dawned rather dull; the clouds were heavy and the day felt humid and oppressive. Very evocative, I thought, the day before a cataclysmic eruption, the weather is getting us nicely in the mood. I had a light meal and then walked around to the stables, the hostler allowing me to hire one of the mares that we had taken out to the villa. Her name was Gemmula, which meant little gem and she was beautiful. I was glad I would be able to save her. I gave him half the payment, the hostler agreeing to bring her round to my home in the early afternoon.

I planned to travel north towards Misenum. I knew the ash would be blown in the opposite direction, and even though Misenum would not escape completely, it avoided being buried. It was the closest, yet safest place I could think of and, I would happily travel during the dark hours, or sleep in a field if I had to. From Misenum, I would make my way to Rome, either by horse, or if I could find a boat that could take me to Ostia, I would risk that route, as I had enough coin to buy passage.

Back at home I packed my leather bag, making sure I had my wooden ornament securely in one of the inside pouches. My clasp I would use to secure my cloak, which would be easier to wear than to pack. I also had a large piece of leather in which I could roll up a change of clothes; it was waterproof and very light. Its long strap could be tied to the horse's saddle, or across my back. I was ready, but before setting off, I wanted to pick up some food for the journey from the bakery half way along the main street. On my way, I popped into the headquarters to ask whether Petronius wanted anything. I knew they made a particular honey-filled bun that he enjoyed. He nodded his appreciation and I said I'd be back forthwith.

With that, I headed along the road. I could hear the sounds of people enjoying the festival, laughter and cheers echoing off the walls of the buildings. I bought what I needed at the bakery and was on my way back when a crowd of people rushed along the pathway towards me. Oh, good grief, I thought, don't tell me we've got drunken mobs already. I stepped up into one of the doorways, hoping to avoid the melee, when one of them grabbed my hand dragging me along with them.

They were in very high spirits in more ways than one — dancing and singing, completely unconcerned about the fact that they were roaring drunk — and I tried in vain to disentangle myself. Without warning, a group of soldiers appeared. Oh no, I groaned inwardly, not again. Desperately, I pulled my hand away, finally managing to loosen my captor's grip. I fell back against a wall, trying to catch my breath, but was almost immediately collected up by two of the soldiers. Assuming that they would escort me back home, I relaxed, only to realise that they were marching me in the opposite direction.

No, no, no, no, no — this could not be happening again. My heart sank. I had no Maxentius to save me, no one knew where I was and if the last time was anything to go by, the mountain would erupt before I was brought before a magistrate. I doubted that any official would be sitting today, since it was a festival day. Attempting to calm my panic, I glanced up at my two sentinels, trying to explain who I was. They weren't listening and I didn't recognise them, remembering that two or three centuries had been drafted in from Rome to augment the peacekeeping force. Now they would be rotating in from the garrison, since Maxentius had required his regular soldiers to accompany him and Marcus to Rome with the rioters.

Dammit! Could I get word to Petronius or to Julius? They were my only hope. If I remained locked in a cell, I would die along with everyone else. About five minutes later, we came to a smallish building and they handed me over to another guard. I made another attempt to get them to listen to me, but I wasn't getting through. I had no idea where we were; it seemed to be down several back streets and I couldn't see any familiar landmarks. The guard removed me to a small cell along a narrow corridor; thankfully one that I wasn't sharing with a bunch of drunken louts.

It was hopeless; I'd never get out. The window was barely a slit in the wall and the door had bars on it. I rattled them but they felt quite sturdy. Useless tears formed. I had promised Maxentius that I would take care, that I would get out. Now I'd never see him again. Slithering to the floor, I brought my knees to my chest and wrapped my arms around my legs. How would it feel to be suffocated by a scorching wind, or buried alive by falling ash? I hoped I would be unconscious before the avalanche of hot pumice flowed into the town; being burnt alive was my worst nightmare.

I waited for hours, but no-one came to check on me. I felt the tremors running under the floor, the earth was moving almost constantly now and I wished one of them would crack the walls. I tried calling out of the window, but no-one answered. I couldn't tell whether I was the only one there or whether there were others who had been brought in. I presumed it was some place where were they brought the drunk and disorderly to sleep off their over-indulgences, but I was completely sober. I still could not understand why no-one came to check on me.

Petronius would think I had eaten his sweet bread bun. I giggled at the thought of his indignation, then clamped my mouth closed realising that hysteria was tickling at my senses. I called for the guard, again, still no response. Frustrated and very scared now, I huddled back on the floor. It grew dark and I worked out that I had been in the cell for about six hours and, although exhausted, I was terrified of falling asleep in case I never woke up — or worse, woke up to find the room filling with dust and ash.

At some point exhaustion overcame my fear and I must have dozed, for someone unlocking the door wakened me. It was still dark; I had no idea what time it was. The bars rattled, as whoever it was jiggled the key and I tried to stand up but found I had grown stiff from sitting in the same position for so many hours. Dazedly, I looked at the door; I couldn't work out what was going on until a familiar voice spoke and someone got hold of my arm, lifting me gently to my feet.

"Come on, Hannah, let's get you home." I stared, trying to make out who was speaking, but there was not enough light from the dim light of the single oil lamp in the hallway.

"Who...what?" My mouth was so dry that I struggled to speak. Swallowing I tried again. "Petronius?"

"Who else? Quickly now, we need to get you out of here."

"Who's we?"

"Julius and me. How on earth did this happen to you twice? Maxentius will have my promotion for this."

"Not your fault," I muttered, "no-one would listen to me." I was starving hungry and so tired that I could hardly stand up. "Please, I don't think I can get home."

"Do not fret, we brought a horse. She's big enough for two. I'll ride with you." We came to a door, the same one through which I'd been brought earlier. Julius was standing there, holding the reins of Gemmula, my beautiful mare. How was this possible? I could see how relieved Julius was and I smiled at him gratefully. He helped me up into the saddle and Petronius jumped up behind me, grasping the reins and wheeling the horse around.

"Wait," I said and leaned down towards Julius.

"You need to run, Julius, the mountain is about to roar. If you don't leave now, you may not be able to." He stared at me but had no chance to respond, as Petronius urged Gemmula into a trot. The last I saw of him, he was gazing after us along the darkened street.

We were home very quickly, which seemed strange, but I had no time to think about it. Petronius slid off the horse and helped me down. My legs buckled and he almost carried me inside, setting me down and helping me to the couch.

"Thank you, my friend, but how on earth did you know where to find me?

"When you didn't come back with my very important bun," he grinned at me, "I started to puzzle over what might have happened. I went to see if I could find you but was unable to. Then, much later I heard that many revellers had been taken to the cells to sober up and considered whether, somehow, you'd been caught up with them. Turns out, my hunch was right. How on earth do you get into such scrapes, Hannah?"

I gaped at him.

"I had absolutely no intention of getting into such scrapes, as you so kindly put it. I was simply walking back from the bakery and ended up in that building. Unfortunately, the soldiers did not recognise me. I think they must have been some of those brought in to supplement you lot." I sighed, leaning my head back against the chair. "Petronius, we have to leave this town. Tomorrow the mountain will erupt and if we do not leave now, it is likely that we will die."

Petronius stared at me in astonishment.

"What on earth do you mean?"

"Exactly what I just said; trust me, it will be terrible. Oh, by the way, how did you get the horse? I had hired her for my journey. I was leaving for Misenum today, or was it yesterday? I don't even know what time it is."

"The hostler brought her here and when he couldn't find you, came next door to check with us. It was then I realised something was really wrong. I knew you would not have missed being here to take possession of her and pay the balance. Then it was simply a matter of hunting you down."

Exhaustion fought with my need to flee.

"I must leave; do you want to come with me?" I asked him. "Or would you prefer to remain here and be buried in hot debris?"

"Hmm...great options there, Hannah," he replied. "So, if we leave, where do we go, Misenum?"

"I think so and from there to Rome."

"Wouldn't it be easier to take a boat from the port."

"I'm sure it would, but the wind will blow the ash out over the bay and I think the water will become too choppy for safe passage. It will be safer to travel north first, then cross overland to Rome." He looked at me curiously and I knew exactly what his next question would be. On cue —

"How do you know all this Hannah?" I looked him dead in the eye.

"I cannot tell you, but you know me well enough to trust that I never speak untruths. Are you coming with me or not?"

"I will come; you do not seem capable of managing on your own." I was about to chide him for his cheek when I noticed that his lips were twitching. I grinned at him and went to finalise my preparations calling through that if he needed to collect anything, now would be a good time to get it.

I changed into more comfortable travelling garb and fastened my light cloak securely with my clasp. I rubbed it absently as I did so and, without thinking, whispered that I would need any protection it was able to summon up. By the time I had gathered my bags together, checking that my wooden pomegranate was in an inside pouch, Petronius was back. He had collected a few things, which he had rolled into one of his cloaks; the other was flung over his shoulders. I had chosen soft boots for my feet and Petronius had done the same; much more comfortable than sandals for travelling in.

Going out to the front of the house where he had tethered the horse, Petronius tied our bags to either side of the saddle. I took one last look around, absorbing the memories and traced the inscription with my fingers.

"Think of me when you see this, Hannah." I murmured.

"Are you ready?" asked my escort.

"As ready as I'll ever be," I replied. He helped me up into the saddle, before settling himself behind me, holding the reins loosely in his hand. Gemmula responded to his light touch and soon we were trotting out through the north gate. The town was quiet; all the party makers had gone home or were lying drunk in the bushes. The moon was bright; the clouds from earlier in the day had been banished by the evening breeze. Looking up at the sky, it was hard to believe that in less than twelve hours it would be filled with choking, black smoke, miles high, so immense that it would create its own storm.

We rode in silence. I was too tired to come up with witty conversation and Petronius seemed engrossed in his own thoughts. Once we were out of the town and had a wide swathe of grass at the side of the road, Petronius clicked the horse into a gallop. She raced along the ground, her mane and tail streaming out, white in the moonlight. The motion was soporific and, unable to stop myself, I fell asleep. Sometime later, I jolted awake to find myself lying on the ground, covered with a heavy cloak. It was dawn. Lifting myself up on one elbow, I spotted Gemmula chewing at the stubby grass and Petronius leaning against a low wall, his head on his chest, snoring gently.

I looked around. I had no idea where we were or how far we had to go. Vesuvius looked to be a long way behind us, but I knew just how far the debris would be flung. I stretched and got up, walking over to the horse and rubbing her long nose. She nickered softly against my cheek, tossing her head. The sound, quiet as it was, disturbed Petronius and I heard him get up.

"We need to get going," I said, wishing I'd thought to bring some food. He nodded putting his cloak back on, then went to the saddle and unrolled his pack. He handed me some sweet bread. I stared at him in amazement. "Where on earth did you get that? Oh goodness me! Thank you, I am so hungry"

"When I came looking for you yesterday, I checked at the bakery to see whether you had made it there and since I missed out on my honey-filled roll, I picked up some of this sweet bread." He winked and bit into his own piece. We devoured it; then, looking around, found a watercourse and without worrying about whether it was clean or not, drank deeply. Gemmula joined us, splashing us as she slurped.

We gathered our things together and re-mounted Gemmula, who set off at a steady trot.

"I'm sorry I fell asleep; it must have made it hard for you to keep me on the horse," I said. Petronius chuckled.

"All I can say is that it's a good job you're so small." I smiled, even though he couldn't see.

"Well, thank you for not letting me fall off."

"I can just imagine what your husband would do to me if anything happened to you, Hannah," he said. "I'd be a dead man."

"We might both be dead if we don't get a move on," I retorted, "then Maxentius wouldn't have to worry; the mountain would have done his job for him."

As Petronius urged the horse into a gallop, the ground surged beneath us; Gemmula reared her head and I feared she might throw us. I twisted in the saddle to look back at Vesuvius. Smoke was spewing from the peak and I searched my memory for information on the time line of the eruption. I thought we had about four hours to get out of the danger zone.

"How far do you think we've travelled?" I asked Petronius.

"I'm not sure, maybe fifteen or twenty miles, we have ridden for many hours." I nodded, looking at how far away the mountain seemed to be and it sounded about right. Tremors ran underneath us, but Gemmula seemed to have settled back into her rhythm and ignored them. We rode without a break until we could see the outskirts of a town in the far distance; I prayed it was Misenum.

Dismounting for a short time, allowing the horse to rest, we stretched aching muscles. I loved horse riding, but I had never spent such a long time in the saddle in one go. I'd be struggling to walk tomorrow. While we caught our breath, I ruminated over the last several hours — my second incarceration, our frantic flight. I felt a bit like a fugitive and grinned at the image that conjured up. I wished that Maxentius were with me; I missed him so much and he always made me feel safe, but he didn't even know where I was.

As we stood, there was a terrible noise; it sounded as though the earth was cracking in half. The ground shook violently causing the trees around us to bend in odd shapes. It was louder than anything I'd ever heard and I had to put my hands over my ears. Gemmula neighed in terror and it was all Petronius could do to stop her from racing away. We hung on to her reins, but couldn't calm her as the roaring sound drowned out everything we tried to say.

Turning to face Vesuvius, we watched as a huge greyish cloud exploded out of the peak. It kept ascending, billowing up, the top dispersing out, its shape reminding me of an umbrella pine, and still it rose. I knew this was the first of several eruptions; the mountain would spew volcanic material higher and higher until it became top heavy and collapsed in on itself. This would cause a series of powerful avalanches of superheated gas and ashes to surge down the mountain, each avalanche burying everything in its path, more deeply than the one before, covering first Herculaneum then Pompeii and its surrounds, vaporising anyone who remained.

"We have to move," I screamed at Petronius. "NOW!" We climbed back onto Gemmula and I kept stroking her, trying to take away her fear. She was prancing and tossing, rearing her head and neighing loudly, trying to get away, but as soon as we pointed her in the opposite direction to the mountain, she flew like the wind. Hoping that we would make it, we urged her on faster and faster; we had to get to Misenum.

As the day wore on, it got darker; the dense clouds hovering over the mountain were illuminated by firestorms and the air was heavy with the smell of sulphur. If I hadn't been so terrified, it would have looked beautiful — a mesmerising demonstration of the incredible power of nature. Just as I noticed that what I thought to be light rain falling on us was actually ash, the buildings on the outskirts of the town we hoped was Misenum appeared in front of us. Gemmula put on a burst of speed and launched herself up to the town's gate. Petronius slid off her back and helped me down. My legs and back were in agony and walking was proving rather difficult. Had I not been trying to escape the fallout from an eruption, I would have seen the funny side.

We trudged, with Gemmula, into the town. It seemed deserted; maybe everyone had already left. The earth tremors kept rolling under our feet, making the horse snort in fear, but she didn't try to bolt. The rumble from the mountain was a constant backdrop. The black cloud had obliterated the sun and going from the timeline of my memory, I worked out that it must be late afternoon. Those people who had the sense to flee Pompeii and the other towns close by still had some chance of escape, but the seismic activity would cause the sea to retreat, stranding many at the docks, trying to leave by boat.

As we walked, I realised that the people hadn't left; they were just hiding in their homes and everywhere was shuttered. I suggested to Petronius that we try to make it to the headland, which was at the other side of the town, hoping that the sea breeze would keep away the worst of the volcanic debris. I knew that sometime in the early hours of the next day, when the cloud finally became top heavy and imploded, Misenum would be blanketed in a thick cloud of ash, but that, thankfully, the surge would not reach the town.

Wearily, we made our way along the main street and out through the gate that would lead us to the headland. It was so dark that it was hard to see, but eventually we made it and came out onto open ground. Far, far out over the water, sunlight sparkled on the waves, which were very choppy, but all around us was gloom. It was very eerie; and although sounds were muted we could still hear, like a distant thunderstorm, the roar of the volcano.

We had come as far as we could; I hoped it was far enough. Finding a low wall, we removed Gemmula's saddle and nibbled on another piece of the bread Petronius had brought. Suggesting I get some rest, Petronius said he would take the first watch and make sure Gemmula did not break her tether. I was so tired that I could barely form an argument, so I nodded and, wrapping myself in my cloak, rested my head on the soft leather of the saddle.

I had no idea how long I had slept but it felt like hours. It was still dark and I didn't know whether it was night-time or because of the volcanic cloud. I could just make out my guardian, resting against Gemmula — the horse had decided to lie down also. Sleep had claimed Petronius too; it was no surprise, for we were both exhausted. I got up slowly, shaking the layer of ash from my cloak and out of my hair and went to stroke the Gemmula's nose. She pushed her soft mouth into my hand and I wished we had something she could eat. Fumbling through the pockets of the saddle I found, to my everlasting surprise, a rather sad looking apple, which she munched on happily.

Desperate for a drink of water, I looked around but there was nothing nearby. Cautiously, I felt my way along the wall until I came to a building. There was a stone trough just outside. I had no idea what it was for but, sticking my finger into the water, I tasted it. It seemed clean enough so I flicked the ash off its surface and, by the simple method of sticking my head into the water, drank my fill. I took the opportunity to rinse my face while I was there, silently thanking whoever lived there for this boon.

By the time I returned to our resting place, Petronius had woken up and was looking around for me. I told him where I'd been and he followed suit, taking Gemmula with him so that she could quench her own thirst. Making his way slowly back, taking care in the darkness, he resumed his seat and we sat shoulder to shoulder chatting quietly. Maybe an hour later, we heard the strangest sound, which after a day of strange sounds was notable in itself. The closest I could come to describing it later was that it seemed like a whoosh, but so much more and was nearly as loud as the initial eruption. I expected to feel a hot wind, or get blown over the wall, but nothing reached us. Gemmula tried to run, her fright or flight mode kicking in, but we managed to control her.

I knew that this must be the point when the cloud had collapsed, creating the surges that would bury the coastal towns and villas. I prayed that the writings of Pliny the Younger, who had witnessed this, were true and that Misenum was not damaged by these surges. I wondered, absently, whether I would meet him. I knew that he and his mother lived in the town, so I guessed there was a chance. How cool would that be? Then I realised that no-one, except perhaps Max, would ever believe me.

Max...where was he? Where was I? Was I still asleep on the couch? Would he be able to bring me back when this was over? His face rose in my mind; his gentle, toe-curling smile and his green eyes deep as a forest, twinkling down on me. My heart thudded as I remembered his touch and, once again, I was torn between the two men in my life, both of whom I loved beyond measure. I needed to go home, but I also needed to know that Hannah, this Hannah, was safe.

We had been sitting quietly for quite some time, each lost in thought, when suddenly I heard the sounds of people shouting and crying. Thankful for something to shake me out of my memories, I glanced towards the gate and could see a crowd of people milling about, seemingly unsure about what to do or where to go. I made my way towards them, encouraging them to join us, thinking that if we could make our way beyond the headland and further north, we might be able to avoid the worst of the ash that would soon fall on us.

Petronius joined me, handing me Gemmula's reins and began to organise the townsfolk into some sort of order. He spoke calmly and with authority and they listened, seemingly glad to have the decision about what to do taken from them. They began to walk away from the town, still panicked, but willing to do whatever was necessary to save themselves. Gemmula was still unnerved, but I stroked her neck, talking calmly to her, before walking her back over to the wall, where I lifted the saddle onto her back. The familiar weight settled her and she steadied. Gathering up the rest of our meagre belongings, Gemmula and I turned to follow the column of people, bringing up the rear, making sure no-one fell behind.

We hadn't been walking for very long when the hot wind I had expected finally reached us. The sky, still dim, went black as though all the light in the world had been snuffed out and a thick deluge of warm ash descended on us. I stood still; there was no point moving, as I couldn't see my hand in front of my face. The thick cloud muffled the terrified screams of the townsfolk, but I could hear Petronius exhorting them to remain calm, stand still and wait it out. I worried about the possibility of fire; some of the ash would be hot despite the distance it had travelled and I batted at my cloak to make sure there were no sparks. After remaining motionless for what seemed like a lifetime, the world seemed to become a little less black and I was able to make out the shapes of the people in front of me.

Gemmula was neighing loudly and I was having great difficulty calming her distress; her eyes were rolling in her head and she kept baring her teeth. I was too small to control a creature in such panic and I yelled for Petronius to come and help me. He was far ahead though and I doubted he would hear me, but I kept yelling anyway. None of the people nearby seemed moved to assist me. Gemmula was a big horse and I knew I would have to let her go if someone didn't help soon. Then with a sigh of relief, through the gloom I noticed a tall soldier making his way along the trail of townsfolk — Petronius had heard. He had almost reached me when a huge earth tremor made Gemmula rear in terror.

The reins tightened, yanking my arm, lifting me off my feet and in her attempts to flee, Gemmula shoved me. I relaxed my grip on her tether and fell hard against something very solid, knocking the air out of my lungs. I gulped, but the air was so thick that every breath was filled with dust and knew I needed to cover my mouth. Coughing and spluttering, I tried to get up, fighting against the thickening layer of choking ash, which seemed to be sucking me down like quicksand. I struggled, but it seemed futile and, I was so tired that it was easier just to give up and rest on the cushiony greyness. I shut my eyes, for just a second and felt that I might float away.

Chapter Thirty Five

"Arrgghhhhhh...noooooo." I jolted awake so fast that I fell onto the floor, which was weird because, I thought I was already on the ground — well the grass, well actually a layer of ash — and the sudden impact took my breath away. "Oooof." I lay flat on my back, trying to get my bearings. Even with my eyes closed, I realised that it wasn't dark; in fact it seemed to be very light and that I could breathe properly again. My lungs didn't seem to be full of dust anymore and I wasn't spluttering. I didn't think Gemmula had knocked me out; her shove hadn't been that hard. Maybe I'd fallen asleep again. Confused I tried to sit up, but found I was trembling too much.

"Hey, you okay there?" A familiar voice, male and full of mirth, spoke from a little distance away. "That must have been some dream." My head swirled, images bounced around and I struggled to grasp what should have been obvious. I heard soft footsteps and felt two hands settle around my shoulders, lifting me into a sitting position. "Hannah?" Questioning.

He leaned me against something soft. I still hadn't opened my eyes, unsure of what I would see. I think half of my mind had worked out what was going on, but the other half hadn't quite caught up. I rubbed my face, expecting to feel dust and ash, but it felt clean and dry. Slowly, I opened my eyes and, looking down, noticed that I was sitting on a rug, not a load of debris and that I was wearing jeans, not a tunic and cloak. I raised my head and locked eyes with the handsomest man I'd ever seen and my breath hitched. He was crouching in front of me, his expression one of mild alarm.

"Hannah," he asked again, "where have you been?" Such a simple question, yet my answer would be far more complicated than his query suggested. I drew a shuddering breath and continued to stare at him, fascinated by the fathomless depths of his green eyes. As I gazed at him, the rest of my brain caught up and I relaxed.

"Max?" I bit my lip, I knew it was him, but I wanted confirmation. My worlds were still entwined and my vision, hazy. Surrounding this man, like a mirage, I could make out a pathway covered with ash, lots of people, a horse and a soldier, faint but defined. He nodded, still uneasy. "Please hold my hand." He grasped my hand, holding it against his body. I could feel the thud of his heart and flattened my hand on his chest, drawing strength from its beat. As my hand rested there, I felt it quicken and his eyes darkened imperceptibly.

I couldn't move and my mouth was having trouble connecting to my brain. I wanted to speak, but the silence was so peaceful that I didn't want to shatter it. The mirage shimmered; it was like the echo of a memory. I thought I saw the soldier pull up a woman out of something thick and grey, brushing her down, but I couldn't be certain. It was fading and I raised my free hand, reaching out to hold on to it, but it dissolved out of time. I felt a tear and scrubbed at my face. No, I was not going to cry.

Max leaned forward and stroked one finger across my cheek. As he did so, I turned my head and kissed his palm; it seemed the most natural thing to do. His breath caught and he leaned closer, brushing his lips against mine. A pleasurable quiver ran through me and I sighed, a gentle sound that seemed to come from a great distance. Maybe millennia. Unconsciously, my hand trailed down his leg and, freeing my other hand from his grasp, slid it up to trace his jawline, feeling the muscle pulse.

Max moved closer and shifting his position ever so slightly, cupped his hand round the back of my head, tilting it so that he could look into my eyes; then whispering my name, kissed me. I felt my heart thud in response and a familiar warmth began to spread through my body. As his kiss deepened, lips firm and cool, I was unable to prevent a low moan, which seemed to come from beyond time. My arms went around him and he gathered me close. Holding me as though afraid I might just disappear again — he gently swung me around until we were both lying on the rug.

I shuffled until I felt comfortable and Max raised himself up on one elbow, watching me. I began undoing the buttons of his shirt, one by one, letting my hands slide across his skin as I did so. In reply, he drew lazy circles across my stomach with light fingers, lifting my T-shirt just enough to stroke the skin at the top of my jeans. Other than those first few words as I'd fallen off the sofa, we hadn't spoken; strangely words weren't needed.

Soon we would talk, but now all I wanted was for him to bring me back to life.

He dipped his head and kissed me again, his lips claiming mine, hands searching, teasing, skimming under my clothes, his touch setting me ablaze. Desperate to feel his skin on mine, I tried to divest him of his shirt, but my fingers wouldn't work. Suddenly Max lifted his head, bewildered I stared up at him. Smiling he said —

"No, not here, I want to do this properly." He stood up pulling me with him and, since my legs refused to work, virtually carried me into the bedroom. He put me down and went out, leaving me feeling rather awkward and not a little confused, but he returned almost immediately, coming around to where I waited.

"What...where?" I asked, words still difficult, all the more so because of his roving fingers.

"Just made sure we're all locked up." He winked. I blushed and dropped my gaze. I have no idea why I was suddenly shy, but I was. He lifted my chin and looked down at me. "I don't want to be disturbed," he growled, his voice husky.

I shivered at the expression on his face. My legs went all wobbly again and I swayed. He caught me to him and resumed that heart-stopping kiss. With delectable slowness, he removed all of my clothes, pausing in between each item to kiss me again, anywhere his lips could reach. I was trembling, desire making my fingers awkward and I fumbled with his shirt, eventually managing to slide it over his shoulders, my breath catching as our bodies touched, skin on skin. Electricity crackled between us and I needed more.

"Please Max," unintelligibly, "I can't...you need to..." Used to my complete incoherence, Max divested himself of the last of his clothes, joining me on the bed. Unwilling to rush, I gazed at his body, drinking him in, stroking his skin, tracing his muscles and delighting in the feel of him. He groaned and reached for me, but I batted him away, leaning forward to kiss all the way down the long length of him. Delicately my fingers tantalised and I heard his breath catch as I moved back up his body. Just as I was about to repossess his lips, he twisted and in one fluid movement pinned me under him. His lips burnt a path along my neck and then trailed all the way over my body.

He raised himself up, looking down at my face, which I knew was flushed. My hair was coming out of its knot, strands falling over my eyes.

"Oh God, Hannah, I don't think you realise quite what you do to me." His voice was laden with need, as he ran his fingers through my hair, smoothing it off my face. I smiled up at him.

"Oh, I think I could make a wild guess," my voice ragged. My control, such as it was, slipped and I shuddered as he lowered himself back on to me; moulding me to his body, curve for curve. As we held each other, the fire that had been burning steadily, suddenly flared into incandescence. "I need to feel you, all of you." I gasped and knowing how close he was, pressed my hips against him, feeling the answering throb through his muscles.

Max held me close and taking his time, made love to me, all the while kissing me almost senseless, sending frissons of delight running along my back. I writhed under him, quite sure that I might actually die from ecstasy, my movements causing a guttural sound, which seemed to be wrenched from his very core. Together we reached the zenith, the world splintering into a million pieces around us. Revelling in the aftermath we lay wrapped in each other's arms, waiting for the pieces to realign themselves and for our hearts to resume something close to a regular rhythm.

Without conscious thought, I began to run my fingers over Max's chest, feeling as though I had to keep touching him, fearing that if I stopped he would vanish and that all this was just my imagination. Trailing his hand across my thigh and over my hips, coming to rest on my waist, Max began kissing me again. Letting the sensations build and weaving his spell, as though each caress, each stroke reclaimed a part of me, bringing me back to him. Under his touch, my other world, which still teased at the edge of my soul, began to relax its hold, fading into the past. With passionate intensity and exquisite tenderness, he took me to heights as yet unsurpassed, holding me there until I was certain we had actually melded into one another. Eventually, we came back down to earth and, as I clung to him breathing his name and whispering my love for him, I knew I was finally home.

Nearly two millennia away, a tall soldier was making his way through a small town, desperately searching for his wife. It was several days after the eruption of Vesuvius and, he had managed to get himself and his second in command, included in the contingency of soldiers accompanying the Emperor Titus to inspect the devastated region. Although the Emperor had since returned to Rome, the two soldiers had remained, determined to find this woman, but they had been looking for a long time and were beginning to think they never would. Neither knew whether she had escaped the catastrophe and no one seemed to recognise their description of her. Even if she had made it out they really didn't know where she might have gone. It was nearly the end of the day when they rounded a corner and came across a narrow backstreet — undamaged but still blanketed under a thick layer of ash.

There were several people in his eye line, but at the far end a woman was leaning over someone sitting on the ground and something about the tilt of her head drew the attention of the taller soldier. Her cloak was covering her hair, hiding her face from proper view, but as they watched, she stood and turned slightly, the hood falling back off her head. Even if he hadn't seen the glint of red sparkling at her neckline holding the cloak secure, he knew.

His heart missed a beat and he muttered her name, a strangled sound and not very loud, but the woman heard and looked in their direction. She just stared, as if unbelieving of whom she was seeing. Then her face lit up and she started to run, her rich chestnut hair falling out of its plait and flowing out behind her. Both men moved towards her, the younger one holding back just a little.

"Max!" Her voice warmed his heart and he struggled to keep his emotions in check. She was alive.

Tears raining down his cheeks, the soldier hurried to meet the woman. She hurled herself into his arms and he wrapped her close, covering her face with kisses, which she returned with interest.

"You're here, you're here. Oh Max, I've missed you so much. How did you even know where to find me? I didn't know when I would be able to get to Rome." Her smile shone brighter than the sun and her husband thanked all the gods that he had found her. Unable to put her down, Lucius Maxentius Valerius told her that they'd come with the Emperor and that they were just searching everywhere, hoping against hope that she'd made it out.

"Although it seems to be my lot in life to find you covered in soot and ash, my Hannah." He chuckled. "Are you sure you're not a fire sprite?" She giggled and squirmed out of his arms to hug Marcus who had waited to one side and, although was grinning at their reunion, the relief on his face was clear. He hugged her tight.

"You have no idea how pleased I am to see you; your husband was becoming quite frantic," his smile softening the anxiety they had both been suffering. Hannah moved back to her husband, needing to touch him again, still struggling to believe he and Marcus were actually there. Maxentius wrapped his arm around her shoulder, drawing her close.

"Oh, and Petronius is with me; he had to break me out of gaol again." She spoke flippantly, but the two men gaped at her in astonishment.

"What?" Maxentius couldn't believe his ears.

"Oh, don't worry, I'll tell you about it later. Suffice it to say that he rescued me and we left Pompeii together. He's with Gemmula just now."

"Gemmula? He's found a woman in all this chaos?" Hannah chortled with laughter.

"No, silly; Gemmula is the horse we hired to bring us here." She sobered up. "Oh, I've just realised that the hostler who owns her might have died." Her face fell and the light left her eyes. Maxentius tightened his arm around her.

"It's no problem, Hannah, one of us will take care of Gemmula. More to the point where's Aliza?" Hannah explained about Aliza's marriage, adding that she had left several days before the eruption, so was probably already happily ensconced in Ostia.

"So, do we have a home to go to somewhere? I really want to go home and see our children." Maxentius kissed his wife on the nose and told her that yes, they had a home to go to and as soon as they could collect Petronius and Gemmula, they would begin making their way there.

Sometime later, Petronius returned to the spot where he and Hannah had set up a sort of basic camp. They had used one of their heavier cloaks to hook it between two tree saplings, anchoring one side to a wall with a piece of rubble and creating a makeshift tent. As he reached the camp, he noticed Hannah was talking to two soldiers who had their back to him. He made his way towards the little group, who turned on his approach. Petronius stood stock-still, shock written all over his face. It was his boss! It was both his bosses!

"Petronius, thank you for saving my wife. It seems that she likes to leave things to the very last minute before fleeing imminent danger. I am indebted to you." Petronius flushed bright red and shook his head.

"No, Sir, it was the least I could do. No debt is owed. I would never have forgiven myself had I let any harm come to your wife." Hannah smiled at the three men.

"Now if it's all right with you all, I'd like to have a few moments with my husband. We'll see you in a little while." She rested her hand on Marcus' arm and grinned at Petronius; then taking Maxentius' hand, led her husband towards the headland to watch the sun set over the bay.

Alone at last, Hannah turned to Maxentius who smiled, his toe-curling, heart-stopping smile. He cupped his hand around her head, tilting it so that he could look down into her eyes and breathing her name, he kissed her. The world around them disappeared. It was just the two of them together and he showed her just how wonderful reunions could be.

Epilogue

Although, we still had a little more time left in Italy, we had decided to spend it all in Rome and today was our last day in Pompeii. It had been fascinating and, despite everything I had gone through, I had learned so much from those I had been assisting. I hadn't drifted between worlds any more, but I had dreamed that Maxentius eventually found his Hannah. I hoped that it was true and not just my imagination filling in the blanks. Max had told me that there was something he wanted to show me before we left and, we wanted to spend the day having a last look around the ruins. As part of the excavation team, we had carte blanche access, which was rather nice.

It was mild for the time of year, the sun was shining and the air felt mellow. We roamed along the pathways between the ruins, revisiting as much as possible. I didn't want to go back into the Gladiators' School. I had no idea whether Tullius had given any of the men under his protection the chance to leave the town and I knew that bodies had been found during early investigations. The fact that I may have known them made it too poignant.

Despite my close connection to a Pompeii prior to the eruption, whole and relatively undamaged, I treasured that day. There were areas of the town that I had never ventured into during my time there — well the other Hannah's time there — and it was marvellous discovering how much had been preserved. Some I recognised, remembering how they had looked, others quite unfamiliar.

Towards the end of the day, as we were heading for the exit near the amphitheatre, Max steered me along a side street and suddenly we were standing in front of the House of the Hebrew. My heart thudded in my chest and I stared at him. Why were we here? Didn't he know the risks? He smiled slowly and opened the door, ushering me through into the cool atrium. Unable to help myself, I traced the inscription. The stone was cool under my fingers but there was no echo today and my ghosts remained quiet — no voices whispering in my head, no images flashing through my mind.

Max walked me through into the ruined courtyard where we had stood the week previously. Now I knew why the amphorae had been stacked in the rear garden and why there had been little to find in this house. I — she — had sent most of it to Rome. Max walked me into the middle of the inner courtyard and turned me to face him.

"Hannah, I have loved you since almost the first time I saw you and have waited a long time for you to catch up. Now that you have finally come to your senses..." he winked at my outraged expression, "...I find that I am unable and unwilling to live without you, even occasionally. Will you do me the very great honour of becoming my wife?" My jaw dropped. Whatever I had been expecting since we re-entered this house, it most certainly wasn't this. He smiled at my expression and added that I obviously needed someone to keep me anchored to this world and he would like to be the one to do so.

I gazed at him; this man who had become my whole life, this man who was the only person — in this world — who knew, understood and accepted my 'other life' and still loved me. I could not help the smile that spread across my face, or the bubble of happiness filling my soul, so big that I thought it might choke me.

"Yes." My voice cracked and sounded husky, the word lost in the breeze. I tried again. "Yes, yes, yes. Oh Max, I cannot think of anything that would make me happier." I flung myself into his arms and kissed him soundly. He held me tightly, kissing me back, causing delicious sensations to tumble down my spine.

He pulled a small, black, velvet-covered box out of his pocket and opened it. Cradled on the inky black cushion was the most incredible ring I had ever seen. It was an emerald, not quite an oval and not quite a teardrop, something in between, dark as a forest and flashing green fire as the sun caught its facets, nestled in an intricate setting, which had been fashioned after a Roman soldier's helmet. It was a replica of my clasp. I looked up at him in astonishment.

"How on earth...?" He lifted the ring and very gently slid it along the third finger of my left hand and then, turning my hand, kissed my palm. The ring fitted perfectly and was unbelievably beautiful. "Oh Max, this is gorgeous, how did you...?"

"I thought we might start our own tradition." He smiled his heart in his eyes. I moved into his arms and we sealed our engagement with a long and very passionate kiss.

Three days later we were standing in the Forum. It was another beautiful day chilly but sunny and the sky was a glorious cerulean blue. This being our second time, we were enjoying being able to dawdle through at our leisure rather than hurrying to fit everything in. We had stopped for a few moments on the Via Sacra, the main route through the Forum, while Max took yet more photos of the ancient architecture. As I waited in the shade of an umbrella pine, I realised that everything had slowed down. My surroundings seemed hazy and the ruins in front of me had been superimposed by a city of bright colour and shining marble. For a split second I was unsure whether I was sliding between worlds again.

As this thought passed through my mind, I noticed a very tall soldier holding the hand of an elfin-like lady walking towards me. The lady spoke to the soldier who glanced up at me, then back at her. Strangely, I was unsurprised and, recognising Hannah and her Roman, I smiled. As soon as they reached me, I was caught up in their embrace; Maxentius whispered his heartfelt thanks and Hannah kissed my cheek. We were both wearing the clasp, she on her cloak and me on the lapel of my winter coat and, I swear each one was glowing. Hannah lifted my hand, running her slender fingers over my ring, showing Maxentius. They glanced across at Max and I nodded at the unspoken question in their eyes. Smiles of delight wreathed their faces.

"I have no doubt that we will meet again," Maxentius said and I grinned.

"I would like to think so, but hopefully in less dramatic circumstances." I paused. "In the meantime, I wish you all the happiness in the world." Hannah looked at me, one eyebrow raised. "Yes, I know. How could I not? Congratulations." Maxentius looked astonished.

"What am I missing, my Hannah?" She grinned impishly at him and whispered in his ear. His face was a picture. They became engrossed in each other and the slender thread binding me to my ancient ancestor relinquished its grasp, for now, leaving only an echo. My world came back into focus and I spotted Max walking towards me.

"Ready, Hannah?" I nodded. He kissed me on the nose, hugging me close, my heart swelled.

"Let's go home."